Cold Courage

Published by Hesperus Nova
Hesperus Press Limited
28 Mortimer Street, London W1W 7RD
www.hesperuspress.com

First published by Hesperus Press Limited, 2013
This edition first published 2014

Original title 'Vilpittomasti sinun'
First published in Finnish by Gummerus Kustannus Oy in 2011,
Helsinki, Finland
Published through arrangement with Werner Soderstrom Ltd.,
Helsinki, Finland

This work has been published with the financial assistance of
FILI – Finnish Literature Exchange

Designed and typeset by Fraser Muggeridge studio
Printed and bound in Great Britain by CPI Group (UK) Ltd, Croydon, CR0 4YY

ISBN: 978-1-84391-496-9

Cold Courage

Pekka Hiltunen

I
Finnish Girls

I

Panic spread through the street, rippling in a viral wave of contorted faces and anxious gestures.

In her morning daze, Lia gazed through the bus window at the unfolding scene. Suddenly it seemed that every pedestrian on the pavement wore the same expression of overwhelming nausea.

It was the beginning of April and Lia was on her way to work. Every morning she performed this ritual of submission, an hour surrendered to the flow of traffic coursing through a city that was too large and too full of people. For Lia, living in London was like living pressed between other bodies, constantly allowing others to invade her meagre personal space.

That morning on Holborn Circus, a short distance before the end of the route at Stonecutter Street, she saw something in the pedestrians she had never beheld before.

The moment before a catastrophe. This is what it looks like.

A car was parked on the pavement, with a crowd gathered around. That was the source of the fear, the ground zero from which the panic was spreading.

The car was a large, white Volvo left sideways across the pedestrian flow, as if someone had abandoned it there in an emergency. Lia couldn't see anyone inside, but the boot gaped open. People were pointing at it, and more and more were stopping to look.

Whenever someone came sufficiently close to see into the boot, their expression changed. That contorted face.

Whatever was in the boot of that car, it made everyone who saw it freeze as though they had been slapped across the face. Many hurried away.

But more people kept coming.

Through the open window of the bus, Lia could hear the pedestrians' exclamations. They were frantic, broken utterances, never enough to tell what had happened. One man was talking to the police on a mobile phone. An old woman had closed her eyes and was chanting, 'Oh my God. Oh my God.'

Lia rose from her seat to try to see down onto the pavement, but at that moment the lights changed and the bus lurched forward. The driver hit the accelerator, beginning to round the Circus.

Suddenly the brakes locked. Lia flew against the seat in front of her and then back into her own. The driver had stopped the bus to avoid colliding with two cars that had cut in front of him, taking a shortcut the wrong way around the roundabout.

The first was a police car. Lia realised she had been hearing the manic siren in the background only once she saw the blue lights, which continued flashing after the car had stopped. The second vehicle was a van with 'ITV Meridian News' emblazoned on the side.

The bus accelerated again. From that distance, seeing into the boot of the Volvo was now impossible. In a second, the strange scene fell behind.

When Lia arrived at work, everyone already knew about the incident. Although *Level* was a bi-weekly and not in the business of reporting news, the computer monitors and large TV screen in the editorial office were broadcasting all the latest updates.

In the boot of the white Volvo on Holborn Circus, police had found the remains of a badly mutilated corpse. It was so badly crushed that initial news reports indicated the police were not able to release any information whatsoever about the victim. Their best guess was that they were dealing with only one body and that it was a woman's, although even that was not entirely certain.

'That's crazy. I was just there. I saw that car,' Lia said to Sam, the writer who shared the desk next to her.

Sam nodded and continued reading the news feeds.

Am I an eyewitness to a crime? thought Lia.

No. I am an eyewitness to eyewitnesses, a person who saw other people's horror at witnessing the aftermath of a crime. That isn't really anything.

She watched the news broadcast on the television showing the white car stopped on the pavement with the boot open. The headline over the image read, 'Brutal slaying in the heart of the City.' Finally Lia felt the wave of nausea she had seen on the street wash over her as well and hurried to the toilet.

2

The murder dominated the Tuesday news cycle, making concentrating on work difficult for Lia. A graphic designer for *Level*, she was currently working on the visuals for two forthcoming articles. Fortunately they were both easy layout jobs: an investigative report on the state of metropolitan Great Britain and a short human interest story on politicians' dogs. She was grateful there was no editorial meeting that day. When she realised she was fixating on any information about the Holborn Circus incident – news agency coverage, tweets, television bulletins – she gave in to her curiosity.

She subscribed to the RSS feeds for news articles about the case so she would receive a notification any time updates were posted. And updates trickled in throughout the day. Usually the new information was just an addition of one or two sentences, including the detail in many of the news articles that the model of the Volvo was an S40.

By the afternoon, the only facts the police could confirm were that the number of victims was one, that she was a woman with dark hair and that she had been mutilated in an exceptionally brutal manner. No information was made available about the killer.

This unsettled Lia, feeling somehow disrespectful to the dead woman.

The online editions of the tabloids used their largest headline font. Because the police had constructed a tent-like barrier around the car, the photographers were unable to get any close-up shots. But the reporters were interviewing eyewitnesses.

'At first you couldn't even tell it was a person. I thought it was... animal innards from a slaughterhouse,' one upset man told the *Sun*.

This idea recurred in the other eyewitness interviews. Few of them grasped that the mass in the boot was made up of human remains until they noticed the hair mixed in and the few fragments only just recognizable as body parts.

Dear God. Whoever did this deserves to burn in hell.

At two o'clock in the afternoon, the *Daily Mail* published a picture from the mobile phone of another witness. Visible in it were the edge of the Volvo's boot and clear plastic surrounding a discoloured mass of black and red.

Fortunately the picture was out of focus.

At half past four, Lia noticed that the *Sun* had, with its typical sense of style, dubbed the corpse 'The Woman Without a Face' in an attempt to make the story more memorable.

By the time Lia left work, she was torn. She could take the Tube home and avoid the whole issue. Instead, she chose the bus so she could see the area around Holborn Circus.

Located on Fetter Lane in the City, the grandiose environment surrounding the offices of *Level* was bound to make anyone feel small. Each day thousands of commuters crammed into the City, the well-dressed, high-powered financial and legal acolytes of the temple of commerce that is the Square Mile. Amid the crowds Lia always found herself trying to convey the impression that she belonged there – focused, striding from one important business appointment to another.

For the staff of *Level*, the location so close to Fleet Street was a point of pride.

Today Lia saw this familiar environment with fresh eyes. Even in the City, some of the most carefully guarded streets of London, brutal crimes could happen.

The large, white police tent was visible from a distance as the bus approached Holborn Circus. Around it was an area cordoned off with white and blue striped tape, behind which people stood staring.

At home in Hampstead, Lia decided to avoid turning on her computer or the television. Her mood was restless, and she didn't know whether she wanted to think about the incident at all any more.

During the night she woke up twice. She had to force herself to calm down.

On Wednesday the story was on the front page of every newspaper and still the first item on the TV news.

One of the police officers had given an anonymous statement to the effect that the victim in the car had been crushed by a large steamroller or something similar driving over her several times.

MOST BARBARIC MURDER OF THE CENTURY? BRUTAL GANGLAND EXECUTION, brayed the newspaper headlines.

Despite her conscience reproaching her, Lia purchased each of the newspapers with a large story on the killing. Placing them inconspicuously on her desk, she read them while she worked.

The gangland-style execution story hinged on the brutal way the corpse had been mutilated and the fact that the car was stolen. 'Using a car of this type is standard procedure for organised crime,' the reporter wrote.

I'm sure it is. But that isn't sufficient evidence, Lia thought irritably.

She was relieved to read online that the cause of death was uncertain. The crushing could easily have taken place after she was killed.

Calling the victim the 'Woman Without a Face' had also spread to several other newspapers and television channels. Lia hated the name and, as she was shutting down her computer and leaving for the day, she thanked her lucky stars she worked for an honourable publication. Yes, sometimes it went fishing for readers with celebrity gossip but it never forced its editorial staff to make up crass nicknames for victims of horrible crimes.

At home that night, she continued investigating the incident online. Her violent surge of emotions had begun to subside.

What had upset her wasn't the actual sight of the crime scene from her bus. What stopped her dead was the realisation that someone had done that to a woman.

I am naive. I am twenty-seven, almost twenty-eight, and I've never really thought that things like this could happen to anyone.

Thinking of the woman's death was horrible. Just the thought produced a nearly physical pain, but Lia couldn't prevent herself from brooding over the details of the crime. Someone had to have driven the steamroller. And then collected what remained.

Only when she noticed the tears falling on her hands did Lia realise she was crying. She felt an oppressive dislocation, a despondency that paralyzed her entire being.

What kind of a person could do that?

Where does the pure evil in that kind of person come from? Did he grow into it or somehow get... pushed into it?

Once, years ago, Lia had feared for her own safety. But that was nothing compared to this.

I have never grieved over something like this before. Am I such a cold person that it takes a brutal murder to make me feel anything?

She looked out of the only window in her flat at the small church next door and the statues in the park, barely visible in the darkening evening light.

No one could help this woman any more. But Lia understood herself in a new way. Herself, and her old fear.

That night she slept a little better.

By Thursday, the story had disappeared from the news. No new information was being reported, and the speculation had shifted to the inside pages.

The *Guardian* published an opinion piece by a criminologist who speculated that the Holborn Circus corpse was part and parcel of a process of 'spectacularisation' of murder in which real life and crime on television and in the cinema were drawing closer together. Making a grand spectacle was the murderer's objective.

'Leaving the body in the middle of the City was pure theatre. In the theatre of brutality, set and staging matter,' the scholar said.

God, he must be right, but do that woman's loved ones really need to be tormented by him saying so?

Then Lia remembered that the police had not yet announced that they had even identified the body, let alone informed the next of kin.

I doubt anyone even knows that they should be crying for her.

That day was the weekly editorial meeting at *Level* during which they went through all the topics for the next edition. To Lia's surprise, at the end of the meeting, Matt Thomas, the editor-in-chief, brought up Holborn Circus.

'So, about the "Woman Without a Face". Any thoughts?'

Lia stared at Thomas. Of course it would just so happen the only person in the office she disliked was the editor-in-chief. The feeling was mutual, and she knew it.

For a long time she had explained her reserve towards Thomas by telling herself that he had to be a bit of a bastard just because of his position. Editors-in-chief laboured under a mountain of pressure to produce results, so they had to have a little leeway to vent frustrations at subordinates. But in fact Thomas had always been unfriendly and routinely collected the praise for the accomplishments of the entire staff. And although he enjoyed talking about 'journalistic ethics', all he ever did was move the magazine closer to the tabloid market.

No one took up Thomas' question.

'This next issue still needs something more hard-hitting,' he reminded them.

'I have a difficult time imagining any reason for us to write about it,' the political reporter, Timothy Phelps, said.

'Gruesome crimes happen. People recoil, and then we all move on.'

'Right you are,' Thomas said, and with that wrapped up the meeting.

Lia disagreed.

I have not moved on.

3

Towards the end of April came a special night.

Not quite one month after Lia had seen the frightening scene on Holborn Circus, it was her birthday. The actual day was Sunday, but she had invited her colleagues to join her at the White Swan, their local, after work on Friday.

Lia had looked forward to the evening anxiously. Celebrating her birthday was not like her but, as it had approached, she had felt the need to do something different this year. In part it may have been due to recent events.

'If you don't have anything else on,' Lia had said as she invited everyone. She wasn't sure whether many would want to come.

Generally they seemed to think of her as that introverted, slightly strange, slightly hard, Finnish woman. But hard in a way that meant they could have a friendly go at her about it.

No fewer than eight of the office's dozen-odd employees turned up at the White Swan. Matt Thomas was not among them, which was a relief for Lia. Two hours later, five of the boys remained.

Lia knew that these men had their own lives, a relationship or a family, so spending a free night drinking with the weird Finnish lady from work was a display of real warmth.

The evening had been fun so far. The boys were displaying openly their affection for Lia, even making toasts.

The mention of her sense of humour in more than one of these especially delighted her. According to the boys, she put an entirely new spin on the blonde joke: here was a blonde who could throw barbs sharp enough to strike fear into the hearts of weaker men.

She received CDs by some of her favourite artists, albums she already had of course, and countless hugs and drinks. She competed with the boys in their silly drinking games.

Around ten o'clock the stage of inebriation Lia loved best began. When the buoyancy of alcohol bears up everything a person does. Leaving the table, Lia went to the toilet.

As she returned, she stopped at the bar, asked for a glass of water and drank it. Water was the best way to draw out the drunkenness in a slow, pleasant burn.

She looked at the table where the five guys sat, her dear and distant workmates. She thought of Finland, her parents and her friends from school with whom she no longer kept in touch.

How many women were celebrating their twenty-eighth birthday tonight? Lia tried to imagine the places they would be celebrating. Bleak Helsinki and countries to which she had never been. What would her party have been like in Australia? Or Mexico?

A woman with dark hair wearing a dark, slim-cut dress approached the bar and stood next to Lia. Roughly Lia's age, Lia took note of how clearly the woman's manner spoke of her self-confidence. She smiled at Lia, and Lia smiled back.

The woman sidled closer to say something, and what she said took Lia by surprise. Not because of the words, because of the language.

'*Onneksi olkoon, synttärisankari*,' she said. Congratulations, birthday girl – in Finnish.

Being addressed in her native language amid the bustle of an English pub was so weird that Lia laughed. She hadn't heard anyone speak Finnish in ages – not since she last called her parents. The woman was speaking a secret language that only they could understand.

'*Kiitos*,' Lia replied in thanks.

Finnish. Open vowels and thick consonants, its taste strong and direct, a language that didn't belong here or, really, anywhere.

The woman said her name was Mari.

'Lia,' Lia said, and they shook hands. Given how tipsy she was, this all felt very formal and thoroughly amusing.

'How did you know it was my birthday?' Lia asked.

'I was sitting near you and heard you all talking.'

'You've been eavesdropping on us all evening then.'

'Yes, but not only on you,' Mari replied. 'You seem to have lived in London for some time now.'

'About six years. And you?'

'Five, but it hardly seems it.'

'I know the feeling. You wouldn't... Would you like to join us?'

'Thank you, I'd be delighted to.'

'Boys, if this girl joins us, will you try to behave yourselves?'

'Anything for you, Lia.'

The waitress brought more drinks. Lia told them that Mari was from Finland. That was all it took.

It was as if the party had started all over again. Having been able to provide her boys with a good conversationalist who was so easy on the eye gave Lia genuine pleasure. Mari brought out both the gentleman and the horny teenager in them. Bombarding her with polite questions, they devoured her with their beer-swollen eyes.

Lia watched the revelling men around the table.

My gallant fools.

These five writers held in their heads an astounding amount of information about politics, sport, high culture and entertainment, and that was another reason Mari enchanted them. She knew all about the current events that came up in conversation. Through the noise of the pub, Lia listened to Mari talk about her background, picking out the words insurance company and personnel manager. The men didn't ask anything more about that, but Mari's political views piqued their interest.

'Bloody hell, Lia, your Finnish friend knows local British politics better than I do!' Sam said with enthusiasm.

As was his way, the political reporter, Timothy Phelps, had to test the newcomer by debating with her. The subject he broached was the Tory chairman Brian Pensley, who had been in the headlines recently.

'Pensley has a problem. Whenever he opens his mouth, all anyone can remember is the Tories' wretched healthcare overhaul. He's going to be carrying the burden of that failure for a long time,' Phelps said as if giving a lecture.

Mari shook her head.

'I think Pensley's problem is his diffidence. He doesn't know how to appeal to any specific voting bloc. He never would have become party chairman if David Cameron hadn't decided to elevate him for some bizarre reason,' Mari said.

'Pensley was chairman even before Cameron assumed office,' Timothy objected.

'No, he wasn't,' Mari said and then expounded from memory: Cameron had begun as leader of the Conservative Party a few years earlier, at the beginning of December. Pensley was promoted to chairman less than a month later, so it was clear that this was done with Cameron's support.

Timothy went quiet, clearly peeved.

'C.Y.F.F.,' Sam said with a grin and then explained the expression to Mari. Ambitious editorial offices valued three things: a feel for language, good networking skills so you could get the scoop on competitors and diligent background work. The last of these had its own acronym, which they used in emails to mock writers guilty of passing on bad information: CYFF, Check Your Fucking Facts.

'By the way, we work at *Level*,' Sam said proudly, but Lia was glad to see that this had no particular effect on Mari.

'I gathered as much,' Mari replied.

Clearly she was intelligent and also capable of holding her own in a debate, which was the sexiest thing in the world to these men. Still they remembered to treat Lia like the star of the show.

Lia had worked as a graphic designer at *Level* for nearly five years, and she got along with the male-dominated staff of the magazine precisely because she held her ground and never let a quip go unanswered. The staff of *Level* were a clever bunch. Founded in the 1960s out of the idealism of a group of young journalists, the magazine had initially focused on politics. Gradually it had added arts and entertainment coverage. Producing astute commentary on the latest right-wing party platform and engaging reviews of hot new pop albums was no trifling task. Circulation had waned of late, but *Level* still remained a small but influential voice.

Sometime after eleven o'clock, Mari asked the waitress to bring a jug of water to the table. Lia realised she had forgotten her strategy. You had to tend inebriation like a campfire.

'And here I was thinking Finnish girls knew how to drink,' Sam said teasingly.

'Drinking,' Lia said emphatically as she raised her water glass, 'is only one of many things at which Finnish girls excel.'

This rejoinder received whoops from the men and a smile from Mari.

The growing intoxication was beginning to show in repetition in the conversation. Timothy even dredged up the Brian Pensley argument again.

'Mari, all credit to your knowledge of politics, but you can't really explain Pensley's unpopularity based on his lack of charisma. Have you ever seen him speak in person?'

'As a matter of fact, I have,' Mari said.

'And you still believe the Tory platform has nothing to do with his problems?'

'Of course it does. But when I saw Pensley speak, I knew his speeches were never going to convince anyone of anything. At most the bedridden residents of an old people's home in a Tory area.'

Everyone waited to see what Timothy would say, but Mari beat him to it.

'Timothy, what if I told you I thought you could know anyone, be it Brian Pensley or any of us, simply based on their speech and bearing? I don't know Lia; I just met her tonight for the first time. But if you ask me something personal about her, I bet I can give you an answer.'

Silence fell over the party. The men eyed each other, and Lia thought, *I like this woman. There's something different about her.*

'Right,' Timothy said. 'Give me just a second to think up a question.'

Mari stood up.

'I'm going to the toilet, and while I'm gone you can come up with three questions. If I can't make it through them, I'll buy the next round. If I get them right, you buy my drinks for the rest of the night.'

From the men's faces, you could see that their drunken brains were struggling to understand what this strange game was all about.

'Challenge accepted,' Timothy said. 'Are there any rules?'

'Well, let's agree that they have to be something that Lia could answer herself,' Mari suggested.

Lia laughed.

What an odd fish. But there is something considerate about it, since the game is about me and it is my birthday. And she also wants to give Timothy a rap on the knuckles.

After Mari left, the men conferred feverishly.

'Where did you find her, Lia?'

After a hushed consultation, they settled on their questions, announcing that the subjects would be travel, money and sex.

'So, basic human needs,' Timothy explained.

When Mari returned to the table, the atmosphere was charged. Timothy stood up.

'Tonight's performance is entitled: "Everything you always wanted to know about Lia but were afraid to ask." And the first question is... We all know that Lia likes to travel. What is her favourite foreign destination?'

Lia smirked. Everyone at *Level* knew what city she had visited three times. Travelling was one of the few personal things she talked about at work. But there was no way Mari could ever guess.

'That's a hard one. Bad luck for me. There are so many possible options,' Mari said.

Everyone expected her to take a long time thinking, but Mari gave her answer right away.

'I'd say a small town in the south of France. Somewhere in Provence.'

The drinking party stared at Mari in shock, Lia most amazed of all.

'That's right! How did you know?' Lia asked.

'From a lot of little things,' Mari said. Lia was probably interested in Europe, and she couldn't travel far on a graphic designer's salary. Lia had used a few words of French during the evening, pronouncing them with a southern accent. Her skin was pale, which meant she didn't go in for beach holidays. During the evening she had talked about her fondness for wine, food and culture.

'And a lot of other little details like that. So what city is it, Lia?'

'Carpentras. In Provence, like you said.'

'Good guess,' Timothy said. 'Impressive deduction. Or a lucky guess.'

That wasn't just luck, Lia thought.

With that, Timothy asked his next question: 'We don't even know the answer to this one: what is the most expensive thing Lia owns?'

'This should be easy,' Mari replied. 'Most people don't have very many really expensive things. But I'll have to think.'

Everyone waited in silence.

Ludicrous, Lia thought. *She can't guess that. Even I would have a hard time saying what my most valuable possession is.*

'Lia could have an inheritance. But I think I'll say that the most expensive thing she owns is an investment holding,' Mari said.

Lia smiled.

'Huh, you're probably right. My parents started a stock account for me when I was at school,' she said.

'Jesus,' Sam said. 'How could you have seen that just by looking at her?'

'I couldn't,' Mari said.

What were people's most valuable possessions usually? A flat, a car, maybe jewellery and investments.

'A graphic designer for a London magazine, moderate salary, maybe thirty-five thousand pounds a year? You can't buy a flat on that in this city. And there's no point owning a car here. Lia mentioned taking the bus to work. And as for jewellery – if you owned a really stunning piece, wouldn't you have worn it to your birthday party? Investments were all that remained. That was just the most likely option.'

'Bravo!' Sam said.

Lia groaned. 'That makes me feel so normal. And boring.'

'Don't worry,' Mari said. 'That's just the safe, ordinary part of you. The rest of you is much more fascinating.'

The men whistled.

'Girl on girl action! It doesn't get much sexier than that!'

'We'll see whether she can answer the last question as easily,' Timothy said.

'The sex question,' Lia said, rolling her eyes.

'The big sex question,' Timothy announced. 'We know that as a beautiful woman, Lia must have plenty of admirers. But how many sexual partners has she had?'

'That's a question an outsider could never answer exactly,' Mari said.

'That's a pretty damn stupid, chauvinistic, revolting question,' Lia said.

'Be that as it may,' Timothy said, 'it's also the most natural thing in the world. Mari's probably right though that getting the exact number would just be chance.'

So he rephrased the question: Was the number closer to one, five, ten, fifty or one hundred?

Among the men the question received boisterous approval, but Lia shook her head. Not only did the inane voyeurism bother her but she also disliked the idea of defining someone by the number of men she had slept with.

'It's all right, Lia,' Mari said. 'Gentlemen, this question is beneath you. But it is within the rules, and obviously interesting to someone on a personal level. Although in a rather lowbrow way. Lia, if you agree, I'll try to answer.'

Lia nodded reluctantly.

She knows. But I don't know if I want her to say it out loud.

'I think it's clear that, like most young women, Lia has a prolific sex life. The closest number is fifty.'

The boys went wild, clapping and hooting so loudly that the entire pub turned to look.

'Fifty men! Fifty men!'

Lia pulled a face at them. Stupid drunks.

'Is that right?'

'Well of course,' Lia said.

Wolf-whistling, the men demanded to know the basis for Mari's guess.

'How can you tell? Was it her neckline?'

Mari looked at Lia and said: 'You can't tell from anything directly. I just have an intuition about these things. And she has the look of an independent person.'

'Shit, you guys are such children,' Lia said.

Leaving the men to their snickering, Lia went to the bar. Sam asked Mari what she wanted to drink after winning the bet, but Mari was not listening. She followed Lia.

'I'm sorry,' Mari said. 'That was in poor taste.'

'It isn't your fault. When they drink, things always get dirty before too long.'

The bartender looked at them expectantly. Mari shook her head and pulled on her coat.

'You are really good at guessing things,' Lia said.

'Thanks. And thank you for including me in your birthday party.'

An odd feeling came over Lia as she looked at Mari, who was preparing to leave. As though their evening ought not to be ending quite yet.

'Are we leaving something unfinished here?' she asked.

Mari smiled.

'Maybe,' she said. 'You want to go somewhere else?'

4

The night was clear, with a sense of impending cold. A faint wind brushed over Lia's and Mari's faces.

Mari hailed a taxi, which took them to Greenwich Park.

A high brick wall surrounded the park, and the gates were already locked for the night, but Mari was not headed for the park. Instead, she began walking along the wall, up the hill.

At the top, Lia had to stop and look. The view was unreal. A magic city.

She had never seen the city she lived in from this angle. Below glittered the meandering Thames, behind it the old Isle of Dogs harbour area, then Mile End, Whitechapel, Wapping. The high towers of the City. Behind them the classical districts of Bloomsbury, Covent Garden, Marylebone, Mayfair.

Even if London felt too big for her, it was beautiful for a large metropolis: instead of disturbing the ambience created by the older buildings, the skyscrapers blended with it perfectly. And somewhere there in the darkness was Hampstead, the streets she now called home.

She wiped her eyes, which were watering from the wind.

Mari continued on. Next to the wall was a small building that looked like a groundsman's shed. There the chilly wind dropped.

Along the wall of the shed was a bench. Mari sat down. From here they could see the dark silhouette of the city and lights, so many lights.

Mari took a small bottle of cognac and two glasses out of her bag.

'Just the essentials, I see. Do you always carry those in your handbag?' Lia asked in amusement.

'Only when I need them,' Mari said.

She poured the cognac and extended one of the glasses to Lia. The silence was almost complete as they watched the city at night.

'OK, now this is starting to feel like a birthday again,' Lia said.

Mari motioned towards the green swathe of Greenwich and talked about the park, an area Lia didn't know well. Behind the trees, out of view, was a famous vantage point, the Royal Observatory. Mari commented on how quiet it was in this spot in the evening and at night. There were none of the people who wander the ungated parks, the drugs and sex trade. Many of the buildings nearby were valuable national treasures, and the police carefully patrolled these streets.

The conversation turned to the thing that connected them. Finland.

'A serious country,' Mari said.

'A very serious country,' Lia agreed, and they toasted Finland. The warmth of the cognac reignited Lia's pleasant buzz, which had begun to peter out during the taxi ride.

Quickly she recognised that Mari had the same complicated relationship with their homeland as she did. Some things they loved, some things they hated, and nowadays their lives were disconnected from it for the most part, and with indifference came a feeling of relief.

Perhaps that was a typical feeling for people who have left their homelands of their own volition.

They talked about Finland, because that allowed them to sound each other out.

'Finland's problem is its need for self-aggrandisement,' Mari said. Like so many other small nations, Finland had taken a few historical events and forged them into an illusion that it had a great past and culture too.

'But the real value of Finland isn't in its uniqueness but in the stability of its society, which makes its citizens good people.'

'Bloody well said.'

'That just came to me once. Whenever anyone asks what kind of country Finland is, that's what I always say.'

Mari spoke about her family in Pori on the western coast and inland in Häme. Lia noticed how Mari spoke of everything with exactness, as though her thoughts were never half-formed.

Mari's second name was Rautee. Two things united the family: leftist politics and a conservative lifestyle.

'You might imagine a conflict there, but they actually combine quite well.'

The family's leftist leanings had faded somewhat, but basically everyone assumed everyone else voted red. At the same time, they always worked to amass more wealth.

'My family are social democrats with big houses.'

Mari seemed to be up to date with current events in Finland. Lia herself didn't follow the Finnish news. Of course she'd read the few stories that passed the test of newsworthiness in Britain. They were usually depressing or idiotic – major disasters, political sex scandals or strange village festivals.

Lia spoke about her family, who had moved to Helsinki from Kajaani in the north when she was small. She didn't remember anything about living in the Kainuu area, an economically depressed region just south of Lapland, other than the winters, which were proper, cold ones, not the months of drizzle Helsinki usually had.

When she had to wake up for school on winter mornings, the world was always pitch black. Lia always went straight from her bed to the window. She pressed against the radiator and dressed herself. The radiator was too hot to stay next to, but the room was too cold. She would try to find somewhere between the two to stand and look outside.

'In the dark all I could see were the tiny, red beacons on the factory chimneys looming in the distance. On the street, little dots moved. Human dots plodding towards the points of light at the factories.'

Lia knew she didn't need to say anything more. Mari understood without her saying what she meant: the Finns' fastidious relationship to work, the atmosphere they had both grown up in – studying hard, the value of honest work, the idea that doing good in the world was an industrial production process.

They drank more cognac.

Neither missed Finland. But still the tangible imprint of their homeland remained on them. In the short space between them on that park bench were the empty byways of Finland, the swathes of sparsely inhabited land, not separating people, but rather bringing inner peace. The pace of their drinking told of the Finnish woman's good head for liquor and appreciation for the fragility of the moment.

'You're thinking about Finnish women,' Mari said.

Lia nodded.

How do you know?

'You were surprised back there in the pub that I could guess the number of men you've slept with more or less correctly.'

Mari said she deduced it from two things. First was that Lia was from Finland. Second was her way of looking at men: intense, appraising, attracted.

'That makes us sound like some sort of conscious consumers of men. But I think you know what I mean. That a woman can openly take pleasure in men.'

Lia knew.

'And the Finnishness?'

Mari grinned.

'How much time do we have? Because, let me tell you, I have a whole theory about Finnish women.'

Laughing, Lia said, 'I would love to hear your theory about Finnish women.'

Mari paused for a moment and then began.

'Most Finnish women are just the same as women everywhere else. Bred to be bland. People resigned to conventionality.'

But there was a group of Finnish women who were something else entirely.

'They're what you get when you raise young girls on rye bread, vodka, good films and equality.'

'Excellent diet,' Lia said.

'These Finnish women are a little like musk-oxen. We are musk-oxen.'

They both laughed.

'For us the world is cold, dark, and windy, but we're still where we are and don't budge,' Mari continued. 'We have a severe attitude towards ourselves and the world. We are harder. More independent and more powerful.'

You could already see this when they were young. Finnish girls had all the gifts and knowledge the world could offer. If you had to entrust anyone with solving the problems of the world, it would be young Finnish women, Mari said.

'And they're also so responsible. They know how to grieve and care for those who need it. Like it or not, we were built tough.'

In the Finnish women of today you see a strength accumulated over generations. Their mothers and grandmothers and great-grandmothers were among the first to stop playing games with men and strike out on their own. They went to school – often more than men – participated in politics, made decisions on their own.

'That's why we have this innate freedom to do anything in the world. Like getting drunk in a London park.'

Lia laughed. Mari had just summarised everything she liked and disliked about herself.

I may belong more to the group living dull lives.

A person resigned to conventionality.

They were silent for a moment, and then Mari said, 'Tell me everything. Start from the very beginning.'

Lia knew what she meant.

'I'm not supposed to be here,' Lia said.

London was the wrong city for her. Admitting this to herself had taken a couple of years, and afterwards she had only decided to stay for practical reasons. And also London was beautiful at times.

She left Finland when she was twenty-two, having already studied graphic design for two and a bit years.

'I thought that if I stayed in Finland, I would just be one more of the thousands of talented women artists all competing for the same low-paid jobs. Teaching jobs or museum appointments.'

She had not chosen London for rational reasons but out of what she had available as a young twenty-something-year-old: dreams. Although this particular dream was embarrassing enough that talking about it made her feel childish.

The memory made Lia smile. When she was fourteen years old, she saw a British television series starring a man with a beautiful face. He wore a wool jumper. At night Lia dreamed about that jumper, about pressing her face against it, feeling the man's chest underneath. Breathing with the man's arms wrapped around her, she felt an uncommon sense of security.

'I thought I would find that same feeling here. That woollen jumper feeling. Silly, I know. Ridiculous. But we do... all sorts of things for ridiculous reasons. I guess that's the normal state for most people – ridiculous.'

Mari nodded and said nothing.

Speaking to anyone this honestly was strange, Lia thought. Something in Mari made her want to open up. But still Lia didn't share all her reasons for leaving Finland. She could tell anyone about the ambitions of her youth yet only a few had ever heard the sweater story. But in Finland there had also been other things she never spoke about.

'Here I had to compete for work in a completely different way,' she continued.

Lia's first year in England had been depressing. She found herself belonging to the global pariah class of the creative arts. In London there were tens or perhaps even hundreds of thousands of people just like her. All of them had training, experience or talent, but in order to get ahead in their industries they had to earn their bread and win their spurs doing crap work. Little jobs done for nothing or for horrid clients.

As an EU citizen, she was able to stay in the country and apply for work, but her combined years of schooling and practical experience in Finland left much to be desired. Her grasp of English was reasonable but limited for what was required of a graphic designer – knowing all the songs of any number of British bands by heart was little help.

She had borrowed money from her parents and taken any design work that came her way.

She had designed advertising flyers for distribution on car windscreens on the street. The pay for that was disgraceful, but she had been able to make some contacts. Next she had found a position as a jobbing designer at a local newspaper. After that Lia had done the layout for a series of anthropology museum brochures and then the museum's annual magazine. With that under her belt, she had managed to land a job as the unpaid graphic designer for a feminist magazine called *Sheer*.

'One day I was in the office, and the editor-in-chief got a call.'

Both of *Level*'s graphic designers were ill, the usual stand-ins could not come in, and there were only seven hours left until the magazine was due to go to press. Lia headed off with *Sheer*'s other graphic designer like a child to a sweet shop: a chance to work at *Level*, a magazine people actually knew about!

The evening was a catastrophe. Just before going to press, they realised that they had made a serious technical error in the page layout, because in all the rush they had misunderstood a key instruction. The magazine was late going to the printers, which cost the publisher money.

Despite all that, something about Lia must have stuck in the art director's mind, because the following summer *Level* hired her as a summer intern. After she finished her degree, they gave her a permanent position.

'That was when I changed my name.'

Lia's real name was Lea. Lea Pajala. Lia had never liked her name, which made her think of an old lady. In any case, the English always pronounced Lea as Lia anyway, so the change was minor in everyone else's eyes. She had changed that one letter just for her own sake. And in some way she felt as though the change protected her from the things she didn't wish to remember about Finland.

The boys at *Level* nicknamed her Miss Finland, which Lia found more than a little amusing. She had neither the beauty nor the radiance of a pageant queen; if anything, she was angular. The name only suited her because she was what the Brits thought a Finn should be: cold and distant.

'Well, I'm not really cold. But I do tend to exercise my right not to participate in pointless chatter.'

Lia joked with the editorial staff, but didn't open up about her life. She did her job. A graphic designer's work was mostly thinking, forming ideas. A lot of people thought that it was all drawing lines and illustrations, but that was only the part that they could see.

Given how long she spent at work, she only had enough time left for two pastimes, both of which she attacked passionately.

Her dearest love was running. She ran three nights a week, sometimes four or five. Always hard and for at least an hour and a half to get her endorphin levels high enough to reach a deep state of pleasure.

Usually she ran on the green, hilly streets and park fringes of her area in Hampstead. She had four standard routes, from which she always chose based on the weather – wind and rain were worse on the Heath, and North End was only good late in the evening when the streets were free of pedestrians.

When Lia ran, she often imagined watching herself from above, high in the air. A slender woman in a navy tracksuit, blonde hair tied in a small bun at her neck. The precise, even footfalls tapping out the route on the tree-lined path or asphalt. Lia saw the pattern in her mind from above, clear and logical.

'Of course that comes from my graphic design background. I've always loved maps and visualising spaces. I always know what direction I'm going, and I never, ever get lost.'

She seemed to like things ordered, Mari pointed out. She looked at things as wholes.

'Maybe too much. A little disorder might do me good,' Lia said.

As Mari smiled, Lia felt as though she could tell her almost anything at all.

Lia never told anyone about her second recreational activity.

'But you saw it just by looking at me.'

Once every month or two, Lia picked up a different man in a bar.

'Fifty might be an understatement.'

Sex gave her the same thing that running did: physical pleasure and emotional release. Since no embarrassment or feelings of guilt or romantic fancies came into it, the feeling of relaxation came quite naturally. All that remained was pleasure for her and the other person.

'Now when I think about it, maybe the thing that attracts me to sex isn't just the pleasure and anticipation but the disorder. You can never be completely sure of yourself or the other person and you don't act rationally.'

Lia had started picking up men after she moved to London, but she didn't mention this to Mari, because it related to events in Finland. The ones she had to get away from. After spending one lonely year in London, she decided she had to make a change.

The men had to be thirty to forty years old and looking for a one-night stand, just like her. No lovesick boys or men searching for a wife. And no restless husbands, because she didn't want any trouble.

'I don't touch anyone at work. No one at *Level* even knows I go to bars.'

Sex made Lia feel strong.

There were many Lias. In the workplace she was introverted, a performer. When she went out at night to meet men, she was open and strong. She was the one who decided. Travelling, she spent her days just walking and reading, enjoying the solitude.

'All these Lias seem very independent,' Mari said.

'Yes, indeed.'

And lonely.

They were quiet, sipping their cognac and looking out over London. This late at night the city divided into two parts: the sleeping neighbourhoods rolling over in the dark and the streets flowing through the spaces in between, channels of living light.

'Now and then I've felt quite alone,' Lia said.

When she turned twenty-five, she went on her second trip to Provence because she didn't want anyone at work to notice that she was not celebrating her birthday. This was a sore point for Lia. Loneliness, family and children – those were things she didn't allow herself to think about.

'I have tried to change things.'

She attended cultural events, exhibitions, guided local walks and even a volunteer course for a mental health patient support association. She found a pub to call her own in Hampstead, The Magdala. Still, there were only fleeting moments when she didn't feel alone, sometimes at work or at the pub or in the crowd at a rock club when everyone was dancing together in one sweaty, giddy mass.

Her home was the tiny flat of a single person, but very important to her.

When she first came to London, she looked for cheap accommodation relatively close to the sights of the city centre. What she found was the Hampstead hall of residence for the venerable King's College, where they rented rooms to non-students during the summer holidays.

In the dormitory laundry Lia met the caretaker, sixty-year-old Mr Chanthavong.

'He's one of those...' Lia searched for the right word. 'One of those Asian British gentlemen. Doubly restrained.'

Mr Chanthavong was born in Laos, but he said he had also lived in Vietnam and China, among other places, moving from country to country before coming to England. Mr Chanthavong spoke polite Oxbridge English which sounded like he had learned it on a foreign language course long ago. Now he had lived in London for twenty years. In the laundry they spoke about what British people's deep love of animals said about the civilised nature of the land and about how learning the Tube map made you feel like you had finally arrived.

A week later Lia could no longer afford to live at King's College. Mr Chanthavong looked pensive. During term time, only students were allowed to live in the hall of residence, but there was one possibility, he said. Mr Chanthavong's caretaker flat was on the ground floor. Beneath it, in the basement, was another small apartment, actually just one room with a kitchenette in the corner and a toilet. A Bosnian couple had lodged there last, starting out in the country as tourists but then applying for asylum after arriving.

'If this option were to interest you, I could let you this room. Initially perhaps for a period of two months, during which you could seek more commodious accommodations from the bountiful offerings of London,' he said.

In the room were only a bed, a desk and a chair. The kitchenette included a hotplate, a small refrigerator and a narrow worktop. The shower was in the toilet, and the space was so cramped that when you were in it you had to stand right up against the bowl. But Mr Chanthavong had asked only £400 for the flat.

Lia had been living there nearly six years now. The rent had gone up, but only to five hundred.

'No one in London lives in such a good area at that price,' she said.

Eventually Mr Chanthavong had become simply Mr Vong. At first the name had only been in Lia's mind – Chanthavong felt so formal – but then when she slipped and addressed him as Mr Vong once and the nickname clearly amused and delighted him, it had stuck.

Lia was not sure whether anyone else was aware of her living arrangements. She never requested a rental agreement and paid Mr Vong in cash. She did her washing in the hall of residence laundry, and Mr Vong helped when she needed tools to repair a socket or a window frame.

'I live like an eternal student.'

For a long time this had been fun. Whenever she saw young students in the stairway she felt as though she were one of them, living in that time of life before you become something. After landing a permanent position, she began feeling a different sort of pleasure: at least something was settled in her life. She had made her exit from the pariah class.

Her flat was small and easy to care for. From her basement window she could see a strip of an early twentieth-century church and adjacent park. The story of the statues in the park was an eccentric one: each had been rejected by the person who commissioned it.

'The Garden of Discarded Statues. Or, more like Rescued Statue Park.'

The pastor of the neighbouring St Luke's Church saved the first statues in the 1920s. Having heard of plans to scrap a statue of his church's patron saint in North London, he rushed to the scene and purchased it. The statue's intended purchasers had found St Luke's face insufficiently virtuous. Next the pastor saved the great Florence Nightingale. This work of art was rejected by a female religious order who found that the sculptor had made the body overly 'carnal' to the eye. Since tradition had it that Nightingale herself once resided in Hampstead as well, the rescue of the statue was considered fitting in all respects.

Over the decades the people and organisations of the area had accumulated a considerable collection of salvaged statuary. Lia was particularly fond of the long-eared dog which, according to the story, was purchased for the price of only one pound. No one knew who rejected it or why. Lia called the dog Poundy.

'This will sound stupid, but sometimes I talk to the statues.'

Whenever she had important decisions to make, she told St Luke and Poundy the dog about them.

Lia emphasised that she was not religious.

'But if I tell someone something, even if it's just a statue, it feels like a promise.'

Sometimes Lia watched the nuns who taught at the nearby school walking into the church.

'They look so peaceful. In films, nuns are always so severe or just one-dimensional. Pious fools.'

But these women looked as though they had found what they were looking for.

'That woollen jumper feeling.'

In the evenings Lia would hear Mr Vong running himself a bath upstairs. Every night exactly at ten o'clock. A moment later she would hear bubbling as he broke wind under the water.

'Of course he doesn't know that the sound echoes from the bath through the floor. But I always get the feeling that everything is as it should be when Mr Vong farts in the bath at ten o'clock.'

Mari laughed and Lia thought, *She's going to know everything about me soon.*

'I love London. I love its size and how uncontrollable it is and that I know a big part of it,' Mari said.

Mari described her life more briefly than Lia had.

In Finland, she studied psychology. That had gone fast, because she had always been quick at soaking up information.

'I would have graduated in less than two years, but I had to complete my internship.'

Mari also lived alone.

'I have men from time to time, but I don't quite match your pace.'

She had circulated through various countries, finally moving to London because Britain seemed to offer the most opportunities. In addition to her degree in psychology, she had studied sociology at the London School of Economics. For three years she worked as a personnel manager at Mend Ltd, a large insurance company. She had got the job based on a recommendation from a headhunter.

'I left there three years ago.'

Mari fell silent.

Lia stared at the city sparkling before them. She wondered what was wrong. At the pub Mari had seemed self-confident and alluring in a strange way.

'One thing has influenced my life more than anything else,' Mari continued.

OK, here we go, thought Lia. *She's a closet lesbian who hits on women in pubs. Or a Jehovah's Witness who proselytises people in public parks.*

'I have an unusual gift,' Mari said, looking at Lia seriously. 'I have a sort of gift for seeing more in people than other people do. I discovered it when I was a child, and that's why I've lived such an unusual life.'

Lia stared at Mari, not knowing what to say.

'Do you know how people notice really tiny things about others, often without realising it?' Mari asked. 'Like when someone glances at a door or fidgets nervously, you conclude that they're anxious to get out of the room or waiting for someone to come through the door. You might call those sorts of deductions semi-conscious or intuitive perception. For me the skill of noticing and analysing things just grew a lot stronger than in everyone else.'

The strongest manifestations related to her sense of sight. When she looked at people, she could see what they were thinking and what they would be likely to do.

'Mind-reading?' Lia said in disbelief.

'No, no. If you think of a number, I can't guess what it is. It doesn't work like that. But I can say what you think of me. And I know what you're probably planning to do this weekend.'

'This weekend I'm planning to sleep off my hangover,' Lia said. 'Guessing that doesn't take any special powers.'

Mari laughed.

'What if I told you how this all started?'

When Mari was eight years old, her great-grandparents held a Rautee family reunion at Vanajanlinna Estate near Hämeenlinna in south-central Finland.

In the elegant old hunting manor were arches, beautiful halls, antique furnishings and a prohibition-era themed bar located behind a secret door in the cellar billiards room. The history of the manor was complicated. Even the Soviet Union had once controlled it for a while, and at the time of the family gathering it functioned as a leftist youth academy.

'Our great-grandparents were such conscientious, ideologically pure supporters of the working class that the director of the school allowed them to rent the entire place for the reunion. It was the poshest leftist party you can imagine.'

Sixty relatives attended, the furthest-flung coming all the way from America. Mari had never met most of them. They were complete strangers, but still very warm people with familiar characteristics.

At the end of the reunion, everyone gathered in the courtyard for a family portrait. Arranging sixty people took time. The great-grandparents and other elderly people sat in the front row. The men wore the dark suits which they only dusted off for weddings and funerals. The women were in their finest gowns with their hair carefully done up. The mothers attempted to clean smudges from the children's clothing using handkerchiefs and spit.

'Then I realised that something strange was happening.'

Looking at the group, Mari knew what many of them were thinking.

She knew that her cousin had just got a new, special drug from an American relative. She knew that Uncle Perttu had just cheated on his wife and wanted to do it again.

'I also knew that my big sister Marja had just decided what she would be when she grew up. She wanted to be a teacher. And a relative she had met there had influenced her decision.'

No one was saying these things out loud, but still Mari knew them all the same.

'Do you know how... crazy that sounds?' Lia asked.

'Yes.'

The group photograph taken at the reunion came in the post a month later.

'Looking at the picture, I noticed more things, and everything I could see in those people made me very sad.'

Soon Uncle Perttu divorced Auntie Minna, and she said it was because he had been unfaithful. Mari's sister Marja did become a teacher and now lived in Porvoo.

'I can understand even a little kid looking at someone and knowing they are using drugs. Or feeling guilty about something,' Lia said. 'Maybe you're just a really good guesser. Like you guessed things about me tonight.'

'No, Lia. That's not it.'

The seriousness in Mari's tone made the unbelievable seem somehow real.

If this woman is a nutcase, she is a very clever nutcase.

'Up until then I had thought that everyone could sense this much about everyone else.'

But at the family reunion, Mari had grasped the power of her gift. As an eight year old, she hadn't known anything about life yet. And yet, she still saw through them all.

Lia shook her head as a surge of mistrust washed over her.

'The effect on my life has been huge,' Mari said.

Mari had seen things as a child that other people only realised in adulthood. She had begun to perceive people's motives and understand why adults ended up doing things that harmed even themselves. And at the same time, she had become a faster learner.

'When I said that I graduated from university quickly – actually I sat for exams and completed the book-based sections in two months. I didn't want to attract attention, so I drew my other requirements out over a longer period.'

'You were some kind of prodigy? A super genius?'

'It isn't intelligence. But this ability – I call it reading people – has brought me luck. And some degree of unhappiness.'

'What kind of unhappiness?'

Mari sighed: it was hard to explain.

'But I'm sure you understand why I quit working at an insurance company.'

Mari had been an outstanding personnel manager. Above all she excelled at recruiting new workers and counselling those already on the staff.

'I could see right off what kind of people they were. Whether they were telling the truth, whether they were a good fit for their jobs. But it wore on me.'

Mari was silent for a moment before continuing.

'Knowing other people's troubles is hard. Or seeing that someone is making a big mistake or doing something wrong but not being able to intervene. For instance, once a guy requested a transfer to another department, supposedly to get more experience, but the real reason was that he was selling information to a competitor.'

'You saw something like that?' Lia asked in astonishment.

'And a lot more.'

'You would be the best police detective in the world.'

Mari smiled.

'A very tired police detective.'

Lia stood up. Her legs were asleep, and the night was growing old.

'You may be able to draw conclusions from people's behaviour better than others, but I still wouldn't call that knowing what they're thinking.'

'OK,' Mari said. 'Do you want me to tell you what you really think of me?'

Lia's mouth remained shut.

This is getting frightening.

'Let me have it,' she finally said.

Mari spoke quickly, without a second thought.

'You like me a lot, more than anyone else you've ever just met. But you're also scared by such a new situation. Most of you believes everything I'm saying, but you won't accept it. You aren't used to thinking that anything like this could exist. Within about fifteen minutes you will have pacified the part of you that's resisting, and then it will be time for us to go home to sleep. You want to see me again. You're curious about what I haven't told you yet and about what might happen between us.'

'Ah,' Lia said. 'I'm afraid it's going to take significantly longer than fifteen minutes for me to believe you.'

'Good,' Mari said. 'A Finnish girl who won't let herself be talked into things just like that. When you were telling me about yourself, you only told the truth, without embellishment. That's rare. Although you did leave out a few things.'

Lia blanched.

What does she know? It's been too long for her to see any of that.

'You also bent the truth when you said that you never go to bed with colleagues,' Mari said.

Lia stared at her.

'How do you know that?'

'I'm going to wager that you've only ever made one exception. Probably the political reporter, Timothy. Being with him was awkward enough that you decided not to do it any more.'

Jesus Christ. She really does see things.

'I have to go,' Lia said. 'It's starting to get cold.'

'OK,' Mari said and stood up.

Slowly they descended the hill, remaining silent all the way. Lia didn't know what to say.

After reaching Trafalgar Road, they turned towards the lights of taxis glowing in the darkness.

'Do you mind if we let this night simmer and then chat again sometime soon?' Mari asked, offering Lia a calling card. It said simply *Mari Rautee*, with a telephone number below.

No title. Like, for example, Extremely Intelligent Loon.

'You came to meet me on purpose,' Lia said.

'Yes, I did.'

'Why? What do you want from me?'

Mari gave Lia a long look, and for the first time after a night that was quickly turning into morning, she looked tired.

'I want you to be my friend.'

5

Mari watches as Lia gets into the taxi.

She waits for the car to begin moving, driving slowly along Trafalgar Road and turning at the first corner.

Mari thinks of Kidderpore Avenue, the street where Lia lives. She has been there. She has watched from a distance as Lia walked down the street, as Lia sat in the small park near her flat, as Lia set out for a jog.

Lia is exactly as she had thought.

Mari turns to look at the driver of the next taxi. South-east Asian, a little past sixty, tired from driving the night shift. Does not raise his eyes from the tabloid he is idly perusing.

Even after all that drinking, the certainty comes automatically.

With her knuckles she gently knocks on the side window of the cab, and the driver turns. Mari climbs in, gives the cabbie her destination in Hoxton, and the taxi takes off with a jerk.

The driver does not attempt conversation. Mari glances at him once more, deciding he does not warrant further thought. Harmless.

The address Mari gave is three streets away from her home. She never takes taxis directly to her building, always getting out at least three streets away.

At her destination, Mari pays the fare and watches as the taxi glides away into the darkness and disappears. She scans her surroundings, waiting one minute. Two minutes.

Always at least three blocks early, always a check to ensure that no one dodgy is behind, always a quick transition from street to home.

No one will invade her home or her thoughts.

6

Lia didn't ring Mari the next day, although she wanted to.

Nursing her hangover, she took it as easy as humanly possible. She didn't even go jogging, only walked slowly around the neighbourhood.

On Sunday afternoon, she climbed up the flight of stairs and rang Mr Vong's doorbell.

Once or twice a month they played cards, sitting facing each other, always in the same seats. The table stood in the centre of the small living room. They spoke little, but smiled a lot.

They had the same style of play, bold but not rash. They took the risks they could afford.

Sometimes as they played, Lia imagined how they must look, such a strange pair. Two foreigners living alone in a quiet corner of a city of millions. From such different cultures, but on these afternoons the background of each was swept away. An older gentleman and a young, well, youngish, woman. Between them the steady, calm flow of the cards.

The next week was busy at work. Thinking about the Holborn Circus murder also took up Lia's time. The incident had nearly disappeared from the major media outlets, but one area of social media would not let it die: the crime enthusiast community.

The postings began immediately after the first news reports, and the killing seemed to provide the posters with material for the most astonishing sorts of musings.

'Woman without a Face the first victim of a ritual killer?'

'Does crushing with a steamroller hurt as much as being burned to death?'

The user TheHardTruth had a theory: The Woman without a Face was part of the 9/11 plot.

Even referring to the victim by that idiotic name was too much for Lia. She only scanned the posts to see whether anything new had come out about the case.

Every now and then the media covered other killings, none of which aroused the same interest in Lia.

The Holborn Circus murder made the news again on 10th May when a police press release revealed three new details. Although the police were still unable to identify the dead woman, they had determined that she was most likely of Latvian extraction and in her forties. Forensic investigators had also found indications of a gunshot wound inflicted prior to the woman being crushed.

Lia read the brief report repeatedly. The new information made the incident more concrete once again. According to the press release, the additional details were the result of exhaustive analysis of the corpse.

How can they tell her nationality from her body? And why don't they give more specifics?

The next day the printed papers didn't run the story, but for Lia it remained important. If the Latvian woman was shot, she could have been dead or unconscious when her killer ran her over. That was scant comfort, but comfort nonetheless.

Latvia – Lia knew so little about Latvia. Actually nothing. Years ago she had visited the capital, Riga, when it became a popular tourist destination following the Soviet collapse.

Riga had been beautiful. Lia had admired the handsome old architecture and taken the lift to the viewing level of the main church tower. She had eaten exceptional *pelmeni* at a fast food place with an amusing name: XL Pelmeni.

Later Riga had become one of the places Brits mobbed in search of inexpensive entertainment. English newspapers published reports describing the raucous stag jaunts of British men and the indignation their behaviour aroused in the local populace.

Lia realised she knew embarrassingly little about a country so close to her homeland and which had experienced such extreme historical upheavals. So at night she began searching for information about Latvia. She visited the library and borrowed two contemporary histories of the Baltic States and sat surfing the internet for hours.

Hardly anyone but the Latvians themselves knew the history of their tiny country, which was simply too meandering for anyone else to follow – at one time or another the Swedes, Poles and Germans had all conquered the area, along with the Soviets of course.

The economy was weak. This was partially a result of the Soviet period: Latvia manufactured nearly all of the carriages for the Soviet rail system and half of the telephones, and this specialization continued to inhibit economic growth to this day. Lia imagined the factories that had churned out railway carriages for the machinery of socialism. That job must have felt as though it would never end.

When she found a blog discussing the most popular books in Latvian libraries, she was delighted. The most popular novel was Lolita Puncule's *Daugavas vizbules sirds*, 'The Heart of a Daugava Violet'. Apparently it featured ill-fated love, Soviet Latvia and the war in Afghanistan. Number one in non-fiction was a book written by the poet Imants Ziedonis with his son Rimants. It told of trees, the forests of Latvia.

The names didn't mean anything to Lia, but that didn't matter. What a fascinating country. People constantly borrowed a non-fiction book about trees.

Perhaps none of this had anything to do with the Latvian woman discovered in the boot of a Volvo S40 on Holborn Circus. But now Lia felt that she could place the woman in some context, that she understood something about her.

Both of them had come to England from the north-eastern corner of Europe, from a place little known in the wider world. Her life had probably been hard, since it ended so brutally.

For some reason this Latvian woman had become important to Lia.

One morning, sitting at her window eating a yogurt, Lia looked out at the dull grey features of St Luke visible in the distance and waved her spoon at him.

I'm so well off that I even have time to think about a perfect stranger who was murdered.

My life has room for all sorts of things.

That day she called Mari.

7

'Don't think for a second that I believe what you were saying. I just want to see how long this bluff of yours will hold out,' Lia said when she and Mari met at the Queen's Head & Artichoke.

To start with, Lia asked about the thing that had been bothering her the most.

'How did you know I would be at the White Swan celebrating my birthday with my workmates?'

'I heard about it,' Mari replied.

'From whom?'

'Martyn Taylor.'

'Huh?'

Martyn Taylor was Lia's immediate supervisor, the AD – art director – at *Level*.

'I know him,' Mari said. 'Not very well, though. We've met a few times at parties and exhibition openings. When he heard I was from Finland, he mentioned you. Since then we've talked about you every time we run into each other.'

'Did you know the answers to those questions in the pub because you'd been prying into my affairs?'

'Tempting theory. That Martyn Taylor might have told me everything I knew,' Mari said and smiled. 'But how would Martyn have known to tell me exactly the things your colleagues asked about?'

That's true. Not a terribly plausible idea.

Martyn had asked Mari about Finland.

'He said he wanted to understand your background. He really respects you,' Mari said.

'He wanted to hear about Finland in order to understand me?'

'That's what he said. Apparently there's something special about you.'

'That's us Finnish women.'

'Indeed. Us Finnish women.'

Lia told Mari her theory that people from small countries adapted to large countries better than people from large countries to small because people from small countries did not expect the world to work the same everywhere as it did at home.

'That does sound logical,' Mari said. 'And then there are countries where anyone would have a hard time adjusting. Like Finland.'

Lia laughed.

Neither of them said so aloud, but they were clearly sounding each other out. Lia had to have time to see whether she could take Mari's claims about her gift seriously.

She let Mari choose where they met, and each place was chic: Foxcroft & Ginger, Le Mercury, an art museum bar.

'Ah, my medium,' Lia might say in greeting. 'Whose mind have you read today?'

The world held legions of people who claimed clairvoyant powers. Why could they not do the same things Mari said she could? Lia enquired.

'I don't know why I can do it and other people can't,' Mari said calmly. 'And this doesn't have anything to do with the supernatural.'

Mari encouraged Lia to compare her gift to those of an artist. Everyone can draw something, and anyone can learn to do it better, but some people are especially gifted and have what it takes to become professionals.

Lia encouraged Mari to read her better: did she need such simple metaphors?

Had Mari ever been examined by a psychologist? she asked.

'No. Of course I've taken hundreds of tests on my own. Just because of my education. But I've never felt any need to let anyone else test me.'

'But if you have such a unique skill, why wouldn't you want it tested? Just for the sake of science?'

'I don't want anyone to start thinking I'm strange; I don't want to attract attention. There isn't anything mysterious about any of this.'

Her brain calculated probabilities about people so quickly that she felt as if she knew what was going on inside their heads. The only unusual part was the amount and intensity of the analysis.

'I've never found a name for it,' she said. 'I've chatted with cognitive scientists about it. They suggested terms like social intelligence and apperceptive observation, neither of which is exactly right.'

Some questions Mari refused to answer. She would not tell Lia where she lived, just the area: Hoxton. And she never said anything about her work.

'I have different things going on,' was all she would ever say.

'You left the insurance company three years ago. Have you just been doing "different things" since then? How do you live on that?' Lia asked.

'I get by,' Mari said, communicating the futility of any further questioning.

But Mari always described her gift openly and as a simple matter of fact.

'I don't think anything special when I do it. There isn't any mental state I have to enter. It's like... eating a sandwich.'

Of course it helped knowing something about the person's background, Mari added. If she wanted to know someone's thoughts in more detail, she looked into that person's actions.

Gradually Lia's resistance crumbled. She heard so many realistic details that believing Mari had just fabricated them became too difficult.

'Last spring when I went home for a visit, I knew my brother had a secret. I saw it immediately,' Mari said.

Secretly her brother had married a woman and adopted her children. This twenty-six-year-old man was now a father of three. He had dated a Chilean woman much older than himself for a year and a half and then thrown a rollicking wedding party in Valparaiso attended by the woman's entire extended family without breathing a word to his own at home in Finland.

'And I had to keep quiet about it the whole time I was there! I couldn't let on that I knew, because he had to have the chance to announce the news himself.'

'Do you mean your family doesn't know about your gift?'

'No, they don't. They think I'm a little peculiar, but just because I live abroad. I've only told a few people about this.'

So why me? Lia thought, but didn't ask out loud.

Mari didn't say much about her relatives at home. Lia, on the other hand, confided openly about her own. She had no siblings, only her parents, and they corresponded only infrequently.

For years now, they had been important to her in her thoughts, but not from day to day. She only missed them for fleeting moments. In their high-rise flat in Espoo, her parents were waiting for retirement. Lia felt as though she were not good enough for them. They were always expecting something from her: a return to Finland, marriage, family.

No one ever said this out loud, or much else of consequence. The feeling was that they should all live with the noise turned down to a sensible volume to avoid any chance of conflict.

Lia didn't tell Mari about the thing she had such a difficult time forgiving her parents for. Before leaving Finland, Lia had some difficulties with a young man. In the end it turned ugly, but her parents never understood.

Lia felt as though Mari might understand the situation, with all its sordid details. But she didn't want to tell anyone about it.

Soon Lia found they were calling each other almost every day and that she looked forward to the times they met. She was having more fun than she had in ages.

To Lia's irritation, Mari seemed to guess that her mistrust had begun to fade.

'Everything OK?' Mari asked, looking at Lia intently.

'Perfectly,' Lia said, looking back.

Lia took Mari to rock concerts, which took some small persuading.

'How old are you, thirty-two?' Lia asked.

'Thirty-one.'

'Too young to live without music,' Lia said and bought them tickets to a Keane concert.

Keane was one of the first British bands Lia had fallen in love with. Singing along to the words in her downstairs flat, Lia regularly subjected Mr Vong to their songs.

Mari was in ecstasy after the concert and, over the summer, they did the rounds of the London clubs. One of the highlights was a show by an American post punk indie band, The Gossip. The front woman was one Beth Ditto, known not only for her big voice and large stature but also for being gay. As she danced in the throng of other women, Lia realised that people might easily take her and Mari for a couple.

Mari is the best friend I have ever had. This is almost like being infatuated with someone.

Sometimes sitting in cafés they would have fun with Mari's gift.

'That one there,' Lia might say. 'What do you see about him?'

Mari looked and then started to tell what she saw.

That young man there studied history and had been doing so for quite some time. He was waiting for his girlfriend; he had something to tell her. It wasn't good news, but he wasn't breaking things off. Perhaps he had to move to another city or something.

That woman had a problem, related to her health, specifically something to do with her lower abdomen. She was afraid.

Upon looking at one man, Mari began, 'He's very focused – some part of his work demands a lot from him, intense concentration like Beth Ditto at her concert...'

'What?' Lia interrupted. 'Did you see what Beth Ditto was thinking?'

Mari looked confused.

'Why would reading a famous person be any different? Whenever I see someone, the perceptions just pop into my head. I can't do anything about it.'

'Well, what was she thinking?'

'When she came on stage, she was in a perfect, nearly fanatical state of concentration, like lots of artists get into. She was thinking of the first words of the songs, because once she got those out everything else would just flow. Then she just went to it.'

'Wasn't she thinking anything else? Like, damn, my panties are riding up, or wow, there sure are a lot of good-looking chicks in the audience?'

'Maybe she was,' Mari said, exasperated. 'I'm not a radar, monitoring every second. I was singing along and was... part of the audience.'

'I was just curious,' Lia said.

'I admit that I'm usually curious to see what I'll find in people too,' Mari said, and smiled.

Soon they developed their own way of talking, their own vocabulary, including the occasional Finnish word that lacked any exact equivalent in English. They spoke English together since both of them had long since begun thinking in English, but at times an idea was simply easier to convey with the addition of a Finnish word.

For example the word *kuuri*: a time during which something is either enjoyed frequently or abstained from completely. *Kuuri* was much more evocative than *diet*, *binge* or *fast*, all of which, paradoxically, apply equally well. They observed a Philip Seymour Hoffman *kuuri* set off by a film they took in at the East End Film Festival. Lia got Mari on a running *kuuri*, but after a few evening jogs, Mari announced she was giving it up.

'Running is your thing,' she said.

'*Kännit*,' Lia said. 'Let's get *kännit*.'

Mari understood. They didn't just want to get *drunk*, and certainly not *pissed*, which was the unfortunate and uncontrolled inebriation of teenagers. They were adult women and took their *kännit* seriously.

'And I mean *kännit* in the plural, not just *känni*. That means drinking together, sociably,' Lia pointed out.

They ordered vodka. Lia's favourite was Polish Zubrówka, but Mari liked the classic Russian Stolichnaya.

Drunken Mari was less serious, pleasantly chatty, Lia found.

But Mari still didn't breathe a word about her gift when others were around. Lia understood that she should not either.

They could talk about social issues for hours, debating and even disagreeing, but the way their intellectual worlds blended gave Lia genuine pleasure.

She especially liked Mari's thoughts about equality.

'It's my personal feminism,' Mari said. 'I've recognised what things in my life make me aware as a feminist.'

This sounded simple, but a surprising number of people – women – had never considered it. Knowing your own problems gave you power to act. At the same time you also saw what you didn't understand about others' problems.

'That individuality isn't just self-interest though,' Mari said. 'Like demanding equality only according to my own needs. You have to have your principles. And a sense that you're doing things for other women too.'

What Mari didn't say was what the problems in her own life were.

But the idea helped Lia. She didn't have to feel guilty over not sharing someone else's version of feminism. And it helped to refine her own.

Over the summer, Lia realised that her life had become happier in a way she had thought lost to youth. Now and then with Mari she even felt younger, as if she were twenty again.

Mari is the friend I was looking for when I moved to London. Together we're doing the things I wanted to do then.

Although they rarely talked about their homeland any more, Lia found herself remembering things about Finland she had forgotten. The silence of an early Saturday evening falling over the city, even one as large as Helsinki. The comforting feeling that no matter whom you spoke to, you knew you were an equal.

She had not thought about those things in years. For the first time she had begun to think of her homeland with warmth.

Finnish girls in the bars of London. A generation bearing the accumulated power of independent women.

8

Lia also told Mari about what had happened in the spring.

'That crazy murder is still running through my head.'

'Has any new information come to light?'

'No, not really. It feels strange.'

After ending her life in such a grotesque way, the killer or killers then brought the woman to the centre of the City and dumped her. You would have expected the police to have identified the woman or someone might have seen the car stopping on the pavement.

'What bothers you so much about this?'

Lia didn't know how to explain why she felt so much empathy with the murdered Latvian woman.

'Oh, I think it's perfectly understandable,' Mari said.

She remembered reading that, at some point in their lives, some kind of crisis stopped most adults in their tracks. Suddenly a disaster or a war in some far-flung country just caught their interest.

'Maybe that need to learn everything about one specific crisis comes from usually ignoring them. You realise you don't think about your own life much either and decide there should be something you understand. And then you start looking at yourself too. The whole thing becomes an opportunity to recreate yourself.'

'Sometimes that degree in psychology really shows,' Lia said.

'Sorry, I didn't mean to lecture. But haven't you ever thought about it like that?'

Lia admitted she had indeed.

Mari had had a similar experience when she was young.

'Have you ever heard of Bhopal?'

'It's somewhere in India, right? And there was an accident there,' Lia said.

In 1984, when Mari was still a little girl.

'It became important to me later, as a teenager, when I read in the newspaper how poorly the company and the government treated the people there.'

The Indian city of Bhopal was virtually unknown to the rest of the world until one of the largest industrial catastrophes of all time occurred there. In the early hours of morning on 3rd December 1984 city residents woke up with difficulty breathing. Their lungs were on fire.

The Union Carbide pesticide plant had released a large cloud of poisonous gas. According to official estimates, the victims numbered some 3,700, but other evaluations claimed many more. As many as 25,000 people may have died of complications resulting from exposure to the gas.

Some city residents began a legal battle, which dragged on for decades. They did receive compensation but complained that it was disproportionately small compared to their loss, and that the investigation into the disaster had been feeble at best. Not only in India but across the world the name Bhopal became synonymous with gross injustice.

'I've been there twice,' Mari said.

'Why?' Lia asked, surprised.

'I know it sounds strange. Disaster tourism. But I wanted to see for myself the marks the accident left.'

Bhopal was dirty white, red, turquoise and grey. The air was thick with dust. Most buildings housed little shops at street level. Motorcycles and powered rickshaws cut through the mass of people and stray dogs. The only unusual thing about the city was that once a large group of people had been annihilated, serious diseases had plagued the remaining populace and the bitterness aroused by the tragedy had been left untreated.

To the locals, Mari had just been one of the hundreds of foreigners who had walked their streets asking questions, another of the reporters, researchers, policemen and government officials. The people of Bhopal told her the same thing they told everyone else. The stories of their families' troubles, the mother who died or the uncle now paralyzed.

'They were telling the truth, but they were also leaving something out.'

On her second trip four years later, Mari already knew what she would hear and what she was supposed to ask afterwards. Some remembered her.

Everyone in the city had known people who had died. Not only had families lost breadwinners but also much of the wisdom and warmth that had once enriched their homes. The accident had become a way to measure time: there was the time before and the time after. It was also a way to measure humanity and justice. As long as the residents of Bhopal had not received real compensation, speaking to them of justice was meaningless.

Perhaps the most fitting word to describe their experience was hopelessness. They were getting over their losses, gradually. However, the loss of their human dignity had not diminished, and they felt that this theft would continue in perpetuity.

The Bhopal scandal was a lesson for Mari in the logic and behaviour of big money.

'And yes, feel free to analyse me,' she added. 'The daughter of a leftist family and the evils of the world.'

Lia smiled at the irony.

It's sad we have to joke about the best parts of us.

She turned the conversation back to the Holborn Circus murder.

'Can you say anything about the perpetrator based on what he did? Can you see what kind of a person would do something like that?' Lia asked.

'If you're thinking that I could guess what the killer is like based only on the news, then no. My gift isn't that strong.'

'I didn't mean exactly that.'

Lia told Mari about the criminologist in the newspaper who had talked about the case as an example of the increasing role of spectacle in violent crime.

'You really have studied this,' Mari said.

'Yes, I have. But do you see anything... more in the murder?'

'This is a subject I don't know particularly well. But let's think about it.'

Mari sighed and thought.

'The killer crushed her with a bloody steamroller and then left her to be found in the middle of London. That has to be a message to someone.'

Lia nodded.

'He didn't just want to kill that woman – he wanted to defile her,' Mari said. 'Someone wanted to wipe her off the face of the earth, to cast her down into the deepest pit of hell. To demonstrate complete control.'

It seemed like a Mafia crime. But not just score-settling: if they didn't want the body identified, then why dump it with such... flourish? The perpetrator wanted this to hit the headlines.

'I'm going to say two things were going on here. First of all, whoever did this wanted to punish that woman. He's obviously a man and more cruel than either of us can really imagine. The second is that he was also probably sending a message to others like her that this is what happens if you don't obey.'

'Do you remember when I said you would make an excellent police detective?'

'Thanks, but I could never work for them.'

After they emptied their final glasses, Lia asked, 'Does it seem macabre that I think about that murder so much?'

'Not to me,' Mari replied. 'Shouldn't people always do things that feel important?'

After recovering from her initial shock, Lia had found that thinking about the murder no longer frightened her. It was still sickening, but the overriding feeling was something new: she wanted to do something to fix the situation, to punish the perpetrator.

'Sometimes I get really angry. I feel like screaming, "Let's nail that bastard."'

Mari smiled quickly.

'I know the feeling.'

9

London at the end of July was sweltering. Most *Level* employees were already on holiday, and the rest were anxiously waiting for their breaks to begin.

Lia, on the other hand, had arranged not to take her leave until September or October. That didn't bother her, but the crush of work while everyone else was away did. Today she was rushing to finish her layouts: ahead was an evening with Mari, bowling. Generally Lia was meticulous in her work, but sometimes you had to take some shortcuts.

When Lia saw Martyn Taylor walking towards her, she quickly tried to hide her work because the art director would be sure to notice the signs of a rushed layout job.

Martyn Taylor was a career professional. Before coming to *Level*, he had worked at a large fashion magazine and helped found two other successful periodicals. He was respected and demanding, and one of the wisest people Lia had ever encountered. Whenever she could, Lia deferred to his judgement.

Taylor leaned against her desk.

'I was just chatting with the boss. Our publisher's board has just held their monthly meeting,' Taylor said.

Lia tensed, waiting to hear what he had to say. The board had approved Taylor's retirement plan, meaning that he would step down in three years when he turned fifty-nine.

'Damn,' Lia said in surprise. 'I never realised you could plan something like that. What will we do?'

'You'll choose a new AD. Or the editor-in-chief will. But Matt Thomas wants to hear who I think would be the best fit.'

The position would be listed publicly, but usually ADs were promoted from within, one of the current graphic designers, Taylor reminded her. Lia tried to act casual, despite a sudden attack of giddiness.

'I think you have what it takes,' Taylor said.

Lia needed to start learning to take overall responsibility though, to think about the whole magazine, Taylor explained. If she succeeded, he might train her to be the new AD. Usually the job required longer experience, but Taylor believed that Lia could grow into it.

'Although you have been slacking off a bit of late.'

Lia swallowed, embarrassed. Taylor was right. Running around so much with Mari had meant a change from Lia's old work-centred lifestyle.

'Thanks. I'll try to get myself together,' she said.

After Taylor left, Lia sent Mari a message, moving their date back by two hours. Now these layouts had to be perfect.

When they finally made it to the bowling alley under the Tavistock Hotel, Lia was bursting with enthusiasm.

'I really like my job, and like Taylor said, I'm not at all shit at it.'

She had thought that she might become an AD somewhere someday, but she had never presumed to think of *Level*.

The euphoria lasted about half an hour. Between increasingly weak bowling performances, Lia's mood began to darken.

'There's no way Matt Thomas is going to choose me. At best he's indifferent towards me, if he doesn't actually despise me.'

Of course the editor-in-chief would promote Lia's male graphic designer colleague ahead of her.

'Thomas clearly has a problem with me being a woman and having opinions. He's the type that still makes jokes about women's abilities and looks. And assumes that women think he's funny.'

They went for a pint in the amusement arcade's bar.

'There are other good magazines,' Mari said.

'Of course,' Lia said. But *Level* was a special place. And if she wanted to be an AD somewhere else, she needed to be making decisions now.

Once she had had the initiative to abandon her familiar home in favour of hunting for work in London, but in recent years she had mostly been waiting around for life to drop things in her lap.

'Work is so important to me. That isn't always a good thing, but there you have it. Now I have to decide whether I hang around waiting at *Level* or try to move somewhere else.'

Mari thought.

'What would have to happen for it to be easier for you to decide?' she asked.

'Good question. I think I'd have to know whether Matt Thomas is going to choose me. I think the answer is no.'

'Why don't you go and ask him? Maybe he respects a direct approach.'

Lia grimaced.

'No. If I look like I want the position, that's sure to increase his pleasure in not giving it to me.'

'Sounds like a nasty old git.'

'Nasty is an understatement. I guess I should be looking online for graphic designer openings.'

'Let me think about it a bit. I may be able to come up with something,' Mari said.

'What do you have in mind?'

'Nothing.'

'Good. Frankly, I'm terrified that Thomas would just say no.'

'That's possible. But then you would know. If I can come up with a way to help, do you want me to?'

'Of course. But if it means you go and sock my editor in the teeth, then no.'

10

In mid-August, Mari called and asked Lia to reserve a long lunch break for the 25th, starting at one o'clock.

They did go to lunch together occasionally, but this invitation was different. Mari hoped that Lia could set aside at least two hours, if not the rest of the afternoon.

Mari didn't explain her request. Lia blocked out the time on her calendar with the words *Something Fun.*

On Monday, 25th August, Mari was waiting for Lia on Fetter Lane. *Level*'s offices were located in a large building with dozens of other companies. Mari hailed them a taxi from the kerb.

'We don't have far to go, but I'm in a hurry,' she explained and then gave the driver an address on Park Street, Bankside.

Lia didn't ask any questions and let Mari have her surprise.

In Bankside, a similar large office building awaited them. Mari hurried into the lower lobby and then led Lia to a lift and the top floor of the building.

There they saw two doors, the smaller of which read *Clarke Holdings*, the larger of which was blank. Mari approached the latter. The locks looked sturdy, but she opened them with an easy turn of the appropriate key.

Behind the door was a long, dimly lit corridor with more doors. Mari opened the second door on the left.

They entered a small conference room. With only a table, eight chairs and a video projector mounted in the ceiling, the sparsely decorated space appealed to Lia's designer's eye.

Tasteful accents beautified the furnishings. The lights had been placed with forethought. A discreet, abstract decorative pattern wound along the walls.

On the table were two laptops, their displays filled only with screen saver waveforms, and next to them two plates, cutlery and Chinese takeaway in pasteboard boxes.

'Is this a working lunch?' Lia asked in amusement.

'In a way,' Mari said as she ushered Lia in and indicated a seat at the table.

Mari looked at her watch and said that they had six minutes to start eating.

'While we have our food, I'll tell you what's about to happen in Hanover Square.'

Opening the boxes, she offered them to Lia and then scooped out portions for herself. Lia began tasting her food, filled with curiosity.

'Right now, your boss, Matt Thomas, is en route to an interview.'

A firm by the name of Elevate had invited Thomas to Mayfair. From the invitation, Thomas had learned that Elevate was a headhunter company that carried out high-powered, confidential background interviews and employment tests.

'In a few minutes, Thomas will enter the company premises and we'll see here, live, how the meeting goes.'

Lia's chopsticks clattered onto her plate.

'What's going on here?'

Mari's face shone with quiet satisfaction.

'As it turns out, the entire company is fictitious.'

In the interview they would hear what Thomas thought of his subordinates, including Lia. And when Thomas left, he would think he had been sounded out confidentially for a position in a company too important to mention by name.

'No, Mari. No.'

Lia was so shaken that she pushed her chair back and stood.

'Now you won't have to ask him,' Mari said.

'Is this a joke? I didn't ask for anything like this. Thomas will guess right off that something is wrong!'

'No, he won't. He'll just have an interesting conversation and never know a thing about why he is really having it. Thomas doesn't know the meeting has anything to do with you; he thinks it's about him.'

'But he isn't stupid – irritating and exasperating, yes, but also clever! If he figures out this isn't real, I'll never be able to show myself at *Level* again.'

'Trust me,' Mari said. 'You've asked what kind of work I do. Well, this is my work.'

Ten days previously, Matt Thomas had received a telephone call. The caller had said he was from Elevate, a company that handled headhunting assignments. He went on to tell Thomas that he was in the initial stages of consideration for the position of editor-in-chief at one of the major British daily papers. The name of the newspaper would only be revealed to the candidates selected for additional interviews. The caller enquired whether despite this necessary secrecy Thomas would still wish to attend the meeting, where he would receive an interview and undergo a battery of tests, with complete confidentiality.

Mari smiled broadly. 'Thomas said he would be delighted to come.'

Lia was speechless. She felt like screaming.

'Just over one minute left,' Mari said. 'Thomas took the Tube. He got off at Oxford Circus, crossed Regent Street and just turned onto Princess Street. He'll be there soon.'

Lia stared in disbelief at the computer screen, which displayed three camera views of an office building lobby. The receptionist, a woman with dark hair, sat at a semi-circular desk.

Seconds passed. Lia swallowed as she watched the surveillance camera images.

'We'll see whether he makes it on time,' Mari said. 'Oh, there he is.'

As a man wearing a sedate dark suit entered the lobby, Lia recognised him immediately. Only donning it as he departed for important meetings, Matt Thomas never wore a jacket at their office.

Thomas approached the desk and spoke to the receptionist. No sound came from the computer, and Lia looked at Mari in alarm.

'Don't worry,' Mari said. 'We'll hear him when he gets up to the Elevate office.'

The receptionist handed Thomas a guest badge. He considered whether to clip the badge to his suit, but then decided simply to hold it. He nodded to the woman and walked towards the lift.

'Does that woman really work there?' Lia asked.

'Of course she does. But the two who are about to interview Thomas work for me.'

Matt Thomas entered the lift.

'Mari, can you still stop this? This is crazy.'

'Now don't fret,' Mari said. 'Let's see what happens now.'

Mari clicked and a different camera image filled the screen, showing another conference room with table and chairs, bigger than the one in which Lia and Mari sat.

A moment later, Matt Thomas entered the room, followed by two other people. Their voices sounded tinny coming from the small loudspeaker sitting on the table in front of Lia and Mari.

Lia scarcely dared breathe.

'They can't see or hear us,' Mari said.

'Please, take a seat,' the woman in the conference room said to Thomas.

Thomas smiled and sat in the chair reserved for him at the head of the table, where there were also a notepad and pen. The interviewers set up at the opposite end of the table, spread out laptops, binders and papers.

The older of the interviewers, a blonde woman of about fifty, led the meeting. Her assistant, a man of some thirty years whose features indicated Indian ancestry, spoke in an accent indicative of time spent at an elite university.

'This meeting will be videotaped,' the woman said, pointing up towards the camera that provided Lia and Mari with their view of the scene.

'The recordings will be carefully stored for six months, after which they will be destroyed. No one beyond Elevate employees will be able to see them. And of course all of us are bound by non-disclosure agreements.'

Matt Thomas nodded.

He was clearly nervous, Lia thought and found herself able to breathe somewhat easier.

'So, for the record, my name is Carol Penn and this is Robert Cansai, interviewing Mr Matt Thomas, editor-in-chief of *Level* magazine. This is a first-round interview, and the date is the 25th of August. Mr Thomas, could you please tell us why you initially chose to work at *Level*?'

The question came quickly, but Matt Thomas was ready.

'It was a mixture of ninety per cent reason and ten per cent emotion. Producing a magazine requires strong financial management, creating principles to guide content decisions and process control, but an editor-in-chief also has to be able to create a unique spirit. In addition to the quality of the magazine, *Level* has a tradition of independence, and that unique voice appealed to me,' Thomas said.

'Ha!' Mari said to Lia as they watched the screen. 'Memorised and grandiose.'

The interviewers took turns asking questions, first about work experience and education. Thomas told of the public school and university he had attended and his working years before *Level*.

Mari continued eating as she watched the interview, but Lia couldn't touch her food, even though everything seemed to be going fine onscreen.

Ten minutes later, the mood in the interview room was relaxed.

It was Carol Penn's turn to ask a question.

'Mr Thomas, do you consider yourself a happy person?'

Thomas smiled.

'Very happy,' he said, and then proceeded to list his professional accomplishments, mention his family and sailing hobby. He talked about the satisfaction he derived from success in leadership.

'He was expecting that. Interviewers always ask a question like that sooner or later to try to throw the subject off. It's an attempt to nudge the interviewee away from the answers he's already prepared,' Mari said.

The next questions Thomas didn't like, as they addressed *Level*'s decreasing circulation. When Robert Cansai asked why Thomas had not been able to halt the downward slide, his face turned sour.

'Circulation hasn't fallen nearly as quickly as during my predecessor's tenure. And you have to remember that I started out with the old editorial team – I wasn't able to bring anyone in with me. I've tried by might and main to add more energy to the magazine and make it more competitive, but the opposition to change among my subordinates is... considerable,' Thomas said.

'That's not true!' Lia exclaimed. 'That little shit. We've been trying to come up with better selling features for years.'

'Listen,' Mari said. 'This is interesting.'

'Mr Thomas, let's do talk about your office for a moment. What sort of group is it you lead?'

'Challenging,' Thomas said. 'Of course everyone has their own special skills that we do our best to utilise, but the dynamism required for commercial success is often lacking. I tend to shoulder responsibility for improving the magazine more or less alone.'

'Do you have any particularly talented subordinates? Is there anyone you'd like to take along if you move to a new position?'

'Not really. Timothy Phelps, perhaps. He's a good political reporter, but he may be at the peak of his career already. *Level* may be just the right size for him.'

'We have collected a list of your subordinates and thought we would ask you your opinion of their potential. This is our way of evaluating how you deal with the strengths and weaknesses of the people you lead,' Cansai said. 'Is that acceptable?'

'Of course,' Thomas said. 'I know all of them inside and out.'

'Sam Levinson?' Cansai began.

'Sam is a very pleasant subordinate and colleague. Good sense of humour. But I wouldn't take him with me. His pieces are too conventional.'

Lia stared at the computer screen. Of all the bloody nerve!

'William Jasper, your entertainment reporter.'

'Jasper is competent in his area. In a sense it's a shame he chose entertainment, because that shows he doesn't have the potential for the big leagues.'

As the list of names continued, Lia heard her boss guillotine one subordinate after another. About each person Thomas first said something good but then immediately added something so biting that the message was clear: good for nothing.

'Lia Pajala?'

'Lia is a diligent foot soldier. But she's a bit outspoken. In order to get ahead she would need social skills. And if she hasn't developed them by now…'

Filled with bitterness, Lia stared at Matt Thomas' crooked smile. The AD position had just moved out of reach.

'Speaking of female employees, the *Level* team has a conspicuous lack of women. Only two in thirteen. At other, similar publications, the proportion of women is closer to forty per cent, sometimes more. Why?'

Matt Thomas breathed in one second too long. He was not prepared for this.

'I would say it has to do with the history of the magazine. *Level* first emerged as an overtly political magazine. In politics women have traditionally played a smaller role, and in political journalism men make up the majority.'

'You have hired five of the current employees, none of them women. Why is this?'

Thomas forced a smile.

'Just chance. But to speak plainly, we're competing in a tough media market, and the best stories come from editorial departments with balls. If you'll pardon the expression.'

'Other publications compete in the same market. And they have women,' Carol Penn observed.

From the look on Thomas' face, it was apparent that he felt the interview had just turned into an interrogation.

'Could you describe your collaborative relationship with the magazine's advertisers?' Robert Cansai asked, changing the subject.

Thomas latched on to the question with obvious relief. Lia, on the other hand, let loose a torrent of rage at the video display.

'Male chauvinist wanker. He's going to pay for this.'

'That won't be possible,' Mari said. 'I'm just sad I can't put this online. This would be sure to go viral. Posh boss badmouths employees smiling all the while. And to top it off he implies women aren't cut out for hard work.'

At the conclusion of the interview, Thomas received an opportunity to share his views on the future of the media business, thus lulling him into thinking that the meeting had gone well.

When Carol Penn announced that the interview was over, Thomas looked relieved.

'What happens from here depends on our client,' Penn said. 'If they select you for the group of final candidates, we will be in touch within two weeks. If you aren't chosen, we won't trouble you any more. However, I will say that we receive similar assignments from media corporations relatively often. These interviews never go to waste.'

Matt Thomas thanked them, seeming satisfied. Then he stood up, shook hands conscientiously with both interviewers and left.

Mari shifted the video connection back to the lobby. They waited quietly until Thomas returned downstairs in the lift and walked to the reception desk, returning his visitor badge and exiting. His steps were faster now than when he had arrived.

He's hurrying back to work. He's going to go back to the office as if nothing ever happened.

'Thank you,' Lia said to Mari. 'I don't know how you did this, and I don't know what I should think about it. But thank you.'

'You're welcome. You should get back to your office too,' Mari said.

Lia nodded.

'And you can't tell anyone about this,' Mari said. 'Not a living soul.'

'I understand,' Lia said.

11

Lia had difficulty concentrating on her work.

The experience had been disconcerting. Hearing someone express so directly things that were usually whitewashed was rare. Suddenly the little community at *Level* looked completely different, and her own future was not feeling particularly rosy any more.

Even more disconcerting was Mari's role in all of it. She said she did this 'for work'. What work was that – luring people into staged job interviews?

Mari had carefully arranged everything in a perfectly planned information-gathering operation.

Who is she really? And who are the two interviewers?

She rang Mari.

'We have to meet again today.'

'Of course. Do you want to come here?'

'I'll be there sometime after six.'

'Call me when you're downstairs. The front door is locked at five.'

Sam, who was sitting next to her, had heard Lia's call and looked curious.

'Was that the same Mari we met at your birthday party?'

'The very same.'

'She was a bonny lass. Do you think I could call her?'

'Sorry, Sam, but she has a boyfriend. Has had for a long time.'

Lia didn't want Mari any more mixed up in her work life than she already was.

It was already seven o'clock before Lia made it back to Bankside. Mari met her at the doors to the Park Street office building and again led them to the blank top-floor door.

'Come right in. Now I can give you the grand tour.'

Mari showed Lia from room to room, and Lia was astonished to realise that the place occupied almost the entire floor.

The conference room they had used during the day was one of the smaller spaces. Altogether eight rooms made up the suite.

Of these, the three smallest looked like employee offices, but the style was the same as the conference room. Lia stopped to look at the large, light orange circle on the floor at each workstation.

They were thin rugs that served several purposes, Mari said. In addition to muffling sound, they contained special sensors that told the office security system whenever anyone moved in the room.

'We call them research rooms,' Mari said.

'Who made the rugs?'

'A man named Berg. You'll meet him later. Let's go to my office,' Mari said and led them to the following room.

As she stepped in, Lia stopped.

The entire *Level* editorial office would have fitted in Mari's room. One wall was entirely glass with a handsome view of the old riverside and industrial quarter of Bankside.

Mari's personal office held so many unique details and pieces of furniture that Lia didn't know where to start inspecting them. There were two large, stylish sofas. The desk was enormous, at least ten metres long, with two computers and storage space for papers and other things. The arching shape of it made it look like a piece of art.

The most startling sight was a floor-to-ceiling shelf full of books and files. In front of them was a large, translucent piece of fabric fixed at the corners to large hooks and at the centre to various shelves. Thin slashes cut through the fabric, making it possible to remove the books. From the sides of the room, beams of light fell on the fabric, highlighting its beautiful texture.

That is the most beautiful wall I have ever seen.

'The same Mr Berg?' Lia asked.

Mari nodded.

'We'll come back here when you've seen the other spaces.'

Nothing could have prepared Lia for what awaited her in the next room she saw. Nearly as large as Mari's office, it had special lamps whose light seemed to change as they moved. The space was like a combination of computer manufacturing R&D workshop and small instrument laboratory. At least twenty computers littered the room. Some had their cases removed, and custom peripherals and bundles of cables bristled from them all.

The equipment in the room would have been a valuable haul for burglars, but strong locks, surveillance cameras and other security arrangements protected the office, Mari said.

'What is this place?' Lia asked.

'Rico's kingdom. He's our CTO.'

'Where is Rico?'

'Today was a short day. Everyone was concentrating on Elevate, and after that it was time for a break.'

'How many people work here?'

'It varies, but usually four or five. But let's go and look at the Den.'

The Den was an open space of a couple of hundred square metres.

'A cosy little den?' Lia asked.

'Berg named it. This is his den.'

The Den would have looked like an industrial hall, but moveable screens of different colours and the same patterns painted on the walls as in the conference room made it interesting. The workstations had various work surfaces, drafting and printing equipment, and even a small press with an endless assortment of tools and materials scattered around. Someone could probably have assembled a small house with the tools and supplies sitting there.

At one side of the Den was a beautiful kitchen partitioned off by more screens. The enormous hooks hanging from the ceiling were the only unique thing about it. Berg loved hammocks, Mari explained.

'I've never seen a better kitchen. You can cook practically anything you can imagine here,' Mari said with pride.

Next to the refrigerators was a wine cooler, from which she retrieved a bottle of white wine and two glasses.

'Let's go to my room.'

Once back in Mari's office, they sat on one of the two sofas.

'So what is this place really?' Lia asked.

Mari poured the wine and offered Lia a glass.

'This is my studio. And that's what we call it, the Studio. Artists and musicians and designers call their workspaces studios. We also create things.'

'Things like that meeting with Matt Thomas?'

'Things like that too. Actually, what I do doesn't have its own name,' Mari said, looking thoughtful. 'At least I've never come up with a single word to describe it. We usually just talk about jobs or gigs. When a job comes up that needs handling, I handle it.'

'Like my troubles at work?'

'That thing we did today probably felt like overkill. And it was. But it worked. Now you know what Matt Thomas thinks of you, and you can decide for yourself what to do.'

'Let's not go there now,' Lia said. 'Too many things are happening at once here.'

Mari told her that the Studio had only been in operation for two years. She had worked for much longer to get it set up and staffed with the right people: an IT professional, a detective, an actor and a carpenter, who could also pull off magic tricks from time to time.

'Here we fix things that are on the wrong track. Or which I wish were different.'

Lia listened with furrowed brow.

'You plan... operations to help people?'

'That makes it sound like we're some kind of do-gooders. But in most cases, we do what we do because I want something for myself.'

Whether the job was large or small, first they investigated the background – better than most police detectives or journalists did. When the plan was ready, they did trial runs, practising everything before taking the operation live.

This way they could prepare for any eventualities that might crop up. For example, if Matt Thomas had thought to demand that he not be videotaped, the interviewers would have flipped a switch on the camera that made it look as though it were shut off.

'We thought through every detail.'

On the table before Thomas were a notebook and pen. If he had looked more closely, he would have seen the firm's name and logo printed on them. In the WC and coffee alcove of the office suite where the interview took place were paper cups sporting the same insignia.

'And what if he had looked the firm up online?' Lia asked.

'He probably did. You can go and look at what's there too. Elevate has a website, and you can find references to the firm on headhunting sites and other places around the web.'

That was Rico's field. Within half a day he could produce a website and online history for anything. If necessary he could also blot out information, although of course he could not completely erase history on the internet.

'And the receptionist? You said she was a real worker. What if Thomas had asked her about Elevate?'

'Also researched and tested.'

The Mayfair office building leased space to dozens of companies, and tenants changed frequently. Elevate had come to the building a week and a half earlier, and the building staff had already received several visitors for the firm.

'We went there ourselves, playing various roles,' Mari said.

'And what if Thomas suddenly decides to go back? What if he's dropped his handkerchief or something?'

Mari laughed.

'You're just as exacting as I thought. Yes, we also took that into consideration. Elevate will still be there tomorrow, and the signs will stay up for another month.'

Studio staff had been through the Elevate office suite after Thomas left. One of them would still drop in from time to time. The reception desk had received notice that the staff were out doing customer visits now, and if anyone came asking about Elevate, they would notify the Studio immediately.

'We're professionals, Lia. And I have my gift to help me. I went to have a look at Matt Thomas so I could know how he might react to different situations.'

She's so good it's scary.

To Mari Lia said, 'I like the firm's name. Elevate. It promises upward movement.'

'I thought that was a good one too. Part of the joy of work like this is in the details.'

Mari asked whether Lia's curiosity was satisfied now and would they still have time to go out.

'Don't count on it,' Lia said. 'I still have plenty of questions. Like, how can you afford this? Just paying for the office space must be crushing, and then there's the equipment and all the people.'

That Mari was unwilling to discuss.

'Not even with you,' she said. 'What I can say is that I'm well off.'

Mari said she had created many good relationships over the years. There were people who were very grateful for the assistance they had received and wanted to thank her for her expertise. That had allowed her to make wise investments and acquisitions.

'You're rich,' Lia said.

Really she was saying it to herself. Mari had never thrown her money around.

'I'm not ultra-rich or anything like that. I just have assets invested in enough ways that I don't have to think about them.'

Lia started laughing.

'What now?'

'I just remembered what you said about your relatives. That they combined a sense of social responsibility with the desire to make money. Social democrats with big houses.'

Mari laughed, and suddenly Lia felt better.

She's still the same woman I've come to know.

Gradually Lia tired too much to continue asking questions. This felt like the hardest working day she had had in ages.

The wine relaxed her mood. When Mari talked about the Studio, Lia felt as though she were listening to stories about any old workplace.

'They're smart,' Mari said of the employees she had hired. 'People with opinions I want to listen to. They have life experience. And the ability to analyse things.'

The Studio staff enjoyed a special solidarity.

A thirty-year-old Brazilian computer geek who had come to London to make more money, Rico had been the first paid employee. Growing up in the slums of São Paulo, Rico learned early on how to crack open old, cast-off computers, fix them and soup them up.

'I've never seen anything he couldn't do with a computer if you just give him a few days.'

Hacking into other people's machines was child's play – Rico was more interested in things like taking control of entire communications systems. At the Studio he had also learned precision mechanics.

Berg, the head of the Den, was sixty years old and from Sweden, but he had lived most of his life in England.

He was a carpenter, but also so much more. He could create anything out of wood, fabric, plastic and metal. And when they needed things printed, for example to create the illusion of a long-established company, his handiwork was flawless.

'You're going to like him. He's sort of a tinkerer,' Mari said.

Carol Penn, the woman Lia had seen on the video feed, had been played by Maggie Thornton.

Maggie had attended RADA, the Royal Academy of Dramatic Art, and had once performed in theatres all across the country. Even in her acting career she had been in the habit of researching every possible detail related to her roles. Maggie also did background research at the Studio and was quick at deciphering information and summarising it for others. Due to the lack of demand for ageing actresses, she had been unemployed for several years. Mari frequently used other actors as jobbers, such as the man who played Robert Cansai earlier in the day.

The Studio's fifth permanent employee was Patrick Moore.

'We just call him Paddy. He's the one who spends the least time here. He also does work for other people, on his own account.'

Paddy Moore was a private investigator, who handled everything for the Studio which had to do with physical security systems and anything requiring police experience. He had also trained the Studio employees in background investigation and human tracking.

Paddy had attended a police college and worked as an officer in London for two years. However, after losing patience with the slow pace of career advancement, he shifted to working for private security firms and developed expertise in escorting VIPs.

'Paddy looks rough, but you'd have a chore finding a more reliable bloke. He either finds you a safe route or he makes one.'

Paddy's past also included a jaunt onto the other side of the law. With two other men, he had robbed a Thomas Cook security van in Manchester. After being caught, he did two and a half years of a six-year sentence and was now out on parole.

'That's one reason he's such a good employee for us. He can't qualify for any of the big security firms, and he's too good for any of the small ones. He's been satisfied with the work we've been able to give him. And I am extremely satisfied with him.'

As Mari spoke about Paddy, she also provided the answer to one of the questions that had been bothering Lia. Everyone else at the Studio seemed like experts in creative fields, and Mari was a psychologist. Perhaps Paddy Moore's police and security experience explained why their work seemed so focused and purposeful. The Matt Thomas interview had looked like the work of a precise military machine.

Mari glanced at Lia.

'That isn't just thanks to Paddy,' she said. 'Don't under-estimate the rest of us.'

'What stops them from running off and giving away the Studio?'

'In theory, nothing,' Mari said.

But the employees had all signed a non-disclosure agreement, and they were paid well.

'And I only choose people I trust.'

The computer on the table beeped, and Mari was suddenly alert.

'Do you mind if I glance at my messages?' she asked, and Lia nodded, standing up and looking around.

In the room's large bookcase, behind the sheer fabric, was an impressive collection of non-fiction books and digital recordings about various subjects, including psychology, information technology, linguistics… A section of the shelves was also devoted to thick binders with numerical codes written on the spines.

'The binders are all of our gigs,' Mari said without looking up. 'I like traditional files. Digital records lack a feeling of reality.'

Lia noticed that the first 'gig' was packaged into seven binders, and case number twenty-four had taken up sixteen. The last number in the sequence was forty-one, and it had five binders.

That can't be the Matt Thomas job interview; they couldn't have had time to archive that yet. What on earth is in all these binders?

Then Lia realised why Mari was still interested in her email this late at night. She still had a job under way.

Lia looked long and hard at Mari, who was completely focused on what she was reading. Even after a long day and a couple of glasses of wine, she still seemed steady and efficient.

Lia noticed that it was already after ten o'clock.

'I think I should be heading home for the day.'

'OK,' Mari said and stood up. 'Will you come back tomorrow?'

'What will be happening here?'

'I was just thinking you might want to.'

'I don't know. We'll have to see.'

At home in Hampstead, Lia would have had plenty to tell the statues in the park, more than ever before. But she was entirely too exhausted and crawled into bed.

The day she had just experienced had changed everything. Her mind was racing, but luckily fatigue won out.

12

The next day, after work, Lia returned to Park Street. When Lia called Mari to open the door to the Studio, she seemed to be expecting her.

A couple of other employees were still around as well.

'Would you like to meet them?'

'Why not?'

Waiting in the kitchen were the woman Lia had seen on-screen, the actor Maggie Thornton, and a slightly older man who introduced himself as Berg.

'How do you do?' Maggie asked as she poured them tea. 'You must still think our Studio is a bit peculiar.'

'You could say that,' Lia replied.

Maggie laughed.

'That will pass soon enough. It's surprising how quickly this work starts to feel perfectly normal,' she said.

With an infectious forthrightness about her, she was dressed smartly in a bold red frock and a shawl folded over her upper arms, but she lacked the self-consciousness typical of actors. When she asked about *Level*, Lia realised that Maggie knew all about the magazine's operations but wanted to hear Lia's opinions about it.

Of course. She's done her homework.

Berg was a real character. Because of his elegant interior design work, Lia had expected a Bohemian artist type. What she found was a portly man in big, sagging overalls.

Berg laughed frequently in a deep, throaty guffaw. When Maggie teased him about the expansion of his waistline, Berg beamed as he presented his beer belly and asked Mari to pat it for good luck.

Lia noted that Maggie and Berg were in no hurry to leave the Studio even at this late hour, seeming content to stay and chat.

They enjoy their work – at least it looks that way.

'I have a word for what you do here,' Lia said to Mari when they sat down together again in her office. 'Deception. You deceive people.'

Mari smirked, not the least bit embarrassed, more amused than anything else.

'Of course we deceive people. But I don't see anything remarkable in that.'

Mari sat lost in thought.

'But deception makes it sound like this is something immoral. I find that a somewhat comical, outdated approach to morality though, the idea that a person should adhere strictly to the letter of the law. Laws and customs often tolerate horrible things.'

The fire of opposition smouldering inside Lia died out. Talking about it as deception did feel stupid.

'I've had dozens of jobs where deception would be a good word to describe what was happening. But deception only brings to mind unpleasant things. Usually our deceptions also result in good for people other than ourselves,' Mari continued.

'I still don't know whether I want to take part in this sort of thing,' Lia said.

'Have I asked you to take part in anything?'

'No, you haven't. But you did that Matt Thomas thing for my benefit.'

To Lia it was clear that one reason Mari had wanted her as a friend was to involve her in the Studio.

A long silence followed. Mari was thinking hard.

'I don't have any intention of trying to draw you into anything you don't want,' she finally said. 'I didn't just want to meet you for… for my own benefit. We're friends. Real friends.'

The intensity of the feeling of relief that washed over Lia was surprising.

'The Thomas interview was my way of helping a friend,' Mari continued. 'I have thought that you might want to join in on something here. But that's your decision.'

'That's good to know,' Lia said.

'It would also be good for you to know that I didn't found the Studio just because I like duping people. What I like is being able to arrange things the way I want them to be.'

Lia listened in silence. For once, Mari was speaking openly.

'I grew up knowing what people were thinking but not having any way to do anything with that knowledge. I chose London six years ago because it was a better fit for what I wanted to do than my previous place of residence.'

Mari related that after completing her psychology degree she had lived in the United States and Spain. She had done gigs on her own. After moving to London, she sought out a team to help her.

'Only in the last few years have I been able to build up any steam. I have resources and space and great people to help me. My gift is being put to use. Instead of selling it to anyone, I use it to gain influence for myself and the people whose side I'm on.'

Lia nodded.

Mari is a natural leader. The sharpest person I've ever met. She knows so much, as if she spent every day just sitting and watching world events. And that strange gift of hers. Of course that would lead to something special.

'What's happening now?' Lia asked.

'How so? Do you mean between us or what?'

'The Studio. What are you doing now?'

Mari hesitated.

'If I tell, you can't talk about it to anyone. Just like everything else we do.'

Now it was Lia's turn to stop and think.

If I say yes, I'm becoming part of this.

'OK.'

'Good. Let's go outside.'

As they walked along Southwark Bridge Road, Mari told Lia what they were doing.

'Did you hear about the Orpheus Telecom mess a little while ago?'

Lia remembered the incident from the previous week, which had stayed at the top of the national headlines for several days. Orpheus, one of the largest telecommunications companies in the country, had announced it was dumping its cheapest mobile accounts because they were not generating enough profit. In their place, the company would be offering more expensive price plans.

This attracted resentment because, first, the company was making a profit and, second, the people who used the cheaper plans in question were the young, the elderly, the unemployed and the working poor.

'Well, I didn't like what they did. Or how they did it,' Mari said.

Orpheus had not expected to encounter any serious opposition. Because the company had the right to terminate the accounts, all the customers could do was try to protest or move to other providers. But they were not terribly likely to complain since they often lacked the tools to do so, such as their own computers and internet con-nections. According to reports, Orpheus had only received some hundred-odd complaints.

'That is about to change,' Mari told Lia as she led her into the courtyard at the back of a large block of flats.

Opening the rear door of the building with her own keys, she marched in. Lia followed. Climbing to the second floor, they found a normal, slightly shabby office.

No one else was present. Mari took them to a room in which around twenty small desks, each with a chair, stood in a row. On each desk was a set of headphones with a thin microphone attached.

'Tomorrow fifteen students will come here and start making calls to Orpheus, beginning a campaign that hopefully will make the company change its mind,' Mari said.

Lia stared at her, not knowing what to say. This was all so strange again.

'You're trying to crusade against a huge telecoms company using a few students making phone calls?' she asked.

'No,' Mari said with a smile. 'We intend to do much more than that.'

13

Two days later, in the early evening, Lia was standing in the same office with a torrent of sound surrounding her.

At the desks sat a dozen students talking into their microphones.

'You are guilty of trampling on consumer rights, and I would like to lodge an official complaint...'

'No, I have read the terms of the subscriber agreement, and I disagree.'

Everyone was speaking calmly and purposefully. Refusing to listen to the opposing side's replies, they interrupted politely and continued their complaints: they didn't accept the cancellation of their budget plans. They expected their complaints to be recorded officially. They intended to raise the issue with the government consumer protection office. Just like all of their friends who had Orpheus contracts.

After each call they rang back, presenting the same issue to another customer service representative. Each time they used a different name selected from an onscreen list, which had been collected from pedestrians around two London shopping centres who agreed to sign a petition opposing Orpheus. Canvassing for a second list of names was currently occurring elsewhere.

Lia listened to the stream of calls, her head full of questions.

How are they not getting caught? Do I want to be a part of this?

Maggie Thornton entered the room, looking satisfied.

'We've been keeping this pace all day!'

Just today they had made more than two thousand calls.

When one of the students took a break to get some coffee, she stopped to chat with Maggie. To the students she was not the actor Maggie Thornton but a campaign manager for the Consume with Care coalition.

If I checked online, I would find Consume with Care and a campaign manager who looked like Maggie. They've thought of everything.

In the other room, Lia found Mari on a computer monitoring the number of calls. Lia noticed that Mari didn't show herself to the students.

'I want you to see something,' Mari said.

Clicking a tab on her browser, she brought up a website with a logo that said *AskIng* at the top of the page.

That same morning, an opinion poll had hit the media claiming that sixty-eight per cent of British residents disapproved of Orpheus' decision to cancel their budget contracts and that fifty-seven per cent said this would prevent them from doing business with the company. AskIng, a small market research firm, had conducted the poll.

AskIng had a website, a phone number and an employee whose assignment was to respond to enquiries regarding the polling data. During the day, six newspapers and one TV station had requested additional information. They were told that AskIng was unable to publish the entire study because it had also involved collecting information related to trade secrets. AskIng sent the newspapers and TV station a concise report showing that the poll had been conducted properly.

A poll that doesn't exist, a polling firm that doesn't exist, and a consumer group that doesn't exist. Fifteen students and a list of names. And they put this together in fewer than two weeks.

'Tomorrow the real fun starts, with Rico taking the lead,' Mari said.

Rico had a computer program ready that would bombard Orpheus' customer service with a continuous barrage of calls.

The calls were supposed to begin slowly with the help of the students so no suspicions would be raised as to the genuineness of the complaints. Rico's computers would call the customer service numbers thousands of times a day. When the Orpheus employees answered, the computer program would ring off. Sometimes the customer service representative would hear a customer begin an indignant complaint, and then the call would suddenly cut out. But the customers didn't exist: the program used voice recordings featuring none other than Maggie Thornton, her voice digitally masked.

'We'll completely clog Orpheus' lines,' Mari said.

Lia looked at her in wonder.

'You're setting up a theatrical performance and enjoying it.'

'Absolutely.'

'And what about real people's calls? How will they get through when they have real problems with their phones?'

'That's a minor inconvenience. We want hundreds of thousands of people to get their phones back.'

On the wall of the office, Lia noticed a pinboard covered with flyers. Mostly they were adverts for Consume with Care consumer action campaigns, mixed in with leaflets from other advocacy organisations. Included was a guide regarding phone worker's rights.

Some of them must be from real organisations. Berg probably collected some and then made the rest himself.

The result was convincing. Some of the leaflets were yellowed as if they had been hanging on the noticeboard for ages.

The AskIng poll fooled the news media, spawning online and print stories in the *Daily Mail*, the *Telegraph* and the *Guardian*. *Level* considered the topic in their editorial meeting, but decided to hold off for the time being.

After the Orpheus telephone exchanges were clogged for two consecutive days, the story catapulted into the peaktime TV broadcasts. A few Members of Parliament seized the opportunity to score public approval points and demanded that Orpheus reinstate their budget connections.

On the phone, Mari revelled in her team's success.

'We're watching the situation in real time on Rico's machine. In two days, Orpheus has received tens of thousands of calls. Even the Queen couldn't get through if she wanted.'

The congestion in the customer service centre and telephone exchange aroused irritation in others besides Orpheus customers. The executives and spokespersons who appeared on the news looked uncomfortable. They had not expected such robust opposition, the lead spokesman admitted.

'Suddenly we're in the crosshairs of the mainstream media even though this is a minor matter compared to the real problems facing the nation,' he said to the BBC.

'Not a terribly intelligent defence,' Mari said to Lia.

Soon news spread that consumer rights groups were also receiving complaints about Orpheus. Lia guessed that the Studio was also arranging these calls.

'Did you hear that Orpheus has been receiving thousands of emails about the problem?' Mari asked.

'Where are they coming from?'

'Real customers.'

The counterfeit consumer uprising against Orpheus had prompted many of the company's actual customers to post written complaints, as the consumer groups recommended. Emails were also coming from other people condemning Orpheus' actions. Criticising the company was becoming something people wanted to participate in just because consumer voices were being heard for once.

Four days later Orpheus executives published a plea to their customers to allow them time to sort out the matter.

'Given the current situation, responding to customer complaints is impossible,' the appeal said.

The Orpheus share price had fallen by one third in less than a week. When the appeal came out, the price fell by one half. The flood of calls and emails continued unabated.

On the morning of the fifth day, *The Times* reported that the Orpheus board had held four emergency meetings during the past week. Three board members had announced their intent to resign if the decision to cancel budget calling plans was not reversed.

At 2 p.m. Orpheus held a news briefing in which they announced that the need for budget mobile phones was real and the company was proud to be able to continue offering these services in the future.

The Orpheus executives who appeared on television looked as though they had not slept for a week.

Mari called Lia.

'Can you come down to the Studio? It's party time!'

Lia finished her work for the day at *Level* and then hurried over to Bankside. The situation felt absurd.

They've just brought one of the largest telecommunications companies in the country to its knees with an enormous, public farce. The whole thing will cost Orpheus tens of thousands of pounds, if not hundreds of thousands. And all with just a handful people.

The party was still on in the Studio kitchen, but only Mari, Maggie and Berg remained – Rico and Paddy had already left. Maggie had popped the corks on several bottles of champagne with the students at the Consume with Care office earlier.

The students had been satisfied. For their work they had received a good wage, and they felt as if they had participated in a real consumer action.

And they had, just not for a real consumer rights organisation.

'Jesus, this has been a good day,' Mari said with a sigh.

Lia felt triumphant as well, even though the whole thing still disconcerted her.

After merrily drinking a couple of glasses of bubbly, Maggie and Berg left too.

Now alone, Lia and Mari sat looking out the windows of the Den at the darkening streets of Bankside.

'One of the more common crimes of our age,' Mari said. 'It just hasn't been criminalised. A big company squeezing people for their last pennies. Just to make larger profits.'

Mari opened a fresh bottle of wine and gradually drank herself into inebriation. Lia sipped hers with more moderation.

'I know you don't like everything we did,' Mari said. 'But I think we had every right to prevent Orpheus from pulling such an underhand trick.'

Finally Mari set her glass aside.

'Now I've got my *kännit* on,' she said to Lia. 'Well, actually, this is something different, since you aren't really drinking. This is my... *kekkuli*.'

'*Kekkuli*. That's probably the best Finnish word ever for getting drunk,' Lia said.

Mari's gaze became unfocused.

'Should I call a taxi?' Lia asked.

'Sure, call yourself one. But I'm staying here with my *kekkuli*. I'll be putting those hammocks to good use.'

Lia helped Mari lower one of the hammocks and get settled in. As she left the Studio, Lia made doubly sure the lock on the door clicked shut behind her.

As autumn began, their friendship changed.

The number of nights they spent in bars dropped off, and Lia got into the habit of calling Mari at the end of her working day to see whether she was at the Studio. She almost always was.

Usually Lia walked the short distance to Bankside. She brought Mari and the others presents, like the roasted nuts which the Southern European immigrants sold from their stalls on the Millennium footbridge.

She spent her evenings sitting with Mari on the couch in her office.

At some point, Lia realised it was her turn to be tested. Over the summer, she had put Mari through her paces, and now Mari was waiting to see how Lia would adjust to the work the Studio did.

Despite Lia's enquiries, Mari was unwilling to discuss past jobs. 'Let's talk about that later,' was her only reply.

Sometimes Mari asked Lia to wait because she had to handle some pressing matter of business. Lia spent hours sitting in the Den and the other rooms, looking out.

She could have stared at the vistas of Bankside from morning to night. Two rooms gave onto views of the glimmering Thames, boats and ships gliding along the grey stream. From the other spaces she could see former industrial buildings now home to dozens of companies, societies and cultural centres. Within a stone's throw was one of the greatest art museums in the country, Tate Modern, the visitors it attracted constantly wandering the nearby streets.

She quickly became acquainted with Maggie and Berg, who always seemed to have time to chat as they worked. Rico she only ever saw in passing and Paddy not at all.

Maggie and Berg seemed unusually sincere. Their attitude towards their own work was understated and relaxed, although Lia understood how expert they were in their fields. But about what the Studio did, they knew how to stay tight-lipped.

Maggie told Lia about her acting career, the major roles she had played and the jobs she had taken just for money. She entertained Lia with her stories about famous directors and the world premiere of *Cats* in London.

Maggie had been in the first ensemble, the one that created the musical's reputation. Every night directors from the great theatres of the world sat in the audience, returning the following day to beg for the opportunity to buy performance rights.

'That show doesn't mean anything to someone your age, but then it was one of a kind.' Maggie explained, her eyes lighting up.

She talked about which of the performers had been given their roles because of their talent, which received them after shagging one of the bigwigs, and how the obscenity of the cat jokes among the cast escalated as the run progressed.

'Starting at the end of the second year, we took a different cat porn picture every night.'

Posing in their cat costumes, the cast created images of ribald feline orgies. In reality none of them had the energy even to think about sex after their punishing performances, but they had to have some way to vent their cat angst.

'We took at least three hundred photographs. Hopefully they'll never end up online or Lloyd Webber's army of lawyers will have a field day,' Maggie said with a chuckle.

'Isn't the Studio a strange place for an actor to work?' Lia asked.

'I love the Studio. Here I'm more than just an actor,' Maggie said.

Sometimes Studio jobs even resembled modern theatre. Maggie used to do experimental performances, like one for an audience of a single person or another where the action was presented solely with lights. Now her job was to create new characters, research background, plan performances, rehearse and perform. The performances were more comprehensive than in the theatre: they created entire worlds to accompany their characters.

'These are much better gigs than most actors get. I don't have to jiggle my bits in adverts wearing some hairy animal costume, hawking chocolate bars.'

Berg also had a background in theatre. He spoke about his father, Bertil Berg, who had worked as a master set designer in Sweden.

'He was in the Dramaten, the Royal Opera and all the big city theatres. He was so good that in Sweden *Bergesque magic* was a common phrase. The sets alone were reason enough for people to come to the theatre. When I was little I thought I would grow up to be a set designer too.'

Berg had received his father's first name, so he was always Bertil Berg the Second. Perhaps that was why he only used his surname now, Lia thought.

For a long time he had done everything but build sets. He studied mechanical engineering and architecture, designed aeroplanes, built houses. After turning fifty, he started again from the beginning and studied theatrical set design, offering his services for free to amateur theatres in order to gain experience.

'I was happy when Mari offered me this position,' Berg said. 'I don't want to be in the theatre, but I still want to stage things. Here I feel like I get to take my work even further. Here just having things look good isn't enough. Now I stage reality.'

Maggie and Berg didn't seem to know about Mari's gift. They respected her, not because she knew how to read people, but because to them she was a smart boss who delivered interesting work.

'Haven't you told them?' Lia asked Mari.

'Why would I?'

'You said yourself how close they were to you.'

'Lia, they do know – at some level.'

Such observant people could not help but notice how Mari thought and did things. But she had never talked to them about it directly.

'It's very personal. And it isn't always easy being able to do what I do,' Mari said.

At the Studio, Lia felt simultaneously inside and excluded. She knew she was close to Mari in a different way from the others.

The others had given Mari nicknames. Berg referred to her as 'Boss Lady'. Maggie gave her name a French flavour, Marie. Apparently Rico amused himself by using alternating versions like Maria, Marilyn and Marjorie.

But Lia pronounced her name as it should be pronounced: Mari. Short vowels, the R short, crisp tap. She was the only person who pronounced Mari's name the way she had heard it for the first twenty years of her life.

This was why she didn't take umbrage at being kept in the dark. She knew that Mari wanted both to keep her close and yet safely at a distance.

The idea came to Lia in September, in the middle of a working day. She called Mari to make sure she would be at the Studio that night.

After arriving in Bankside she was impatient to sit down.

'I have a proposal,' Lia said.

Mari's eyes focused.

'Well? Let's hear it.'

'You could investigate the Holborn Circus murder. Figure out why that Latvian woman had to die.'

Mari looked at Lia silently.

'I thought we would come back to this,' she said finally, looking serious.

'I know that solving a mystery like that has to be terribly difficult. But you could probably get somewhere with it,' Lia continued.

'How do you know the police haven't made any progress in their investigation?'

Lia stopped. That was true – she didn't know.

'But if they had found anything important, they would have announced it.'

Mari shook her head. The police didn't continually update the media about ongoing investigations; sometimes making progress meant calming the situation down. Getting mixed up in a serious crime could also be dangerous. Not to mention that they might hinder the police in their work.

That was all true, Lia admitted.

'But you see so much even in little things. And if we find something, we tell the police. I'm not asking you to chase criminals, just to see what you can see.'

Mari was not enthusiastic. One of her most important principles was never to get involved in several undertakings at once. At the moment she already had a project in progress.

The work usually divided into two phases, a long, slow process of background research and preparation, and then a short, intense execution. They had to give the execution phase space.

'You never know what will happen. Everyone here, especially me, has to be able to concentrate one hundred per cent. Criminal cases like that aren't something you can control. Something can pop up at any moment, and then you have to be able to react quickly.'

The second principle was that although Mari led each project, she stayed in the background when it came to hands-on implementation. She didn't want attention or to be connected to the results of her work.

Above all Mari wanted to keep away from the police.

'Why?' Lia asked.

'You name it! We're not criminals here, but plenty of things we do are illegal or at least borderline. Just think about Orpheus.'

With the police there was always the risk they would start asking questions. Some detectives really did get 'hunches' from noticing little details. That was close enough to Mari's gift that she didn't want anyone like that getting too close.

'I've also been involved with professional criminals before a few times. Unpleasant is too mild a word. I'd rather not do it again if I have a choice.'

'OK,' Lia said. 'And what if we arrange things so you don't have to go anywhere near the police? Or criminals. You could investigate from a distance, and I'll help where I can. If we don't come up with anything, we drop it.'

Why did Lia want this so much, Mari asked inquisitively.

'I don't know. Let's call it a hunch, or whatever you want. That woman deserves someone to investigate her case properly. You could do that.'

Mari thought silently, but Lia could see that her words had set something in motion.

'Well, let's do this,' Mari said finally. 'But you really are going to have to help. If we ever have to contact the police, you're going to do it.'

'Agreed!'

'Give me two weeks. After that we'll decide whether we proceed. And you have to accept my decision, whatever it is,' Mari added.

'Got it. Great,' Lia said, so excited she stood up.

'Hold on now,' Mari said. 'That was only part of the deal. I want a favour in return.'

'Fine, what kind of favour?' Lia asked, sitting back down.

'I want you to help us stop Arthur Fried.'

II

A Better Britain

14

Lia glanced at the clock on the wall of the offices of *Level.* Only 7.55. Still a little time until the others would begin showing up at work.

She had come in early in order to have time to read everything she could find in the magazine archives about Arthur Fried. Sipping from her mug of vending machine coffee, the bitterness of which no amount of milk could take away, she clicked on another story: 'Fried promises record number of candidates for party lists.'

In addition to its own stories, *Level*'s electronic database contained a sizeable collection of reports from other British publications. *Level* had purchased the rights to browse them so the reporters could find background material for their stories. Material about Arthur Fried was in plentiful supply.

A noted, perhaps notorious, politician and the leader of the small far-right Fair Rule Party, of course Lia had already known Fried's name.

He was famous for his ability to whip up his supporters into political frenzy with his words.

Lia had never bothered to research the party's policy platform, since her own political stance was mostly that she didn't have one. She found ideas she could support in what the Conservative, Liberal Democrat, Labour and Green parties said, and had only been relieved when, as a foreigner, she could not vote. But she disagreed with Fair Rule instinctively.

Maybe that's where the major dividing line in society runs today. It hasn't been between left and right in ages.

Reading the news stories confirmed her prejudices. Fair Rule stood for law and order, racial cleansing and Christian principles. It opposed a huge number of things, beginning with most of what happened in cities and encompassing everything related to youth counterculture, gay rights and social support for single parents. The party even disapproved of such an innocent activity as football clubs for schoolchildren: they claimed to support sport as a hobby, but opposed immigrants having their own teams and uniforms.

However, the position that had aroused the most discussion was the party's strict stance on abortion laws. They wanted to ban abortions outright. Even those most people would allow, for victims of rape or incest. For the representatives of Fair Rule, life was sacred – which was a fascinating contradiction of the party's other main goal, the reinstatement of the death penalty. About this the papers had written significantly less than about the party's position on abortion, apparently because no one believed they could ever succeed in returning judicial hangings.

Ever the smiling party leader, Arthur Fried had a penchant for colourful turns of phrase. Like many politicians, he tended to repeat a few favourite lines in his interviews.

The catchiest of these – and the one that annoyed Lia most – was 'Get Britain Back'. Even though reporters tried to remove obvious slogans from their stories, Fried nearly always succeeded in slipping this one into his press interviews.

Let's get Britain back. What the hell did that actually mean?

Fried used this catchphrase to add emphasis almost regardless of the topic. Once, *The Times* had asked Fried to explain the motto, and the result had been a long explanation about the 'dire consequences of the modern culture of multicultural thought and irresponsible loose behaviour'.

They either want Muslims to live in slums or get out of the country so the white British population can rule.

This train of thought seemed to be increasingly popular. Support for Fair Rule in the previous parliamentary and local elections had been in the range of one to one and a half per cent. However, in the most recent polls, that had risen to three per cent.

Lia looked at the picture of Arthur Fried. Quite tall, blond hair, pleasant face. Not handsome per se, but certainly engaging when he performed. His rather serious demeanour was softened by the broad smile he wore in the photograph. His teeth had been straightened and whitened.

What was it about this that worried Mari so much? Fried is like an American import, a right-wing evangelical. No politician like that has ever become very significant in Britain.

'Why do we have to stop Fried?' Lia had asked Mari.

Because Arthur Fried was a much bigger phenomenon than people guessed, Mari explained. The next general election was predicted within six months, and Fried was very likely to win a seat in Parliament himself, probably dragging a few party cronies along on his coat-tails.

How did Mari see that? And why did they have to stop it? If the people wanted to vote for them, was that not just one of the usual irritations of democracy?

'I've seen Arthur Fried up close many times. He is the devil incarnate.'

Mari spoke of Fried in a tone that indicated long-held concern. She had seen Fried once, years before, at an exhibition of classical paintings at an art museum. He was giving the opening address. It was part of a project meant to create dialogue between art and politics. In his speech, Fried had praised the important 'examples of true beauty' that the paintings offered contemporary society. Mari found that the realistic depictions of landscapes, Victorian upper-class hunting scenes and posing maidens mostly just made her want to take a nap.

Mari had watched from close range as Fried shook hands with the attendees, smiling all the while.

'His eyes were so cold.'

In his mind, Fried classified the people he was greeting into two categories: a small group of useful people and a large group of useless people, for whom Fried held nothing but contempt.

'Watching that was horrible.'

'Sounds like a reptile. But a calculating politician isn't exactly out of the ordinary – what's so dangerous about him in particular?'

There were things about Fried you couldn't see on the surface, Mari said. Lia would just have to trust her.

'Read everything you can get your hands on about Fried. We have to know him completely.'

That was why Lia had started sifting through all of the reports about the Fair Rule party. First she wanted to research the objective sources before she started wading into the more colourful offerings of the internet.

The picture forming was of a man who had tried many different things in the course of his life, finally channelling his energy into politics.

Arthur Fried hailed from Wales. His family was originally from the United States but had moved from there to Swansea and then to Newport. There Fried attended comprehensive school and then immediately went to work doing manual labour in a large foundry. His family were deeply religious. Fried enjoyed describing these parts of his history because they gave him an opportunity to talk about his faith background and demonstrate his affinity for the common man.

Quickly Fried escaped the factory, leaving to study marketing at Gwent College in Newport. After graduating, he tried out various professions: estate agent, radio announcer, sales representative for an arms importer, hotel chain service manager, chamber of commerce chairman.

All speaking professions, Lia noted. Selling guns was probably more of the same. The quick moves between careers told of enterprise but also restlessness and perhaps hinted that no one had wanted to engage the young Fried with a more permanent employment contract.

Next, Fried founded a couple of companies, an estate agency and a business consultancy. Then he moved to the US for a few years, a time about which the newspaper articles had nothing to say other than vague references to more business activities. Clearly his religious fervour grew during his time in America. After returning to Britain he developed an interest in social issues and the Fair Rule party.

'That was a decisive moment. As if I had stepped out of the darkness into bright sunlight. I realised that Britain lacked a true voice of the people, a party that could restore the honour of the nation. I knew that, despite all of my personal shortcomings, this was the mission God had in store for me,' Fried had told *The Scotsman*.

The pastimes of this 'voice of the people' were golf, shooting, volunteering and church service. His wife was an American, Anna Belle Fried, whom he had met in New York, and every article remembered to mention that she had once won her home state's beauty contest.

Lia frowned. Shooting, parish work, founding companies and a much younger Miss Ohio. Not exactly the path of the average Welsh lad.

Lia managed to get through all the major stories in which Fried appeared before small noises at the front door of the office began to announce the arrival of the others.

When Timothy Phelps showed up, Lia decided to see if he could add any insight.

'Morning, Tim.'

'Good morning, darling.'

'What do you know about Arthur Fried?'

'That's a strange question to start the day,' Timothy said, looking at Lia curiously. 'Why are you interested in Fried?'

Lia had already cooked up an explanation.

'An illustrator is offering us caricatures of political figures. He sent me his drawing of Fried as a sample. I was wondering whether we might have any reason to do a larger story on him.'

'Well, with the general election coming up, that's possible. Fried's lot are gaining popularity. It is interesting.'

Britain had always had its conservatives, Timothy observed, but Fair Rule was trying to unite all the voices shouting at the fringes, from the young yobs in the housing estates to the older generation of right-wing Christian moralists.

'A difficult but intriguing combination. I'm not exactly hankering to go to their party conference. But Fried is a very powerful personality.'

'In what way?'

'He's a strong speaker. Never afraid to spread his opinions around. He's a reporter's wet dream. But I still get the feeling he has bigger plans. Once there were whispers that he would defect to the Tories, but it stayed only a rumour. And he's doing better as the leader of his own gang than he would as rank-and-file in a big party that would try to control what he said.'

'And his private life? Any skeletons?'

'Not that I've heard. His wife is quite the bombshell. She's a leggy bottle blonde doll who works in some parish church. They have two little kids. So all the ingredients of a normal family, but still there's something plastic about those two that'll send shivers down your spine. Like they're robots carrying out some set program. Presumably God's vision for the future – I don't know.'

'It's great to be coming up with topics for stories and series we can do,' Timothy added. 'That's one of the best things about Taylor – he's always producing new ideas that none of the rest of us think of. Given the success he's been having, a profile of Arthur Fried would definitely be in order.'

Walking back to her desk, Lia wondered whether Timothy's reference to Taylor was a coincidence. Timothy was Matt

Thomas' right-hand man in the office. Had he heard something about the plans for a new AD?

Lia was on a roll during their morning meeting, which yielded an idea for a series of stories on books and musical albums of social significance from the Noughties. When the editorial staff started trickling off to lunch, Martyn Taylor said, 'Well done, Miss Finland.'

When Lia arrived at the Studio that evening, Mari was tied up with work.

'Paddy and I are having a meeting. Maybe you could go and see Rico in the meantime. If you're going to start bringing us more work, then it would be best for you to know the whole gang.'

Mari opened the door for her into the IT kingdom, and Lia slipped into the dimly lit room.

Seeming to snap awake, Rico left his computer to come and greet Lia as though he had been waiting for her.

'You came at a good moment. I'm just opening the Well. It takes time, so you can have my undivided attention.'

Rico led her to his machine and resumed typing for a moment, giving Lia time to observe him.

At thirty years old, with his black, curly hair cropped short, Rico was as thin as a rail. His Brazilian features would have been most prominent around his eyes were it not for the strange glasses he was wearing, which could have belonged to Elton John or some drag performer with an eyewear fetish. The frames pulsed with light, the lenses had points that turned into tiny reflective surfaces when viewed from a certain angle, and above all this wobbled colourful bits of wire projecting from the frames towards the wearer's temples.

'My friend makes designer art glasses,' Rico said when he noticed Lia's gaze. 'I'm his guinea pig. The name of these is Web 7.7. They work pretty well on me, don't you think?'

This was the first time Lia had exchanged more than a few words with Rico. He was fun, lively and an impossibly fast talker.

As Lia stared at the screen filled with scrolling lines of code and bits of text that meant nothing to her, the talk turned to computers.

'What is the Well?' Lia asked. 'I've never heard of it.'

'That's no surprise.'

Some IT pros knew about the Well, Rico said, but even among that group it was more legend than reality.

'Access is guarded carefully to keep from ruining it.'

The Well was an opening through which the top tier of computer wizards tiptoed into places where they should not be. It was an online meeting place for hackers. After breaking down a system's defences and figuring out how it worked, they would add to the Well the information they had gleaned and then sometimes do a little mischief or strike a blow for peace and freedom. The Well was a website full of secret files describing back doors into hardened networks. When someone gained access to a system, a corporate intranet for example, he would post information about what to look for and how to cover your tracks once you were in. The files changed rapidly and access to any given target was fleeting.

Recently the Well had offered access to the data systems of several large banks and the internal network of a French army unit, the Gendarmerie Nationale. Using these holes, you could have looked at what was happening in the accounts of the richest people in the world or what secret memos were changing hands in the Directorate-General of the gendarmerie in Paris on rue Saint-Didier. The Gendarmerie Nationale was a favourite target of hackers because it had once become mixed up in the sinking of a Greenpeace ship in New Zealand in which two environmental activists died. Although hackers were not generally interested in politics, getting one over on the French military police was a matter of honour.

The location of the Well changed frequently, generally being housed either on old, disused servers or servers whose operating systems used outdated technology and which the companies or government authorities in question no longer bothered to protect. Using servers like this was a hacker's bread and butter. Usernames for the Well and access to its files were encrypted and stored on yet another separate server.

One of the important features of the Well was that cracked security systems only stayed visible for a short time. What was available in the Well was different every day. The purpose was not to make money or do damage but to share information.

But you had to work in the field for a long time and catch the eye of more experienced operators before you could even get close to the first gateway. When someone did finally gain access, he felt a responsibility to use the Well's information with due respect for the work of those who gathered it.

'What happens if someone talks?' Lia asked.

'Nothing like that has ever happened. If someone did that, he would never work in the field again. Angry computer wizards would track him down and pummel his every movement on the net.'

'Can they really do that?'

'Yeah, you can track just about anything a person does if you have enough firepower behind you.'

Rico nodded out into the room, and Lia realised he meant his computers.

'Aren't you breaking the rules by telling me about the Well?' Lia asked light-heartedly.

'Yes, actually,' Rico said just as cheerfully. 'But you don't have access to it. And if you told someone else about it, they would probably just think you were paranoid.'

Even most experts who worked at computer security firms considered the existence of a site like the Well impossible.

'And besides,' Rico added as if stating a truism, 'the fact that you're here means Mari has decided you're safe.'

'And I am,' Lia said. 'I know so little I couldn't be a risk to anyone.'

Rico smiled, taking off his bizarre glasses and rubbing his eyes.

'These things make my head feel funny,' he admitted. 'Maybe they need a little more refinement.'

Rico showed Lia around the machines in the room. Some of them were programmed to track people or organisations whose information could be of use to the Studio. Rico didn't want to name them, but he proudly mentioned that they included two British police forces and three international communications companies.

A few dedicated machines secured Mari's, Rico's and the others' computer traffic, monitored possible attempts to break through their security and kept watch over the office. No one outside could circumvent the measures he had put in place, Rico assured her. He also had a backup electrical generator, so the only thing that could crash the system was an explosion that took out the entire floor of the building. For internal Studio communication, Rico had developed an instant messaging application with direct access to all their computers and mobile phones so they could stay in constant contact.

'And here are my Mills.'

The Mills were machines Rico used to produce websites, online discussion boards and web histories for use in organising gigs. He showed her an example of how a program was monitoring aeroplane enthusiast discussion boards and using them to create new content. If you read the messages that the Mills created closely, you might notice that some of them were linguistically simplistic or copied from other online discussions. But these creations served their purpose: people usually only glanced at web pages, and if they didn't look very high quality, they moved on to other pages – believing they had seen genuine discussion threads.

'So if we wanted to create discussion online about you, for example, the program would sprinkle mentions of Lia Pajala here and there. Your name would appear in an old message on one of these aeroplane sites and a list from five years ago of people someone remembered attending a convention.'

And thus Lia would have an online history, which it would be difficult to prove was fake.

Lia listened, her head spinning. Finally she changed the subject.

'How did you and Mari meet?'

A smile flitted across Rico's face.

'Hasn't Mari told you?'

It had happened four years before.

'I was a lazy hacker bum. I wasn't really doing anything, just spending most of my time hanging around BigSmoke.'

BigSmoke was one of London's hacker spaces, the type of semi-public meeting place for hackers you could find in any metropolis around the world. Any hacker who joined could come and sit, mess around online and trade information.

'Of course almost all of us were young men.'

Sometimes hackerspaces held open houses when anyone could drop in. Usually there weren't many guests, but one day Mari turned up. A whole room of men fell silent in an instant.

'Because she was a woman?'

'No, because she was a *woman*.'

Attractive, under the age of thirty, and coming to ask about computers, Mari elicited an almost comical reaction.

'There wasn't a bloke there who wasn't falling all over himself to help her. And get her phone number. Except me.'

'What do you mean, "except you"?'

'I could tell just by looking at her that she wasn't interested in that. She was really looking for someone to work.'

Mari had said she was looking for a person who knew websites and information systems. That had failed to narrow the range of potential helpers at all. But she chose one from the crowd.

'They exchanged numbers. And then you should have seen the winding up he got the rest of the night.'

Mari called the next day, but not to ask the man for help.

'She asked him for my number,' Rico grinned. 'That's how it started. Pretty quickly I knew I wanted to be a part of this.'

In the middle of Rico's story, Mari appeared at the door and motioned for Lia to follow her.

'Rico is lovely,' Lia said.

'I knew you would like him.'

Paddy was waiting in Mari's office.

'Patrick Moore,' he said, hand outstretched.

He was large, with broad shoulders; keen eyes peered out from below Paddy's buzz cut and strong brow.

'What do you think of the Studio?' Paddy asked.

'Hard to say. It's the most unique workplace I've ever seen. Confusing and exciting.'

'I think this is the best place to work I can imagine,' Paddy said and smiled at Mari. 'Unfortunately for me there just isn't enough work here for me to live on it.'

'Yeah, yeah,' Mari said. 'I pay you better than anyone else. It just isn't enough to support your wanton lifestyle.'

Paddy laughed.

'I play poker. And sometimes I like to fly to far-off places,' he explained to Lia.

'To escape gambling debts,' Mari said.

Paddy laughed again, and Lia almost thought she could sense some sort of tension between them.

Soon Paddy excused himself, and Mari collapsed on the sofa next to Lia, pulling her legs up under herself.

'I'll get right to the point. Arthur Fried – did you find anything?'

Lia spoke about the vanilla offerings of the news archives and her conversation with Timothy Phelps. Mari was interested in Timothy's thoughts.

'The marriage is a good observation. There is something fake about them, some kind of acting. We'll have to dig into the wife as well.'

Lia said that even after reading so much about him, she still didn't understand why Fried was supposed to be Satan. What was this all about?

'I can't say yet,' Mari said.

For the time being she simply had a firm conviction that Fried was worse than he looked.

'I don't want to ruin his personal life. What I want is to cut off his political career so thoroughly he could never make a comeback.'

'And if you're wrong? What if he's just one extremist conservative politician among many?'

'I know that this sounds strange, but so far I've never been wrong. If we just dig deep enough, we'll find some dirt on Fried. But just one revelation won't be enough; an operator like him could recover from that.'

At its apex, politics was extremely unkind, but, based as it was on reputation and charisma, politicians often survived crises. If one unfortunate thing came out about a popular elected official, the party protected him and the electorate didn't necessarily lose confidence. After several scandals, however, supporters started trickling away. No one working in politics wanted to have anything to do with someone who had lost his reputation.

'And I want Fried out of the game permanently.'

Making a brilliant return after stumbling was not at all unheard-of for politicians. All they needed was to wait a year or two for people to forget. Strangely enough, surviving some cock-ups could even be seen as a benefit for a politician. As if in losing his position a decision-maker also gained life experience.

Mari asked Lia to continue, encouraging her to make note of everything that might lead to evidence that Fried was not as squeaky clean as he made himself out to be. Mari and the others at the Studio were also researching other channels.

'And what about Holborn Circus? Have you had time to think about that?' Lia asked, changing gears.

'Actually, I have a meeting at a pub tonight related to that. Do you want to join me?'

They walked to The Rake. Along the way, Mari told Lia about the man they were going to meet.

He was not a particularly charming person, but he had one important virtue: he knew people in the London underworld, and he sold his information to anyone who had money and whose own connections could be useful to him. Mari had acquired information from him before.

'He collaborates with the police too; he's an informer.'

They ordered sandwiches and beer. Mari said that the man's nickname was Big K.

'Don't ask why, because I haven't the foggiest. He isn't even very big.'

About fifty years old, Big K was fleshy but not rotund. As he sat down at their table with a pint in hand, Lia thought he looked relatively normal, if you didn't think an earring and a ruddy complexion were abnormal.

'Evening. Long time no see,' Big K said.

The Rake was a very small pub but so full of people and noise that they didn't have to worry about other customers overhearing. Mari greeted Big K and introduced Lia as her friend.

'The price is the same no matter how many people listen,' Big K said.

He said he had made a few phone calls.

'The results weren't great. Of course, the value depends on how you interpret it,' he added.

No one in any of the usual professional crime circles seemed to know who was behind the brutal Holborn Circus murder. The visibility and unorthodox nature of the act made it unusual.

'People who do things like this generally put the word out, or you just recognise who did it. The big gangs have established methods, and the little capers that junkies get up to are always the same, you know.'

But no one knew why anyone would crush a woman with a steamroller.

'Or whatever they used. Maybe a city highways department workman who was sick of his wife nagging him did it.'

Lia glanced at Mari. What a pleasant chap.

But he did have one potential scrap of information.

'One friend had heard that the woman was from somewhere in Eastern Europe, Poland or Estonia or Latvia.'

Lia said nothing, despite a strong desire to correct him.

That was already in the news, that she was probably from Latvia. But I don't imagine criminal types keep up with the police beat.

Big K continued.

'I heard that there were several whores involved, maybe from Latvia. That would explain how she got into such nasty trouble. And even though no one knew anything about the guy who did it, they said the body was a message. They didn't want to make all of London shit its trousers, just one specific person or group.'

And that was all, he said and took a slurp of his beer.

Mari nodded, removing from her bag an envelope and offering it to him. Big K glanced in the envelope, nodded in turn and left without a word.

Lia waited for Mari to say something, but she was concentrating on her sandwich.

'It seems like you were right,' Lia finally said. 'I can't think how that could help us move forward. She may have been a Latvian prostitute, or Eastern European. Plenty of those around.'

'No, there was nothing concrete in that to follow up on. That's what this is like – you put out feelers in different directions and wait for something to break,' Mari said. 'I could ask Paddy to ask his sources about Latvian prostitutes, but Big K is better in that respect. Paddy knows former criminals, Big K knows current ones.'

They were silent again for a moment.

'Any ideas?' Lia asked.

'Yes, one,' Mari said. 'The best thing would be to speak with the detectives investigating the case.'

'But you didn't want to contact the police!' Lia said.

'And I don't. But this seems like a dead end. If this is important to you, we have to look at all the possibilities. Even the difficult ones. Go and see the police.'

'Why would they tell me anything? I'm a complete bystander.'

'Maybe they won't. But when people ask direct questions, they get direct answers surprisingly often. That trait seems to be inbuilt in us somehow. We want to give people what they hope for from us.'

Lia was hesitant.

'What if they just take me for a daft woman obsessed with lurid crimes?'

'That isn't very far from the truth,' Mari said grinning. 'Care for another?'

15

The grey office block of the City of London Police at 37 Wood Street had probably been an imposing building in its time. Crushed between the modern business towers of the Square Mile, it looked small and insignificant.

Lia had taken the morning off work for this. Two days before, she had rung the police telephone exchange and enquired which unit was investigating the Holborn Circus murder.

She was told that each area of London had its own homicide unit. The City's own detectives always investigated murders that occurred within the district.

'Do you have information to offer related to the case?' the woman asked in a routine tone.

'No. I just wanted to talk to a detective,' Lia answered.

Prior arrangement was always required for any meetings, the operator informed her. They didn't connect phone calls directly to detectives.

Even so, Lia had decided to drop in at the police station, trusting she would be able to meet someone.

Once she reached Wood Street, however, her hope diminished. The building's reception area was tiny, with a group of people crowded before a counter of worn, dark wood. No chairs, no turn numbers, not even organised queues. Standing behind the counter, two police officers did what they could to straighten out the crush of clients. The place oozed with boredom and wasted time.

Lia felt as though she were in entirely the wrong place, adrift despite her focused mission.

She decided to queue in front of the older, male officer; the younger officer, a middle-aged woman, looked too bored. She waited twenty minutes or more. For one patron after another, the two civil servants sought forms and quickly scribbled on scraps of paper numbers for them to ring.

When Lia's turn came up, she greeted the policeman warmly. 'Good day.'

'It's just got much better,' the man said with a smile. 'How may I be of service?'

'If I could, I'd like to see one of the detectives investigating the case of the body found in the car on Holborn Circus.'

'That sounds like a perfectly reasonable request, but it may be difficult in practice,' the officer said, explaining that detectives didn't take tip-offs from citizens face-to-face – she would have to ring or send an email to the police central office.

'I don't have a tip. I just want to ask a few questions. It won't take long.'

The policeman looked at her more closely. The woman next to him also glanced at Lia, and Lia could see from the motion of the policewoman's head what she was signalling to her colleague: get rid of her.

Lia looked the man straight in the eyes.

'Is that so?' the man said. 'Is that so?'

Lia comprehended how thoroughly he evaluated her in those two seconds.

'What if we do this?' he continued. 'I'll try to call one of the detectives, and if he decides to give you a moment, you can ask your questions. If he says no, you have to be satisfied with that. What was your name?'

'Lia Pajala. And yes, that would be lovely,' Lia said with relief. She smiled at the policeman again, adding an extra sparkle for his stern colleague.

After looking up a phone number on his computer, the officer made the call. Lia waited, looking at the man's soft, friendly face and ears, from which grew long hairs that he, like so many other ageing men, for some reason felt no need to trim.

No one answered.

Lia was sure that the man standing behind the counter was also a little disappointed.

'And Detective Chief Inspector Gerrish hasn't noted any information in his public calendar,' the officer said. 'He simply may not have arrived yet, or he may not be coming in at all today.'

'Is only one detective investigating the case?'

After glancing at his computer screen again, the officer explained the process of an investigation. Such large cases in the City were always dealt with by one of the larger criminal investigation units, which consisted of around twenty police officers. When a body was found, they set up an incident room, a physical location where all the information was collected. All leads received by phone or by police patrols were directed there. But since the case had gone so long without any resolution, at this point only two detectives were working on it any more, one of whom, Detective Chief Inspector Gerrish, was leading the investigation. For one or two officers to take sole responsibility for a case after the initial crime scene investigation and other large-scale operations were finished was perfectly normal.

'Britain doesn't seem to have the resources to do it any other way.'

'Fortunately Britain seems to have excellent police officers in her service,' Lia said. 'Would there be any use in waiting a moment for Gerrish to arrive at work?'

'No telling. But go ahead if you like.'

Lia flashed the man her most beautiful smile, thanking him and moving aside.

While she waited, she watched the creeping press of patrons. Some of the visitors were exasperated, but the officers serving at the counter seemed to have a superhuman ability to keep their cool.

Lia had never been forced to transact any complicated business with the British authorities. As an EU citizen, she had not even needed to request a work or residency permit when she moved to England. At the police station, she quickly saw how happy her position was: the greatest problem facing the people crowding the reception area was not crime, it was the paperwork jungle.

Another twenty minutes passed, and Lia considered leaving. The policeman noticed and motioned for her to jump the queue.

'Let's try one more time,' he said and punched the number into his phone.

When someone answered immediately, Lia perked up. The policeman explained the situation and then waited. The reply was clearly negative. But the policeman winked at Lia and continued the conversation.

'Listen, Gerrish, are you any more busy today than any other day? This young lady says she'll be quick, and she looks like a woman who keeps her promises. S-3, I would say.'

Lia's eyebrow went up upon hearing this code word. The line went silent. Then from the other end came a resigned, 'OK.'

'You can have fifteen minutes,' the policeman said to Lia.

Lia extended her hand.

'Lia Pajala,' she said, introducing herself again. 'Graphic designer from Finland.'

'Lionel Rowe,' the man replied. 'Copper from Croydon.'

A few minutes later, a man of about thirty appeared in the reception area. Lionel Rowe waved Lia over to him.

'Detective Chief Inspector Peter Gerrish. What was your business?'

'I'd like to ask you about the Holborn Circus murder.'

'Why?'

Lia was flummoxed. She had prepared a snappy answer to this obvious question, of course, but now, confronted by the impatient police detective, it eluded her.

'I've just been thinking about it a lot,' she finally said.

'I hope you aren't one of these women who think they can guess who murderers are in their dreams,' Gerrish said. His tone said that he had met more than one person who fitted this description.

'No, I'm not,' Lia said. 'Just fifteen minutes.'

The detective eyed her mistrustfully.

'That balding bloke wobbling behind the counter over there is one of the best policemen I've ever known. If Lionel Rowe thinks that I should let you ask your questions, I'm inclined to do so. Follow me.'

Without waiting for a response, Detective Chief Inspector Gerrish started across the lobby. Lia hurried after him. Briskly they proceeded to the other side of the building, through a door the man opened with a pass he carried around his neck, and then up two flights of stairs. Lia only had time to read the sign on the door into the corridor that led to Gerrish's office: Major Investigations Team.

'Sit,' Gerrish said when they entered his office. 'Ask your questions.'

The room was full of papers and files. Lia sat in the visitor's chair, the upholstery of which was so worn that the stuffing showed through.

'I saw the car on Holborn Circus. I don't have any eyewitness testimony that would help you though, because I only saw it from the bus,' Lia began.

'Did you see the body?'

'No. But the case has stuck in my mind, and I wanted to come and ask about it because... Because it just felt like someone on the outside needed to be thinking about this woman too. Everyone else has already forgotten her.'

Gerrish said nothing; he only looked at Lia seriously.

'I've read all the news reports about the case, and they've contained almost no information. Have you discovered anything about who she was?'

Gerrish sighed, growing even more sombre.

'This was such a brutal murder that it's anyone's guess,' he said. 'This is also an unusual case in that the body was dumped during morning rush hour in the middle of the City, but we still don't have any real leads. Every deadline my superiors give me for getting results passes with nothing new to report. And now I'm going to have to ask for more time again. Is that sufficient?'

Lia shook her head.

'I'm sorry to be taking up your time. But I'm not a crackpot, and I'm not a murderer groupie. If you don't want to tell me anything, I can leave.'

'Are you a reporter?' Gerrish asked.

'No,' Lia replied. She had intended to tell him she worked at *Level* but now left it out. 'I'm a professional graphic designer. Just a normal person who wants to think about this case.'

Gerrish asked to see Lia's identification and jotted down her national insurance number on his computer. Instead of returning her card immediately, he stared at it.

'All the bells in London,' he said, a little wistfully.

Lia stared at Gerrish in confusion, and he continued.

'All the bells in London, all the cells in London. All the tears in London, all the fears in London.'

'Where is that from?' Lia asked.

'I don't know. Part of a longer rhyme. They read it to us when we were young. Not here in London, in Manchester. Seemed to me it was saying something about how short life is and how much trouble a person can find in it. Don't borrow sorrow from tomorrow, our old vicar used to say.'

'I like that. It sounds like something that would have brought a lot of people comfort over the years.'

'What I'm saying is that you don't have anything to do with this crime. But you're still choosing to carry this sorrow,' Gerrish said, unable to conceal the ridicule in his voice.

Lia flinched, as if he had slapped her across the face. A stinging, naked shame filled her.

She realised how tired Gerrish must be.

His job is accepting death. And then trying to explain its logic to others.

Yet still, Lia's small sorrow didn't merit such condescending treatment. True, she had chosen this sorrow, but his disdain was unnecessarily hurtful. Indignantly she stared at Gerrish.

The smile disappeared from the corners of his mouth. He squeezed his eyes shut for a moment and then opened them again.

'I'm sorry. People should think about crimes and what can be done about them. Too few people bother.'

'I read that the woman may have been Latvian. I've also heard that she may have been a prostitute,' Lia said.

'That's a reporter's trick for trying to get a detective to shoot his mouth off,' Gerrish said sharply.

Lia went quiet.

'If I tell you something about what I know, can I be sure I won't find it online or in the news later?' Gerrish demanded.

'Yes, you can.'

'Right, then. As you know, we determined that the victim was Latvian. We publicised that because we expected the uncommon nationality to prompt more tips from the public. It didn't. You said you saw the Volvo. Do you know how the body looked, exactly what was in the car?'

Lia swallowed, remaining silent.

Gerrish spoke quickly without waiting for any reaction.

'When a person is crushed with a steamroller, nothing stays intact. It's like everything bursts and loses its shape.'

He described the pathology findings in detail. The woman's tissues, her organs, everything had been flattened. Whoever did it had driven over the woman several times – the medical examiners had deduced that from how the body was smashed: the tissues showed stress marks in different directions. Most of the victim's blood had been squeezed out and flowed away, and of course the large bones were crushed to powder.

'But, oddly enough, many of the smaller bones weren't pulverised, they just broke into smaller pieces.'

The detailed description made Lia feel ill, but she ordered herself to get a grip.

The forensic pathologist had determined that the surface on which the woman was crushed influenced the result, Gerrish told her. The terrain had been soft, fresh asphalt that gave a little under the body.

'That was why parts of the skin were preserved and some small things like the fingernails were almost undamaged. Both the fingernails and toenails were painted.'

Lia felt tears welling up.

I'm not going to cry. I can cry about this later but not right now.

'Do you know anything about the place where it happened?' she asked.

Not much, Gerrish admitted. There had been fresh asphalt, but the particles that adhered to the body mass were a composition used all over the country. The presence of the asphalt and the use of the roller indicated a road construction site had been the scene of the murder.

'But in theory it could have happened anywhere tarmac had been resurfaced recently. Even in the drive in front of a house, if they might have been able to do it without the neighbours noticing.'

The police had investigated all the building sites in the Greater London area, because the remnants of the body had only been in the car for about twenty-four hours. There had been sixteen such sites, but none of them had shown any evidence of the crime.

Gerrish still believed that it happened at a construction site though. The perpetrator had shovelled most of the body onto a plastic tarpaulin, which he then lifted into the boot of the Volvo.

'He probably covered his tracks by spraying down the road with water or maybe by laying down more asphalt. If we could open up all the roads at those sixteen sites, somewhere we would find blood and other evidence. I'm almost sure of that. But we can't get the permission or resources we would need for such an extensive investigation of only one murder. Not even in a case like this.'

The police had assumed that CCTV would have recorded the dropping off of the white Volvo, since the City was one of the most closely watched parts of the country. But the police were out of luck. If the car had been a few metres closer to the bus stop, it would have been within the field of vision of a camera. As it turned out, there was no surveillance footage of the drop-off, and determining who the driver had been, based on the other images of the street, was impossible.

Detective Gerrish seemed to have warmed to her, so Lia quickly continued her questioning.

'And the nationality? How did you decide that?'

'Luck,' Gerrish said.

Nothing about the body or the car had revealed her identity. As it turned out though, the woman had been in relatively good health. In the blood tests, the tissues, the bones and the hair there were no indications of disease or long-term drug use. The killer had chosen what would be left of the woman. Nothing identifiable, just scraps of clothing and such like, and one commonplace gold earring.

Finally the results from the dental analysis had come in. The forensic dentist had reported that the woman had several fillings. Some of them contained a material which, according to the international registries, was only produced in the Soviet Union and only in the early 1980s. The material had fallen out of use because of high production costs, but the final batches had been sold to Latvia, where its use continued into the 1990s.

Of the fillings in the woman's mouth, some had been done around that time. The forensic dentist could not remember any comparable case in which the use of the dental filling material of a body's teeth could be dated so exactly. It was a result of the rarity of the material, the mothballing of the factory that made it and the recorded sale of the remaining stores.

'How do you know the woman didn't just happen to get that filling material by chance? What if she was a traveller who visited Latvia and had a dental emergency?'

'Good question,' Gerrish said.

Of course they had studied all the teeth they found, discovering other filling materials used in Latvia at various times. DNA analysis also supported the result: current analytic techniques were able to narrow down possible areas of origin, and the woman's DNA pointed to the Baltic States.

'Do you have any suspicions about the perpetrator? Have you done some sort of analysis of him?' Lia asked.

Gerrish glanced at Lia pointedly, and she realised she had gone too far.

'Of course we've profiled him, but I can't talk about that.'

Lia saw that her time was up, and Gerrish's willingness to help was waning.

'Doesn't the nationality help move you forward? Latvia is a small country,' she said.

'No missing person reports have been in filed anywhere in Britain for a Latvian woman of that age. We've contacted the authorities in Riga, but the woman doesn't match anyone missing there either.'

The British immigration database contained relatively few Latvian women in their forties, and the police had begun going down the list. But that was a slow process.

'Most likely she was an unregistered immigrant, and there

are certainly more of those than legal ones. But by definition we don't have any information about them. Most of them are prostitutes.'

The woman had been wearing a considerable amount of make-up, Gerrish mentioned. The make-up itself was no help in establishing an ID, because the brands were standard mass-market ones.

'The amount of make-up fits the Latvian background. And of course it also lines up with the guess that she may have been a prostitute.'

Gerrish snapped out of his thoughts and glanced at his watch. 'Now you've got all you're going to get. S-3.'

Lia looked at him questioningly.

'S-3?'

'Security 3,' Gerrish said.

They categorised information on a sliding scale of secrecy. S-5 was what they told anyone.

'S-3 is what I tell trustworthy reporters. Everything I've told you is something I can tell the news media at this stage. But we only talk about things at this level with serious journalists we collaborate with on a regular basis. And you can imagine why none of them have been coming around asking lately. If we can't solve the crime, they aren't interested.'

'And the car?' Lia said, trying to keep the conversation going.

'Leads nowhere,' Gerrish said impatiently.

Stolen in Kensington the night preceding the discovery of the body, the car had only confirmed that the act was premeditated. It bore no fingerprints included in the police database. The owner, a lady approaching seventy, was so shocked about the use of her car in committing the crime that she had been forced to move in with her daughter for the time being. Thieves stole dozens of cars in London each day, some of which they used in committing other crimes, so the stolen car suggested the involvement of organised crime, but this was not conclusive by any means.

Standing, Lia thanked DCI Gerrish for the information and his time. On a side table, she noticed three transparent, tightly sealed plastic bags in amongst the stacks of papers. In them were dirty pieces of paper and shreds of fabric, as well as some small bits of metal.

'Are those her things?' Lia asked.

Hesitating for a moment first, Gerrish rose from his chair and moved the plastic bags so Lia could see them better.

'This is everything that was left of her besides the body,' he said. 'These are strictly S-2. But you've heard most of it, so I imagine it's all the same if you see these.'

Lia didn't dare to touch the bags, but stooped to get a closer look at the contents. In the bags she saw shreds of clothing and a handkerchief, all of which were stained dark with blood. There was a small key, a heart-shaped necklace pendant and some sort of plastic bits. After a moment, Lia realised that the fragments of plastic were parts of a comb. Among them were some teeth and faux mother-of-pearl from the handle, which featured a simple, white-flowered pattern. Daisies, Lia guessed.

'The key hasn't been any help identifying her. Nor has any of the rest of it. The crazy thing is we can't even be sure this stuff belonged to the woman. Maybe the perpetrator just shovelled a key off the street that somebody else had dropped,' Gerrish said.

'What sorts of things get stamped S-1?' Lia asked as she left.

'That I can't tell you.'

'Naturally, information or suspicions about who killed her. And the body, of course?'

Gerrish smiled dryly.

'Do you have much S-1 about this case?' Lia asked.

'What S-1?'

16

Lia had learnt too much from DCI Gerrish to review it all over the phone with Mari. She had to wait until the end of the day when she could get to the Studio in person.

Mari listened carefully, asking questions from time to time. Had Gerrish said what colour nail varnish the woman wore? Had he commented on how expensive the make-up was?

'No, I didn't think to ask,' Lia said.

'If he didn't mention anything, then it probably wasn't significant. They do good work. They get more information out of tiny details than you might think. And it's great that he told you all that.'

'I was a little surprised. I could have been some crazy lady who was just going to put it all on her blog.'

'Well, for whatever reason he decided to make an exception for you. They develop a good feel for human nature, and he seems to have put you in the same category as a serious reporter.'

The amount of time that had passed since the murder had probably also influenced his decision, Mari guessed.

'Had you gone in with your questions in May, they would have ignored you. But now you made them curious: why would someone come round asking about this body after so many months? Right now Gerrish is searching their databases to see what your name brings up.'

'Fortunately he won't find anything in particular. At least I hope not.'

Now that Lia had heard as-yet unpublished details about the case, she took the Holborn Circus murder even more personally. In a strange way she felt as though she were party to it.

'Have you thought of anything we could do?' she asked.

'The police are investigating all Latvian women registered in the country, so of course that leaves the unregistered immigrants,' Mari said. 'But you can imagine what a nightmare that is. Women sneaking or being brought secretly into the country, most of them prostitutes. London must have the most, but surely they live in other cities as well. I would guess that most of them live in hiding, especially if they work for brothels or pimps.'

'Sounds pretty impossible.'

The woman was likely to have lived in the Greater London area, Mari suggested. That was only an assumption, but they had to start somewhere. How could they trace a Latvian woman living below the radar? By doing the things that she had done.

'But a Latvian living in England wouldn't necessarily do anything specifically linked to her homeland. I don't think I do anything specifically Finnish here,' Lia said.

'This is all conjecture,' Mari replied. 'But it may be that Latvian culture is more important to them here than Finnishness is to you.'

'In what way?'

Free Latvia was a young country. In the tiny Baltic States, culture had been the glue that held the nations together through hundreds of years of oppression. A Latvian living in London might very well try to find ways to recreate her homeland, if only for a moment, in the foods she ate or the celebrations she attended.

'Perhaps she missed the flavours of home or used to go out to places where other Balts or even Russians gather.'

That sounded logical, Lia agreed.

'If she was here working illegally, she probably didn't go to any of the Slavic restaurants in London, since they're so expensive,' Mari continued. 'But she might have visited the stores that sell Eastern European food. Or the bars where Eastern European prostitutes work or Balts spend their free time.'

'Should we go looking for Latvian prostitutes?'

'No, *we* shouldn't,' Mari said. 'This is your thing, and if you want to move forward with it, you can do it on your own. I have to concentrate on Arthur Fried.'

Lia fell silent, thinking.

'So what I need to find out is where there are food shops and nightclubs like that.'

'Well, actually, I think Maggie could do that much more quickly,' Mari said.

Lia considered whether to take offence – she did work at a magazine, the whole point of which was gathering information – but then decided she could not afford to indulge her vanity.

'You continue with the Arthur Fried news stories. You're definitely the best person for that. I think there's still hope that might turn something up,' Mari said.

She's moving me like a pawn on a chessboard. And I actually like it.

The rest of the night Lia spent at *Level* reading what felt like an endless stream of articles about Arthur Fried.

From midnight onwards, reading required serious effort. Her eyes began to ache. Because her stomach could no longer handle it, she changed from drinking coffee to tea and eventually to just water. Her brain came up with three categories into which she placed the articles she read: Routine, Pointless and Absurd. Routine stories just reported events. Pointless stories gave Lia nothing. In the Absurd stories, the reporter allowed Fried and his party to sound off without bothering to check the facts.

Lia was reading a short piece in a local paper called the *Lincolnshire Echo*. She hadn't been able to find any connection to Fried in the story, and had begun to think that it had probably popped up in her archive search by mistake. So, Pointless.

But something made her return to it. 'Wave of bankruptcy sweeps away six businesses,' the headline proclaimed. After reading for a moment, Lia realised why her search had hit this article: Fried was the founder of two of the companies in question. Lia had included the names of his businesses in her list of search terms, even though Fried had founded them long ago.

Gordion Ltd and Fellowship Ltd had been located in Lincoln. According to the paper, the Lincolnshire Chamber of Commerce had noted with concern that liquidations of small and medium-sized businesses had been on the increase, the evidence being the six companies mentioned in the article.

Information on the bankruptcies had not appeared in any of the other articles about Arthur Fried. As a party leader, Fried was obliged by law to disclose publicly his financial connections, and Gordion and Fellowship Ltd appeared in those reports year after year.

Lia dug out the pile of papers she had received from Mari containing all the basic information they had collected about Fried. They were still there: as recently as the previous year, Fried had declared his ownership of both companies.

Lia didn't know what the bankruptcy notice in the *Lincolnshire Echo* meant in practice. Obviously the bankruptcies meant some sort of legal complications she did not understand, and she was too tired to sort it out that night. But on the Tube on her way home, the feeling came to Lia that a small tear in the carefully woven fabric of the Arthur Fried Story had just formed before her eyes.

Is this how Mari feels when she's researching her jobs? As if information gives her a hold over a person?

First thing in the morning, Lia told Mari over the phone about her discovery.

'Really? Both went out of business?'

How could that be possible? Mari wondered. She had read the information Fried gave to Companies House, and no mention existed there about any bankruptcies or even suspension of the companies' activities. Both businesses still existed online: they had websites, clients, continuity.

Lia had to concentrate on her own daytime work, but Mari was more than keen to continue digging herself.

'Thank you, Lia,' she said.

That evening they met at the Studio. Mari's face indicated that it had been a good day.

'Your find is a real bombshell,' she said.

From the amount of printed pages scattered on the desk, Lia saw that Mari had found plenty of information on the topic. Mari and Rico had been working on it all day.

'Sit down and have some wine,' Mari said and then began her account of events.

Years earlier, Arthur Fried had founded two businesses, Gordion Ltd and Fellowship Ltd. According to the official register, Gordion's lines of business were property sales and communications and Fellowship's were business consulting, travel services and logistics.

'Excellent choices. That basically covers everything under the sun,' Mari said.

The listed places of business were both Lincoln, and a later entry in the records disclosed a new injection of equity capital and added Anna Belle Fried as a principal shareholder.

'That was around the time they got married.'

The county employment register revealed that Gordion Ltd listed sixteen employees and Fellowship Ltd nine. On this basis, they had also received county business subsidies. During the early years, the companies had delivered to the authorities annual reports and accounts which showed the firms were successful. In one year, Gordion had even made a profit of some quarter of a million pounds.

'But then, as you discovered in the *Lincolnshire Echo*, they notified the county authorities that the companies were entering bankruptcy. Just like that.'

No one had ever reported the bankruptcies to Companies House. And Fried had had an important reason for that: when he reported in Lincoln that the businesses had failed, he didn't need to return his business subsidies or pay some of the council tax the companies owed. Businesses experiencing insolvency were exempt unless the failure was deemed the result of dishonesty or negligence.

'One year later the story picks up again.'

Lia heard from Mari's tone that she was enjoying the narrative and the work of uncovering it.

Gordion Ltd and Fellowship Ltd had moved to London. This came from the Greater London official register whom the companies had needed to notify about their employees and activities.

'They were essentially the same firms. They just had some new staff and new offices.'

'So they never actually stopped doing business,' Lia said.

'Exactly.'

'How can that happen? That's supposed to be impossible.'

'We don't know all the details yet, but we don't have to. We only have to know that he did it and it was illegal. The police can sort out the rest.'

Mari had a hunch about how Fried had made it work. Fried had probably fooled the Lincoln officials by simply claiming that he had filed all the proper declarations. Perhaps he paid someone off so fewer questions would be asked. Of course the national registers were supposed to receive information directly from the counties, but the bankruptcy process was often so complicated that years could go by before information travelled from one office to another, and sometimes they never passed it along at all. Since the businesses claimed to be entering liquidation voluntarily and there was no angry mob of creditors clamouring for payment, there would have been no need for an official liquidator to review the books. Apparently no media outlet beyond the *Lincolnshire Echo* had ever publicised the bankruptcies.

'And because the article didn't mention that they were Fried's businesses, he has never been publicly connected to their problems.'

Mari paused for a moment before slamming her damning conclusion down on the metaphorical table. When Fried lied about the bankruptcies, he and his wife had in effect stolen some £320,000 from the public coffers. That was only a rough estimate, and the real value was greater, because that figure didn't include all of the employment and other taxes never collected from the companies.

'Why did no one in Lincoln ever wonder why the companies continued operating in London?' Lia asked.

'Fried wasn't famous yet, so hardly anyone would have noticed.'

If someone had happened to ask, Fried would probably just have said that they were new companies with the same names. In the business world, recreating old firms was common. Sometimes the name of even a failed company could be a valuable asset. But for some reason Fried hadn't bothered establishing new companies.

'He wanted to save the bother and expense. He assumed that he wouldn't be found out because they're such small companies. White-collar crime detectives' nets usually aren't that fine.'

'Three hundred and twenty thousand pounds. That's a lot,' Lia said.

'If you ask the editor-in-chief of one of the newspapers how much that is, I bet he'll say, "About one Arthur Fried's career's worth."'

They had found what they were looking for. Mari had been right. Arthur Fried was a criminal.

'But this isn't enough,' Mari said. 'Fried is good enough that he could get around this. We need two more things just as bad.'

This surprised Lia. Mari's dogmatism felt exaggerated. How could she know that they would find anything else this damaging?

'I believe he's done much more like this and worse. I just don't know what,' Mari said.

Frustrated, Lia fell silent, but Mari still had more to say.

'I have something for you,' she said.

Maggie had spent the day concentrating on places where they could try identifying the Latvian woman.

Two London nightclubs had reputations for specifically attracting Eastern Europeans. Some of the club patrons were wealthy foreigners who visited London while travelling, but most of them lived there. A certain taste in music and an expensive style of dress united the regulars, wherever they hailed from. Eastern European prostitutes also frequented both clubs because Russian businessmen were reliable clients.

'Some Russian men want their sex in Russian here too.'

Concentrated in Ealing and Leyton, there were any number of Slavic grocery shops. But only some of the stores sold Baltic goods.

'Now we have to start going through those,' Lia said, realising herself how discouraged she sounded.

'It's hard work,' Mari admitted. 'Weeks might pass with no results. It could also be as far as you ever get. But you have to start somewhere.'

The supermarkets seemed like a more remote possibility than the clubs, because few people created personal connections at a supermarket. But at a nightclub you chatted with other patrons and the staff constantly.

'So I'll start with the clubs,' Lia said.

She would have to invent a cover story, Mari reminded her. Eastern mafia types frequented these places, so marching in and starting to ask questions about dead women wasn't a good idea. Lia's appearance clearly showed that she was not a police officer, but she had to have a reason for her questions.

'What if I were looking for a friend from Latvia?'

'Too vague. The explanation has to be more specific to be believable. They'll be able to hear from your voice that you aren't a Brit, so say you're a Finn. Say maybe that you have a sister or stepsister who was born in Latvia and is missing, and you've heard that she came to London. Do Latvian women come to the club often; does anyone know who you could ask?'

'What do I say if they ask why my sister hasn't contacted me?'

'Because she's sick. That's why you're worried: maybe your sister is so sick that she can't contact you. But think the story through thoroughly beforehand. You have to believe it too. The sister has to have a name and an age, habits and flaws, and of course you have to know what she looks like. She has to have a fully fledged life in case someone asks something unrelated.'

The enormity of the undertaking began to dawn on Lia.

One thing did feel like a stroke of luck amidst it all though: Lia's work leave was starting. She had arranged to begin her three-week holiday at the end of September, and hadn't had time to think much about what she would do. Visiting Finland held little appeal. Now she could concentrate on her search for the Latvian woman.

'Don't use your whole vac now,' Mari suggested.

'Why not? Right now is when I need the time.'

She should perhaps take one week off now for this, Mari explained. The rest of her holiday allowance she would do best to store up.

'If you start getting somewhere with your investigation, time will be the thing you need the most.'

At first this idea was difficult for Lia to get her head around, but after considering it for a moment, she saw the upside.

Maybe I should start demanding more at Level *instead of just waiting for what they're going to say.*

'Do you want Paddy or someone else as a minder at the clubs?' Mari asked. 'I know good people in that line of work.'

'Thanks, but I have no intention of getting myself into a situation in which I would need a bodyguard.'

Later that evening in Hampstead, Lia was finding it hard to fall asleep. She had spent a good hour out jogging, but that had done nothing to calm her down.

Deciding to go back out for a walk, she stepped into the churchyard. Security cameras kept watch over the area, Lia knew, but she had always assumed she could walk there freely whenever she wished. A young woman strolling calmly through the church grounds has never set off any alarms.

Kidderpore Avenue, her home street, was like that. Most of the buildings in the area were either large houses or old, beautiful edifices housing schools and businesses. The residents were predominantly families who had lived there for years, students and cultural types. A small oasis of peace and quiet amid the hubbub of London.

Lia gazed at the familiar statues. St Luke and Poundy the Dog, which she could see from her own window, and, further off, the composer Edward Elgar and his wife, the author Caroline Alice Elgar. Lia sat down on Florence Nightingale's plinth, which was only just wide enough.

What am I doing? Visiting the police and prying into a murder investigation. Staying up at night reading news articles to catch a smug politician up to no good. Cooking up a cover story about a sister in Latvia I don't have.

I'm not the person I used to be.

The Studio felt familiar to her now, no longer like an extraordinary or special place. Coming and going freely, she knew the details of every room, like the paintings on Mari's walls and the way the sunlight moved across the spaces.

She knew the care with which Berg built his projects in the Den and how deliberately he tidied up. Once he had arranged the chips that flew off while he was planing wood into small, artistic ornamental piles. Just the sounds of machines echoing from the Den made Lia think of Berg grinning in his overalls.

My peculiar home away from home.

Rising, Lia gingerly touched the cold surface of the statue. She liked how the marble was always hard and soft all at once.

17

Mari sits in her office at the Studio reading the news on her computer screen. After reviewing all the headlines, she goes back and rereads the information Maggie has unearthed about the Baltic shops and nightclubs in London that Lia intends to visit.

She thinks of the Eastern European population of London, its customs and sense of humour, the unemployment and jobs and the unspoken dreams that brought these people here.

Lia will fit in well with the Russians and Poles and Balts at the clubs – in that crowd in this city, a Finn wouldn't stand out much at all.

And Lia will manage.

Mari likes the change visiting the Studio has brought about in Lia and done for their friendship. Lia still is not committed to the Studio emotionally, but she doesn't need to be. That will come in time.

Mari knows how it will happen. That was why she planned carefully how and when Lia would meet each person there.

Maggie and Berg, charming and safe. Lia got to know them first. Thinking of them, Mari feels a surge of joy. Her cornerstones.

And Rico and Paddy, whom she allowed Lia to meet gradually – weapons she couldn't parade around until a person was used to their presence. Just a little more time and Lia would stop thinking of them and their skills as anything remarkable.

They all have their reasons for being here. Over the years, Mari has done a favour for each of them: Rico, Maggie, Berg, Paddy and now Lia. Each of them has been the subject of one of her operations in his or her own time. She helped them, asking nothing in return, giving each space to receive the gift. She allowed each of them to see the effect of the assistance they received and decide for themselves what they thought. Perhaps they are repaying her by giving something back.

Instead of being beholden, they are simply more satisfied with their lives.

Changing as a person and finding a community you want to work in creates a bond stronger than most.

Mari has chosen them well. With each of them, it began slowly. When she heard about Lia, she knew it was more than a coincidence. Out of all the Finnish women living in London, Lia was the one whose background had placed her in Mari's path.

Mari has learned to trust her instincts. That was how she chose Rico out of a room of hackers and Maggie from a small London stage where she was brilliantly screaming a Greek tragedy.

Once at the Studio, Maggie mentioned her acquaintance Berg and his staging skills, and Mari knew that she wanted to meet him. Paddy she encountered in a bar. On the surface she could see his gambling debts and prison background, as well as the warmth that would gradually develop between them.

There are things that Mari doesn't tell any of them. Rico knows the most – he was the one Mari sought out first and his are the skills she calls on most frequently. But even Rico doesn't know everything.

And Lia knows least of all. But the trust between them will grow to become something different from that with the others.

Lia sees herself as introverted, even a bit lost. In reality she is strong and capable. She has achieved a promising position in the London journalism scene, no small accomplishment for a young foreign female. But she keeps her world small, living alone in her tiny apartment and falling into a rut doing the same things every day. Because her Finnish background is what it is.

Lia is becoming strong. She just needs time, time to do things and time to learn. That Lia is worth it, Mari knows.

18

Flash Forward was not a place Lia would normally have chosen to spend an evening. Everything was harsh: the sounds, the lights, the colours, the people's eyes.

A brazen pickup joint. There was something ironic about it: Lia had been prowling the London nightlife circuit for men for years, but here she felt like a kitten by comparison.

She was looking for information, not company, and she worried it was too obvious. She was also dressed entirely too conservatively.

By ten o'clock, at least two hundred people had filled the club, more than half of them male and all of them wearing suits. Unlike the British men in the clubs that Lia went to, these men could wear bright white, red or even green suits with complete nonchalance.

The women were something else again. Not since the parties of the 1980s had Lia seen such a parade of iridescent fabrics and gaudy jewellery. The make-up was garish and hours had gone into each coiffure. Lia had guessed that glitz might come with the territory and had donned a blue top with demurely sparkling stripes, but in this company her sequins were like dying embers surrounded by raging wildfire.

Flash Forward was the playground of London's Eastern European community. Standard music ranging from Madonna to U2 set the tempo for the game in the early evening, but Lia knew that as the night progressed the music would switch to hard dance beats. Maggie had said as much as she described this and all the other Eastern European haunts.

What Maggie had unfortunately failed to factor in was how Lia could afford to drink for the whole night. She ordered a coke for almost £5. Bottles of champagne and flamboyant mixed drink concoctions flowed across the bar. The patrons were doing well for themselves, or at least they were prepared to pay to have a good time.

Lia looked around and tried to determine whether any prostitutes were present. She guessed that a couple of the women must be, based on how they approached a group of men, but whether there were more was impossible to say.

She had spent the last few days reading up on Eastern European human trafficking. Estimates indicated that prostitutes from these areas were particularly prevalent in Britain and Germany, and hundreds of women were thought to leave Latvia alone for other parts of the world to work in the sex trade every year. But no precise figures were available for obvious reasons.

Media coverage had perhaps exaggerated the scale of the problem. Exposés of human trafficking in Britain claimed that thousands of women and young girls had fallen victim to forced prostitution. However, academic and government research showed far fewer cases coming to the attention of police investigators. Dozens, perhaps hundreds. Only a few human trafficking cases had actually ended up in the courts. How much prostitution and human trafficking remained undetected was impossible to know, but no one could deny that it was a serious problem.

Lia had found two reports that focused on Latvian prostitutes. For a small country, prostitution there seemed surprisingly prevalent. Selling sex was not illegal in Latvia, and some researchers claimed that the shame associated with it was less than in many other nations. Some even referred to Riga as the Bangkok of the Baltic. This was a crude comparison but not completely inaccurate. Due to the weakness of the Latvian economy, some women considered prostitution their best way to achieve a more comfortable life.

Perhaps we Finnish women live in a bubble of equality. We can afford to be horrified by prostitution. Our standard of living protects us. And the illusion that we possess a morality they supposedly lack.

As she did the rounds of Flash Forward, Lia realised that if there were prostitutes present, considering notions of morality or the lack of them was the wrong way to approach the situation.

This is about money. And desire, the fulfilment of desire.

After a while, just waiting around started to get on her nerves. Approaching the bar, Lia made eye contact with the barman.

'I need something fun,' Lia said.

In his bow tie, the man smiled.

A moment later, he returned with an enormous drink containing three bright, plastic female figures with flashing lights inside.

'The Lovelight, eighteen pounds.'

Lia gave the barman her credit card and tasted the drink. With a considerable alcohol content, its effects were rapid. The Robbie Williams echoing from the loudspeakers started sounding more fun, and Lia began noticing the men whose glances brushed over her.

A few minutes later, one appeared at her side.

'You look like a woman who knows how to have a good time.'

Aljoša was from Russia and had a strong accent.

'You can call me Al,' he said.

Lia laughed. 'Like the Paul Simon song.'

'Huh? Who?'

'No one. Where are you from in Russia? I'm from right next door in Finland.'

By half past eleven, Lia had collected four business cards, accepted three drinks and laughed a lot.

Aljoša had turned out to be a salesman with a loud, brash streak who wanted to show off his dance moves. With his help, Lia had met two parties of Russians and one of Estonians, but no one seemed to know any Latvians or where to ask about women from Latvia. Her cover story had worked brilliantly – a search for a sister seemed to be sufficiently personal and serious that no one asked any questions.

Lia decided to try the same barman again.

'I'm looking for a Latvian woman who lived around here. Do Latvians come to the club often?'

The barman's eyebrow went up.

'Latvia? I don't think so.'

Lia motioned to the barman to lean in closer.

Offering the man a folded twenty-pound note, she asked, 'And Latvian prostitutes? Are there any here tonight?'

The barman laughed and took the banknote.

'Everyone here!' he said, spreading his arms at the crowd.

Lia cast him a sharp glance.

'Don't fool around. I have an important reason for asking.'

The barman slipped the note into his pocket and then looked around until he found the person he was looking for.

'She knows,' the barman said, motioning towards a tall woman with red hair.

Lia thanked him and moved aside.

The red-haired woman was dressed conservatively given the surroundings: black leather boots, black skirt and a red frilly blouse. Her party consisted of two other women and one man.

Lia noticed that the man was not participating in their conversation. With dark hair and dressed in a black suit, he appeared to be there for reasons other than carousing.

If they are prostitutes, he's their protector. Or pimp. Neither is good.

Lia couldn't think of a natural way to approach them. Aljoša was waving to her to rejoin him on the dance floor, but Lia only blew him kisses.

About ten minutes later, the women set off towards the toilet in a group. The man stayed put.

Lia hurried after them. There was a long queue outside the women's loos, and as Lia arrived, the red-headed woman and her friends were just turning back.

Now. Come right out with it.

'Hi, my name is Lia. May I ask you a question?'

The redhead smiled, surprised but friendly.

'Of course. What do you need?'

'This is my first time here. I'm looking for my sister. She used to live in Latvia, but now she's here in London. Do you happen to know any Latvian girls here?'

'I don't think so,' the woman replied suspiciously. 'My family is from Latvia, but I'm British now.'

'Could we talk for moment? I could offer you a drink.'

'I don't think so,' the woman repeated. 'A lot of Latvian women live in London. I don't know if they come here.'

The woman said something to her girlfriends in Russian, which Lia guessed probably meant something along the lines of: 'Crazy bitch. Let's go.'

The trio began to leave, but the redhead still said, 'I'm sorry. I hope you find your sister.'

'As a matter of fact, I think she's in trouble, and I need some advice.'

This piqued the woman's interest.

'What trouble? What kind of advice?'

'I don't quite know,' Lia said. 'I think she's been working in a business where a woman can get into trouble... with clients or the boss.'

The red-headed woman's gaze hardened.

'Please. This will only take a minute,' Lia continued hastily. 'Sisters have to stick together.'

'Of course...'

Lia looked at the woman pleadingly.

'There are a lot of Latvian women in London. In that business where you can get into trouble,' the woman said. 'But they always have a boss who handles their problems. I don't know any Latvian girls who work alone. I doubt there are any. So if your sister is here, her boss will help her. Goodbye.'

Turning, the woman walked away, followed by her friends.

Needing a moment to gather herself, Lia stayed in the toilet queue. She knew that nothing the woman had said gave her any new leads.

It was only midnight. She still had time. She just had to work out how to proceed.

Lia peered back out towards the dance floor and bar. The red-headed woman and her girlfriends were huddled together, talking intimately and glancing in Lia's direction. Their male companion was gone.

Then Lia noticed him barging his way through the dancing crowd directly towards her, accompanied by another, younger man. Bald and muscled, the second man stared her straight in the eyes.

Fear swept over Lia. She retreated back to the queue.

The men would reach her any moment. She had to get away, anywhere.

Jumping the queue, Lia stepped towards the toilet holding her stomach and repeating, 'Excuse me, excuse me! Emergency!'

Irritated exclamations followed her, but Lia was already inside. The room was so full that there was barely space to move.

She looked around. No way out but back through the club. On a side wall were two small windows, but metal grilles were visible behind the frosted glass. Going that way without attracting attention was impossible.

Outside it was cold, and Lia's coat was hanging in the cloakroom.

She could ring Mari. But whatever Mari came up with would take time. Lia just wanted out. The crush in the toilet was stifling.

She had to appeal to female solidarity. She glanced at the women standing by the mirrors.

That sporty blonde looks like she doesn't take any nonsense from men.

Lia sidled up to the woman.

'Excuse me. I'm so sorry, but I have a problem,' Lia said in a low voice. 'There's a man out there who's been bothering me. I'm afraid to go back out. I think he's going to try to force me to go with him or something.'

'That's outrageous,' the woman exclaimed.

She looked at Lia appraisingly.

'Can I help? Shall I call the police or the bouncers?'

'I don't want anything like that unless he gets aggressive. But could you leave with me? I just want to get out. Just walk me to the door. Then he won't dare try anything.'

After hesitating for a moment, the woman made her decision.

'Of course.'

Taking Lia by the arm, she squeezed reassuringly. Lia smiled quickly, and they began moving towards the toilets' door, arm in arm.

Lia caught her breath as the door opened: the dark-haired man and his bald partner were right there waiting.

'That one, in the dark suit,' Lia whispered.

'Right,' the woman said, holding her tightly by the arm and glaring at the man. Pressed against each other, they set off through the nightclub.

In order to reach the exit, they had to force their way through the mass of dancing people. Lia tried to keep her eyes down and move as quickly as she could. The woman understood from her grip that now they just had to move.

At that moment, Lia was yanked back, her left arm feeling as though it might be torn from its socket.

Lia cried out in agony and tried to break free from the man in the dark suit who was dragging her aside. The blonde woman Lia had been walking with stared on in shock.

Lia screamed.

'Help! Rape!' she shrieked, her voice cutting through the din of the club. The people around them came to an abrupt stop, as if they had been struck.

'Help! Someone help!' the blonde woman shouted.

With that, the man in the dark suit released Lia's arm and left, quickly melting into the crowd. The bald man was nowhere to be seen.

Lia held her arm, which was numb and possibly dislocated. Her whole body tingled with shock and pain.

'Out. I have to get out,' Lia said to the blonde woman.

Lia could see the fear in the blonde woman's face, but she still came to Lia's aid and made a path for them by waving the dancers away. The crowd parted instinctively. In a moment, Lia was at the cloakroom with her escort.

She realised she was gasping, as if the jerk backwards had knocked all the wind out of her lungs. Lia handed the woman her handbag.

'My coat,' Lia managed to say, and the woman dug Lia's ticket out of her bag.

Noticing that something unusual was afoot, the attendant eyed them.

'Is anything the matter?' he asked.

'No,' Lia said quickly. 'No, there isn't.'

With some effort she managed to get her coat over her shoulders. Her left arm was too sore to put the coat on properly.

'Thanks,' Lia said to the blonde woman. 'What a dreadful night.'

'That was just awful,' the woman agreed. 'You will notify the police, won't you? There were a lot of people there who saw that man and what he did to you.'

'Yes, thanks. Of course I will.'

As she stepped out into the air, she felt her legs wobbling.

On the street, Lia had to stop and brace herself against a wall. She had to catch her breath. Despite her idiotic attempt to the contrary, she was still alive and in one piece.

Perkele! *What a stupid Finnish girl! Now there's another perfect Finnish word.*

No free cabs were visible on the street. After waiting a moment, Lia started walking towards Waterloo Tube station. She glanced behind her and made sure to keep to the better lit parts of the street. Thankfully no one was following her.

At Waterloo there was a long stagnant queue for taxis. The trains would be running though.

Dozens of people stood on the Tube platform, kissing couples and young club-goers. Lia was starting to feel more secure, and the train would be coming soon, in three minutes.

She had thirteen stops to travel, about thirty minutes. From Hampstead station she would have to walk home, since getting a taxi at this time of night would be like winning the lottery.

The Tube carriage was full to overflowing, so Lia had to squeeze her way in. She set her back against the wall to keep herself firmly upright and protect herself from anything hitting her arm.

The train arrived at Embankment. Lia carefully watched everyone entering the carriage. No man in a dark suit, no bald thug.

As the train picked up speed again, the screeching of the tracks mingled with the mirthful buzz of conversation. At a bend in the tracks, the carriage rocked, and Lia could see back into the rear of it. A bald head momentarily flashed into view.

Lia felt as if she had been slugged in the stomach with a lead pipe.

Frantic, she closed her eyes. When she opened them, the man was no longer visible in the mob. The carriage rocked. Again the man came into view.

He was in the same car as Lia and trying to stay out of sight.

Perkele, *what a stupid Finnish girl.*

Heart pounding, Lia began running through her options.

Get out at the next station? He'll follow me.

Get out at Hampstead? He'll follow me and see where I live.

Call the police? He'll definitely run away, but I'll have to explain why he was following me. And they'll record my name.

Lia looked at the time on her mobile. Almost half an hour to Hampstead station.

What if I ring Mari? Maybe I could stall for time in the Tube station. I should be safe with people around. Mari could send someone to help. But that would take time.

Then she remembered Mr Vong. Mr Vong always helped when one of the young students ended up locked out on the street at night. And Mr Vong had a moped. But how could she contact him?

Phones only worked in the parts of the Tube network that were above ground and sporadically in a few places underground near the stations. Lia glanced at her mobile. No signal.

For station after station her phone stayed dead. The Northern Line was just too deep.

The Tube train hurtled on. Lia stared ceaselessly at the corner of the phone. No bars.

As the train slowed on its approach to the next station, a sound further up the carriage caught her attention. Someone had received a text message. As Lia thought, she remembered the same thing happening to her once or twice even though the stations here were so far underground.

A text message only required a momentary connection. It would be nothing short of a miracle if the SMS got through, and she would have no way of knowing if Mr Vong had received it.

Growing ever more anxious, she quickly typed a message before the next station arrived: LIA. NEED HELP. BAD MAN ON TUBE. HAMPSTEAD STATION. MOPED.

The carriage stopped. Lia extended her mobile towards the open door, knowing how empty a gesture it was.

She pressed the green button and waited.

A status bar. After a few seconds, the display of her mobile went black. Lia frantically pressed another button to wake up the phone but was returned to a different screen.

The couple standing next to Lia glanced at her as if she was mad, but she didn't let them disturb her.

Then the doors closed and the carriage moved again.

Now all Lia could do was wait twenty minutes and seven stations for the train to arrive in Hampstead and then dash to meet an aged saviour who probably wouldn't be there. Twenty minutes was plenty of time for her to imagine herself kidnapped and beaten bloody or mashed to a pulp in the boot of a white Volvo. She wondered what sort of resistance she would be able to put up against the bald man. At each station she felt an almost uncontrollable desire to rush out of the carriage. She thought of the year in Finland when the fear of physical violence had become a normal part of her life. How on earth could she have let her relationship with her parents grow so distant? Mentally she reproached Mari, who had suggested that she visit clubs looking for evidence of the Latvian woman. She reproached herself for rejecting the offer of a minder. Why had she wanted to pry into this whole ugly business anyway?

She tried to calm herself by breathing deeply, but it didn't work.

In all of those twenty minutes, Lia never glanced into the rear of the Tube carriage. This required a significant effort, but Lia knew that if she saw the man staring at her, she would instantly start screaming.

The train braked at Hampstead station. Lia edged closer to the exit. Finding that her left arm was almost completely useless, she realised that she had not thought of it once during the whole journey.

When the doors opened, Lia was among the first to push her way out.

When she glanced to the side, she saw the bald man exiting from the other door of the carriage. Now she could see him properly. It was definitely the man from the nightclub, the same face, the same thin, sunken cheeks. Cheeks drawn tight by years of hard training, Lia knew instinctively.

The man cast a glance at Lia as well. For a moment their eyes locked.

The Underground platform had two routes out: the slow lift or the long, difficult stairs. Lia chose the safety of the crowd and joined the crowd queuing for the lift.

She saw the bald man off to the side of the crush. Perhaps he wouldn't fit in the same lift.

Suddenly there was jostling and shouting. The bald man was trying to force his way towards her, elbowing people out of his path.

The doors opened, and Lia was among the first to shoot in. She turned to watch as the bald man roughly cleared his way towards the lift. Most people sidestepped him in outrage, but a couple of men stood their ground and grabbed him by the coat.

The lift doors closed.

The trip to the surface took ten seconds, but Lia knew the man would not stay to wait for the next lift.

Lia dashed out of the lift towards the Tube station's barriers, Oyster card in hand ready to touch out. She heard running steps echoing from the stairs.

When the bald man arrived at the gates, Lia was already on the other side.

Now came the moment of truth as Lia ran through the doors.

There on the street in front of the station was Mr Vong. Small, old and frail, Mr Vong sat in the saddle of his blue moped, waiting. He raised his hand.

As Lia rushed towards the moped, she saw how Mr Vong looked on in stupefaction at the man charging after her.

'Let's go,' Mr Vong yelled and kicked the moped into motion.

Throwing herself onto the small scooter, Lia felt pain tear at her left shoulder.

As Mr Vong swept around the street corner, Lia turned to look back. The bald man stood on the pavement anxiously looking for a means of transport to continue the pursuit. The other people in front of the station stared, aghast at his strange behaviour. Some stared at Mr Vong and Lia, the aged Asian gentleman fleeing the scene with a young blonde riding pillion.

Holding on tightly to Mr Vong, Lia swore an oath.

No more of this ever. Not ever.

19

'That was a bad mistake,' Mari said.

The next day when Lia related how the evening had ended, Mari repeated this several times.

It was Thursday. Lia was glad that she was on holiday and didn't need to try to work with her sore arm. And she was happy to be alive.

'I should have thought this through more thoroughly. I'm sorry, Lia,' Mari said.

'It wasn't your fault,' Lia said. She had wanted to go to the club herself, even though Mari had warned her and even offered her a bodyguard.

'I was being stupid. I'm not the secret agent superwoman I've been imagining. I almost lost my mind, I was so afraid when I saw that bald guy in the Tube,' Lia said.

'I can believe it. I'm sorry. This thing of trying to have two different jobs going at the same time doesn't work. It doesn't give me enough time to think. Now we have to proceed carefully,' Mari said.

'Mr Vong is quite the hero. I feel like hugging him,' she added.

'So do I. Of course I thanked him last night, but everything happened so fast. There wasn't time for anything else. I'll get him something nice as a thank-you gift.'

As Mr Vong sped off into the Hampstead night, Lia had thanked her lucky stars. The bald man would have been able to catch her easily on those dark little streets.

At Kidderpore Avenue, Lia had motioned to Mr Vong that he shouldn't drive straight up to the hall of residence in case the man had succeeded in following them. Mr Vong had driven his scooter a few yards further and from there walked her to their building, entering through the other stairwell.

Mr Vong was too polite to press her for details of how she had ended up in such distress, but Lia had felt the need to explain.

'That man and his friend tried to attack me at a club and then started following me.'

'Clearly the kind of person from which one should keep one's distance,' Mr Vong observed.

Lia had gone to her flat, and Mr Vong waited for her to lock the door. Lia had listened and waited as Mr Vong returned home and gradually returned to bed.

She didn't turn on any lights: for the first time, her basement room felt unsafe.

But after Lia had sat shivering in the dark for some time and then gone looking for a torch so she could find some painkillers for her shoulder, the situation began feeling absurd.

Why am I afraid?

She had sat down on her bed. In all probability, she had shaken the man off her trail. How long was Lia intending to huddle at home alone in the dark then?

I'm going to stop being afraid now. I've done this before. I can do it again now.

She thought of the woman found murdered in the white Volvo and her agitation abated. Determination rose in its place.

Whoever you were, I'm going to find you. Fear isn't going to stop me. Fear is only an emotion.

The feeling of numbness had begun to abate. She switched on the lamps and brewed a couple of cups of tea.

She had taken a sleeping pill with the painkiller. As she waited for this to take effect, she searched the back of her cupboard for a book Mr Vong had given her.

It was an old guide to London written in Hong Kong for Asian travellers. At first, Lia hadn't bothered even to browse through it because it looked so cheap and simplistic. Once she looked at it more closely however, she changed her mind.

The name of the book was *London, Good For You!* and it contained such chapters as 'Why London?' 'London for women', and 'Remember to shake hands'.

The book was silly, its language clumsily translated, rote English. Representing a mixture of 1960s London and an Asian view of British customs unfamiliar to Lia, many of the things the book described had almost died out, such as gentlemen's clubs and travelling salesmen. But the book also had a disarming sincerity.

Lia had lain on her bed looking at the guidebook, immersing herself in its world, which was in such stark conflict with the events of the past evening. It helped her re-examine her feelings towards her environment. Emotions could be controlled. The innocent, good city the book described did not exist, but somewhere out there were its remnants.

She had slept soundly through the night.

In the morning Lia had visited her GP so he could look at her shoulder, which still hurt but could be moved. The muscle was badly strained but her shoulder wasn't dislocated. Lia made up an explanation involving a run-in on the street with a motorcyclist. The painkiller the doctor prescribed took away the remainder of the aching.

'I got off with a scare. But what I don't understand is why those thugs reacted so aggressively,' Lia said to Mari. 'A couple of questions about Latvian prostitutes and they're immediately trying to beat up a lone woman.'

If the men were running a pimping business involving a good number of customers and a lot of money, she could understand the heavy-handedness, Mari observed. Anyone who came around asking questions could be a risk.

'Well, I'm certainly not going back there ever again,' Lia said.

'No, you aren't. And investigating nightclubs alone isn't a good idea at all,' Mari said. 'But we'll come up with another way. Maybe Paddy could go to the clubs. I have to think.'

Lia looked around at Mari's office, thinking how safe she felt at the Studio.

Silly. Just a few weeks ago this place felt so strange and mysterious.

'You're thinking about how your attitude towards this place has changed,' Mari said.

'Yes, I am.'

'Since you're coming to the Studio so often now, would you like your own key? Then no one has to come to open the downstairs door for you any more.'

Lia couldn't come up with any reason to say no.

'And you can choose a research room to start using. Maggie is using one of them, but two rooms are usually free.'

That Lia had to consider longer. Having an office sounded sensible because then she would have a place for all of her papers. But then would she be working as one of Mari's employees like everyone else?

'I don't think of you the same way I do the others,' Mari said. 'You aren't working for me. We're friends.'

That sounded good to Lia.

'Right then. I'll take an office, but I don't work for you. I'll do what I want here.'

Mari smiled, satisfied.

'What next?' Lia asked.

'Wouldn't a little rest be in order?' Mari asked.

'No,' Lia replied.

If she got stuck at home nursing her wounds alone, she might think too much about the man with the bald head and end up being scared of going outside at all.

'Well, since you ask, tomorrow evening there is this one event. I was thinking you could attend.'

'Arthur Fried?'

'Arthur Fried.'

20

Standing in the ice rink car park, Lia looked at the building welling sound and light into the evening twilight.

The Streatham Ice Arena was not a particularly grand place, but it was a big step forward from the little halls where Fair Rule had been holding meetings barely a year before.

This evening's event was not an official party conference for making decisions about platforms or programmes. It was a spectacle for the faithful. A rally for the supporters who would be going out before the election to talk voters into getting behind the party.

Entrance was free, and even two hours before the event was due to begin, the place was already buzzing. No one paid any attention to a woman entering the arena alone.

In the entrance hall, Fair Rule workers bustled around a line of tables, putting out brochures and stash bearing party slogans that would be sold to raise campaign funds.

Lia climbed the stairs from the entrance hall towards the ice rink. Cardboard and plastic mats covered the rink, and more helpers were setting up chairs so that seating would be available for the audience elsewhere than in the stands surrounding the ice.

Lia sat in the stands to watch as volunteers hung posters on the walls.

Get Britain Back. Fight for Your Rights.

This would be an interesting evening.

On the far side of the rink was a large platform upon which a pair of young men were doing a sound check of the microphones. Behind them over the stage hung two large flags, and a third was being raised into place.

Lia had read about them as she prepared for the event. Pride of place behind the rostrum at Fair Rule gatherings was always reserved for these cloth banners bearing no text, only an image:

the face of Arthur Fried. The flags had cost a lot given Fair Rule's resources and had sparked no small controversy.

A reporter for the *Independent* had named them the 'Great Leader Flags' and observed that they injected a strange 1970s Soviet or Chinese air into British politics. All parties used images of their leaders as they campaigned, but only Fair Rule had gone so far.

Arthur Fried had defended the flags in several newspaper interviews. He had been the architect of the party's recent rise in fortunes, and the mainstream media constantly overlooked small parties, never inviting them to participate in televised debates. What else could a beleaguered group of concerned citizens do to elevate the profiles of its leaders?

Lia sauntered around the rink watching the party workers and volunteers hard at work. Whenever an opportunity presented itself, she lent a hand. She carried boxes, hung placards and helped an older woman named Dorrie set out her trays of biscuits and paper coffee cups. This gave Lia a chance to ask various questions about Fair Rule business and the schedule for the evening's event.

The ice arena provided ample space for more than a thousand visitors, but the workers didn't think it would fill to capacity. Fair Rule had never turned out that many supporters on a weekday night. The party had booked the large hall for other reasons.

A year earlier, Arthur Fried had initiated a change in policy. Support for the party had been static, and its political initiatives had not been able make a media breakthrough. Fried had crafted a new strategy: the only way to get big fast was to start acting like you already were.

So, Fair Rule began grinding out opinions on every issue the main parties dealt with, and Fried poured oil on the rhetorical fire. Incendiary words like *deception*, *threat*, *crime* and *destruction* served as a challenge to the powers that be and netted new voters. The party began to organise its events at ever larger venues and with ever more pageantry. At every opportunity they focused media attention on Fried in hopes of making his face universally recognised.

This new, theatrical approach had succeeded in drawing larger crowds.

There was also a practical reason for booking the Streatham Arena: they had got it cheap because the party's financial secretary knew the arena's marketing director and had managed to convince him that the party meeting would attract a new clientele.

Lia wondered whether the marketing director would really have wanted this particular customer base. Low-skilled, working class, mostly ageing white males. Lia believed she understood why they came. The only thing in their lives over which they had absolute control was what pub they spent their money in. Here they felt powerful.

Fifteen minutes still remained until the event was set to begin. Lia slipped into the long corridor that ran behind the rink and offered access to the locker rooms and storage spaces.

There was a commotion at one locker room door. Lia recognised the reason from his pictures in the news: Arthur Fried.

Dozens of men were pushing, trying to reach the party leader, most of them lacking the patience to queue. Fried was stuck in the corridor shaking hands.

Arthur Fried had a knack, Lia had to admit. He listened to the beginning of each supporter's story, then interrupted and answered briefly. He sounded decisive but did not promise anyone anything.

Each man had what he thought were brilliant campaign ideas that he had to tell the party leader about. They expressed deep concern about vague fears, such as the spread of Islam in Europe.

Some just felt impelled to tell Fried, 'Go and show them, Arthur.'

Although Lia found it impossible to share their opinions, she recognised their feelings.

They want Fried to kick the shit out of the world for them.

When the background music in the hall faded and the first speaker of the evening was announced on stage, Arthur Fried said goodbye to his supporters milling in the corridor and disappeared into a back room. The corridor emptied in next to no time as the men moved into the stands.

Lia chose a seat near the platform, a little to one side.

The first speaker was a man in his sixties who said he worked for a warehousing company and that he had lost faith in politics until he read the Fair Rule party literature and heard Arthur Fried speak. He reiterated the party's key objectives – no social support without work requirements and the reining-in of special rights for immigrants – to raucous applause.

Lia listened to the rhythm of the speech rather than the content. She knew the pattern the evening would be built around, beginning with untrained speakers and moving towards more skilled orators until Fried himself took the stage.

Articles about Arthur Fried often touched on how good he was at inspiring a crowd. He described it himself as surrender. He said that when he was younger he tried to be anything but a politician. He had tried to make his living leading companies, making money. But, over time, he had realised that what he knew best was speaking in front of people and raising their hopes. This had been an important insight for him, he said. He had known immediately that he would succeed at it. Once he had surrendered himself to this fact, his career had taken off.

Forty-five minutes and three stiff speakers later, Lia was wondering whether the evening would ever get going at all. She could not think of any reason for choosing such conventional presenters other than that each of them came from a different part of England.

A young man in a black blazer came onstage and the announcer introduced him as Andy Cargill, the assistant director of the Future Rule youth programme. He took the microphone, and the volume of his voice was startling.

'We've seen what isn't working in Britain, and we know how to respond. We are Future Rule, and we have a question. What are we waiting for?'

Cargill's roar made the young men in the crowd spring to their feet.

Lia watched the crowd. The uniformity of their dress was plain frightening. Black jeans and black jackets, short-cropped hair and burning eyes.

Cargill and his ferocious followers played a specific role in the show – to raise the pulse of the crowd. They focused on one theme only, the restoration of the privileges of the white race.

Actually they didn't use the word race. Lia knew that the party leadership had banned its use since the term would have brought universal condemnation. But they didn't need the word.

Cargill's performance also energised the older generation. For the last minute of his speech, he simply repeated one slogan. The scene resembled a rock concert with the audience howling in adoration.

'GET BRITAIN BACK!'

The audience responded: 'Get Britain Back!'

'WHAT DO YOU WANT?'

'Get Britain Back!'

'LET'S DO IT NOW! GET BRITAIN BACK!'

After Cargill finished, most of his audience appeared willing to march out onto the streets to do battle that very moment. But two more speakers remained in the queue.

'Next we will be pleased to hear from the chairman of Fair Rule North, Mr Simon Lord!'

Lord continued on the same themes at nearly the same volume as Cargill. The main message was that Britain should withdraw from all international agreements that allowed immigration from poor countries.

Preventing herself from getting worked up was impossible for Lia as she listened to this. The idea recurred often in the party's public statements and represented their vision of a new period of independence for Britain. Of course there was no practical way to carry it out – but Lia had no interest in discussing that with this audience.

She glanced at her watch. Almost half past eight. Lord started revving up the audience for the final speaker of the evening.

'We have the man who will get Britain back! Who is he?'

'Arthur Fried!' the audience shouted.

The passion that filled the ice arena made Lia's heart pound. She felt like covering her ears.

When Fried appeared on stage, the entire audience stood as one man, bellowing Fried's name and pumping their right fists rhythmically in the air.

Lia surveyed the frenzy.

This is his power. This is why Mari thinks Fried is so dangerous.

Arthur Fried made a show of calling for calm, but allowed the chanting to continue for a full minute. Then he took the microphone and raised his hands in the air. The audience fell silent before their leader.

'Friends,' Arthur Fried began. 'Friends, thank you for your faith.'

Fried spoke well, in short sentences, pausing frequently to allow the audience room to call out in response, which served further to charge the atmosphere.

Fried used the introduction of his address to describe the rise of the party. Polling figures, TV appearances, statements quoted in the media. This was not a new story, but he made it sound as though it was a credit to them all.

Fried moved to a small news item. Lia knew to expect this as standard procedure at party events, bait for any journalists in attendance.

'Friends, I am happy and proud to be able to tell you that I have just completed drafting my programme for Britain's new defence policy. It will be published next week. This will be our trump card next year when we enter Parliament in an unprecedented landslide at the ballot box.'

They would publish the details later, but Fried wanted to tell his 'friends' the main points. The programme was called 'A Better Britain' and promised to restore the honour and influence of the native peoples of the United Kingdom.

'We demand that Britain enter into defence agreements only with those countries that share our values.'

The audience clapped uncertainly, not knowing precisely what this meant.

'For all of this, we need you. Every single Briton you can recruit to our cause of creating a new, better Britain. Everyone's contribution is important. We need every man and woman,' Fried said, motioning to one side of the stage.

Out walked his wife, and the howling of the audience returned to fever pitch.

Anna Belle Fried walked to her husband and extended her hand. Away from the microphone, Fried said something sweet to his wife. They knew the choreography by heart: Lia had already seen it online in videos of previous Fair Rule events.

Anna Belle Fried was a heavily made-up, buxom woman. Her blonde curls, a thigh-revealing slit skirt and high heels made her look like a doll.

Anna Belle, you would have been beautiful without all the dressing up too.

Turning to the crowd, Arthur Fried took a step towards the front of the stage, leading his wife along. Fried laughed and winked at the audience: my woman. In the glow of the bright spotlights, they looked unreal, as if everything they did appeared in slow motion.

Some of the black-clad young men in the front row whistled and barked astonishingly lewd suggestions at Anna Belle. Lia saw her freeze, staring somewhere into the middle distance, trying to ignore the shouts.

Arthur Fried set his wife in motion with a jerk of his left arm and raised his own right hand, clenched in a fist. He smiled at the black jackets in the front rows. They shouted even louder.

Lia stared at Arthur Fried's hand holding his wife, squeezing tightly.

Anna Belle took a step to the side, intending to retire from the stage. Arthur Fried did not look at his wife, but Lia saw how his grip made her flinch. Her struggling ended instantly.

Fried likes this. He likes them treating his wife like a whore.

The loudspeakers carried Fried's voice over the roar of the audience.

'We are going to Parliament! And you, you and you, all of you here, are coming with us!'

21

Lia opened the door to the Studio with some effort: she was carrying two large boxes of papers and newspaper clippings, and her left shoulder was still sore. The papers dealt with Arthur Fried and the Latvian case.

Entering one of the free offices, she set her load down on the desk. She wondered whether she should go and tell Mari she had arrived but then remembered: the orange circle on the office floor had already told the surveillance computer.

A moment later, Mari arrived to greet her.

'It's nice you're moving in.'

'I think so too. Nice and weird. Less weird and more nice as I get used to the idea though,' Lia said.

She reported on the frenzied party rally of the previous evening.

'Fried is even more talented in front of a crowd than I had expected. The news stories, videos and TV appearances can't show you what he's like in person. He has this ability to unite the aspirations of such different people and make it sound like he supports them all,' Lia said.

She described the young paramilitary-looking men in the front rows. As they called Arthur Fried out onto the stage, they looked like neo-Nazis ushering on their saviour.

Mari asked about Fair Rule's Better Britain programme, but Lia didn't have any more detailed information. The event had only received a brief mention in the papers because no reporters had been in attendance at the ice arena.

'It's strange how they can make it sound as if their bunch had some sort of ability to shape political programmes,' Lia said.

'Well, when they publish it, the commentators will make sure that all the most absurd parts receive plenty of coverage,' Mari said. 'But that's still publicity. They don't have to make sensible proposals to increase their popularity.'

Channelling people's mistrust, anger and disenchantment was enough.

'And I'm not so blind that I can't see why you wanted me to go there. You wanted me to see Arthur Fried so I would want to fight him too,' Lia said.

'Well, do you?'

Lia admitted she did. Sitting in that audience, the sickening dread that Fried and his shock troops might actually enter Parliament had been all too real.

How could it be possible for a party like Fair Rule to win even a single seat? Lia wondered out loud. Of course, believing that they would be able to accomplish much in Parliament was difficult, since the other parties would hardly stand for Fair Rule's outrageous declarations.

'Their ideas definitely do offend a lot of people. But that won't stop them from growing,' Mari said.

The rise of tiny right-wing extremist parties had been one of the greatest political changes Europe had seen in recent years. Mari reeled off the countries where groups like Fair Rule had gained representation in town councils and Parliaments: France, the Netherlands, Austria, Hungary, Switzerland, Italy, Bulgaria, Slovakia, Denmark, Sweden, Norway... Of course the parties were different in each country, but two things united them. First, they were built around a strong leader and, second, they opposed immigration, ethnic minorities and gay rights. Mari reminded Lia that Finland had its own version of the phenomenon. The 'True Finns' were not a blustering far-right party, but they were populist, reactionary and racist.

'The problem is that there are a lot of people who think that things should just be allowed to play themselves out,' Mari said. 'No matter what bad things happen, they don't intervene. They appeal to freedom of speech and claim that we should always be civil to others and respect their opinions. So to all intents and purposes Fair Rule can do and say almost anything.'

Educated women like Mari and Lia were especially likely to oppose the issues pushed by parties like Fair Rule. But most of them did nothing about it.

'I'm not going to stand around waiting for Fair Rule to grow. Some things need protecting. Social order, for example.'

Lia nodded. She recognised herself in Mari's words, her own unwillingness to intervene.

They had to get closer to Fair Rule's operation, Mari said. By this point they had sifted through more or less everything ever written about Fried. They needed more material. They needed someone who could observe the party's work at close quarters.

'Like a volunteer,' Mari suggested. 'All the parties use them. There were a lot of them at the ice arena, weren't there?'

Lia took a few seconds to realise what Mari was suggesting.

'You want me to join Fair Rule?'

'If you want to. But we can find someone else if we need to.'

'I don't want to be anywhere near that crowd,' Lia said. 'What could I do there anyway? Isn't this more Paddy's territory?'

Paddy would be a good fit for the job, Mari admitted. A big white man with a buzz cut would fit in perfectly. But Paddy was frequently tied up with other assignments for long periods of time. He also avoided gigs where he had to work with people as himself. That didn't sit well with a private detective.

Mari listed the reasons Lia was a good candidate. She seemed so normal that she wouldn't arouse any suspicions. She had already met party workers at the arena. And any party would welcome with open arms a volunteer who knew graphic design. Parties needed placards, brochures, bulletins and websites.

'And besides, if I have you there observing things, I'll feel almost like I'm looking at the place with my own eyes. You see the world almost the same way I do.'

Lia understood but still hesitated.

'I don't know if I'm up to it. I've never done anything like it before. Spying on people.'

'I know,' Mari said. 'And no one is going to force you to do it. I'm just giving you the opportunity. We agreed that you always get to decide what you do.'

Lia thought for a moment.

I must be crazy. Mari definitely is. But I'm going to do it anyway.

'OK,' Lia said. 'If it starts feeling too hard, we'll handle it some other way.'

This time she did not want to make up any complicated cover story. Perhaps her own background would do.

'Hmm, that could work, but we have to think through the basics,' Mari said. 'At least don't tell them your real name or any other personal details. Tell them you're a graphic designer. If they ask anything else, change the subject. Maybe say that your boyfriend got you interested in Fair Rule.'

'Sounds good,' Lia said. 'My boyfriend is a neo-Nazi. I just love a man in uniform.'

Mari smiled, but Lia noticed how quickly her smile evaporated.

The Fair Rule party offices were crammed into three rooms above a shop on Epping High Street at the end of the Central Tube line. Apparently the party lacked the funds to pay London rents. Lia had rung ahead to ensure they were taking volunteers for office work.

'Miss, if you'd like to help, come on down,' the man who answered the phone had said.

Since she was still on holiday, Lia didn't bother getting up early, so she didn't arrive at the office until eleven o'clock.

The place didn't look like the efficient command centre of a political movement. What it looked like was a tatty office with people trying to cope with the issues flooding through the door and out of the telephones and computers. There was no shyly making her way in all alone. If anything, she had to dodge the flow of traffic to avoid being knocked down.

Arthur Fried was nowhere to be seen, but Lia had expected as much. The party had to have other uses for its leader's time than sitting in an office.

She presented herself to the man whose desk was closest to the front door.

'Hi, I'm Lia. I've come to volunteer.'

'Great, Lia. What can you do?'

'I'm a professional graphic designer. I can do newspaper layouts and...'

'What you are is an angel from on high,' the man said and pointed to the next room. 'That's the media centre. You can find coffee and tea in that corner there. Welcome aboard to helping us get Britain back.'

He had clearly repeated this greeting hundreds of times.

The media centre consisted of two desks, three computers and three busy people. The two older men in collared shirts and jeans were Stephen and Simon. The younger one, Tim, had the same kind of buzzcut as the men at the ice arena, but his clothing was not so dominated by black. They were delighted to hear that Lia knew graphic design.

'Excellent,' Tim said. 'I've been trying to handle the design work, but what I do always comes out pretty crap. Now I can concentrate on writing.'

Three hours later, Lia had designed the poster and flyer for Fair Rule's next London event, chatted with a couple of party activists she had met at the arena and realised to her relief that no one in the office had time for delivering harangues about putting immigrants in their place or closing the borders. The political content came out of meetings between party operatives, and the day-to-day work of the office was just getting the message out the door.

'Is Arthur Fried here much?' Lia asked.

Stephen smiled. This was obviously a typical question for newcomers.

Fried was at the office for a brief time almost every day when he was in London, Stephen explained. Usually he popped by in the evening after his various appearances and meetings. He usually sat in the back room, where the party secretary, Tom Gallagher, worked.

'They always say that anyone can come back and talk about anything, politics or new ideas. But no one ever bothers. Still, it's good that they're around and available.'

Lia worked until six in the evening, but Fried did not appear.

'Will you come again? Please say you will,' Stephen pleaded when he saw her preparing to leave.

'Yes, I think I will. I may have time at weekends.'

'You're welcome anytime. Come tomorrow or Sunday, if you can. We have to prepare materials for three more events.'

'Do you work on Sundays too?'

Stephen snorted.

'With a potential election looming, there's no such thing as a day off.'

Lia returned to the Fair Rule office on Saturday evening. She had verified online that Arthur Fried was supposed to be in London. He had a public meet-and-greet session and three party discussion forums.

At the party office, Stephen was delighted to see her, immediately dumping the templates for the upcoming events in her lap and telling her where to find the pictures and text that needed setting.

It's strange how easily people can adapt to almost anything,

Lia thought as she placed and resized slogans for Fair Rule events in Glasgow, Manchester and Edinburgh.

As they worked, Stephen asked Lia what had got her interested in Fair Rule. Lia told him briefly about her boyfriend, who had been to a party event and convinced her to join too. This explanation seemed to pass muster.

At half past nine, Arthur Fried stepped into the office. No one could fail to notice his arrival, and many of the workers rushed to ask him about various situations they were dealing with.

'Arthur, do you want people to come up to Manchester? We need to reserve the buses if we're taking a big group.'

'Arthur, there hasn't been any activity on your blog for more than a month. We're already getting complaints. What should we write?'

Don't these people have any operational leadership? Do they ask Fried about everything?

The operational leadership walked in after Fried. Lia soon saw that Party Secretary Tom Gallagher was the one who had all the answers, but everyone still wanted to have contact with Fried.

Fried smiled and answered briefly. Tired-looking Dorrie, who was saddled with the cleaning, making coffee and other office chores, he patted on the back. Lia thought Dorrie's job was pure torture, because everyone else was always leaving a mess. Fried praised Stephen and Simon for the news release they had sent to the foreign press about the Better Britain programme.

Fried also noticed Lia.

'A new face? Arthur Fried. Glad to have you aboard,' he said, shaking her hand and looking her in the eye.

'Good to be on board,' Lia said, looking at Fried carefully.

In a second he had lost interest in her and moved on.

He works like an assembly line. That was a fine show of human warmth. What would Mari have seen in him just now?

Fried continued into the back room with the party secretary. They left the door open, but as Stephen had observed earlier, no one went in to continue any of their conversations.

As she worked, Lia walked past the door a few times, looking in as she went. Gallagher sat at the desk making notes on the computer while Fried sat in an old armchair dictating short instructions. A secretary and a boss, Lia concluded. The party secretary was an influential figure, but he stayed in the background to allow Arthur Fried room to shine.

A lot of what Fried says probably comes out of Gallagher's head. Interesting. The devil in the detail.

As the evening wound down, Lia found that she had not made much progress in her intended assignment. She had worked obediently, but except for some superficial acquaintance with the people in the office, she did not know much more about the party.

On Sunday morning, she rang Mari.

'I don't know if this is going anywhere.'

The brainwork and real leadership seemed to happen somewhere other than at the party office.

'If you want to stop, stop. How about we go out tonight,' Mari suggested.

'No. I want to try a little more. I have a sort of... *vihi*.'

Mari laughed at the Finnish word.

'Are you my bloodhound now?'

She knew how Lia felt: she had a sense there was something to find, so she just had to soldier on.

Lia set out for the Fair Rule office in the morning this time. The supply of layout work showed no signs of running out.

On Sundays fewer people were around the office and the pace was slower, which left Lia time to wander around holding a coffee mug listening to people's conversations.

Dorrie was happy to have someone notice her other than to ask for more coffee or toilet rolls.

She said that her husband had been one of the founding members of the party. He had died four years ago. Dorrie was a widow of limited means in her sixties and childless. She did not know what else to do but come to the office. She had been coming there most days for more than ten years.

'I don't care much for politics,' she said. 'But after Lee's death, I was away for two months, and then when I came back I realised that I felt better for it. Being involved in something does the head and the heart good.'

'I know what you mean,' Lia said.

Early in the evening, a heated exchange came from Gallagher's office, making everyone raise their gaze from their work in surprise.

'I'm not changing one bloody word. If you can't accept it, go and find another party,' Gallagher shouted.

The door flew open, and Lia saw a young man by the name of Gareth Nunn march out of Gallagher's office. Lia had only exchanged a few words with Nunn and did not have any connection to him, but she noticed the other workers lowering their eyes as he fetched his coat.

'Cheers,' Nunn snapped, his face pale, as he stormed out the door.

Lia only had seconds to make her decision. Grabbing her own coat, she yelled to Stephen that she was going out for some air and went after Nunn.

Not particularly smooth, but I have to try something.

She caught Nunn on the street and grabbed him by the shoulder.

'Hey, what was that all about, Gareth?' Lia asked.

Nunn stared at her angrily.

'What the hell business is it of yours?'

'It isn't really. I've just been wondering whether I really belong with those people either.'

Nunn eyed her, surprised at her response.

'Do you really want to know what kind of people they are?' he asked.

'Yes, I do. Let's go for coffee,' Lia said, leading him further down the street.

After half an hour chatting with Gareth Nunn, Lia knew she had something significant.

The young man sitting with her in the café was quite impressive. Nunn had studied social policy and political science, travelled the world doing charity work and finally devoted himself to politics. Lia felt like asking how such an intelligent young scholar could get mixed up with this kind of crowd at all, but he told her himself.

'I joined Fair Rule because our immigration policy isn't working. Everyone can see the problems, and it's the one thing the party is right about. But they don't really want to solve the problems. All their political thought is about is giving the masses a false impression that someone is listening to them. Their solutions to the immigration issue are stupid, or, more like, they don't have any solutions.'

Nunn had been looking for a conduit for formulating a new, better-managed immigration system. But his ideas were not good enough for Tom Gallagher and Arthur Fried.

'Fried is a façade for hanging everyone's hopes on, and he purges all attempts at deeper thought from the party's statements. Fried tells Gallagher what the people want, and Gallagher writes it.'

They had hoped Gareth Nunn would be the party's ideas man, and he had been able to participate with Gallagher in writing statements, but the two had quickly fallen out. Arthur Fried had not shown any sort of interest in Nunn.

'They don't even think about what they would do in Parliament if they got there. All their energy is channelled into making the party a popular movement. Riding xenophobia all the way.'

Nunn sipped the last of his already cold coffee. He said he was going to make his way home.

'I have no intention of coming back to Epping. It's clear now that there isn't any place for me in this party.'

'I understand,' Lia said. 'Thank you for telling me. You've made it easier for me to think about whether I want to go on too.'

Did Nunn have any other reasons for leaving besides differences of opinion on politics, she asked in parting.

Nunn glanced at her quickly.

'Yes, there are other reasons. But I don't know whether I can talk about them.'

'Why not?'

'I don't know anything for sure, but I have my suspicions.'

Lia restrained her desire to enquire further.

'I wouldn't recommend staying with them,' Nunn said and left.

Lia returned to the Fair Rule office and continued making up advertisements until evening, but her brain was actually focused on trying to process everything she had just learned.

On Monday at the Studio, Lia delivered her report to Mari, who asked with interest about Gareth Nunn and the other workers in the office, especially Tom Gallagher.

'Excellent,' she said once Lia was finished.

In the span of just a few days, Lia had collected a lot of practical information about the party.

'Do you want to go back?'

'No, not unless it's absolutely necessary. Every time I think about what those leaflets are really saying, I start getting angry.'

'Great. It may be good for you to go back once or twice more until we figure out what Nunn meant about the party's other problems.'

'I was thinking that Maggie, Rico and the others could work that out.'

Lia wanted to move back to the Holborn Circus case.

Mari studied her thoughtfully.

'Surely you don't intend to go back to those clubs?'

'No, definitely not.'

She would visit the supermarkets that sold foods imported from the Baltic. At least no one was going to attack her in a food shop.

'If we don't keep it alive, the case is going to die,' Lia said. 'Even the police aren't getting anywhere.'

Mari lifted her mobile.

'I'll be right there with you.'

'I know,' Lia replied.

22

Lia had never previously encountered the smell that she noticed in the Ealing Slav Market. The smell was not bad, but it was pungent.

Sour and sweet. As though someone had mixed minced meat, fish and spices and pickled them in vinegar.

Lia browsed the selection on the shelves as she glanced at the other customers, who were few in number since it was the middle of the afternoon. Most were women, some clearly Eastern European. The shopkeeper was a small man with dark hair, also apparently with family roots in that corner of the world.

Picking a few tins from the shelves – Estonian sprats and Latvian fish paste – Lia attempted to strike up a conversation about them with another female customer.

'Excuse me, but do you know what the difference is between these?'

The customer was an older woman, with dyed blonde hair.

'That Estonian one is whole fish and very strong. The other one is a paste. Quite mild.'

'Thanks. Do you happen to be from there, since you know so much about it?'

'I am from Belarus. But I have lived here in England for many years now.'

Feeling emboldened, Lia jumped to her actual question. Did any Latvians come here? Did the woman know any Latvians in London?

Taken aback, the woman expressed her regrets that she was unable to help and hurried to the cash desk. When Lia followed, the shopkeeper eyed her suspiciously. Lia met his gaze unwaveringly.

'I'm looking for an acquaintance from Latvia, a woman. Do any Latvian customers visit your shop?'

'Perhaps. I don't know,' the man said.

'It's important that I get in contact with her. Is there any way you could help? You must know a Latvian I could ask.'

'No, I don't,' the shopkeeper said. 'This is a grocery shop, not a post office.'

With that, he motioned for her to make way for the other customers.

This is clumsy, Lia thought as she left. *I'll have to come up with a more workable approach.*

Just one street down was a shop with a grandiose name, the Mirage Gourmet, but it was even smaller than the previous place. Behind the counter sat a Chinese-looking woman reading a newspaper.

'Good day. My name is Lia Pajala. I'm doing research for my master's thesis in marketing about customers of ethnic shops and how they make purchasing decisions. Do you mind if I interview a few of your customers?'

The cashier shrugged.

Digging out of her handbag the questionnaire she had made up at the Studio, she surveyed her prospects. An Asian man, an English-looking woman and another, more nondescript woman.

Lia chose the last. Introducing herself, she repeated her explanation.

'Are you here looking for foods from a certain area or culture?'

The woman's gaze only flitted over Lia.

'Russian.'

The woman pushed the survey form back.

'I don't want to do it.'

Lia attempted to approach another female customer, but she just said 'No' and turned her back.

What's with these people?

Lia had to force herself to calm down.

They're here shopping. They might have good reasons for not answering questions from total strangers. I'm coming across too pushy.

Lia returned to the counter and tried to engage the cashier in conversation. She asked questions about the tins of mango on the counter and the game show flickering on the television on the wall. She mentioned looking for good ingredients for a meal she was preparing for friends that evening.

The woman answered with a few grunts Lia had difficulty understanding.

She began losing hope. Unless she got herself a job at a shop like this, starting conversations was going to be like pulling teeth. She had just reached the pavement from the shop when her mobile rang.

'We have an idea,' Mari said. 'About Fair Rule. Can you come in?'

Two hours later, Lia was sitting on Sprowston Road in Forest Gate in the front seat of a large, grey delivery van staring at a red-brick house a hundred metres away. Next to her in the driver's seat sat Berg, whose calm attitude gave her to understand that this was just another night.

But for Lia, it wasn't.

They were staking out Gareth Nunn's house. Mari's plan was simple: they were to follow Nunn's movements and break into his computer while he was away.

Lia liked the simplicity and directness of the plan. Not so much the illegality.

'Of course it's illegal,' Mari had said. 'It's absolutely positively illegal in every way.'

But it was also practical, and the best way to move forward.

In the rear of the van sat Maggie and Rico. Not Mari. Of course not.

Everyone sitting in the vehicle had an assignment. Lia's was the easiest: she was there to identify Gareth Nunn. Actually, they only needed her to confirm the identification. Rico had looked up pictures of Nunn online, including Facebook.

Mari had suggested that Lia could just point out Nunn and then leave while they handled the rest.

Lia didn't want that. The thought of breaking into Nunn's home and computer and really the whole idea of such a blatant invasion of someone's privacy terrified her. Still, she wanted to be with them.

Lia knew she wouldn't be able to control the situation, but it felt important to her not to leave this for others to do.

They had been waiting nearly an hour when Gareth Nunn stepped out of the house and set off up Sprowston Road.

Lia did not have to say anything. Berg had noticed Nunn and saw from her expression that the man in the grey jacket walking away from them was definitely the right one.

'Maggie, dear,' Berg sang out into the back of the van. 'We have work to do.'

They sounded like an old married couple going out to do their shopping, Lia thought.

Maggie jumped out the side door, closing it and hurrying after Nunn.

Lia, Berg and Rico stayed put. They had agreed to wait until Maggie called with permission to move out.

'Simple, old-school tradecraft,' Mari had said about this part of the plan. All Maggie had to do was shadow Nunn as Paddy had taught her.

Paddy was not with them. They didn't need him, Mari had explained.

The time they waited for the call felt unnervingly long to Lia, even though fewer than ten minutes actually passed. When Berg's phone finally rang, Lia breathed a deep sigh of relief.

'He's ordering pizza,' Mari reported. 'Eating in.'

Maggie had followed Nunn into the restaurant and taken a table from which she could easily keep tabs on him.

'You have at least twenty minutes. But I would say more like half an hour, maybe forty minutes.'

'Thanks, dear,' Berg said and rang off.

Gareth Nunn's name did not appear on the door, but they were sure of the address since they had crosschecked it from several sources.

No one else was about on the stairs. Still Lia was constantly preparing to make a getaway. She watched nervously while Berg and Rico inspected the door to the flat, located on the ground floor.

Berg ran a small, black device along the edges of the door, keeping his eyes on the display.

They had researched Gareth Nunn's background with care. He was unmarried and no other residents were registered at the address. Nothing indicated that he had so much as a domestic pet.

'But we have no way of knowing with certainty,' Lia had argued. 'What if his mother or sister happens to be visiting?'

'We'll find out soon enough when we go into his flat,' Mari had said dryly.

Berg nodded: the door was clear. The device display stayed dim, not registering any signals. If a burglar alarm were located in the hall of Nunn's flat, the device would have detected its power source.

Berg pressed the doorbell.

Lia held her breath as they waited. The others were more accustomed to situations like this, but for her it was all was new and frightening.

If someone were to open the door, they had an explanation ready. In his dungarees, Berg was a maintenance worker doing the rounds checking on the gas cookers. Someone had complained of a small gas leak, and all the flats had to be checked. Rico was Berg's assistant.

'And me?' Lia had asked.

'You're a passer-by, a resident of the building making her way up to her flat. All you have to do is walk up the stairs. If a conversation starts, ask what's happened. Berg and Rico will handle the rest,' Mari had answered.

No one came to the door, despite Berg pressing the bell several times.

They waited for another moment, listening. Not a sound. From the floor above, they could hear music, a radio, filtering through the walls, but Nunn's flat stayed quiet.

Opening his toolbox, Berg removed a bunch of key-like metal tools and began working with the lock.

Within a minute, he had it open. Lia stared at the flat through the doorway, still expecting something to pop out at them. Berg and Rico entered the hall confidently, and Lia hurried after them.

They were inside. Five minutes had passed since Maggie rang.

In the hall, Berg took a small bag out of his toolbox. Out of it he dug thin, transparent rubber gloves and white, plastic shoe covers. They slipped the covers over their shoes and pulled the gloves onto their hands.

Like in a hospital. Ready for sterile work.

The brief shot of relief this amusing mental picture brought made Lia realise how tense she was.

They surveyed the flat's two rooms and kitchen. Nunn was not the most organised man in the world. The sink and table in the kitchen were full of dirty dishes. The whole flat stank of rotten food.

The bedroom was small and dark, but they were not interested in it anyway. In the living room was a wall full of books, a large sofa, two armchairs and a desk with a laptop.

Rico smiled as he sat down in the desk chair and inspected the computer.

'Wow,' he said. 'I didn't know people still used things like this.'

Rico turned the machine on and, while he waited as it whinged into life and booted up, opened his own toolbox on the desk. In it were wires, small tools and electronic equipment Lia did not recognise. And a collection of memory sticks.

'Nine minutes since Maggie rang,' Berg announced.

'I don't think this will take long,' Rico replied.

The next twenty minutes were a lesson for Lia in how astonishingly easily difficult-seeming things could be if someone knew what they were doing.

Of course Nunn's computer requested a username and password. That took Rico two minutes.

Not even attempting any usernames, he simply plugged one of his memory sticks into a USB port, bringing up a window filled with lines of letters and numbers. Rico watched in satisfaction.

'This is a hacker kit,' he said in hushed tones as he began typing commands.

Lia stared at the words on the screen. *Acunetix Vulnerability Scanner. MD5 Cracker. MSN Freezer. MySQLi Dumper. Passstealer – Istealer. Zero Server Attacker.* Program names, she decided.

These were hacker tools: programs for breaching passwords, monitoring network traffic, scanning databases and servers, Rico explained. All hackers used them and updated versions were distributed online regularly.

'The most important thing is getting to the machine,' Rico said. 'Once you're there, you can get past the user security in an instant.'

And, a moment later, a familiar tune announced that Gareth Nunn's operating system was open for business.

'In,' Rico said.

He looked at the folders and icons on the screen.

Lia didn't dare speak. She feared that despite their precautions, someone would surprise them, the computer would start sounding alarms or something else unexpected would happen.

Rico selected a second memory stick, putting it in the computer and waiting for the machine to recognise it. Once it did, he started the program that would copy the contents of the hard drive onto the stick.

Three hours, twenty-eight minutes and sixteen seconds, the program estimated the copying operation would take.

'It won't be that long,' Rico said. 'I'd say fifteen minutes.'

The program had calculated the size of all the programs and files on the computer, but Rico had set only the emails, pictures and other web browsing information to copy – just the content that was relevant to them. The archiving program would skip everything else.

'Will Nunn be able to see that someone has been on his machine?' Lia asked.

'No,' Rico replied.

Covering up the break-in was actually more demanding than getting in in the first place. That was what separated real operators from 'script kiddies', 'newbies' who blindly used hacking tools written by others. A computer's operating system was supposed to log everything that took place, but a professional could change the log to remove all traces of his visit. Copying the files would change their timestamp, a record of when they had last been read, but Rico could restore the timestamps as well.

While they waited, they browsed the thousands of works on the wall-covering bookcase. Nunn had amassed an impressive collection of books on political history, communications and psychology.

'That's where he puts his money,' Lia said 'not into computers.'

Rico made his opinion of that clear with a roll of his eyes.

Once they had tidied up after themselves and left the apartment, Berg rang Maggie.

'No rush. He hasn't even finished his pizza,' she said.

They picked Maggie up from the restaurant, with Lia sitting in the rear of the van in case Nunn happened to notice the vehicle.

On their way to the Studio, Lia thought about how quickly everything had happened. When they had made it from the flat to the street, she had almost been reeling.

But she also felt satisfaction.

As Mari had said, it had all been practical and simple. And completely illegal. But they had not touched anything else in Nunn's flat, as if they had just popped round for a quick visit to his private life, politely and without leaving a mess.

In the lift up to the Studio, Lia's satisfaction began giving way to triumph. She could have gone right back out and done it again.

The amount of information to analyse on the memory stick was considerable. Maggie and Berg left, but the remaining trio wanted to continue. Rico took the text files and Mari the emails.

'The intimate things are probably in the pictures and browsing history,' Rico said. Lia should take those.

Lia found porn, but just the soft variety. She did not inspect the pictures very closely, since that would have been voyeurism. The other pictures were the normal stuff: trips, parties, Nunn with his friends. He had had a couple of girlfriends in recent years. The browser traffic was largely political. Nunn had been a diligent student of what was being said about Fair Rule.

Rico found material Nunn had written for the party. Especially interesting were numerous versions of the Better Britain programme.

The first presentation had not had anything to do with defending the rights of indigenous Britons. It had been Nunn's vision for improving the immigration system and the position of the immigrant community. Nunn had proposed moderate, humane changes. The latest version of Better Britain was closer to what Fried had said at the Streatham Ice Arena.

Version by version they had forced Nunn to change his text until it became something else entirely.

Mari said she could see why he wanted out.

'It probably happens in most parties. The person who originally came up with the ideas can't stand what they're being twisted into.'

Reviewing the email traffic took hours.

Why was Nunn involved in the party's finances? Mari asked Lia in an instant message.

The email chains showed that a few months earlier Party Secretary Gallagher had asked Nunn to help divvy up funds for the party's various branches and member organisations. The job was largely number crunching but also involved some serious politicking.

Soon Nunn had begun complaining to Gallagher how tired he was of arguing with the party's pig-headed leaders. Gallagher didn't care.

Perhaps he had intended to tire Nunn out, Mari suggested.

In order to make decisions on applications for funding, Nunn had access to copies of the party's financial records. He had started raising questions.

There are recipients here not listed in the registers. Money transfers every month. To whom? he had asked the party secretary.

Gallagher had not answered, but the next day Nunn was informed that he would no longer be responsible for fund distribution. He had protested angrily. *WHAT do you want me to do if I can't even do THIS?*

'This is it,' Mari said. 'This is what was bothering him about Fair Rule but he didn't want to tell you about.'

Perhaps Gallagher and Fried were slipping some of the money into their own pockets. Or maybe they were distributing money to entities they didn't want anyone else knowing about.

'Bloody hell,' Lia said.

They went through everything related to financial transactions, but the results were meagre. Nothing indicated where the shadowy money transfers had gone.

'Dead end,' Rico said.

'We have to get at Gallagher's messages and the bank records,' Mari said.

Lia stared at her, exhausted.

'Do you want to break into Gallagher's house?'

'Not necessarily. You mentioned that he uses a desktop computer in the Fair Rule office. That's probably where they distribute party funds from.'

'Couldn't we break in remotely?' Lia asked Rico.

'Not easily.'

At the least they would have to install a trojan horse on the machine first.

'How on earth would we do that?' Lia asked.

'We'll think of something,' Mari replied.

23

Strange holiday, Lia thought.

She was investigating food shops that sold products from the Baltic again. As long as she was looking for a connection to Latvian women, even the tiniest scrap of information about the murdered woman, she felt like she was doing something meaningful.

She was glad to leave the Fair Rule job for Mari to stew over. Lia was interested in Arthur Fried and his party, but they were still mostly Mari's concern.

Lia searched one grocery shop after another, falling into conversation with customers and chatting with shopkeepers. She varied her tactics: at times she posed as a regular customer asking about Latvia out of simple curiosity, and sometimes she was a student doing market research. But making any real contact with anyone was difficult.

Five stores were a complete wash-out. Lia did not find anything that would help her move forward. Her expectations fell.

The Eastern Buffet located in Leyton on the High Road was the largest store she had been to so far. There were customers in abundance, most of them Eastern European-looking women. The shelves boasted more Baltic products than in any of the previous shops. Duna bread, Magus mixed grains. Laima chocolate, Selga cookies, Dzintars make-up. Here they even stocked Baltic dairy products, whose shelf-life was relatively short.

Lia greeted a woman standing alongside her inspecting the selection of dried meats. Fortunately the woman did not rush away, instead praising the store's selection and chatting openly. Lia even had a chance to ask whether the woman knew any Latvians. She was from Estonia and worked for a diplomat. She only met Latvians at official embassy receptions.

This information did not help Lia, but her mood improved.

The shopkeeper was a burly man with a broad face. He didn't smile, but he did bother to exchange a few words with each customer.

At random, Lia took a jar of something from a shelf and picked up a small bottle of vodka, and then joined the queue at the checkout.

When her turn came, she placed her purchases on the counter and said, 'I also need some information. I'm looking for a Latvian woman living in London, an old acquaintance. Do you know any of your Latvian customers?'

Glancing at Lia's purchases, he keyed the prices into the cash register.

'We don't ask our customers' nationalities,' the shopkeeper replied.

'Where are you from yourself?' Lia asked to keep the conversation going.

He did not reply.

'Anything else?' he said finally.

Lia handed him a banknote and waited while he calculated the change. Then on the edge of the counter she saw a row of small combs and mirrors with a familiar pattern around their edges. Pearly white flowers.

Lia would have recognised them anywhere. She had seen pieces of exactly the same type of comb in a plastic bag on Detective Chief Inspector Gerrish's desk.

'And I'll take two of those,' Lia said, pointing at the combs and brushes.

'One of each?' the man grunted.

'Yes.'

The shopkeeper took a mirror and a comb, recalculated the total again and offered Lia her change.

Moving away from the counter, Lia felt alternating waves of confusion and triumph pulsing through her.

If that woman visited this shop, someone here might know her.

Lia looked by the exit at the noticeboard filled with advertisements for local events. She noticed a surveillance camera high up in one corner of the room.

So many possibilities were opening up. All of them distant, Lia knew. But now there was a direction she could follow. She and Mari would not be able to access the shop CCTV camera, but the police would.

She hurried out. As she sat on the Tube, Lia held the flower-bedecked comb and mirror in her hands. Strange that anyone would ship such simple objects all the way to Britain. Did the flower pattern have some special significance?

Lia had seen the same flower somewhere else. Where?

She strained to remember. She had sifted through such an enormous amount of information in the past few months. She stared at the flower pattern. Daisies.

Finally a picture from a website returned to her mind. The daisy was the national flower of Latvia.

Waiting to get to the Studio to tell Mari everything she had found was difficult.

Mari listened, holding the comb in her hand. How likely was it that the woman had got hers from that shop? It was at least possible.

'This is an excellent find. We should almost give it to the police,' Mari finally said.

'What do you mean "almost"?' Lia asked.

'We can do that later. First we should investigate it ourselves.'

'I could go back to the shop. Maybe I'll meet a Latvian.'

'What if you take a break? Maggie and I can see whether we can find out anything more about the comb or the food shop,' Mari said. 'I want you to go back to the Fair Rule office. Rico has come up with a way to get into Gallagher's computer.'

Mari led Lia into the computer room.

'It works!' Rico announced when they appeared at the door.

'Excellent,' Mari said.

Rico asked Lia to log in to her email or some other webpage using her own username on one of the computers.

Lia thought for a moment and then chose Traveldame.com, a travel service where single women could find information about discounts and budget one-person accommodation. Showing Mari and Rico a more personal site would have felt strange. On the front page a slew of semi-spam messages were waiting for her, all starting with the words 'Dear Lia'.

'Hmm, I guess you've been to France a few times. The adverts are all about Paris and Loire wine tours,' Rico said with a grin. 'But now log back out.'

After Lia closed the website, Rico grabbed the keyboard, removed it from the machine and connected it to another computer. A moment later letters and numbers were streaming down the screen.

'There you go,' Rico said. 'Lia's username for Traveldame is *missfinland* and her password is *nicedog44*. Lia, your password is OK, although not terribly difficult, but your username would be easy to guess.'

Lia snorted, embarrassed. There they were, lit up in pixels, her username and password.

Rico explained that he had installed an extra chip in the keyboard. Whenever someone typed, the chip recorded the keystrokes and the time they were entered. When Rico connected the keyboard to a certain program on his own machine, it regurgitated everything it had recorded, showing every message written, every password entered and every word googled.

'Unbelievable,' Lia said.

'Well, a hardware key logger isn't exactly a new idea, but I've added some improvements of my own. The hardest part is on the software side, since there can be so much text to sort through,' Rico said.

'Wouldn't it be easier to infect his computer with a virus or something?'

'That's a good thought, but we don't have any way to know what security programs might be on the machine. This is much harder to detect and disable,' Rico explained.

'How are we going to get this connected to Gallagher's computer?' Lia asked.

Rico had a plan all worked out.

'Gallagher has a standard desktop. All we have to do is swap his keyboard for another one just like it with the key logging chip installed. Then we switch the keyboards back and bingo!'

'Sounds easy,' Lia said. 'But there are always people in the party offices. If someone sees me messing with Gallagher's computer, I'll have some explaining to do.'

'Don't worry,' Mari said. 'We've done replacement operations like this before.'

Lia had to get at the computer three times. First to photograph the keyboard so they could be sure of the model. She also needed to check it for any obvious wear or other identifying marks. The second time she would swap the keyboards. And finally she would switch them back.

'Sounds easier and easier all the time,' Lia said. 'Bingo.'

The campaign workers at Fair Rule were surprised when Lia turned up at the office on Sunday morning.

'I thought you weren't coming any more since we hadn't seen you,' Stephen said.

To Lia he sounded almost accusatory, but she let it go.

'So what's on the to-do list?' she asked.

'You can choose. There's lots to get done.'

The options were an information pack destined for Ireland and advertisements for two party events. Arthur Fried had also announced that he wanted all the old placards re-designed.

'We've only got twenty plus different ones,' Stephen said.

'The information pack, please,' Lia said.

I don't want to see posters I designed on the street pulling in votes for Arthur Fried.

Lia guessed that the party secretary would not come in until later on a Sunday morning. She guessed right.

Trying to work out how she could get in to photograph Gallagher's keyboard, she walked back and forth past the room, glancing in at the paper-strewn desk.

Then a simple idea popped into her head.

'Stephen, I need to make a personal call. My boyfriend and I had a fight. Is there any way I could use that back room while I ring him?'

'Just close the door, and no one will bother you,' Stephen said.

Lia stepped into the room and closed the door behind her. Quickly taking out her mobile, she began snapping pictures of the computer keyboard. She tested each key individually, as Rico had requested. If any of them were worn or moved strangely, he would have to build the same idiosyncrasies into the substitute.

Luckily the unit was quite new, with no visible marks of wear on the keys other than the spacebar.

Lia felt calm and confident as she returned from Gallagher's office.

'Everything OK?' Stephen asked.

'Better,' Lia said with a smile.

Rico was satisfied with the haul of photographs.

'A basic Dell keyboard. I can have one ready by tomorrow.'

'How do you intend to make the swap?' Mari asked. 'I wouldn't recommend trying the phone trick again.'

'I'll come up with something,' Lia replied.

She had to visit the Fair Rule office three times before a night came when Tom Gallagher was not on the premises. Every time she had to carry in her bag Rico's modified keyboard with its embedded key logging chip and design new party information materials.

But she also had time to plan how to switch the keyboards. What she decided was to fall back on Dorrie.

'The work here's never-ending,' Dorrie said with a sigh.

Someone had dumped food scrapings in the paper bin again. Could you really entrust political decisions to men who did not have the nous to separate their rubbish? they wondered together.

'Dorrie, what would you say to coffee and cake?' Lia asked. 'I have a reason to celebrate.'

'You sweet little dear, congratulations! What's the occasion?'

'Let's keep that secret for the moment. I'd like to organise a little surprise for everyone.'

Handing her some money, Lia asked Dorrie to fetch a cake or two, leaving the exact amount up to her discretion. Dorrie collected her coat and left for the supermarket.

Lia retrieved her bag.

'Could I have everyone's attention for a moment?' she asked, raising her voice.

The dozen-odd people in the office stopped to listen.

'We'll be having coffee and cake for everyone shortly!'

'Hurrah! What's the occasion?' Stephen asked.

'You'll see soon enough. Just give me five minutes to prepare.'

Lia moved with her bag into Gallagher's office. Closing the door, she set a chair in front of it. She took the keyboard out of her bag. Rico had done good work, even darkening the spacebar.

Lia switched the keyboards, hiding Gallagher's in her bag before pulling out a roll of streamer material, colourful paper plates and paper hats. She threw streamers over the shelves, ceiling light and desk. Then she stacked the plates and set the paper hats in a row on the desk.

Cracking the door and peeping through, she saw Dorrie just returning with two cakes.

'Oh, how lovely,' Dorrie said when she saw the decorations.

When Lia called everyone else into the back room, they were excited.

'Well, will you tell us why we're celebrating now?' Stephen asked.

'My boyfriend asked me to marry him. And I said yes!' Lia announced, showing off the new ring flashing on her finger.

Shouts of jubilation ensued. Everyone wanted to congratulate Lia and Dorrie kissed her on both cheeks.

Thanking them all, she said she was in a complete whirl but happy. Stephen and the others asked all about her fiancé, and Lia recited the story she had prepared. Michael was an engineer and worked dreadful hours, which had made Lia hesitate at the idea of marriage. They would hold the wedding later, when the time felt right.

Merrymaking filled the back office. As she sampled her cake, Lia realised that she had not thoroughly thought through everything that would follow her made-up story.

As the others returned to work, Dorrie came to hug her one more time.

'I just know you'll be so happy,' Dorrie said.

Lia remained silent as they embraced. She felt despicable.

When Mari heard the story, she was less than overjoyed.

'You should have told me in advance. It was creative, but there are problems with it,' Mari said.

'What problems?' Lia asked.

The workers at Fair Rule would now associate Lia with the party secretary's office in their minds. The story about the engagement focused attention on Lia and her personal life. They would remember her. Operating without creating emotional relationships would have been better.

She's right. Again. But it worked.

'If I'm going to help, then I'm going to do things my own way,' Lia said.

'That's fine,' Mari said. 'But that isn't going to stop us from talking over how to do things, is it?'

'Well, no,' Lia admitted. 'And you're right. I feel like I'm deceiving them. In a bad way.'

'We've all learned that same lesson at one time or another,' Mari said, waving at the binders lining the wall.

'What kind of jobs do you have in those anyway? When will you tell me about them?'

Mari suddenly looked serious.

'Maybe someday. You already know a lot, Lia.'

In the following days, Lia visited the Fair Rule office often, but always briefly. They had to make sure Gallagher had been using the keyboard for several days before retrieving it.

Gallagher was at the office every day, and the keyboard did not seem to have aroused any suspicion.

Lia's biggest problem was remembering to wear her ring and to respond casually to questions about her engagement. Word had got around the office. Every now and then someone who had not been in when they had the cake came to congratulate her. Even Tom Gallagher expressed his congratulations, as Lia swallowed her mortification.

After five days, Mari decided that the time had come to bring in the keyboard.

'Don't worry. This time no one will notice anything,' Lia promised.

She had decided to simply be the last person to leave the office. In advance, she arranged with Stephen that she would put the finishing touches on the campaign materials.

‘I won’t be in until late though,’ she said.

Lia went to the office at nine o’clock at night, when only Gallagher, Stephen and a couple of others were still around. One after another they left, until at half past ten only Stephen and Lia remained.

‘I have to go,’ Stephen said finally. ‘Shouldn’t you pack it in for the day too?’

‘I really want to get this done. I don’t know if I’ll be able to come in for a few days,’ Lia said.

After showing her how to set the burglar alarm, Stephen wished her good night and departed.

Lia finished the designs. She circled the office to verify that no one else was present. She visited Tom Gallagher’s office and replaced the old keyboard.

She placed the substitute keyboard in her bag, turned off the coffee maker and lights and switched on the alarm as she left.

If this works, I’m never coming back. No more anti-abortion slogans for the walls of Glasgow.

When Lia texted that she had the keyboard, Rico replied that he would pick it up from her at home immediately.

Lia brought the package wrapped in a plastic bag out to the street in front of her building.

‘Thanks,’ Rico said, eyes all aglow.

‘Are you going back to the Studio?’ Lia asked.

‘One guess. And Marge is coming in too. She wants to see what we got *tout de suite*.’

Lia smiled at Mari’s latest pet name.

‘Sweet dreams,’ Rico said.

Lia watched as Rico set off down Kidderpore Avenue in the Studio’s familiar grey delivery van. Curiosity won out over exhaustion. What would they find on the keyboard?

Quickly she dug out her mobile and rang Rico.

‘Stop. I’m coming with you.’

24

'Lots of coffee and hard information. That'll keep you awake,' Rico said.

They were at the Studio again, the same threesome, Lia, Mari and Rico, sitting in Rico's office reading the data they had obtained from Tom Gallagher's computer.

It was clear that he exchanged messages with Arthur Fried daily.

'I kicked Stephen and Simon in the backside. The media value of the new posters is pathetic. They're trying to be artists.'

'If the money doesn't show up in the account tomorrow, I might just forget the whole fucking election.'

Specific themes were repeated in the passwords Gallagher used: the party, polo, Tube station names and dogs.

But how could they know what websites he was logging in to with each username and password combination? Lia asked. The sensors didn't record what pages he visited.

'That's surprisingly easy to track,' Rico explained.

He could find the right pages by searching the web for the passages of text the user entered. Even if the pages were private, the subject matter was obvious from the messages, making identifying things like discussion boards quick work. They could confirm the identification by logging in with the usernames grabbed by the key logging chip.

'And what if the page records the last time someone logged in?'

Most web users never look at that, Rico said. And changing log information like that was a basic hacking skill.

Prying into Gallagher's messages was interesting, but there wasn't anything particularly secret in them.

'Let's look for bank details,' Mari suggested.

Quickly Rico determined that Fair Rule had accounts with at least six different banks Gallagher had visited over the past few days.

Rico's software showed them what Gallagher's usernames and passwords were at the various banks, but it was unable to show them the next codes in single-use PIN sequences.

They knew what banks the accounts were with, but could not get into the accounts themselves.

'Is this a dead end?' Mari asked.

'I don't know,' Rico said thoughtfully. 'The Well has had back doors into almost all of these banks' systems. It's just been a while.'

An hour passed, during which Lia started falling asleep in her chair, Mari read printed copies of Gallagher's information and Rico bore down on his computer.

One by one the banks' defences began to crumble.

'I can't get into two of them. And if I start burrowing into them myself, it'll take days. But we have credentials for four banks,' Rico said.

This news woke Lia up again.

They scanned through the account entries. Most of the amounts were small, and the payees and recipients seemed unremarkable: materials suppliers, payments for advertising space, support payments to party member organisations.

'Using the web interface is too slow,' Rico said.

To speed up the process, for each account he downloaded spreadsheets of all available transaction information. From these he easily separated the normal, monthly fund transfers. Lia and Mari looked up information about the recipients and payees online and compared them to the transactions. Gradually they whittled the list down until all that was left was a small number of money transfers lacking any obvious explanation.

'A few of these do seem suspicious,' Mari said.

In all likelihood, some of the transfers had gone to expenses the party did not want publicised. They were mostly small sums though, a few pounds at a time.

'This name comes up several times,' Mari said. 'Penitent Catering.'

Several transfers of a few thousand pounds each had been made to this strangely named account, at more or less regular intervals of two or three months. The account was held in the United States, at a bank called Danford Trust.

They tried to search for the company in the international business register. The chairman of the board of Penitent Catering was recorded as Thomas Andrew Gallagher in London, and it gave the impression of being a relatively new shell company. The business had no employees and little activity in the US or anywhere else.

'Can we get into Danford Trust?' Mari asked.

'I'm almost in already,' Rico replied.

When they got the account open, it turned out that the only thing Penitent Catering had ever done with its money was to transfer it to the same three recipients.

'They're all on this side of the pond,' Rico announced.

In the space of only one year, Gallagher had transferred over £20,000 to three British accounts. Each time he entered the account numbers by hand, apparently not wanting to mark the accounts as regular recipients.

'That's stupid,' Lia said. 'It's obvious from the transaction information where the money is going.'

'People do unnecessary things thinking they're covering their tracks all the time. It makes them feel like they're being careful,' Mari said.

Rico listed the transfer recipients in the UK. The accounts belonged to organisations named Battle 88, Gallows and the Nordic Guild.

Mari recognised only one.

Battle 88 was a racist, far-right hooligan group in Leeds. The courts had convicted some of its members of throwing Molotov cocktails at mosques and other equally serious crimes.

Staring at Mari in shocked disbelief, Lia was suddenly completely awake.

'I know,' Mari said. 'We found what we were looking for.'

Gallows and the Nordic Guild operated out of London; Battle 88 was lying low after the judgements against it.

The organisations' websites did not make pleasant reading, being filled with coarse slogans and pictures glorifying the white race and demeaning everyone else.

Lia made the mistake of glancing through the image gallery on the Gallows page, which included pictures of black people being executed and female victims of sexual assault – all also from ethnic minorities. Lia found herself physically unable to look.

'Aren't these pictures... against the law?' she asked.

'Some of them are,' Mari said. 'Catching someone for distributing them is another matter though.'

The Nordic Guild had ambiguous connections to Scandinavian groups that used old Germanic and Norse symbols in their speeches and images. The mythology made their troublemaking seem 'deeper', Mari observed. Most of them were little more than disorganised clubs, but some had full-on hierarchies, online networks, fundraising schemes and profitable enterprises of their own.

But why would Fair Rule give money to borderline-illegal groups like this? Lia wondered out loud.

'They can't openly. Supporting people like this is pure poison for a legitimate political party,' Mari said.

However, openly racist groups were useful. They did the dirty work the party couldn't. They made Fair Rule look moderate. Through them, young supporters could channel their aggression. They kept the immigrant population in a state of fear, thinning the ranks of their supporters and creating an image of constant chaos surrounding foreign-born minorities.

'I'd bet the Fair Rule leadership has regular contact with them. They probably have specific requirements in exchange for their support. But we don't have to figure that out – just the knowledge that a party trying to get into Parliament is supporting illegal activity is enough.'

'Why does Gallagher go to all the trouble of circulating the money through an American bank?' Lia asked.

Rico had the answer. While they had been talking, he had reviewed Penitent Catering's financial statements. The company had made investments in the United States and taken tax deductions for charitable donations. Deductions had been granted for the past three years at least.

'Can you guess to which three companies they made their charitable contributions?' Rico asked.

'You're kidding me – the same white supremacists?' Lia said.

'Exactly.'

All three groups were registered as 501(c)(3) charitable institutions. In London and Leeds, Battle 88, Gallows and the Nordic Guild harassed immigrants and caused disturbances in ethnic restaurants. In America, they claimed to produce special education materials for disabled children and organise cultural events.

Lia couldn't believe what she was hearing.

'Why the charity mask?'

'I bet that was Fried's idea,' Mari said.

Fried had lived in the US and knew local business practices. Using charitable tax deductions, his party was probably saving many thousands of dollars every year.

'And the name Penitent. The whole thing had to come out of Fried's brain,' Mari said.

Penitent was an extremely peculiar name for a catering business. The company certainly never had any intention of operating publicly given a name like that.

'This is going to be the biggest political story of the year,' Lia said.

'One of the biggest,' Mari said. 'Now we have two strikes against Fried. We still need a third. And a timetable and plan for rolling them out.'

'How can we publicise this without our role coming out too?' Lia asked, thinking of her visits to the Fair Rule office.

Rico assured her that no one would be able to trace the story back to them. Of course Fried would realise that the information came from Gallagher's accounts, but that would be as far as the trail led.

Planning how to release the information would come later. Now was not the time.

'Now we all need to go home and get some sleep. Let's take a few days off in honour of this find,' Mari said.

At four o'clock in the morning they all stood, groggy with exhaustion, waiting for cabs on Park Street. None were in sight.

'I had been waiting to tell you this. But now is as good a time as any,' Mari said.

Mari had asked Maggie to investigate whether the comb Lia found meant anything.

Maggie had visited all the stores that sold Baltic goods, checking whether any of them carried the same combs. None of them did. She had also paid visits to British shops that sold similar cheap little sundries. None of the shopkeepers recognised the comb.

'Thorough work,' Lia said, astonished.

'It usually helps.'

The murdered woman had probably bought her comb from the Eastern Buffet.

'I've been thinking I could pay it a visit too,' Mari said.

Lia looked at her in surprise.

'We agreed that this was my case, but that would be a big help.'

'You've given me two weapons against Arthur Fried. Now I want to help you,' Mari said.

25

Lia's spent the last day of her holiday sleeping.

When she returned to work at *Level*, she tried not to think about anything related to the dead Latvian woman, Arthur Fried or the Studio.

It did her good.

In their editorial meeting, they talked about story ideas. Sam had a series of articles in progress everyone was excited about. He had been asking the family members of famous politicians their opinions on social issues, a subject which usually only the politicians themselves got asked about.

Lia worked on illustrations for her series about socially important books, albums, films and television programmes.

She enjoyed the whole day. She felt like a normal person doing proper work. Nothing mysterious or special.

As she left for home, she wavered between the bus and the Tube. The bus was more peaceful, but she had not been able to take it in months without remembering the murdered woman.

She chose the bus, and when it arrived at Holborn Circus, she tried to stay calm. She had to be able to move through the City without her emotions paralyzing her.

She went for an evening jog on Hampstead Heath. As she returned, she saw Mr Vong in the hall of residence garden, looking up at the gutters.

'Evening, Mr Vong,' Lia said. 'I hope you aren't still thinking about work at this time of night.'

'We old men tend to believe the world would fall apart without our watchful care,' Mr Vong admitted.

Lia popped in to her flat to get a package. It was the present she had purchased for Mr Vong to thank him for his night-time rescue mission.

'My goodness,' said Mr Vong. 'A gift is certainly too much. But it is very kind of you.'

He opened the package. In it was a small, waterproof radio fashioned in the shape of a floating rubber duck.

'Now you can listen to the radio anywhere. Even in the bath or outside in the rain,' Lia said.

'I cannot remember the last time I received such a delightful gift.'

Lia was already on her way inside when Mr Vong said, 'Seeing you looking so at peace is nice, Ms Pajala.'

'Thanks. The feeling is mutual.'

26

In Leyton, Mari walks towards the Eastern Buffet. The name makes her smile. That's good. Smiling is a good thing. She knows she's too serious these days, too caught up with trying to control what might happen. She has been wondering for a long time whether she could come here.

The summer has gone swimmingly, especially because of Lia. She has made Mari smile every day. But during this autumn, Mari has had a hard time keeping her head clear.

She owes Lia this visit. And the Latvian woman, killed and mangled by someone so brutal. Unforgivable.

Mari has feared coming to this shop. If that barbaric, evil person is there, the visit will be hard. Sometimes she reacts so strongly to what she sees that she can't conceal the surge of emotion. That has happened before when she's dealt with criminals.

Mari has only told a few people about her ability. Even them she hasn't told how the gift has changed over the years and how it has changed her.

She can't always decide whom she reads. Sometimes it just happens. Sometimes she feels like an antenna obliged to receive and feel every signal from every person that comes her way.

There are days when Mari has complete control over her thoughts. But in recent years she has felt more and more often that the gift controls her. Limiting it takes all her willpower – or a few drinks. That is another reason why she has enjoyed her evenings with Lia. And their little *juominki*.

Juominki. She must remember to say that to Lia. An old, rakish word. The moment when a person feels truly alive.

Mari stops at the threshold of the Eastern Buffet and breathes in. Strange smells, an entire foreign world. She steps inside. The place is exactly as Lia described.

Mari sees the customers, four women, and sees immediately that they are not simply buying food, aromas and tastes. They are seeking something to fill an empty space. The void formed by the gradually fading memories and feeling of home, of belonging somewhere. Of a world they have lost.

Mari's eyes fill with tears, the feeling is so strong.

She has not missed her own homeland, but now, in the middle of this shop, whose shelves are filled with real and artificial mementos of these people's origins, she is ready to burst into tears.

She tries to calm herself. She looks at the calendars and magazines on a rack against the wall. They are written in languages she doesn't know, which keeps them closed to her. Having something that does not cause an avalanche of thoughts and stays unknown feels good.

Mari sees the pearled combs and mirrors. The sight startles her. Here, in the middle of so many useful and so many other useless things, their significance is suddenly perfectly clear.

They are part of a tradition: small girls sitting still in the evening while their mothers comb or brush their hair. One hundred strokes. Mothers sitting next to their daughters at night, every night, even if the day has been busy, the daughters learning the peaceful rhythm of the comb and carrying it with them always. The daughters feeling something which perhaps never takes shape as a conscious thought: if they ever have daughters of their own, they will pass these moments on to them.

On the combs and brushes are white daisies made with cheap imitation mother-of-pearl. Whenever a woman buys them, the memories of her childhood make her smile as she completes her purchase.

That was what the Latvian woman did.

At the back of the shop a curtain moves, the shopkeeper stepping out into view. The motion makes Mari reflexively look at him.

A second passes, perhaps two, and then the man looks back.

Mari just has time to stop her reaction. She holds back her cry but not the pain, which slams into her.

The man looks at her, and Mari knows that he is thinking of the full shelves in the back room, of all the goods he has ordered from thousands of kilometres away, and then of how many women are in his shop who will not buy anything, who are just looking. And Mari knows that the man has a dark side, a side as black as pitch. So cold and brutal. Panic grips her.

This man has killed many times. He has killed men and women, with steady hands and the efficiency of a postman delivering letters. If he did not kill the Latvian woman whose body ended up in the white Volvo, it is only a matter of chance.

The man looks at a woman moving down an aisle, and Mari sees him think how much he would like to strike her down – and the thoughts that follow become too excruciating for Mari to bear.

Mari rushes out onto the street, the door to the shop banging closed behind her as everything floods out of her in a panicked deluge.

She waves down a taxi, looking at the driver only for a fleeting second, but that is enough. Collapsing into the back seat, she asks him to drive to Hoxton.

Mari gets out of the cab before reaching home. Always at least three streets early.

All her strength has cascaded away, but she must walk the last few blocks to make sure that no one is following.

The man who has killed goes with her, inside her, in the terrible certainty growing within her.

Now there are two. Arthur Fried and this man. She must stop them both.

Before her building stands an older gentleman, slow movements, walking cane, decades-old cap upon his head. Looking at him, Mari sees something that takes a moment to recognise –

what it is, what remains, when a person begins to slip away. Forgetfulness.

She is filled with compassion and envy for the old man. She does not have forgetfulness as her aid.

Two men who require action.

At home in her top-floor flat, she looks out the window. She sits there for a long time, minutes stretching into hours. Fear burns in her. Anger hardens her. She sits there until she can control her thoughts.

That night she doesn't sleep. She thinks.

27

'We have to start following him,' Mari said.

Lia knew immediately that something had frightened her.

Nothing concrete had come out at the shop, Mari assured her. She had just looked at the man behind the counter and known that he was dangerous. That was all.

'Do you think he killed the Latvian woman?' Lia asked.

Mari had nothing to go on but her own impressions. So there was no use going to the police. A comb with flowers on it was not sufficient evidence.

Still, Lia knew that something had happened.

Mari had resolved the main issue: now they had something specific to investigate.

Now this is a job for Patrick Moore, Mari said.

'A stake-out. If you want, you can join him. If he's willing to take you along.'

Lia thought.

'Yes, I want to.'

Mari's second suggestion felt more difficult. She asked Lia to go back to the Fair Rule office.

'If you stop going all of a sudden, they'll wonder where you disappeared to. Better for them not to suspect anything. Maybe tell them that you aren't going to have so much time any more. Besides, something new could always turn up.'

'They could always catch on that I don't share their Nazi ideology,' Lia responded.

After another few moments of hesitation, she agreed. She did not have any logical grounds for refusing, just an unpleasant feeling.

The following day after work, she went to the party office in Epping. Stephen was happy to see her, but disappointed when she said she would not be able to come for the next couple of months.

'My fiancé and I have started looking for a new flat, and it's taking an unimaginable amount of energy,' Lia explained.

'You're easily the best graphic designer we've ever had. And you'll miss all the best times as the elections get closer,' Stephen said, trying to coax her into reconsidering.

'Thank you, but I'm going to have to be content to watch the elections from the sidelines.' Lia designed an information flyer, but when there was no sign of Arthur Fried and nothing else in particular happened, she said her goodbyes.

'For now,' she said. 'Who knows? Maybe I'll be back sooner than I think.'

'I hope so,' Stephen said.

'Stephen, I've always wanted to ask you: what do you think of these slogans? Do you agree with all of them?'

Stephen looked at her in surprise. 'Of course. I wouldn't devote all my time to this if I didn't.'

Lia nodded and quickly left.

A few days later, Patrick Moore rang Lia and suggested a meeting over lunch.

'Mari said that you'd like to learn certain skills from me.'

'Oh she did, did she?'

They met at The Real Greek in Bankside, around the corner from the Studio. The restaurant was full, but Paddy landed them a table in short order. Something about his burly physique and commanding presence made people unwilling to argue with him, Lia noticed.

Paddy got straight to the point.

'I've been following the target for two days now. This is going to be interesting.'

The target. Lia understood that it was time learn the lingo.

Paddy told her the background information he had gathered up to that point. His name was Kazimirs Vanags. People called him Kazis. Age forty-six, birthplace Latvia, moved to Britain in 1997.

'Latvia!' Lia said.

'I know,' Paddy said. 'And there's more.'

Vanags was registered as the owner of the Eastern Buffet, and other firms also appeared under his name in the Companies House register. One of them, Salmina, imported products from the Baltic and Russia and had a turnover of nearly half a million pounds per annum.

'We'll have to look into that more closely. Taxes, employees, import licences. Everything he brings in and from where.'

Paddy worked quickly and rigorously. He also wanted to agree on some ground rules before Lia started shadowing the shopkeeper.

'I say what we do. You're Mari's friend, but here you're a spectator. I'll call off the whole operation instantly if you start getting your own ideas. Two reasons: first is security – yours, mine and everyone else's. The second is the success of the mission.'

Lia nodded.

Paddy encouraged her also to prepare for it being boring. Usually the work was just sitting for hours on end. Then when something happened, you had to spring into action immediately to follow and try to predict what would happen next.

Lia listened seriously. She had a lot more to learn than how to talk the talk.

After work, Lia hurried to their meeting place on the High Road in Leyton.

She had imagined Paddy watching the shopkeeper directly outside the grocery, but instead, he took her to his car parked one street away. In the car, he showed her the screen of his laptop, which featured a high resolution shot of the shop entrance.

Nowadays trailing was more remote surveillance than anything else, Paddy explained. But you still had to be close enough to the target to follow him if the need arose.

On the building across the road from the food shop, Paddy had installed a miniaturised WiFi camera, one of Rico's gadgets. It was unbelievably small, perhaps the size of a screw, and you could stick it to any metal surface with a magnet or use a special adhesive strip. Paddy had installed it at night with a telescoping pole, high on a wall so passers-by wouldn't notice it.

The camera could even see into the shop when someone opened the door. At times Lia made out the shape of the shopkeeper behind the checkout counter.

'Unbelievable,' she said. 'Such a sharp picture from so far away.'

Buying something comparable would cost in the range of £5,000, Paddy said. But the basic components were common enough in mobile phones, so Rico had built a dozen of them. The most expensive part was the miniaturised high-capacity battery, which still cost less than a portion of fish and chips.

Normally the camera would operate for about a day. However, they could turn it off remotely when they weren't watching, allowing it to transmit for longer. When the time came to change the battery, Paddy would dress up as a worker pasting up advertising hoardings so he could move around without arousing any suspicion.

Paddy described how Kazis Vanags had been in the shop each day from morning until closing time but had immediately left in his car at six o'clock and driven around for the rest of the evening, making the same circuit for the past two days. First he drove to Oval and visited a flat on the top floor of a three-storey building on Vassall Road.

'It's a brothel,' Paddy said. 'There are always men coming in and out, and they're always acting in a certain way. Glancing from side to side.'

Paddy had seen two women in a window smoking. They looked Eastern European. There were probably more. They didn't go outside much, since presumably their movements were restricted. They were not prisoners though: one of the women had gone shopping down the road.

After visiting Vassall Road, Vanags drove to a supermarket and purchased a whole bag of food. Then he drove to Catford, to Sangley Road, and entered a terraced house using his own key. Vanags stayed in the house only about ten minutes. The grocery bag he left inside. Paddy could not see into the house, but the previous night he had caught a glimpse of Vanags switching on the light in the hall and a figure flashing by before the door closed shut.

'The size of the shopping bag says that there are probably at least two people living there,' Paddy added.

From Sangley Road, Vanags drove to the Assets strip club in Hackney. They had had problems with their business licences for years, and it was known for being the kind of place you could get your wallet nicked. There had been beatings.

'A regular dive,' Paddy said.

Vanags seemed to be in the habit of spending an hour there before going home. Paddy had seen him going into the back room and chatting familiarly with the proprietor.

'The same route each night,' Paddy repeated. 'What do you make of it?'

'Is he picking up money? He might be running the brothel and be a partner in the bar too,' Lia suggested.

'Highly probable,' Paddy said, casting Lia an approving glance. 'And I also doubt that's his ageing mother living in the terraced house in Catford, unable get out to shop for her own groceries.'

The time was just past six when Lia and Paddy saw Vanags closing up. After retrieving the poster stand from the pavement, he carefully turned the key in both locks.

Paddy waited until Vanags had disappeared from the reach of the surveillance camera and then started the car.

'We'll give him space to get moving. I'm guessing he'll make the same rounds again.'

Paddy guessed right. When he turned his dark blue BMW onto the Leyton High Road, they saw Vanags stuck in traffic.

'Will he recognise your car?' Lia asked.

'I've used a different one every night. Mari never complains about expenses like that.'

They stayed a good hundred metres back.

'At this distance, he would have a hard time recognising anyone,' Paddy explained. 'When people are far away, we recognise them by their body shape, clothing and hair colour, which is why I've been wearing different clothes every night and a hat yesterday. If we follow him tomorrow, you should change your clothes too.'

When they arrived on Vassall Road, Paddy stopped his car a long way from the building Vanags drove up to. They watched while he exited the car, locked the door and entered the block of flats.

'Now we just wait.'

Lia wondered what Vanags could be doing.

Is he collecting last night's takings? Is he talking with the manager about the market situation? Is he screwing prostitutes?

The evening was already dark, and Lia noticed that Paddy was watching the whole area using the car mirrors. Whenever someone walked by on the street, Paddy turned his face away.

'Thinking that sitting here this long wouldn't attract anyone's attention would be silly. But we also shouldn't try to look too inconspicuous. That would just arouse more curiosity,'

Paddy explained. 'Usually it's a good idea to get out and walk around for a minute. But I think tonight we can just wait.'

To pass the time, Paddy explained surveillance techniques.

'It isn't enough to know where the target is going and what he's doing when you can see him. That's just the beginning.'

What was important was figuring out what kind of person your target was. How did he think and make decisions? Did he panic easily? If Lia had to capture him, what would she do? When you learned to recognise things like this, you knew a lot about your target instantly. Surveillance was not just about following people but about being able to predict what they would do.

This all sounded sensible to Lia, but difficult.

I don't have a clue how a person like Kazis Vanags thinks.

The little tricks Paddy shared impressed Lia, such as avoiding eye contact. People remembered best those with whom they made direct eye contact. Keeping your own expression blank was also surprisingly difficult when you met the eyes of the person you were following. You learned how to avoid eye contact by watching the rhythm of your target's motion and how often he glanced around.

Paddy laughed when Lia practised avoiding his own eyes. The laughter helped her relax.

They also had time to chat about other things. Lia would not have brought up Paddy's past crimes and prison sentence, but when he mentioned them himself, she said aloud what had been bother-ing her.

'I don't understand why a man like you would turn to robbery.'

'I understand it a little too well,' Paddy replied.

The thought of robbing an armoured car had come from one of his old workmates. Neither of them had ever committed a serious crime before. But the third man who joined them had been to prison already, serving long stretches for robbery and forced entry.

'We were too close to big money. Sometimes bankers cheat and investment company managers stick their hands in the till. And when you work with big companies and rich people, you get to see what a good life you can have if you have the cash. We didn't do it to be clever; we wanted the good life.'

As their target they had chosen Thomas Cook, a large multinational corporation, so no little people would suffer unduly from their theft.

'We did it as cleanly as a robbery can be done. We didn't run in waving guns. We knocked out the guards with diluted chloroform onto mattresses. That's why we got caught: we were too careful.'

The handcuffs they used to bind the guards were padded to prevent bruised wrists. Because of the padding, one of the guards squeezed free from the handcuffs much more quickly than they had planned.

The alarm sounded within six minutes. The police surrounded them.

'I thought I was a real player. Taking risks is the only way win big. But it doesn't really work that way. Life is too short for shortcuts.'

Paddy's tone changed.

'Stay cool. Don't stare at the building. A woman just walked out.'

Lia slowly moved her eyes to the building and saw a woman approaching along the pavement.

'Take this,' Paddy said and pulled a large, folded map out of a door pocket.

Lia opened the map. Paddy grabbed his mobile and held it to his ear so that his hand covered his face when viewed from the street.

The woman passed by without stopping. Lia glanced at her in the rear-view mirror. Bleach-blonde hair, shapely body, long coat, clicking heels.

'One of them?' Lia asked Paddy.

'I saw her yesterday too. I'd say it's ninety-nine per cent sure she's an Eastern European prostitute.'

'How can you tell?

The whole package, Paddy said. Over the years he had hired dozens of prostitutes for his customers when he was working as a bodyguard.

'Some customers think that a bodyguard's job is getting them whatever they want at any hour of the night or day, not just monitoring their security. Drugs, prostitutes, whatever.'

Lia watched as the young woman entered the corner shop.

'Can we go and talk to her?'

Paddy stared at her in astonishment.

'Using what cover story? The job is to shadow Kazis Vanags, and if that woman knows him, he'll be sure to hear that he's being followed.'

'OK, OK. This is all just so slow. It could take weeks before we get anywhere.'

'Welcome to the first stage of your training. Working slowly is usually a requirement for success.'

They waited quietly, and, after a few minutes, the woman returned. Lighting a cigarette, she walked casually towards the building from which she had come. She clearly had no interest in hurrying back.

As the woman passed their car, Lia was pointing out to Paddy a point on the map of London. This time the woman glanced at them but showed no further interest.

After reaching her building, the woman stubbed out her cigarette on the pavement and disappeared inside.

'I really feel if we talked to her or one of the other women, we could find something out,' Lia said.

'Perhaps. But we don't have the opportunity for that now.'

A few minutes later, Vanags appeared and walked towards his car.

'Exactly one hour and twenty minutes. About ten minutes longer than on the previous nights,' Paddy said.

Vanags set off, with Lia and Paddy in pursuit.

'The same route every night,' Lia said. 'He has an important task to accomplish in these places, some sort of responsibility. He probably owns the properties and the businesses.'

'I've been thinking exactly the same thing. He seems like a bloke who could keep a pretty big ring going,' Paddy said.

On the way, Vanags drove into the multi-storey car park at the Lewisham Shopping Centre. Paddy parked in a space near the exit.

Eleven minutes later, Kazis Vanags' car pulled out of the car park and turned south.

'Quick shopper. He knew exactly what he needed,' Lia said.

'Good,' Paddy said.

When they came to Sangley Road, Lia and Paddy watched from a distance as Vanags parked his car in front of number 182. Vanags entered carrying his bulging Sainsbury's bag.

'Pulls out own keys,' Paddy recited. 'Glances around. Opens door. Moves inside quick, without waiting for anyone to meet him.'

This time Vanags did not turn on the hall light, and Paddy and Lia did not see anyone else at the door.

'Let's get out,' Paddy suggested.

Driving the car around to a neighbouring street, Paddy found a narrow space after a little searching.

As they walked towards the house on Sangley Road, Lia noticed that Paddy was constantly scanning their surroundings. He didn't seem nervous, just very focused. For Lia this was all so exciting that she felt all of her senses were heightened.

They stopped on the other side of the street, about fifty metres from the front garden of number 182. It was unlikely anyone would see them from the house, Lia thought.

She tried calmly to evaluate what she saw. A two-storey terraced house on a quiet residential street. Few people were about: mostly coming back from work, a few from shopping.

Number 182 looked abandoned. Lia guessed at its size. Downstairs perhaps three rooms and a kitchen. Upstairs a couple of bedrooms.

This is not a place where anything could arouse neighbours' suspicions. Whoever is inside wants to stay out of sight. Or someone else wants them to be kept out of sight.

Lia understood from Paddy's sedate manner that he wanted them to be as quiet as possible where they stood. When someone went by, Paddy looked at his mobile, as if searching for the address they were going to.

When they had stood on the street for nearly ten minutes, Paddy motioned to Lia to follow. They walked back to the car.

'He'll be coming out soon. It's best that he doesn't see us.'

They waited around the corner where they could still see the door to the house.

Vanags came out without the shopping bag. After pulling the door closed, he walked to his car. Rapidly pulling out, in twenty seconds he was gone.

'No rush,' Paddy said. 'Next he'll go to Assets.'

The Assets strip club was easily distinguishable from the surrounding business premises, which were already shuttered for the night. The glow of the neon signs flashing in the windows was visible from a considerable distance in the twilight.

Paddy stopped a couple of hundred metres from Vanags' car, which was parked directly in front of the bar.

'Just a quick check,' Paddy said, getting out, and Lia understood that he expected her to wait.

Approaching it on the opposite side of the street, Paddy stopped directly across from the bar. There he dug out from his pocket a packet of cigarettes and a lighter and a moment later blew a wisp of smoke into the air.

Paddy looked at the bar and then crossed the street. His face illuminated by the advertisements, he looked in for a moment and then quickly returned to the car.

'Good performance,' Lia said. 'Bloke who wants to go into a strip club but can't work up the nerve.'

'Vanags is in there. He's at the bar talking to the proprietor, with a pint in front of him. He'll be there for a while,' Paddy said.

They waited patiently. Paddy turned the conversation to Lia.

'How did you and Mari meet?'

Lia described that night at the White Swan the previous spring. She did not tell how the evening had continued on the border of Greenwich Park, but Paddy did not enquire any further. He just laughed hearing how Mari had answered Lia's colleagues' questions at the pub.

'Mari's understanding of human nature is something else,' Paddy said. 'An exceptional woman in every respect.'

'How did you meet?' Lia asked.

'She hired me for a job. I can't say what, but as the client she can if she chooses to.'

The next question surprised Lia.

'Can you tell me about Finland?'

'Of course,' Lia said.

She told Paddy about the Nordic welfare state, which Finland still was in many ways. Having a social conscience was often a distinguishing characteristic of people who grew up there.

'Although I imagine that's changing now,' Lia said.

The dominant mood for Finns was a melancholy placidity, she said. Melancholy in the sense that people did not dream much there – they weren't in the habit of fantasising about grand or extraordinary things. Placid because life was good.

People's cares could mostly be solved. In Finland you had every opportunity imaginable, but most people's goals were commonplace and practical.

Lia found herself getting caught up in the topic. They compared the differences between their countries, and Lia analysed Finnish women.

Paddy listened carefully. When Lia finished, he said, 'I've thought a lot about what it is about Mari that's so exceptional. Is it her or her Finnishness?'

Lia smiled.

That's the same question Martyn Taylor seems to have asked about me.

'I think Mari is pretty exceptional even among Finnish women,' she said.

They both liked Mari. This thought vexed Lia somewhat as she felt a fleeting twinge of jealousy. Here she was sitting with an attractive man. They could be talking about anything and getting to know each other better, but instead they were talking about their friend.

Lia was not looking at Paddy directly, but she was still strongly aware of his virility, the woollen jumper and the man inside.

When the memory came, Lia found herself utterly disoriented. The woollen jumper feeling. The reason she had chosen London all those years ago.

Paddy is a man I could feel safe with.

Lia nodded a few times as Paddy talked, to conceal her discomfiture.

A man I could have a family with.

Lia had never thought with any seriousness of starting a family. She had met precious few men who could have made that dream concrete for her.

With the men she dated she was usually just trying to learn how to be close to another person. She had lost that ability once, during the year when she learned to fear. Brief encounters with men in London had meant sex and overcoming her physical self, taming the fear lurking within.

But sitting with Paddy she felt stable.

They had been waiting for Vanags for more than an hour. Lia wondered how long she could sit there with her mind so befuddled with all these thoughts.

Of course she realised that she was not dreaming of a relationship or family with Paddy specifically. She was thinking of some other man in the future.

I've never thought of myself as a woman who could become a mother. And a wife. But perhaps it is possible. Someday.

She had had to live for twenty-eight years in order to be able to think of herself starting a family.

In the end she was forced to push these thoughts aside as Kazis Vanags walked out of the bar.

Lia and Paddy followed his car, even though Paddy already knew that he was going home to Romford. To Lia's surprise, Vanags' residence was a well-kept terraced house in a wealthy-looking area with a lovely view onto a narrow river.

'Whatever he's doing, he makes good money,' Paddy said.

He made an entry about Vanags' schedule on his mobile.

'That's it for today,' he said. 'Off to Kidderpore Avenue then.'

With that they drove to Hampstead in a tranquil, weary silence.

'Pretty place,' Paddy said as he parked his car in front of Lia's hall of residence.

'What do we do now?' Lia asked.

They knew Vanags' evening routine, Paddy observed. Now they needed to discuss with Mari how to proceed.

Lia thanked him for the lift and walked to her door without looking back. She heard that Paddy waited until she entered the stairway before starting the car and driving off.

For hours Lia lay awake, waiting for exhaustion to overcome her, but sleep didn't come. She tried to read her books about Latvia, but nothing came of it. She searched for her *London, Good for You!* travel guide, but reading that was just as impossible.

Chaos swirled in her head. Sitting next to Paddy, that surprising feeling of security had triggered it.

Not just daydreams about a family. No, there was also that fear that she had never fully shaken.

Lia went to her computer. After hesitating for a moment, she typed a few words into the search engine. She had never allowed herself to do this, not once in all the years she had lived in London.

She looked for the person who was the reason she had left her home.

Finding the familiar name took time, but not much. The search results were few, but the person did still exist. He was doing things, living life in his own way.

An old, familiar feeling rose in Lia's mind. Not fear as such, but instead the memory of its power, the memory of how living with it had felt.

She had got over it. Or had she?

She shut down the computer and went to her bed. The tears that came were only a physical reaction. She knew the crying was a result of the surge of emotions. She was just processing.

This was the second time in a year that she had cried. The previous time had been because of the Latvian woman.

The crying only lasted a moment, and in its wake came weariness and sleep.

28

The following evening, Mari called Lia to the Studio. They went through the information they had on Kazimirs Vanags. Paddy had briefed Mari about everything he had found out about him.

Lia was relieved that Paddy was not present now though.

I'm not infatuated with him. But too many things came at once yesterday, too much to think about.

One of Kazis Vanags' companies, Dynos, owned the flat upstairs in the building on Vassall Road. In recent years a neighbour had lodged three complaints with the property management company, complaining of the number of people coming and going and the screams that frequently emanated from the flat. The complaints had not led to any action. The property company had called Vanags, who claimed that he had rented it as a shared flat to some students.

Vanags owned the terraced house on Sangley Road in his own name, and another company he controlled, Riga Trade, owned Assets. He did not have any unpaid taxes, but the registered information about the companies' employees and social security contributions was woefully incomplete.

With the help of his acquaintances in the police, Paddy had checked Vanags' criminal record. Over the years the authorities had interviewed him three times, twice on suspicion of assault and once as a witness in an assault and battery incident. None of these cases had gone to court.

'The Eastern European criminal network protects its own,' Mari said.

In two of the cases the victim had been a woman, one involving a large knife and the other strangulation. In the third case, a young Russian man had been found beaten in an alley near the strip club. As the police investigation proceeded, the man stopped talking, and the case dried up.

Vanags had money, as his expensive flat, expensive car and

payroll of several employees demonstrated.

'What do we do now? Do we give this information to the police?' Lia asked.

'I'm torn,' Mari said.

If they arrested Vanags, he probably already had some plan in place. His associates would probably destroy any remaining evidence. If they got him for pimping, something bigger might go unsolved – like the Latvian woman's murder.

'Let's not give this to the police yet then,' Lia said.

'I agree,' Mari said.

They decided to revisit the issue later.

Teasing, Lia told Mari how Paddy had asked about her the previous night.

'What did he ask?' Mari enquired with obvious interest, and Lia gave an account of the conversation she had had with Paddy about Finland.

'What's really going on between you two?' Lia asked.

'I don't know. Neither of us has made any moves. It's hard to say what might come of it.'

Paddy knew an immense amount of the Studio's business, Mari reminded Lia. That complicated things.

'And how are you doing?' Mari asked.

'Well, I'm feeling pretty drained.'

That was putting it mildly, but Lia did not want to tell Mari everything: not her dreams of a family, getting over her fear or her sorrow. Maybe Mari saw it all in her anyway.

Not long had passed since her holiday, but her days working at *Level*, the running around chasing Vanags, her work at the Fair Rule office, her evenings at the Studio – it had all sapped her energy. At the same time, she wanted to get things off her mind and rush forward with them.

'Then I have a difficult choice for you,' Mari said.

'What do I have to do?' Lia asked, feeling a wave of exhaustion roll over her.

'You don't have to do anything. But you can if you want.'

Mari had reviewed everything they knew about Arthur Fried's private life.

'I realised that there is something similar in him to Vanags.'

This had dawned on her when she had seen the Latvian. He was clearly a criminal, but Mari had recognised the same sort of emotional coldness as in Fried.

As she considered this, Mari had noticed that Fried had not married Anna Belle until he was thirty-seven years old.

'It clicked that I had overlooked something really critical.'

Arthur Fried had been married before. They had divorced years earlier, a little before his current marriage. No mention of his first wife appeared in Fried's biography.

Mari had only found the information in the marriage records at Fried's former church in Shoreditch. She doubted that this was a coincidence. Why the information remained in the congregational records was difficult to say. Perhaps Fried lacked the temerity to have the information removed.

Fried had however managed to purge record of the union from the General Register Office. This was quite a stunt, since they tracked all officially sanctioned weddings and divorces in Britain.

The previous wife had not appeared in even one newspaper article Mari had read about Fried. Of course the reason could be that during his first marriage he had only been in the first stages of his political activity and neither he nor Fair Rule were widely known. And since he was attempting to court Christian voters, he didn't want to appear as a divorcee.

'Do you know anything about the first wife?' Lia asked.

Mari rattled off what little she had found out: Sarah Hawkins was born in Suffolk, and her marriage to Fried had lasted seven years. Nothing else appeared in the congregational records or online.

'So what were you thinking?' Lia asked.

'We have to talk to the ex-Mrs Fried. I was thinking you could go.'

'You don't want to do it yourself? If she was involved in covering up the marriage, she may not want to talk about it. Wouldn't that be a case where you could use your ability?'

Mari did not want anyone to be able to connect her directly to anything involving Arthur Fried. When they started releasing their information about him, he would realise quickly that someone was out for blood. Better if Fried didn't know his adversary.

'Right then. Do you know where to find Sarah Hawkins?'

At her home in Lambeth, Mari said. Based on her phone records, Rico thought that she was likely to be home at that moment.

'How did he find that out?'

'A very old fashioned way. In addition to a mobile phone, she also has a landline, and it's been busy for hours at a time over the past few days. She's probably been online all the time.'

'Well, I don't have anything planned for tomorrow,' Lia said. 'Wow, dial-up. Does that still exist?'

29

Number 204 Ferndale Road, Brixton, was a two-storey terraced house. The area was full of council flats and the children they contained. Parts of the district may have been on the rise, but this street was still the London of open drug trafficking and gang attacks that the travel bureaus did not show visitors.

It was Saturday morning, and Lia was looking from the street at Arthur Fried's ex-wife's house. The paint was peeling from the walls, and the front garden fence was leaning. Two scratched and battered plastic chairs fulfilled the role of garden furniture. Sarah Hawkins' life looked meagre.

One window was open, and Lia could hear the sounds of a TV programme or perhaps a video game coming from within.

Children?

If Fried had a child with his ex-wife, he or she would be a teenager at most. Lia waited, thinking about how to make her approach.

Someone came to close the open window. A woman, past forty, with dark hair pulled back in a ponytail. Face devoid of make-up and slightly puffy.

She noticed Lia standing on the street. For a moment their eyes locked. Collecting her courage, Lia waved and entered the garden.

The woman met her at the door. There was no curiosity in her eyes, as though she were too tired to be interested in anyone standing in front of her house.

'What do you want?' Sarah Hawkins asked.

Lia had an explanation ready, but the bluntness of Hawkins' question made her abandon the window dressing.

'Ms Hawkins, my name is Lia Pajala. I came to talk to you about your ex-husband.'

Sarah Hawkins' eyebrows went up.

'You know Arthur?'

'Not really. I've just met him. I have some questions for you about him.'

The woman looked at Lia appraisingly.

'Are you a reporter? You don't look like a political reporter. Or a gossip columnist.'

Lia smiled. Sarah Hawkins might look like a tired housing estate mother, but, as Arthur Fried's sometime wife, she clearly knew how the media operated.

'Actually, I'm a graphic designer for a magazine,' Lia said. 'But I'm interested in Arthur, and I'd like to talk to you about him, Ms Hawkins.'

Hawkins hesitated. She was still looking at Lia narrowly. In the end she nodded.

'If I let you in, you have to leave off that Ms Hawkins rubbish. I'm Sarah. And I'll decide what we talk about and what we don't. I say when we're done and whether I want to talk about a subject or not.'

Lia nodded.

'Absolutely.'

'I'll put the kettle on,' Sarah said and opened the door the rest of the way.

Lia followed her into the small kitchen, sitting down on a chair and looking around. The house was relatively tidy, and piles of washing showed that Sarah had been in the middle of doing the laundry. She could hear the sound that had been audible from outside better now as well: it was a video game, with booms and rapid-fire bangs filling the back room.

Lia looked at Sarah questioningly.

'My nephew. He's eleven,' Sarah explained. 'He spends a lot of time with me. My sister does shift work at the hospital and I'm... I'm not currently working.'

She prepared a plate of biscuits, laid out cups and a pot of tea and encouraged Lia to help herself.

Lia thanked her. Into her mind popped the little bottle of vodka she had bought from the Eastern Buffet, which she had been carrying in her bag for days.

She pulled the bottle out and set it on the table next to the tea service. Sarah smiled sourly.

'You aren't going to get much out of me with that little thing. And getting people drunk isn't very posh.'

'Oh, it's not about that,' Lia said. 'I'm from Finland, and we have a tradition of having a nip with our coffee or tea when we're talking business.'

Sarah laughed. It was a small, satisfied giggle, but Lia guessed that the ice-breaker had been timed just right.

'From Finland?'

Sarah didn't really know anything about the country. Only that the capital was Helsinki.

'But you didn't come here to talk about that. What do you want to know?' Sarah asked.

'All sorts of things. For starters, why did you divorce Arthur?'

Sarah sipped her tea.

'Before I do that, you tell me what your impression was of Arthur when you first met him.'

'I thought that under his polite shell he was a very cold, calculating person,' Lia said.

Sarah nodded.

They had not seen each other since the divorce.

'We had problems,' Sarah said.

She looked out the window.

'Or, Arthur had problems,' she added. 'And his problems became my problems.'

Sarah continued nursing her tea. Only the racket of the game in the other room broke the silence.

Lia tried to put her thoughts into words, but she knew how strange they would sound.

Your ex-husband is some sort of villain. But what kind?

'I don't know how to ask what I want to know,' Lia said.

Sarah snorted.

'Just spit it out.'

Lia swallowed.

'I believe that Arthur is not what he seems. There's something nasty hiding under the surface. But I don't know what.'

Sarah stared at her teacup as she weighed Lia's words. She offered her more tea. Lia shook her head.

'It may be that he's changed. But during our marriage there was a lot wrong with him,' Sarah said.

Lia saw that Sarah was collecting herself.

'No one knows about this. Not my sister, not anyone.'

Sarah squeezed her cup, which was shaking. She had to set it back on the table.

'I hope that Arthur has changed, because when I lived with him, he was a cruel rat bastard. He beat me so much that in the final years I had to escape to a women's shelter three times.'

Lia inhaled deeply. Everything was falling into place. Her observations about Sarah Hawkins and her home. Everything about Arthur Fried.

'Do you want to know more?' Sarah asked.

Lia nodded.

'Where's your recorder? You must have a recorder if you're doing a newspaper story.'

'I don't have a recorder. I want to hear your experience so I can decide what to do about it. Whether it deserves a newspaper story or something else.'

'Fine. It's all the same to me.'

Sarah said she had waited, expecting that someone would come and ask her about her marriage to Arthur Fried. But no one ever came.

'Maybe it's because Arthur wasn't famous when we were married.'

At that point, Fair Rule's supporter numbers had been so humble that they did not even register in the national polls, and instead of few invitations to televised debates, Fried received none. Sarah had been pleased to see Fried forced to understand that he was not the leader he imagined himself to be. But Fried's frustration had sent him out of his mind at home and he started beating her.

'No one came to ask about your marriage because almost no one knows about it. No record of it exists even in the national database,' Lia said.

Sarah was amazed. They had been married and filed for divorce in the usual ways, signing all the forms at the proper offices.

'I think Arthur had the records erased somehow,' Lia said.

'That must be it. I'm sure he's never regretted what he did to me.'

Lia listened on the edge of her seat as Sarah spoke, the careful consideration and confidence of her words telling of years of thought directed at this moment.

'My sister says someone would probably want to write a kiss-and-tell book about our story. But I don't want to blow it up into something larger than it was.'

They had been married seven years, the first three of which had been reasonably good and the last four of which were pure hell. Thousands of women went through the same thing. That was why Sarah had always intended to talk about it publicly someday. These men shouldn't be able to get away with their violence without suffering the consequences.

At first, Fried had only hit Sarah once or twice a month. It usually happened when he had drunk a couple of pints too many and wanted sex, but Sarah never wanted to when her husband was being aggressive.

'But after the first few times, he didn't need the excuse of being drunk any more. He would just hit me for anything.'

Sarah talked for more than two hours. Lia listened in anguish. The situation was absurd: all the while, as this tragic story was flowing out of Sarah, the sounds of simulated car chases and random death echoed incessantly from the living room.

Fried had usually begun by slamming Sarah into the floor. Sometimes she did not even see the blow coming and ended up with bruises just from the fall. Then she had to huddle on all fours as Fried circled her, lashing out at her at will.

'Usually with his fists. Sometimes he used his belt. On my back or my breasts so no one would see the marks.'

Sarah had not let anyone see her body, even in a swimsuit. At times even now in her dreams she would feel her body covered in bruises. For years she had simply become accustomed to the reality that another attack could come at any moment.

Once it was so bad that she lost consciousness and fled to a shelter when she came to. Fried was both drunk and angry. The party was doing badly. Another time the parish failed to appoint Fried to its governing board.

Once they were on holiday in Italy, on a road trip around Tuscany. Just before arriving in Volterra, Fried had suddenly flown into a rage.

'He stopped the car on the side of the road and started beating me. Not in the face, just everywhere else. I tried to get out, but he held me with one hand and hit me with the other.'

Sarah had been numb with shock and anger that he had dared to do it even when they were travelling. But she had no way to defend herself. Then her head jerked back so hard from the force of a blow that something cracked in her neck. For a moment she thought the torment would end there, on the side of that Italian motorway. She would never get to see Volterra or anywhere else ever again.

Suddenly Fried had stopped, urged Sarah to control her crying and started the car. After driving the rest of the way to

Volterra, they walked around seeing the sights, but Sarah had no memory of it.

'At night in the restaurant, Arthur ate larded veal with truffle sauce and I ate painkillers.'

Sarah noticed Lia shudder.

'Have you ever seen domestic violence up close? No? I could give you a definitive lecture on the subject. It's a strange drama of repetition and promises that things will change. But they never do.'

Sarah had waited for years for Arthur to stop. If only she loved him enough or he got help from a therapist. The violence clouded the victim's judgement: when someone close to you does something that terrible, you go into lockdown. Thinking that your situation was different from everyone else's was typical.

'In the beginning I made the same mistake as most women by thinking that I was to blame. It took two or three years for me to realise that it had nothing to do with me.'

They were a textbook case.

'Arthur was sick. Not deranged, but he did have some sort of personality disorder.'

It had dawned on Sarah that although Arthur Fried had exceptional social skills, he was utterly cold. Not only did he see himself as the centre of everything, he also derived extreme pleasure from subjugating others.

Sarah discovered that she was not the only woman Fried was doing this to. He had been visiting prostitutes the whole time they were married. This only came out after the violence had become commonplace and Fried no longer felt like pretending and concealing his whoring any longer. Not only had he been acting out sadomasochistic games with the prostitutes, he had really been hitting them too.

'He had to pay them to keep quiet. Once some girl got hurt so badly the payoff had to be in real money. I heard him arranging it with his party secretary.'

'Tom Gallagher?'

'No, then it was a man named Bob Hewitt. Slimy toad. But he only had the job for a couple of years. Working under Arthur is hard, so turnover has always been high.'

Some forms of violence were a strong sexual fetish for Fried. He had wanted Sarah to praise how well-endowed he was.

There were things she was supposed to say, things she could never say aloud again.

Sarah could not even think of reporting her husband to the police. She was too afraid. There were days when she was unable to leave the house, and working was impossible. When she first met Fried, she was working as a secretary for a labour union, but after the first few years of the marriage that fell by the wayside.

'I was so messed up. I kept having crying fits.'

After the divorce, as she gradually began to recover from Fried, no jobs were open to her. She had been out of the workforce for more than ten years.

Arthur Fried paid his ex-wife a small amount of maintenance each month, just enough for her to scrape by.

'I know that Arthur pays me because he's afraid. Now that I'm telling you everything, he's sure to stop giving me money. But I'm thirty-eight years old. If life has anything left for me, it has to start sometime.'

Lia was shocked. Sarah looked nearly fifty.

It was strange that no rumours had got out about Fried's violent tendencies, Lia observed.

'He's very good at what he does,' Sarah said. 'In the beginning his self-sufficiency was charming. Sounds stupid, doesn't it? But I had never met anyone before who shines the way he does.'

Fried could talk for an hour without expecting anything from his conversation partner other than the occasional nod of her head. And after one session like that, anyone would be prepared to vote for him. In fact, he had all the elements required of a good politician: he knew how to inspire, his energy was boundless and he knew how to play the game.

'But he has no heart – he knows how to fake warmth, but he doesn't feel any. Ever.'

All politicians were narcissists to some degree, Sarah suggested. It went with the profession. They had to believe in themselves, in their own omnipotence, in their ability to act as representatives in others' stead.

But Fried was unique in one respect. According to Sarah, he didn't even agree with many of the key Fair Rule policy positions. Fried had joined the party because he had seen its appeal to a type of voter he could control.

'He despises most of them. He would come home from party meetings and yell: "I fucked them all!"'

This meant that Fried had got one of the statements he wanted onto the party agenda.

'Do you know what his ultimate goal is?' Sarah asked.

Lia shook her head.

In the beginning it had felt like pie in the sky, Sarah said.

'But not any more, not now that his numbers are up.'

Fried's goal was not simply to get Fair Rule into Parliament. He saw himself leading something much larger.

'He speaks out against the EU, but he intends to be in the EU Parliament before long himself.'

Fried's objective was to unite all the fragmented far-right parties in Europe. To create a coalition that would make them even stronger and larger.

Lia shivered. She thought of the fanatic zeal she had seen in the Streatham Ice Arena.

Sarah glanced at her watch. It was already half past one.

'I have to make lunch for the boy. Food is one of the only things that will get him to take a break from his games. But you can stay if you want to hear more.'

Sarah Hawkins loaded chicken nuggets onto a baking tray and boiled them a fresh kettle. She seemed lost in thought. The stillness of afternoon fell over the kitchen.

Lia thought about Sarah's life and her own.

When Sarah placed the teapot on the table and sat down, Lia made a decision. She felt obliged, in return for all that Sarah had just told her. The time for her to face her own fears had come.

'I don't know anything about domestic violence,' Lia began. 'But I know what it feels like when someone you think you love becomes someone you hate.'

Sarah listened in silence. This was the first time Lia had ever spoken about her experience to anyone in England. No one knew but her parents: not her old friends in Finland, not anyone at *Level*, not even Mari – although Lia was unsure whether she could actually keep anything secret from her.

His name was Matti. Lia had been twenty-one and Matti a few years older. Perhaps it was his fascinating restlessness that had interested her first.

'He had such a different energy than everyone else.'

Matti's deep infatuation with her flattered Lia. He worshipped her. He gave her gifts and sent her letters – long, impassioned missives. He promised to build them the old Finnish dream, to fell the logs for their home with his own two hands, to fill the shed with a winter's worth of wood and build them a bed.

Before long his manic ardour became exhausting.

When Lia began showing signs of reluctance, Matti enlisted every tool he could invent. He sent her more gifts. Whatever she wanted, he wanted. But when he started writing letters to her friends and fellow students, Lia balked.

'He went to extremes you wouldn't believe. He was a stalker.'

When she came out of her block of flats in the morning, that tall, slim figure was always there on the street corner. He tried to call her hundreds of times a day. When she didn't answer, he called the people he saw her with.

Matti only drew the line at calling Lia's parents, who were surprised to see the relationship falling apart. He seemed like a lovely boy. He was good with his hands and wanted to start a family.

One night a small cot appeared in Lia's bedroom. With a baby doll lying in it.

'That was the main reason I left Finland. I haven't talked to anyone about this in years.'

'I can tell,' Sarah said quietly.

Sarah's eyes told that she understood. Something of what they had experienced was the same.

'He never hit me,' Lia said. 'He wanted to though. Sometimes I wonder if someday he'll come here from Finland and do what he wants to me. Finish the job.'

Sarah took her by the hand. A quick squeeze, strong and reassuring.

Would Sarah be willing to speak publicly about everything she had told her about Fried? Lia asked.

'Yes. If we do it the way I want and I get to see the story in advance,' Sarah said.

She didn't want anything that made her look like the bitter old ex-wife of a famous politician. She only wanted to tell her story. And she wanted facts about domestic violence victims to accompany it.

'Sometimes they list the statistics in the newspapers and on the telly, but not very often,' Sarah said.

And besides, it was only a couple of weeks until Christmas. Families did more hitting at Christmas than those who hadn't experienced it would believe. Whenever a newspaper or TV programme dealt with domestic violence, the women's shelters saw a spike in calls.

Thanking Sarah, Lia said she would get back to her within a day or two. She stood up to leave.

'You forgot this,' Sarah said, pointing at the vodka bottle.

'Oh my God!' Mari said.

Lia had asked Mari to meet her immediately at the Anthologist Bar. When Mari heard Sarah Hawkins' story, all she could do for a while was repeat two phrases. Oh my God. That poor woman.

A determined look came over her face.

'Fried will never recover from this.'

The three weapons they now had would send the sainted Arthur Fried to the bottom of the ocean. Corporate tax evasion, material support for racists and years of domestic abuse.

'Do you understand why stopping Arthur Fried has been so important for me?' Mari asked.

'Yes. Now I do.'

Fried's goal of becoming a force to be reckoned with in Europe was perfectly plausible, Mari said. He really could create a coalition of right-wing extremists from different countries that all supported xenophobia, the limiting of women's rights and a return of the European police state. A conservative coalition already operated in the Euro-Parliament, but fractures weakened it: the groups belonging to it were too different, and speculation was rife about the eventual withdrawal of the extreme right wing into their own caucus.

Did Sarah seem balanced? Mari asked.

'She looks tired. And you can see how limited her life has been,' Lia said. 'But when she talks about Fried she seems sincere.'

'Good. Instead of a print story, we'll do a video. And then spread it all over. When people see a woman talking directly about being beaten, they'll have to listen. This will stop everyone in their tracks.'

Mari created the plan right then and there. They would record Sarah Hawkins' full account of Fried's violence and then compress it down into a clip that was only a few minutes long.

Preserving the anonymity of the person making the video was important. Rico would take care of that.

For distribution they would give the final recording to an organisation with a good reputation so Fried would have fewer grounds to question its veracity.

Lia saw the tension release on Mari's face.

'We did it,' Mari said. 'We stopped Arthur Fried.'

She called the waiter.

'This calls for champagne.'

The following morning, Lia called Sarah Hawkins from work.

'Yes, a video is fine with me,' Sarah said.

She had thought it over during the evening. When the story came out, she wanted to have a professional agent to help her, to answer all the media inquiries, as well as a lawyer just in case.

'For a few days Arthur will be all the news can talk about. And I'll be fair game for the tabloids. They'll dig into all my business. They'll go over every single visit I've ever made to a health centre looking for evidence that I'm disturbed and trying to prove whether this really happened. And Arthur will deny it all. But I have the nights I spent in shelters and the medical records of my injuries as evidence.'

Lia promised a media advisor, a lawyer and even a make-up artist so Sarah could look her best. Mari had thought of this the previous night as well.

'And can we put a women's help hotline at the end of the video?' Sarah asked.

'Absolutely,' Lia replied. 'You have my word on that.'

III

Fairness

30

The large television screen on the wall of Mari's office flashed once.

'This is how it's going to play out,' Mari said.

Lia and all the other Studio regulars looked at the diagram that appeared on the screen. Organised within it was a list of dates and times outlining when they would release the revelations they had collected about Arthur Fried and what each person's duties would be.

Like fighting a war. Nothing left to chance.

For Lia this was the first time being with the whole group together. She looked around as each person examined his or her list of responsibilities.

Maggie in her relaxed flowery dress, the carefully groomed dame of the theatre. Rico in his sagging jeans and T-shirt. Berg cheerful in his familiar loose overalls. Paddy had deemed the day worthy of a sports jacket in addition to jeans and a sweater.

And Mari, stylish and self-assured in her pencil skirt, like the boss of a large corporation ready to lead her troops in a hostile takeover.

They were all different but formed a cohesive team. Lia did not feel she was at their level. Not in her abilities or in her attitude.

This team meant to bring down Arthur Fried and the entire party he ruled.

They could destroy an international mega-corporation if they wanted to. I wouldn't be one bit surprised to find one in the archives.

The first date was five days hence, 11th December. That would unveil revelation number one. By that time, Lia was to have found a reporter to leak information about Fried's tax shenanigans. She would only give the information verbally, but with enough detail that the reporter could confirm her claims.

The reporter would receive the information on condition that it be publicised in the manner they requested.

One week later would come revelation number two. That was the day when a private investigator Mari had hired would turn over to the police the information about Fair Rule's support for racist paramilitaries.

Mari said she was using a PI who had a good relationship with the police. He would also get word quickly about what the authorities intended to do.

'If the police don't begin an investigation immediately, we'll give the package to a reporter.'

To cover that eventuality, Mari would find an appropriate journalist at a different media company to the newspaper reporter Lia would leak the tax evasion story to. They had to use different outlets to avoid the impression that this was all just one organisation with a vendetta against Fried.

Revelation number three would go to the press just before Christmas. Rico and Berg would have the video of Sarah Hawkins' story prepared well in advance.

They had to film it with a camera that no one could trace in a place no one could recognise. They had to take Sarah Hawkins to the shooting location in a way that would prevent her from knowing exactly where she had been. They had to mask any ambient sounds so police experts could not track them down.

'We can do it,' Rico promised.

He had already practised by removing background noise frequencies from old Britney Spears videos.

'Britney sounds funnier and funnier the more sounds you remove,' Rico said.

Lia laughed, and Rico winked at her.

Before the release of the video they would move Sarah Hawkins to a hotel for the duration of the saga. When Arthur Fried realised that someone was leaking damaging information about him, he would start trying to block any possible new sources. They could not let Fried get at Sarah to change her mind.

'And when the video comes out, Sarah had better not be home. The media will surround the house,' Mari said.

The video they would give to an organisation named The Wall that campaigned against violence against women and whose name was well known all around the country. The organisation had been founded in the 1990s after the rape of a young woman in Birmingham. The rape occurred in broad daylight in the centre of the city when three men dragged the woman into the ruins of a demolition site where only one wall remained of the former structure. Passers-by heard the woman's screams behind the wall, but no one went to help. The girl's mother had founded the organisation, with the motto 'Break the Wall', and now their work consisted of exposing rapists and domestic abusers. They also waged pitched battles in the media if the courts found perpetrators guilty but let them slip away without punishment.

The women of The Wall would be happy to publish the video.

'What if Arthur Fried makes a comeback even after all this? What if he shows up again in a few years?' Lia asked.

'That's always a possibility,' Mari said. 'Then we'll just have to see.'

When a public figure's reputation begins to crumble, other skeletons tend to fall out of the closet as well, Mari pointed out. People got up the courage to talk. Who knew what ugly secrets Arthur Fried still had buried?

After the meeting ended, Lia remained in Mari's office.

She was nervous about the operation against Fried. What might happen when the revelations started flowing? And she still thought about the case of the murdered Latvian woman every day.

'We'll have to get back to that later,' Mari said. 'You remember when I said we can't handle two big jobs at once, right? Now we need all our time for Arthur Fried.'

Lia understood. But something else was bothering her too.

'I don't know what to think about you and me.'

A while ago they had been friends, plain and simple. Now they were something else. Lia was not sure what. Conspirators of some sort.

'I miss when we had time to go out at night and have fun.'

'Do you want to go out tonight?' Mari asked.

'Yes!'

'There's a place I've been meaning to show you. Let's meet at eight,' Mari said and wrote an address on a slip of paper.

Lia smiled.

Again, something new, like in the beginning after they had just met.

At eight that evening, Mari was waiting for Lia in Fitzroy Square.

The place was a minor disappointment for Lia. There were beautiful Georgian buildings and a garden fenced off for residents only, but no particular ambience or other reason for stopping.

'I'm taking you to one of the most important places in the world for me,' Mari said.

Lia laughed at Mari's seriousness, until she realised that Mari meant it.

Mari led them onto a side street and from there into a large, white building, the Fitzroy Art Museum.

At the ticket desk, Mari flashed a card that gave her free admission, and the worker obviously knew her. Lia made a move to buy a ticket, but the woman waved her hand.

'Go on in. We're only open for an hour yet.'

They walked up the stairs to the first floor. Mari nodded

briefly to the guard they passed.

Between the fourth and fifth galleries was a lobby with one piece of art and a bench placed in it.

They sat and looked at the installation, which was made up of two three-metre high fans. They were placed facing each other, several metres apart, blowing a strong current of air towards each other.

Between the fans, supported by the air current, were two thin black circles of ribbon. After inspecting it for a moment, Lia realised that the ribbon was some sort of film.

The large black circles of film whirled in the air against each other, occasionally parting. There was something magical about them. They never fell. Although they frequently rippled wildly as they morphed, they never slipped loose from the grip of the air currents buffeting them from either side, locking them in an eternal aerial gyration.

Lia lost herself watching it.

'It's wonderful,' she finally said.

'Isn't it?'

The name of the work was *Double O*. The circles of film formed two large noughts, or perhaps two letter Os. The artist was a Lithuanian named Zilvinas Kempinas.

Quite a coincidence, Lia pointed out.

'The Baltic is well represented in London,' Mari said. 'Just as is every other country and corner of the world. If you know where to look, you can find things from everywhere.'

'Do you come to look at this often?'

'Whenever the urge takes me. For some reason it gives me a very comforting feeling.'

Lia had loved visual art since she was a child and had studied it as part of her graphic design training. These sorts of contemporary art installations had always represented two specific states of mind for her: they were clear and analytical yet at once open to intense emotions.

This is how Mari is. Impenetrable when you look at her from the surface, intelligent and implacably purposeful. But inside she's all churning waves of grand emotion and ideals.

The museum was open on weekdays until nine o'clock, and Mari usually came late in the evening when few other visitors remained. She sat there when something troubling was going on in her life and she had to think clearly, or when she was feeling down.

'It's like it contains the rest of the world for me. It's over there, and I'm over here. I don't have to control it. It moves along its own trajectories. It can't be controlled.'

Lia thought she understood.

Mari moulded the world to be how she wanted, one piece at a time. That must be hard. If it was possible to change things, what of all the possible things did you choose to change?

'You can't and shouldn't intervene in everything,' Lia said. 'The world will keep turning on its own.'

'Yes,' Mari said. 'That's how I see it too.'

Watching the circles of film whirling in the air, they forgot the passing time.

Finally Mari stood up.

'Now I want to go to a pub. Is the Queen's Head & Artichoke OK?'

'Sure, thanks,' Lia said.

31

Arthur Fried's corporate fraud would make the front page of any newspaper in the country. Lia just had to choose which reporter would get the byline.

She decided on the *Star*'s political reporter, Thomas O'Rourke, whom she had met through work. The *Daily Star* used more of its space for reality TV interviews and photos of topless models than actual current events, but lurid scandal was exactly what the Studio was looking for. The *Star* also had a reputation for reaching precisely the audience that Fair Rule pandered to.

Lia's call surprised O'Rourke, but he agreed to a lunch meeting when she hinted that there was a story in it for him.

At Café Blend, Lia chose a corner table. Once the waiter had brought them their meals, she went straight to the point.

'I have an unusual proposition for you. I have a big political exposé I can give you, but only if you publish it at a certain time and keep the source to yourself, no exceptions.'

O'Rourke immediately forgot his steaming plate of penne.

'May I ask why a *Level* employee is offering me a scoop?'

It was complicated, Lia explained. The way she had come by the information made it impossible for her to use it in her own office.

'And I don't want the story connected to me or *Level* in any way, shape or form.'

O'Rourke pried no further – he was used to writing stories based on anonymous tips and expedients that had to be kept under wraps.

'It's about Arthur Fried,' Lia said. 'I have evidence proving that he has defrauded the government to the tune of hundreds of thousands of pounds.'

O'Rourke's eyes lit up, and the sparkle in them only grew as Lia related what she knew.

'This is big,' O'Rourke said once she was done. 'Really big.'

He said he had wondered more than once about Fried's rapid rise and how he managed to stay so squeaky clean. When this story broke, Fried's campaign would get a right drubbing.

'When can I release it?'

'At the Fair Rule press conference four days from now.'

O'Rourke burst out laughing, and Lia knew that she had chosen the right man for the job.

Mari's strategy sat perfectly with O'Rourke. The *Star* would be able to publish the headline on their website simultaneously with O'Rourke presenting his questions to Fried at the press conference. The paper would have exclusive access to the background information – the rest of the media would be forced to quote the *Star* because digging up their own sources would take time.

'Why such a precise time for the embargo?' O'Rourke asked.

Lia said that was what she had promised her own source. She described in detail how O'Rourke could confirm the claims she was making using Lincolnshire County Council tax records. O'Rourke wrote all this down, impressed that Lia could recite all the necessary information from memory, including the file numbers of the necessary documents.

'Are you sure you're in the right line of work? I'd say you'd make a brilliant investigative journalist.'

'One never knows when one might need a new job,' Lia said.

'This is where it begins,' Mari said in satisfaction when Lia called in at the Studio to report on her meeting. 'The next few weeks are going to be busy.'

To Lia's relief, Mari was so focused on the Fried case that she didn't seem to be paying any particular attention to Lia's comings and goings.

She didn't want Mari to realise what she had decided to do. As she left the Studio, she slipped the comb and mirror from the

Eastern Buffet into her bag, along with a copy of an article about the Holborn Circus murder.

When Lia arrived in Oval, Vassall Road was wet from the cold rain, which thankfully had now let up.

She had come to continue the investigation. She wanted to try to talk to one of the prostitutes. They must know something about what had happened.

Lia knew she was also here for selfish reasons. Arthur Fried was Mari's business. Of course, Lia wanted to help. A person like Fried had no business in Parliament. He belonged in prison. But the Holborn matter was her case.

She was standing out in the chill evening air on Vassall Road because she wanted to do something for herself. The Studio employees were strong, somehow larger than life. Larger than Lia, in any case. It was time for Lia to grow too.

Fear had been directing her life. Working for the Studio, she had faced danger and survived. She had no intention of letting fear take hold of her again.

Lia had to keep moving to stay warm. She kept her eye on the cars and the people that walked past. One of the most important things Paddy had taught her was that you had to stay aware of your environment.

There was no sign of Kazis Vanags' car. As it seemed he always made his evening rounds at the same time, he was probably on his way to Assets right now.

Lia stopped diagonally across the road from number twelve. She reckoned that seeing her from the building would be difficult because two lorries were parked in the way.

She saw two men entering stairwell A and one coming out. Each was alone.

Residents or customers?

The cold of the evening began to chill her through. She didn't see any more men, and the street was quiet.

At twenty minutes past eight, a woman walked out of stairwell A. In an instant Lia forgot her restlessness and the cold. It was the same woman as Lia had seen when she had been there with Paddy.

The woman walked with purpose in her steps. Based on her smart appearance, Lia would never have taken her for a prostitute, even though Paddy had said it was obvious.

Of course they can look perfectly normal. Is she supposed to wear a sign that says 'tart for hire'?

The woman walked towards the corner shop. Lia hurried after her. Once they had crossed the side street and she was sure no one could see them from the building, Lia came up alongside the woman.

'Excuse me,' Lia said.

The woman glanced at her but carried on.

'Excuse me, miss,' Lia said, touching her lightly on the arm.

The woman made a sound of irritation and quickly turned back the way she had come. Lia tried to keep up.

'I'm not with the police. I'm not with the police!' Lia hurried to say. 'Have you seen this before?'

In her hand was the pearled comb. The woman stopped and stared.

'Whose is that?' she asked in nearly unaccented English.

'I don't know her name,' Lia said, pulling out the newspaper story. 'This woman's.'

The presumed prostitute glanced at the clipping but did not seem to recognise what it was about.

'Where is she?' the woman asked, pointing at the comb.

'Dead.'

The woman's whole body stiffened. Lia could see in her eyes that something painful had just clicked into place. She stood there for a long time, neither of them speaking. Finally the woman began moving more uncertainly towards stairwell A.

'What's your name?' Lia asked.

'Elza,' she replied.

'Are you from Latvia?'

'Yes,' Elza said, glancing at Lia in confusion. 'I have to go.'

'Take this,' Lia managed to say, handing her the newspaper article. Elza snatched the clipping, shoving it into her pocket before disappearing back into the building.

Lia turned and started briskly walking off. She had a difficult time containing her excitement. She felt like running.

Elza. And she knows her.

Elza had recognised the comb. She must have known the murdered woman. Every other possibility would be too great a coincidence.

Lia was already unlocking her mobile when something made her change her mind.

I don't have to tell Mari yet. I can tell her when I've found out a bit more.

Lia walked to the Tube station. As she waited for the Northern Line train to Hampstead, she felt a wave of triumph.

The following evening she returned to Vassall Road earlier.

The encounter with Elza the previous day had made her cautious. She watched number twelve from further away, from a shadowed spot on a corner down the street. She held her mobile in her pocket with Mari's number on speed dial.

Lia watched as Kazis Vanags arrived, parked and disappeared into the building. About half an hour later he came out and left.

When Elza stepped out a few minutes before eight, Lia felt her pulse accelerate. Once again, Elza headed towards the shop in the next row.

Instead of following immediately, Lia waited to see whether anyone was following Elza. Then she hurried after her and entered the shop.

Elza showed no surprise at seeing Lia but also showed no sign of recognition. Her shopping basket contained a fashion magazine, cigarettes and a packet of tampons. When she moved further into the shop, between the aisles, Lia followed.

'Did you read the story?' Lia asked.

Elza nodded.

'Who are you?' Elza asked.

Lia told Elza her first name and that she was from Finland.

Elza thought for a moment.

'Did you know Daiga?'

Lia blanched.

That was her name!

'No.'

'Why are you asking about her then? Who do you work for?'

'No one. Daiga was murdered brutally. Whoever killed her deserves to rot in prison for the rest of his life.'

Elza frowned, looking uncertain.

'Now is not the time to talk,' she said. 'I can only be outside for ten minutes or I get in trouble.'

Monday was the only day each week when she and her friends went unwatched for a time. They always went to the Westfield mall. One man did follow them, but he usually didn't bother to keep up.

'He goes to a pub and sends a carder out to follow us.'

Lia looked at Elza questioningly: 'A carder?'

'The boys who paste up our pictures on the walls of bars and phone boxes.'

Of course Lia had seen cards and stickers around the city advertising female companionship. She hadn't realised that tart card distribution had its own specialised labour force. The everyday life of a prostitute in London was gradually dawning on her.

'Come to Westfield on Monday,' Elza said. 'There's a café there where we can talk.'

They arranged to meet at two o'clock. Lia decided to ignore her own work. Maybe she could take another day's holiday.

Before Lia left the shop, one more question popped into her mind.

'What was her whole name?'

'Daiga Vītola,' Elza answered quietly.

Smiling at Elza, Lia left.

Daiga Vītola. I've found you.

As she exited the shop, Lia glanced around. No sign of anyone.

She started walking towards the Tube station. Inside her a giddy, almost dizzying feeling of triumph mingled with the dozens of questions running through her mind.

The evening had grown darker. All she saw before her was a hint of movement and then it was too late.

The bald man. The same burly man Lia had fled from at Flash Forward and from whom Mr Vong had rescued her. This was no carder. This was a grown man whose job description Lia had no desire to become more familiar with.

She had no way of defending herself. And the street was empty except for the two of them.

The man approached her. He was close. There was no way to escape.

Lia was distantly aware of her arm rising with her mobile in her hand. Pointing it at the bald man, she snapped a picture.

The man stopped a few metres away and stared.

'I have a picture of you,' Lia said, surprised by the sound of her own voice. It was hard, as if she were in control of the situation.

'And now that picture is going to my friend,' Lia continued and pressed a button on the phone, exaggerating the gesture.

She knew all too well that the whole trick was a bluff. Pictures like that never turned out sharp, especially in the dark. And no picture went anywhere with just one press of a button.

But the stunt made the man stop short.

'What do you want here?' he asked.

Lia recognised the accent. Elza's was the same. The man kept one hand in his coat pocket, and Lia didn't want to think what he was holding there.

'What do you want here?' the bald man repeated.

Tell your story. The same one as at the club.

'I'm looking for my sister. She moved to Latvia a long time ago. I heard that she was in London.'

The man stared at her.

'You're looking for a whore?'

'I don't know what my sister is doing here. We haven't had any contact for several years.'

Lia heard a car approaching from behind.

I have to say something. Anything.

'Have you seen my sister?'

The man snorted.

'You can come with me and we'll talk about it.'

When he made his move, Lia guessed that the car was only ten metres behind her to the right. Turning, she rushed into the street.

A metallic shriek of brakes. Lia did not allow herself to stop, pelting forwards with all her strength. Skidding out of control, the car's front bumper grazed her leg. Then she was on the other side of the street, running.

A glance back. The bald man had been forced to dodge the moving car, losing several seconds.

Lia had never run so hard. She ignored the slipperiness of the street. She took no heed of anyone who might cross her path. One thought only pounded in her head: *Get away.*

After passing two side streets, she allowed herself a second look back. The bald man was following her but was rather far behind. That gave her renewed strength to increase her pace.

Lia saw the lights of the Tube station, with two taxis waiting parked in front. As she jumped into a cab, she turned and saw the bald man stopped a good hundred metres back.

Lia gestured for the cabbie to drive off. She couldn't catch her breath to talk, but the cabbie understood, starting the car and driving away. When Lia's breathing slowed, she asked him to take her to Bankside, Park Street.

When they arrived, she paid her fare, opened the door to the building with her key, entered the lift and pressed the button for the topmost floor. The lift doors closed, and Lia took a few deep breaths.

Safe.

She closed her eyes. What did it mean that in an emergency like this, she fled to the Studio?

This is my second home now. A strange home that makes me stronger than I am in any other place.

When the doors opened again on the top floor, she realised another fact. She was not afraid. Once the immediate threat had passed, in an odd way she liked the way she felt.

I shouldn't feel like this. I was in mortal danger. But I feel strong. In fact, I feel pretty damn good.

Lia walked straight into Mari's office.

She said she knew the Latvian woman's name. She told her about the bald man who had chased her once again.

She sat down on the sofa. Mari came to sit next to her and listened without uttering a single word. Lia showed her the blurry picture taken with her mobile phone: the bald man, coming for her.

'It was completely insane. But it worked. It worked,' Lia said.

She was waiting for Mari's reproach to come. But, without a word, all Mari did was hug her.

'Daiga Vītola,' Lia said.

Mari knew who she meant. She squeezed Lia's hand. Then she stood up and started her harangue. This was to be their first fight.

'You selfish idiot,' Mari said. Lia had almost ended up at the bottom of the Thames in a pair of cement overshoes courtesy of the eastern mafia. And here she was sitting expecting Mari's praise.

'That was so fucking dangerous,' Mari said.

Lia did not say a word.

I solved it. She was Daiga Vītola.

'You've probably cracked the case,' Mari said. 'But what if he had caught you? What then?'

'Then things would have gone badly for me. But they didn't.'

The Fair Rule press conference where they were going to start releasing their revelations about Arthur Fried was only two days away, Mari continued. What could they do with this Elza and the knowledge of the dead woman's name now? No one had time to focus on it given everything else they had planned.

'Someone does. Me,' Lia said.

They needed Lia for handling Fried, Mari argued. They couldn't risk endangering the operation's complete success.

'Getting Sarah Hawkins' story on tape depends on you. You have to be there when we make it. She trusts you.'

They had to give the information about Vanags, the bald man, the comb, Elza and Daiga Vītola to the police, Mari said.

'No,' Lia objected. 'Not yet.'

She thought Elza would talk to her but not to the police. If the police didn't arrest anyone for the murder, what would happen to Elza and the other prostitutes? Lia had to keep her appointment at the Westfield London shopping centre on Monday.

'When everything is ready, when we know how the whole thing went, I want to be the one to tell Daiga Vītola's name to that policeman, Gerrish.'

As they continued to argue, the volume grew.

'You asked me to solve the Latvian woman's case,' Mari reminded her.

'Yes, I did. But I didn't ask you to decide everything for us, everything I can and can't do.'

Can't you see how hurtful it is that you aren't excited about what I found? This might be the key to solving a horrible murder, and that's supposed to be a problem?

Mari looked at Lia for a long time. 'OK.'

Lia could go and meet up with Elza. But first she would help with Fried.

But Lia was not going to go alone, Mari said firmly.

'We'll see who can go with you. Probably Paddy. We're going to be up against the wall with Fried, but we'll make do.'

Although it was late, Mari decided to ring Paddy and tell him the situation. Lia guessed he would be angry, but could never have predicted the reaction that poured out from the other end.

Mari handed the phone to Lia.

It was her second sermon of the night, but Lia listened without complaint. Paddy and Mari were both right. She couldn't deny it.

'This ends now,' Paddy said.

He would no longer be willing to work with Lia. This startled Lia, and she saw that Mari was worried too.

Lia had not only endangered her own safety, Paddy said. She had endangered everyone at the Studio and the prostitutes on Vassall Road.

'The same thing happened once with Mari,' Paddy suddenly said.

A few years before Mari had been accompanying him, learning shadowing technique. They had been following a particular man all day. In the middle of everything, Mari decided to go and talk to the target's neighbour.

'I said no, but she went anyway. Mari happened to be right that time. The neighbour told us a critical piece of information about the target, which saved us several days. But Mari could have just as easily been wrong.'

Lia breathed deeply, but did not say what she thought.

Mari knew she was right. She saw it in the neighbour's face. I don't know whether I was right. Clearly I have to learn to analyse risks better, but I also need to figure out how to trust my own instincts.

'No one else has done that,' Paddy said. 'Why you and Mari?'

'Because we're Finns?' Lia suggested. Mari grimaced: this was no time for making jokes.

'You both have a problem accepting other people's authority,' Paddy said coolly. 'In Mari's case there might be good reason. She seems to have what it takes. She knows how to balance risks. You don't.'

Lia became aware that her entire future at the Studio was at stake. 'I'm sorry,' she said.

Talking Paddy down took time. He started softening when he heard in her tone that she really did want to try again, with a new attitude.

When Paddy finally believed that Lia was serious, he put the whole argument behind them.

'I'll see you on Monday. Let's talk before we go to the shopping centre, and I'll decide how we go in.'

It was already past ten o'clock, but neither Lia nor Mari wanted to go home. Mari stayed to work on her own research, and Lia went to see what she could find online in relation to Daiga Vītola's name.

There were plenty of Daigas and lots of Latvians with Vītola as their last name. But she couldn't find a single Daiga Vītola.

Going to the kitchen and fetching two glasses and a strong Syrah from the wine cabinet, she returned to Mari's office. The warmth of the wine coursed right through Lia's body as she sat on the sofa.

'My life has changed,' she said.

Lia was running around talking to Eastern European prostitutes and the battered wife of a redneck politician. Instead of hoping something interesting would happen at work each morning, she looked forward to getting back to the Studio. Having escaped the bald man twice now, she felt stronger than she ever had.

Her experience moving around London had changed as well. She had never felt in control of her environment before. The rivers of people agitated her. Now she felt as if the city was there for her. On the bus or on the Tube she wasn't just along for the ride – she had a goal, a mission. She knew something that others didn't, and she had seen more than they had or ever would.

'I understand why you want to do this now,' Lia said. 'It makes you feel powerful.'

Mari nodded.

'It comes and goes. But usually it's there.'

Mari filled their glasses and raised a toast. 'To Daiga Vītola.'

'To Daiga Vītola.'

32

Sarah Hawkins was waiting at the door of her terraced house.

When Lia arrived in her taxi, a completely different woman was waiting from the one she had met before. Sarah was dressed in a two-piece suit and high heels. A packed suitcase waited at her side.

She said she had not used the suit or the luggage in years.

'Haven't had any money for trips. And I never like staying the night anywhere, not even at my sister's house, because I can't sleep in strange places. That started while we were married.'

Sarah had tidied up the front garden and moved the shabby plastic chairs out of sight.

'I cleaned up a bit. Just in case the press comes,' she explained.

After locking her front door, she walked with Lia to the cab.

'Are you ready?' Lia asked.

'I am.'

To her sister, Sarah had said that she was going for a two-week retreat organised by a women's refuge. Her sister had been overjoyed to hear that Sarah was finally getting out.

After a ten-minute drive, they switched from the taxi to the Studio's grey delivery van.

'We found a place to do the taping that isn't far from your hotel,' Lia said.

Driving the van was Rico, whose laid-back conversation helped Sarah relax and feel at ease. They took a circuitous route, and Sarah was seated on the middle bench, where she couldn't see much.

Only one day remained until Operation Arthur Fried was scheduled to start. They had to get Sarah onto tape and then into hiding.

The set for the taping was an industrial hall Berg had rented, and he was waiting in the car park. Lia was amused to find that this was the first time she had ever seen him without his overalls. Although today's outfit was not all that great a change: baggy khaki trousers and a waistcoat full of tiny pockets. He looked like a jungle explorer.

'Welcome!' Berg said while they were still a way off. Lia knew that Berg's warm manner would do Sarah Hawkins good. Making the video would be emotionally draining.

Berg took Sarah's suitcase and led the group into the nearly deserted, cavernous hall. In one corner was a small cubicle, some sort of office space with a coffee machine, and at the other end of the hall they had built a set.

Maggie was waiting there, also impressively transformed. In her denim outfit and enormous jewellery, she gave Sarah the impression that she was in the hands of a true professional. When Maggie spoke, Lia knew she was hearing the dozens of make-up artists and hair stylists who had prepped Maggie for the stage over the years.

'Dearie, now you just trust me. You look fabulous, but I'm still going to wash all that off. Taping under these powerful lights requires special materials and secret tricks.'

An hour later, Sarah looked as though she could walk into a business meeting or official reception anywhere.

The hairdo suited her, and Maggie had softened the jacket suit with a sheer scarf at the neck. She looked style conscious. The heavy studio make-up was skilfully done, and Sarah could not help but stare at herself in the mirror. She looked younger than before, like a woman her own age.

They ran through how the taping would progress. Lia would ask Sarah the questions she had written up beforehand, which Sarah had received a week earlier. Rico would remove Lia's voice from the video. They could do as many takes as they needed.

Sarah sat in a chair with a white backdrop behind. Rico and Berg arranged and metered the lights and then checked the sound levels. Rico was in charge of the audio and Berg the video, which was being filmed simultaneously with three cameras.

Sarah sat and waited. Lia let her concentrate. In the end she received the signal from Rico that it was time to start. Lia smiled at Sarah reassuringly.

'To start off, could you tell me who you are and why you're making this video?'

'My name is Sarah Hawkins. I'm Fair Rule party leader Arthur Fried's first wife. We were married for seven years. For the last four of those years, Arthur Fried abused me. He beat me regularly, systematically and brutally. I want to tell my story publicly because constant abuse nearly destroyed my life, and I know that many other women live in that same hell. No one needs to put up with it. I've never got over what Arthur did to me. Arthur, I'm sure this is going to cause you problems but nothing like the ones that you caused me.'

Lia could scarcely breathe as she watched Sarah talking to the cameras, seeming as though she had been practising for this moment her entire life. And yet none of it sounded memorised.

Sarah was serious, calm and sincere. Only in her eyes could you see the emotion that relating her past suffering evoked.

'How did the abuse start?'

'I remember the first time, of course. You never forget things like that. It was a Friday night at home in Shoreditch. He had been drinking and wanted sex. He was groping me and it hurt. Our relationship had started out of love, but little by little a more aggressive side had been coming out in Arthur. I didn't like it. I told him I didn't want to. And he just knocked me to the ground with his fist, onto our kitchen floor. Then he took his belt and tied one of my arms to the handle of the fridge so I couldn't get away. Then he started beating me.'

The silence of the industrial hall swallowed individually each of Sarah's words. Lia, Rico, Berg and Maggie looked on in shock.

Sarah told how Arthur Fried liked to hit her, and showed the places on her body where he aimed his blows. She spoke about the trip to Tuscany and her visits to the women's refuges. She described how problems and struggles for power at Fair Rule had made Fried vent his frustration on her at home.

The time came for Lia's final question: 'Do you have anything you would like to say directly to Arthur Fried?'

'Arthur, I don't think you ever regretted for a moment what you did to me. You begged me to forgive you often enough. You tried to smooth things over with flowers and buying me things, but you just kept hitting me. I don't know what you're like now, since we haven't seen each other in years. I don't want to see you. I've never been able to get over what you did to me. I'm still afraid of a lot of things, like loud noises and people arguing. You beat that fear into me. When I see you on the telly, to me it looks like you haven't changed. During our marriage you enjoyed hitting me. But you're never going to do that to anyone again. Arthur, our marriage stole my life from me. Now I'm going to go looking for a new life to live. This video is my first step.'

They recorded Sarah's story in one take. Only the last part, where she recited lines she had written up beforehand, did they have to film twice. She repeated the expert estimates Maggie had gathered about how much violence occurred against women in Britain, and gave the contact information for two long-established support centres. Finally she encouraged everyone suffering from domestic violence to ask for help.

Berg switched off the camera and the bright tungsten lights.

Remaining seated, Sarah asked with some relief, 'How did it look?'

'Good. Really good. We'll show you the finished video in a couple of days,' Lia said.

Maggie walked over to Sarah and wrapped her in her arms. The hug lasted a long time, and neither of them spoke.

Once everything was done, Berg drove Sarah directly to her hotel, where she would stay for the next several weeks. Lia, Rico and Maggie stayed behind to watch the recorded interview.

'This is going to go viral instantly,' Rico said. 'Sarah's face says so much. I have a hard time imagining anyone voting for Arthur Fried after this.'

Lia watched as Rico and Maggie deftly edited the video. Maggie was the more skilful of the two at seeing where they should cut Sarah's answers and which camera angles they should choose.

'Instinct, dear, instinct,' Maggie said to Lia in her make-up artist voice.

Instinct coming from the years Maggie had spent making adverts and more artistic cinematic fare.

When Berg came back, he brought Mari along as well. The video made a profound impression on her, gluing her to her chair even in its incomplete state.

The video was done by that night. They were exhausted but satisfied with the end result. It was four minutes, six seconds long in all, and even after viewing it so many times, the effect was hypnotic.

People can tell when someone is telling the truth straight from the heart.

Berg drove them to the Studio. The others scattered towards their homes, but Lia and Mari stayed and sat together.

'Tomorrow it starts,' Mari said.

This would be the first time Lia had been on board during the execution phase of a long-term operation. She should enjoy it.

'I'm sure I will,' Lia replied.

Lia went to fetch drinks and snacks from the kitchen. When she returned, she found Mari standing in front of the sofa, her face drained of blood. On the television was a news report.

Together they watched the live broadcast from Ludgate Hill in the City of London. On the screen was a blue car parked on the pavement. Around the car, police officers busied themselves cordoning off the area.

Mutilated body found in car boot in central London, said the news ticker at the bottom of the screen. *Similarities with victim found in the spring. Crime scenes in close proximity.*

For a while they sat watching as the news report repeated the few available details.

'That's quite close to here,' Mari said. 'Do you want to go and have a look?'

'No. Or, yes. I don't know.' Lia thought for a moment. 'Let's go.'

Mari shook her head.

'Not me. I'm pretty sure the police take pictures of crowds gathering around crime scenes. And besides, the Arthur Fried countdown starts tomorrow.'

The street corner on Ludgate Hill looked like the set of a disaster film. Bustling, uniformed officials, large vehicles, floodlights.

Traffic had been rerouted. The police had sealed off the area with tape, behind which even at this late hour gawked a hundred-strong crowd of onlookers and several TV crews.

Inside the barrier, officers were searching the vehicle and nearby ground. Three enormous lights on telescoping stands had been positioned around the car. The strobes of the crime scene investigation team's cameras flashed. Only a few detectives and other police personnel were within the roped-off area, but more were in two large vehicles that looked like crosses between a camper van and an ambulance.

The area was filled with noise: hooting car horns, traffic police whistles, commands from the detectives, TV broadcast commentaries and the hum of the gathered crowd.

The strangest thing was the fear hovering over it all focused on the blue car, with its boot gaping open menacingly. Everyone stared at the car, even though no one could see in from so far away.

An unexpected evil had appeared before their eyes. Proof that anyone's life could be taken at any time.

Lia watched the incident unfold on this cheerless corner – Pageantmaster Court. And a pageant it was indeed. Fear really had made the slumbering street a stage, she thought. Everyone there knew they were watching something they would never be able to forget.

One police officer after another shook his head after looking in the car's boot. The faces of the investigators were set, gravely determined to work with speed and accuracy.

Lia recognised one of them. Detective Chief Inspector Peter Gerrish wore a translucent white protective suit and sterile gloves like all the rest. Gerrish was too far away for Lia to speak to him.

But after a few moments, Gerrish approached the police officers waiting behind the tape. As he scanned the crowd, he noticed her and for a moment pulled up. Then he walked over. The rest of the crowd stared at the detective and his examination gloves. They bore smears of red.

Ducking under the tape, Gerrish motioned for Lia to follow him. He found them a quieter place behind the throng.

'Why am I not surprised to see you here?' Gerrish asked.

Lia did not know how to answer, so she told him the simple truth.

'I saw the news and came to see if there was anything here connected to the Latvian woman's death.'

Gerrish nodded.

'I may have some information that will help you soon,' Lia said.

'Playing amateur detective, are we?' Gerrish asked.

That familiar crooked smile flashed across his lips but quickly disappeared.

'When you visited the police station, you lied to me. You denied being a reporter. But you work for *Level*.'

Lia was taken aback.

'That's true. But I didn't come to talk to you as a representative of the press, and I haven't written a single line about what we talked about. I'm not even a reporter. I'm a graphic designer.'

Gerrish's gaze was penetrating.

'I'm a bit busy now. What information do you have that could help us?'

Lia weighed what she could reveal.

'I can't say yet,' she said. 'All I have so far are guesses that still need looking into.'

'You do that then,' Gerrish said and turned to leave.

'Is this case the same?' Lia asked quickly.

Gerrish snorted.

'The next press release will be out soon. And I'm sure *Level* will get it too. But yes, it's very similar. The remains of an adult female in the boot of a car. This body is more intact though. She was shot, but more brutally than I've ever seen.'

Gerrish walked briskly back to the investigation area. Lia stayed to watch for a few more minutes. The police detectives' overalls shone in the glare of the lights.

Something horrible had happened, and now they had begun to pick up the pieces, laboriously, one by one.

The blue car was a Hyundai, and so the media called it the Hyundai Murder.

Lia watched the news until long into the night.

The police announced that the victim was approximately thirty years old, but positive identification had not yet been made. She had been shot extremely savagely, with a large-calibre automatic weapon. Simply killing her had not been enough. Parts of the body had come loose due to the force of the blasts, and it was clear that this had been the perpetrator's intent.

'I'm hard-pressed to think of any previous cases like this in Britain,' a tired-looking DCI Gerrish said in a BBC interview around midnight. 'Except one.'

The victim's head had been separated from her body by shooting her neck at close range with an automatic weapon for so long that the neck tissues and cervical spine had broken down. The murder had been loud and bloody.

Lia felt the same wave of nausea as she had in the spring.

The media quickly dug up their footage from the case of the Woman Without a Face.

How long will it take for the Sun *to give this victim a crass name too?*

It only took a moment. The first story to refer to her as the Headless Woman appeared online at 12.36.

Lia went to sleep at 3 a.m. when she couldn't stand to watch one more news report from Ludgate Hill.

In the morning all of London seemed to be thinking of only two things: the Headless Woman and the Woman Without a Face. Two murdered women, both left in the boot of a car in the City. The crimes were so unusual that they made the reporters resort to ever stronger metaphors. On the BBC morning news, a newsreader spoke of a 'new era of brutality', a phrase which was then repeated on show after show throughout the day.

In their reports, presenters considered it obvious that a serial killer was behind the crimes because the police had already found connections between the cases. What those connections were, the police did not wish to say since the investigation was ongoing.

'I have a hard time believing it's a serial killer,' Mari said to Lia on the phone.

The perpetrator was probably the same, but that didn't necessarily mean that he would follow a serial killer's logic, fulfilling some inner appetite.

'This is someone who kills for a living. He's probably killed many more people than these two. Dumping the victims in a public place is a message. The cars and the locations. They're supposed to tell someone something.'

They were still mulling over whether Lia should tell DCI Gerrish about the prostitutes on Vassall Road and Daiga Vītola. They didn't have any actual evidence to back up their suspicions.

'And besides, Gerrish has plenty of other work to do,' Lia said.

The media had started pointing out how little progress the police had made in the case of the Woman Without a Face. The lead editorial in the *Daily Star* said the situation was embarrassing: a victim had been found in the middle of the Square Mile, within spitting distance of the Old Bailey, but the police could not track down the murderer.

In one interesting way the Hyundai Murder differed from the Holborn Circus case. No one knew who the first person had been to see the victim in the white Volvo that spring. This, even though the police had interviewed more than 160 eyewitnesses.

But in the Hyundai Murder, they knew who had been first on the scene, a seventy-one-year-old maintenance man who had been on an evening shift monitoring the mechanical systems of a nearby shopping centre. He noticed the blue car parked carelessly on the pavement and went to look. When there was no sign of the car's owner, he tried the doors and found them unlocked.

'The car was empty. That was strange too. Usually people have things in their cars. I even looked in the glove compartment, because that's where people keep log books and other papers, but nothing,' the maintenance man told the BBC news when interviewed.

He happened to try the boot as well. It had opened, releasing a nauseating stench.

'I had to hold my hand over my mouth and nose. It was wrapped in plastic. A big... figure. So much blood. Straight away I remembered the Woman Without a Face...'

The man had slammed the boot shut and rung the police immediately. No one else had had to see the body.

Hauling the corpses into the City must have been a brazen operation, Mari said. The perpetrator had to drive the car onto a pavement in the middle of London, park it there and leave. Someone must have seen the driver, but without realising what they were seeing. People were constantly parking cars illegally as they ran quick errands.

But what did the discovery of the second body mean for Lia and Mari? And for the prostitutes in the flat on Vassall Road? Lia had her meeting arranged with Elza, but anything could happen before then.

'Perhaps the police will discover something before Monday,' Mari said.

They had to be extremely careful, she added. One murder might be a single, brutal act. The second victim made it clear that they were dealing with hardened criminals.

Lia had to hurry back to *Level*, and she knew that Mari's mind was on other things apart from this new murder case: the first revelation about Arthur Fried was set to be made today. Lia had no intention of attending the press conference herself. She planned to watch the event on her phone. She and Mari agreed to return to the murders as soon as possible.

'Fingers crossed for a good start to our political campaign,' Lia said.

'I'm sure it will be fine,' Mari said. 'It won't be as big a story as the Hyundai Murder, but it will be plenty big enough.'

In spite of how busy she was, Lia kept an eye on the news at work. Deep down, underneath it all, was the same sorrow and shock as the previous time, but now she evaluated what she heard as an investigator as well.

At 11.05 a.m., her mobile began to ring. It was Maggie. The Fair Rule press conference had just begun.

33

The sound was tinny and the picture was small, but the connection through her phone over the office WiFi was good. Lia watched the press conference sitting at her desk, listening through earphones. She knew that Mari, Rico and Berg were watching at the Studio and Paddy from somewhere else.

In the briefing at Westminster's Broadway House sat more than forty representatives of the media, even though the announced topic was something as dry as Fair Rule's new social programme. There were more reporters than at any of the party's previous news event, a result of the latest opinion poll numbers, which showed Fair Rule breaking six per cent.

A small lure had also been thrown to the media in the form of an announcement that the party would proclaim its opposition to the government's current income tax policy and propose a tax relief initiative. That bore Gallagher's trademark, Lia thought. Taking a stand on the tax burden was a tool for bolstering the party's position in the eyes of journalists, commentators and other political professionals.

Looking at the audience in the hall, Lia remembered something she had heard Fried say in Epping at the party headquarters.

'Reporters hunt in packs,' Fried had said. 'They think they're independent, autonomous defenders of truth and justice, but in reality they always just follow whoever happens to be winning.' Now the pack had started to realise that Fried was a rising star in the upcoming elections, and the pack wanted to get a piece.

Two TV news crews were also in attendance, Sky News and ITV. So far Fair Rule policy statements had failed to make the TV news, but that situation might be changing.

In amongst the reporters sat Maggie, who had gained entrance using a bogus press card. She was Susannah Thurman, from a paper named *The Public*, and if anyone had decided to check on her background or the paper she purported to represent, they would have found online every indication of a long and distinguished career for Thurman along with several of her articles.

The paper actually existed, but Susannah Thurman did not.

Maggie focused her smartphone's video camera on Arthur Fried, who had just stepped up to the podium.

'Dear friends, a lot has been written about Fair Rule in recent months. We've begun rising fast because we've been a real challenge to the status quo from the very start. We've challenged the politics of cowardice and cover-ups. We've shown the public what isn't working under the current leadership and dared to say out loud what the majority thinks but does not express to avoid being unfairly labelled politically incorrect. We don't think any of this is politically incorrect. What is incorrect is the collection of crushing taxes from British entrepreneurs who work tirelessly in service of their country...'

Lia had to smile. Fried had no idea the turn that was about to take place.

As he always did, Fried ended his grandiloquent speech by repeating the party's slogans: Get Britain Back, No Way but Our Way.

Then he asked the reporters for their questions. Ten hands went up at once, and the party secretary jotted something down. Usually the larger outfits were called on first, and Gallagher indeed began with them.

'The *Sun*, please go ahead.'

The tabloid reporter's question had nothing to do with the issues at hand. Instead he asked about a recent case in Sheffield in which CCTV had recorded a black man robbing an aged, fair-skinned woman. Arthur Fried observed that the incident was a regrettable yet instructive example of how domestic politics that rode hobbyhorse on multiculturalist ideals were driving the nation into chaos.

Gallagher gave the second question to the reporter from *The Times* who wanted to know why the social programme the party had just announced sounded so much like a programme a German conservative party had promulgated during their previous round of elections. Some portions were borrowed word for word.

The irritated glance Fried cast Gallagher spoke volumes. Apparently Fried hadn't known Gallagher had stolen the text of his programme proposal.

But Fried's answer was smooth nonetheless.

'We're extremely happy that the issues our party has raised are supported by other groups. Fair Rule has never followed anyone else. We begin conversations.'

As the third questioner, Gallagher pointed to Thomas O'Rourke from the *Star.*

Lia's heart pounded. She watched as O'Rourke stood and smiled.

He's really enjoying this.

'Mr Fried, I have here copies of some documents I was hoping you could explain. I'll pass out copies to everyone so they understand what this is all about,' O'Rourke said

Fried and Gallagher watched in surprise as O'Rourke sent a stack of papers circulating down the aisle.

'There should be enough for everyone, I think,' O'Rourke said jauntily.

A reporter sitting on the front row handed a copy to Arthur Fried, who barely had a chance to glance at it before O'Rourke continued.

'Mr Fried, these are copies of your corporate financial reports from 2000 and 2001, copies of the information submitted to the tax authority and a copy of the Lincolnshire County Council business register annual report for 2001, according to which both of your companies filed for bankruptcy in the same year…'

'I can't see what this has to do with Fair Rule,' Fried said in an attempt to stop O'Rourke, but instead the reporter simply raised his voice.

O'Rourke related how Fried's companies had faked bankruptcy in Lincoln and then continued operating in London virtually unchanged. Fried had never returned the business grants he had received during 1997–2001 and had, for example, failed to deliver some £70,000 in social security payments owed to the state. The final page was a document showing that Fried was the chairman of the board of both companies and controlled one hundred per cent ownership of each along with his wife.

'That means that you are individually responsible for their activities,' O'Rourke observed.

Even the mobile phone video connection showed how Arthur Fried's face began to twitch.

'So, the question is,' O'Rourke said, 'have you swindled the British Crown out of some three hundred and forty-six thousand pounds through bankruptcy fraud or is there a more honourable explanation for all of this?'

A surge of noise rolled over the briefing room. It began when some forty reporters simultaneously picked up their mobile phones and rang their editors to say that the Fair Rule press conference had suddenly become extremely interesting. One TV cameraman moved closer to Fried to record his reaction from a better angle, and the other TV camera followed right behind.

Arthur Fried did not look at O'Rourke. He was staring at Tom Gallagher, who was staring back. Their faces showed disbelief and a frantic effort to catch up with the situation. To this, Fried's eyes added pure hatred.

Finally Fried turned his gaze to O'Rourke and his eyebrows rose.

'Well now, Mr O'Rourke. You certainly have a dramatic way of presenting your shocking claims. It's almost as though you're trying to paint me as some sort of tax evader.'

Fried assured them that both companies had always conducted their business honestly, and he was sure that once he had had time to look more closely at the information that had been presented in such an oddly defamatory manner, a perfectly legal explanation would appear.

'This event is meant to be a discussion of the new Fair Rule policy programme, and I'd like to concentrate on that,' Fried said, attempting to change the topic.

Another wave of noise ran through the hall. Some of the reporters were demanding a turn to ask follow-ups, while others relayed Fried's response to their offices and the rest expressed their astonishment at O'Rourke's allegations.

Fried and party secretary Gallagher looked at each other again. Lia saw Gallagher mouthing words. He did not want to say anything to Fried in front of the cameras. Lia was unsure what Gallagher was trying to communicate. It could have been: 'Stop now.'

Arthur Fried turned again to look at the crowd of reporters, who were now rising from their seats, eagerly awaiting the next turn that events would take. They all wanted a comment from Fried on O'Rourke's papers and the charges he had made.

'Thank you for your attendance,' Fried said in a loud voice. 'We'll issue an announcement soon about our next press conference. I wish you all a good day and may God bless this great nation.'

Turning, he walked out of the hall with Gallagher behind.

Maggie's phone transmitted the chaos that broke out as the reporters stampeded after Fried and the party secretary and porter attempted to hold them back.

Reporters hunt in packs.

34

The fact that Arthur Fried had been accused of corporate fraud made the headlines at every news media outlet in the nation. It was, ironically enough, the most press Fair Rule had ever garnered.

Mari and Lia watched from the Studio as the story swelled. Thomas O'Rourke had done his homework. The documents he had distributed were so convincing that no one dared claim they were a fake. Because only the *Star* knew the entire story, the other editorial offices were forced to turn to them for facts. By the early evening, the story had spawned so many hits that the tabloid's web server crashed.

O'Rourke sent Lia a text message around eight o'clock: 'I've given sixteen interviews today. I can't remember the last time I had this much fun.'

But Arthur Fried and Fair Rule were lying low. Because the TV stations didn't have their own interviews with him, they were still airing clips filmed at the press conference, showing how Fried's face froze as O'Rourke posed his question and the sorts of quiet, dark looks Fried and the party secretary exchanged. The videos closed with Fried exiting as the reporters shouted after him.

Lia imagined the feelings of confusion and panic hanging over the party headquarters – if Fried even had the nerve to go there and thrash the matter out.

How will Stephen, Dorrie and the others react to this?

Sky News showed a feed from the Fair Rule office in Epping High Street. The faces of Stephen and Simon flashed across the screen. Lia swung between empathy and irritation. She expected to experience some pangs of conscience over what she had done to these people she had come to know, but they never came.

The BBC Nine O'Clock News began with the headline 'Right-wing Leader Tax Scandal' and the commentators proceeded to express their astonishment that a person with such an impeccable reputation as Arthur Fried could become the target of such serious accusations. A BBC crew had interviewed the head of the Lincoln economic development office, who said this was the first he had heard of Fried's businesses' continued operations. In his personal view, this was a case of unusually egregious fraud.

'Fried was a highly esteemed businessman here several years ago. His enterprises received support above and beyond the usual limits. Apparently we experienced a significant failure in judgement,' the official said.

Arthur Fried released his own statement the same evening, at 10.39 p.m. He announced that he would cooperate fully with the authorities in any possible investigation. If any confusion had arisen during his companies' move to London, he would endeavour to rectify it in full. The statement came too late for most of the morning papers – they would only have time to quote directly from it in their paper editions without any further commentary. And Fried was not giving interviews.

When the morning papers did appear, expert opinion was unanimous in predicting a significant blow to Fair Rule's support.

'What was to be a standard press conference turned into Arthur Fried's final kamikaze dive. What will remain of a party based on talking straight when no one else would dare now that its leader has been accused of such an astonishingly brazen con? If the accusations turn out to be true, this case will be a triumph of investigative journalism sure to influence the upcoming parliamentary elections,' wrote *The Guardian*.

Over the next few days, Fried continued to refuse any interviews, but the reporters on the political beat succeeded in prising comments out of the rest of the Fair Rule leadership. And of course representatives of the major parties were eager to comment. His own people still supported Fried, but others were more than happy to criticise his 'messianic' appearances and populist pandering.

'Cool-nerved damage control,' Mari said.

Fried knew that he had to calm his own troops first. He would probably attempt to draw the investigation out beyond the election. The party's popularity would not necessarily collapse if the public remained in the dark as to whether he had committed a crime or not.

Lia listened to Mari's analysis. It was almost as though she knew what was happening inside Fried's mind.

Fried most likely still believed that this was a game of politics, that the information had come out by chance, dug up by one reporter, Mari continued. When they released the next revelation, Fried would know that someone was attacking him. Then he would start the fight for real. They had to be one step ahead.

Lia called Sarah Hawkins at the hotel where they had taken her after taping her interview. They had given her a new mobile phone so no one else could reach her.

'Have you seen the news about Arthur?' Lia asked.

'Yes. This is unbelievable. Of course I knew about his businesses, but nothing like that,' Sarah said.

Lia warned her that more sensational news stories were likely to follow soon.

'The media will start digging into Arthur's and Fair Rule's dealings in an entirely new way,' she explained.

'Good. When my video comes out, that should give them something to talk about.'

Sarah had received a copy of the final interview. She had watched it dozens of times.

'Seeing myself on the telly is so strange. But I feel better than I have in years. If only this could all be in the past. I could get on with my life again.'

'It will all be over soon.'

35

At two o'clock on a Monday afternoon, the Westfield London was surprisingly peaceful. The lunch rush had passed, and only the occasional shopper walked here and there.

Lia was sitting at a window table in the café, sipping her coffee and waiting. Now and then she glanced at Paddy Moore, who was sitting a few tables back.

Although they had patched things up, they still regarded each other more carefully. Paddy wanted to see how dependable Lia was.

Lia had arrived at the café alone, once Paddy had first checked the place and scanned who was nearby. They showed no sign of knowing one another.

Lia had asked for two days off. Martyn Taylor, the AD, had agreed after Lia had showed him how the layout work could be divided so her leave would not muddle anything terribly. Lia had expected Taylor to object to her sudden absence, but he seemed to respect her purposefulness.

At 2.25 p.m., four women walked into the café. One of them was Elza, and the features of the others also showed they were from the Baltic. A boy who had been following the women remained outside. Perhaps sixteen years old, he was dressed in jeans and a leather jacket and wore oversized earphones. A carder.

The women bought pastries and coffees at the counter. Listening to them chat, Lia wasn't sure but thought the language was Latvian.

The women claimed the table next to her. Elza did not greet Lia, but after a few minutes cast a long glance her way.

Then she got up and said to her friends in English, 'Ladies, do excuse me while I powder my nose.'

The others laughed at this affectation, and in that moment Lia realised that Elza had not told them about Daiga Vītola's death or about herself. The humour and warmth between the women was a pleasure to see, in spite of the situation.

Elza walked to the ladies' room. After waiting a minute, Lia grabbed her coat and handbag and followed. Elza was waiting, looking serious.

'Tell me your name,' she asked.

'Lia Pajala.'

'Elza Berklava,' Elza said, proffering her hand.

This must be terrifying for her. She lives every moment with thugs like Kazis Vanags and that bald man.

'If I tell you about Daiga, what will happen then?'

Lia admitted she didn't know.

'But whoever killed her must be brought to account.'

Elza nodded.

'I'll help how I can, but then you have to help me too. If they find out, the same thing will happen to me as to Daiga and Anita.'

Lia did a double take.

'Anita?'

'Anita Klusa. The woman they found shot last week in the Hyundai.'

Lia tried not to show her agitation.

Elza said she had cried the whole night after reading the newspaper clipping Lia had given her.

'I had to rip it to bits and flush it down the toilet because they search our things all the time. They look for drugs – they know we have them, but they don't want us using them too much. The customers complain if a girl is high.'

'Tell me about Daiga,' Lia said.

Elza smiled. When she spoke, her eyes filled with tears.

'Daiga was a crazy girl.'

She was from the Riga suburbs and had come to Britain two or three years before any of the other prostitutes. When they met, Daiga had given Elza pointers about working in London. She had taught several other girls as well.

'In most of the houses there's a more experienced girl who gets the others started.'

When Daiga was still at the flat in Vassall Road, five prostitutes had been working there. Four remained.

Daiga had been the only one who ever dared contradict the brothel operator, Kazis Vanags. Daiga took fewer clients than the others because she wanted to keep herself healthy. She wouldn't buckle under the strain of bullying. She had always been the intellectual leader of the girls on Vassall Road, making sure that their conditions were tolerable.

'Daiga always told us that life is shit but at least our shit life was in London.'

They had done the same work back in Riga too.

'Daiga and me used to turn tricks in the parks, two or three nights a week. Our area had the best parks with the most traffic. We could choose our clients ourselves.'

Having to work year after year like prisoners here and take anyone who came was a hard blow for them.

Daiga had thought that something else would come along someday, a better future in London. She had done everything with rare fortitude. A common problem for most prostitutes was that their minds couldn't take it and they had to numb themselves. Daiga Vītola had not drunk or taken drugs. Because of her the girls had been able to see a doctor regularly. Even though they used condoms, they would still have inflammation and infections.

'Who killed Daiga?' Lia asked.

Elza's lips pursed in a bitter line.

'It must have been Vanags.'

Kazis Vanags had hated Daiga's lack of fear. However much he railed at her she gave it back in turn. Once she even laughed in his face.

'I had a bad feeling after that. Kazis wouldn't hesitate to kill a baby.'

Elza had no evidence against him though. She did know that Vanags had been apoplectic at Daiga just before she disappeared.

The toilet door opened and an elderly woman entered.

Elza and Lia fell silent. When the woman entered the toilet stall, Elza quietly said, 'I'm going to go back to the table so the other girls don't wonder where I am. Wait five minutes.'

Before she left, Elza dug into her handbag and then handed Lia something.

'I brought this for you.'

Lia looked at the piece of paper. It was a photograph, the small type you might get from a self-service booth.

In the picture was a dark-haired woman. Lia knew who it was. Daiga Vītola.

The woman in the picture was smiling, laughing actually. She looked strong but also like a person who could take pleasure in small things. For example how silly it was to sit in a photo booth and pose.

She looked like a mother, Lia thought. Strange that a woman like that had prostituted herself, first in Riga and then in London.

Or perhaps that was precisely why a woman like that left her home. She probably had to earn a living for her family. She wasn't doing it only for herself.

Looking at the small picture in her hand, Lia thought about all the many choices people make.

If you've never had to make a difficult decision in your life, you can't know what it's like for someone else.

As she exited the stall, the older woman eyed Lia suspiciously, but Lia didn't give her a second thought. The woman left, and a little later Elza returned.

'I think the girls guess something's up,' Elza said. But Elza's friends were afraid, and they knew better than to ask why she kept traipsing off to the toilets.

Elza continued her narrative. Four days before Daiga's disappearance, Vanags had flown into a rage at her.

'The two things must be connected. I thought Kazis forced Daiga to go somewhere else. But now I know he killed her. And in such a dreadful way.'

Elza's eyes filled with tears. Lia had a hard time keeping her composure too. Both leaning on the sink counter top, Lia listened as Elza went on.

The four women of Vassall Road were all from Latvia. In London there were four brothels where the girls were Latvian, and all had come to the city the same way.

Six men ran the brothels, most of them from Latvia as well. They also had a group of collaborators, the descendants of Eastern Europeans living in London now.

'There are three lower bosses. Each one takes the profits from one house, but Vanags gets the most.'

Vanags handled the importing, making him the de facto head of the operation. He had a large network of transportation specialists in Eastern Europe, and the Eastern Buffet food shop was a perfect front for the rest of his businesses. The real money came from weapons and prostitutes.

'They don't do drugs because the police investigate that the most.'

Before 2004, when Latvia joined the EU, trafficking women had been more difficult. First they were all smuggled into Poland from Latvia. That had been the easiest part of the journey, since they could simply bribe the border guards. Elza had ridden across the border in the back seat of a car in broad daylight for everyone to see.

Then they had to hide the girls. A car drove them overland to Sweden, and from there they came to Edinburgh on a passenger ferry. Some of them were given false passports and visas so they could travel more comfortably.

But forging documents was expensive, so most girls had had

to stow away. Elza had spent the two-day sea voyage in the boot of a car under a false bottom.

'It was terrible. I felt like screaming my lungs out the whole time, but I couldn't. It would have been even worse if I had been found out.'

They had just had to cry into their hands to muffle the sound. They travelled in complete darkness in that tiny confined space. Air came from a small tube under the car. The driver gave them a couple of bottles to pee into. A little food and even less water.

No one had told them about the journey in the car boot until right before they had to go. And there were no other options. The driver simply ordered the girl into the boot and then told her she had to stay there if she wanted to get to London. If the girl refused, he said he would shoot her on the spot.

'Daiga and me and a lot of other girls had to go through that. Sit in the boot of a Volvo and look straight down the barrel of a pistol. We knew we were staying in there dead or alive. We call it a Volvo berth.'

The car was always the same model, a Volvo S40, because it had space for a false bottom difficult to find in a superficial inspection.

This was why Elza was sure that Vanags was the one who had killed Daiga Vītola.

'Daiga tricked him on one of the transports. Kazis got so angry at her we were all afraid.'

Bringing new prostitutes into the country was much easier now because it was all EU territory. All they needed was a Latvian passport, which was only a problem for Russian girls. Vanags sent for two or three new girls a year, and they came in a lorry. In Latvia they put the woman up front next to the driver, who ensured that she couldn't escape or talk to anyone.

In one particular transport, two girls were supposed to be coming from Latvia. Daiga had come up with the idea of using this to get her mother and daughter into the country. She had not seen either in years. They had only kept in contact over the phone, and she could only ring them occasionally, with the pimps mon-itoring her.

Daiga had no need for her husband back in Latvia. 'He's a bad man,' Elza said, and Lia felt as though she understood without elaboration.

Daiga promised a large sum of money to an acquaintance in Latvia for substituting her mother and daughter for the prostitutes. The lorry driver wondered about a sixty-year-old woman being exported as a prostitute. The sixteen-year-old daughter was easier to believe.

'But the drivers don't ask too many questions. He brought the grandmother and daughter to London, straight to the flat on Vassall Road.'

When Vanags discovered them, he blew his top, immediately taking the mother and daughter away. They only saw Daiga for ten minutes. Daiga went insane with regret and fear.

She screamed at Vanags and refused to take any clients. She had really thought that after so many years of work, Vanags would have felt pity for her and allowed her family to stay. She offered Vanags money, but he was too angry to listen.

Four days later, Daiga disappeared.

Elza had asked about her, but in vain. She had hoped that Daiga had just been moved to a different house.

How did Elza and the other girls not hear about it in April right when the body was found? Lia asked. 'It was the number one story in the whole country. It was in all the papers.'

Elza shrugged.

'We don't follow the news. We don't have any use for it.'

Some of the prostitutes did not even speak much English. They only knew the vocabulary they needed with customers. But they had read about Anita Klusa's death.

Daiga's body was found in the same kind of Volvo used in smuggling the prostitutes, except that the car lacked a false bottom. The body was put in the boot, which was a message to them all. The Volvo berth.

Daiga had been left on Holborn Circus and Anita on Ludgate Hill, and it was clear what that meant. Another brothel, on tiny Creed Lane, was nearby.

'Two girls escaped from there last year. They tracked one down straight away and killed her. The other was Anita. They didn't get her till now.'

Lia understood. They had killed Anita Klusa as a sign that they always caught escapees sooner or later. Daiga was a sign not to defy the pimps.

Lia was relieved that out in the café, just a dozen metres away, sat Paddy Moore. Then she realised something.

'Elza, it's possible that I know where Daiga's mother and daughter are.'

She then explained about the house in Catford where Vanags took food every night.

'It could be that Vanags is keeping them hidden there.'

Elza covered her mouth with her hand.

'Oh my God! I was afraid Vanags sent them right back or something worse. Maybe they've been there the whole time.'

'Can you go to Catford?' Lia asked.

'I don't know,' Elza said, clearly startled. 'Just talking to you is so dangerous. What can we do if they're locked in there?'

'At least try to talk to them. Maybe they'll be willing to risk talking to you.'

Elza thought. Near them in the shopping centre was a beauty salon. She could get out through the back, which offered access to the loading docks and car park. No one would know about it unless they had been inside the shop.

'I've thought that if I tried to escape someday, it might be possible through there. The boy waiting outside the café is so stupid that if the girls and me go into the beauty salon and I come out the back, he's bound not to even notice. We could have an hour and a half. Maybe two.'

Two hours. In London traffic! I guess that's better than nothing.

'Let's do it,' Lia said.

Lia opened the door a crack and watched as Elza returned to the other women and suggested that they go straight over to the beauty parlour.

This suggestion surprised them, but no one objected. They could see that Elza had her reasons.

There is no question who their leader is.

The women collected their shopping bags and coats and left the café. Slipping out of the toilet, Lia saw Elza explaining something to the waiting boy. The whole group set off up the escalator to the beauty parlour.

Paddy still gave no sign of knowing her, but Lia heard her mobile beep. The text was from Paddy.

'Situation resolved?'

Lia controlled her urge to march straight over to talk to him. Someone might still see them. Returning to the toilets, she rang him.

'No, the situation is not resolved,' she said. Quickly she summed up Elza's story.

'I have to go with her to Sangley Road. I don't know whether you should come with us. Elza might lose her cool. Can you follow close?'

Paddy asked about the risks of visiting the house, but since it was clear that Vanags only went there in the evenings after closing up the shop, Paddy didn't see any specific obstacle to their visiting.

'But you have to remember we don't have any real information about who is in that house. There could be someone there who isn't being held prisoner and they could attack us. Or someone could be surveilling the place from nearby,' Paddy pointed out.

'And this time no genius brainwaves,' he added.

She left the café and made her way down to car park. Paddy kept Lia just in sight as she looked for the beauty salon's rear door near the loading docks.

Soon Elza appeared at a door. She smiled, but Lia could also see the mixture of fear and tension in her face.

'For six years I have wanted to do this and been afraid of doing it,' Elza said.

Quickly Lia directed Elza to the taxi rank. Out of the corner of her eye, she saw Paddy head towards his own car.

They found a queue of black taxis and no other customers waiting.

'I've never taken a cab in London. They always take us places in their own cars,' Elza said.

First they navigated smaller streets to reach the Chelsea Embankment and then cross Vauxhall Bridge. Elza watched with dull eyes as the scenery passed.

She looks more resigned than unhappy. People can get used to almost anything.

She asked Elza about her working conditions, quietly so the cabbie couldn't hear.

Elza and the other women in the flat on Vassall Road had come to London to make money. An elegantly dressed woman with expensive jewellery who visited Riga from England, also a prostitute, had promised them they would. Afterwards they had realised that Vanags had hired her to lure them in.

'I know there are a lot of girls in prostitution who have been forced into it, but we knew what we were coming to London to do,' Elza said.

What she and the other girls had not known was that they would be forced to live in a virtual prison.

'Kazis likes to screw three or four nights a week. We just have to put up with it. But we don't have to sleep with their little thugs. Kazis says we don't have to. He wants to keep us in good shape.'

They had a few rights, mostly based on practicality. The pimps avoided hitting them so they would look good for the customers. But there were certain clear limits. You couldn't tell the clients about yourself. You couldn't lock doors inside the flat, not even the toilet. You didn't leave the flat except to visit the corner shop. You couldn't keep in touch with anyone outside.

'They have guns, but they don't have to use them. We know what they can do.'

The conditions for the women in the brothel on Creed Lane were worse.

'It's because they're in the middle of the City.'

'How is it possible for there to be a brothel there at all?' Lia asked, surprised.

Where could they maintain a flat like that in amongst all the office buildings and government agencies? And the rents in the area were so high.

'There are at least a dozen, in basements and back rooms,' Elza said.

Creed Lane was a pedestrian precinct. Every morning a large, black van drove to one of the buildings there. From it the prostitutes were taken under careful guard to an office where they accepted male clients in two rooms in the back. Customers flowed through the place, including businessmen, lawyers and maintenance workers.

'The girls' conditions are terrible,' Elza said. 'They have to work like conveyor belts.'

The women were never allowed out of the office, and all they had in addition to the back rooms was a bathroom. Breaks only came occasionally, when the offices in the Square Mile were closed.

That was why Anita Klusa ran away, Elza said. It must have been unbearable there.

When Lia and Elza arrived in Catford, Lia noticed Paddy's car already parked on Sangley Road. That was when she noticed her uneasiness: the entire taxi ride she had been out of breath, and her heart was racing.

The drive from Shepherd's Bush had only taken forty-five minutes since it was still the middle of the afternoon. They couldn't hope for the traffic to hold, so they could stay at the house only for perhaps twenty minutes.

After asking the cabbie to wait, Lia showed Elza number 182. Elza looked at the covered windows and nodded.

They walked around behind the end-of-terrace house. Lia had decided with Paddy that the back garden was the best way to approach whoever was living there. Lia checked that no one else was in sight as they opened the gate and stepped in.

Slowly they walked up to the back door. Lia moved to the side, up against the wall, and motioned to Elza to do the same. This was one of Paddy's precautionary measures: if someone discharged a weapon from inside, they would be out of the line of fire.

The house looked completely empty. Blackout curtains covered the windows. None of them even twitched.

Lia had thought about trying to get the attention of those inside by knocking on the door, but Elza got straight to the point.

'*Labdien*!' she yelled in a loud voice.

'*Labdien! Te Elza Berklava.*'

They waited for a moment. Nothing came from inside.

Elza repeated the greeting as well as her own name.

Silence. Lia looked at the other gardens in the row. The chilly December weather was not luring anyone outside. She saw Paddy standing behind a fence, a few dozen metres away.

Elza looked at Lia and then spoke towards the door again. And although Lia did not understand anything but the name – Daiga – she realised what Elza was relaying.

Daiga was dead.

The silence lasted for a moment. Then suddenly from inside, directly behind the door, came a woman's cry. Lia did not need any help to understand what was going on.

Time stopped. All that existed was the wail of a mother, a cry of agony choked behind a hand.

Elza placed one of her hands on the door, caressing the dark, painted surface.

She said something in Latvian, comforting Daiga Vītola's mother.

From behind the door came another voice, a young woman, who said something to Elza.

'Ausma?' Elza exclaimed.

Elza spoke feverishly, and someone replied from inside. Questions flew in both directions. Over this exchange of words floated the mother's hoarse lamentation, which she continued to attempt to stifle with her hands.

Elza interpreted the conversation for Lia.

The women had been prisoners since the spring. Vanags had brought them there directly. He had told them he would kill them instantly if they attempted to escape, made a noise or did anything else that might make others notice them. Vanags had said that the doors and windows were wired with explosives that would detonate if they tried to get out.

'But I don't believe that,' Elza pointed out.

Lia instinctively took a step back. However, she had to admit that the explosives threat sounded unlikely.

Elza continued the conversation. Daiga's mother's name was Henriete and the daughter was Ausma Vītola – Daiga had been using her maiden name in recent years because she wanted to forget her husband.

Henriete and Ausma were not in any distress, but they were very afraid.

Ausma believed that Vanags would force her into prostitution. He had made advances at her several times, but by screaming the women had made him back away. Vanags had announced that if the girl wasn't any fun, he intended to get his money's worth for her.

Lia checked the time: already twelve minutes had passed.

She considered what to do. Could Paddy get the grandmother and daughter out of the house? That would take tools and was unlikely to go unnoticed in the neighbourhood.

'The problem is that if they stay here, Vanags may realise they have been in contact with us. And if we take them away and report it to the police, Vanags could do something to you or the other women on Vassall Road,' Lia said.

Elza stared at the ground, her face turned white.

'I don't believe they can stay quiet about this long,' she said, motioning at the mother and daughter behind the door.

Henriete asked Elza with whom she was speaking.

'She's a Finnish woman, Lia, who wants to help you. She found you,' Elza replied in English.

Behind the door, they understood.

'Thank you, Finnish Lia,' Henriete said in English.

'We need time to decide what to do,' Lia said. 'Tell them they have to wait a little, but we'll be back soon.'

'*Nē*!' Ausma's shout came straight away. 'We aren't staying here!' she continued in English.

Elza said something to the girl in Latvian, and she quieted down. Lia pulled Elza to the side.

'Convince them to be quiet just for tonight,' Lia said. 'When Vanags comes to bring them food, he mustn't notice anything. Tomorrow we'll help them get out.'

I have no idea how we're going to do it. But do it we must.

The convincing took some time. While Elza calmed Ausma down, Lia phoned Mari and reported on the situation.

Lia looked at the clock on her mobile: twenty-one minutes. They had exceeded their time limit.

'Now we have to be hard,' she said to Elza.

Elza nodded. She ordered the women to be quiet and wait.

'We're going to come back,' Lia said, knowing she was saying it as much to herself as to the two women who were to remain behind the locked door.

As they climbed back in the taxi, Elza said nothing. She simply cried.

Lia calculated they were six minutes late already.

'Please do hurry,' she said to the cabbie as she asked him to take them back to Shepherd's Bush. He replied that he would do his best.

As they started back the way they had come, towards the Old Kent Road, Lia wondered at what seemed a circuitous route, but assumed the driver knew his trade. But after travelling for only twenty-five minutes, the traffic took a turn for the worse. Apologising, the cabbie informed them that it appeared an accident on the roundabout at Elephant & Castle had snarled up the entire area. There went their timetable.

Lia asked Elza to call her friends at the shopping centre to tell them she was going to be late. Elza did not have a phone – she and the other prostitutes were not allowed anything like that – but she rang the beauty shop on Lia's mobile. There the staff called one of Elza's friends to the phone. The conversation was brief.

'They'll be fine,' Elza said after ringing off. 'They can tell the carder whatever they want. But if Olafs comes looking for us, things will go wrong.'

'Olafs? Who is he?'

Olafs Jansons was the gangster who ran the women at the Creed Lane brothel. He frequently drove Elza and her friends to the Westfield mall and back to Vassall Road. Elza described Jansons: he was a tough bodybuilding type with a shaven head.

The bald man. Of course he had to come from somewhere.

Jansons was the number-two man in the gang that maintained the Latvian brothels. He had started as a guard but had risen to manage Creed Lane. Above him was only Vanags.

'I know he's beaten people to within an inch of their lives,' Elza said. 'Customers who didn't pay and an enforcer from a rival gang.'

The taxi was moving again, but still at a crawl. Lia felt as though her brain couldn't process all of her questions quickly enough. Where was Paddy?

'Give me a sec,' Lia said and rang Paddy.

Paddy answered immediately, informing her that he was just a few cars back and had been watching them the entire time. Lia explained the problem. The line was quiet for a few seconds.

'How far do you think the budget will stretch?' Paddy asked.

'I don't know,' Lia replied. 'Quite a way.'

She thought of Mari and the wealth she never wanted to speak about in specific terms but which seemed elastic enough to allow her to accomplish whatever she wished.

'All right,' Paddy said. 'We'll stop at the roundabout. There is one faster way to Shepherd's Bush, but it will cost six thousand pounds. I'm ringing off now. I have a call to make.'

Lia turned back to Elza, whose eyebrows were raised.

'Now you are just going to have to trust me and my bodyguard,' Lia said.

At Elephant & Castle, Paddy edged ahead of the cab and led them to a car park, where Lia threw some banknotes at the bewildered driver.

They gathered on the pavement and Paddy pointed at the roof of the next building down.

'There.'

They ran into the building, one of London's countless office blocks. In the lobby, Paddy cast about for the lifts and led them to the closest one. They sped up to the topmost floor.

Once there, Paddy went out first, glancing to either side and nodding for them to follow. They passed two office doors. All the time, Paddy was scanning for something. Finally he found what he was looking for: a plain door with a sign that read 'Staff only'.

The door was locked, but Paddy pulled from the inner pocket of his coat a jangling bundle of small metal implements, somewhere between keys and tiny tools. Lia recognised the bundle, since it was just like the one Berg had used to open the door to Gareth Nunn's flat.

A moment later they heard a click and the door opened. Behind it were stairs leading upwards.

The door that opened onto the roof was unlocked. Running out into the light, they instinctively bent double as a wave of ear-splitting noise and pressure washed over them. A helicopter was landing on the middle of the roof.

The landing was not entirely smooth: the pilot was forced to correct his angle of descent several times before he dared set down the entire weight of the helicopter.

When the skids touched the roof, Paddy told Lia and Elza to follow him. He opened the side door of the chopper and they climbed up into the shaking and thudding machine.

Sitting on the benches, they fastened their safety belts as Paddy directed the pilot to take off.

Only after they had been flying through the skies of central London for about a minute did Lia realise that none of them had said anything. Paddy was concentrating on the route. Elza's serious expression revealed that she was simply trying to keep her wits about her amidst all the confusion.

Lia herself was too astonished to speak. She had never flown in a helicopter. She stared at the London Eye to their left and the skyscrapers of the City to their right, which from this perspective looked new and smaller.

'Two minutes,' Paddy announced. He almost had to shout to make himself heard over the din.

'I didn't know that ordering a helicopter was this easy,' Lia yelled back.

'This is illegal. Or, the flying isn't illegal, but the flight path and landings are. That's what's costing us. And the short notice.'

They passed over Marble Arch.

Might they get caught? Lia asked.

'Of course. If anyone notices.'

Almost immediately the helicopter reached Shepherd's Bush. It didn't land on the shopping centre roof, since the sight from inside of a helicopter flying so low over the glass roof would attract unwanted attention, but the pilot found an appropriate spot on the top of a neighbouring building.

When the chopper's skids touched down again, Paddy was already opening the door. Lia and Elza needed no admonition to move quickly. They were all out within seconds.

Paddy gave the pilot a thumbs-up, and he rose back into the air.

Then they ran to the rooftop door and down the stairs.

The block was another large commercial building, the top floor of which was used by an asset management company. The guard at the door stared at them as they charged down from the roof to the lift. But the lift arrived quickly, and they got away without any trouble.

Paddy took a few deep breaths and evaluated the situation. The building security cameras would have pictures of them, but the helicopter had touched down on the roof so quickly that that was unlikely to cause any problems.

'The whole trick is that it has to happen instantly. So quickly that the air traffic control authorities don't have time to start asking questions.'

How had he managed to hire a helicopter so quickly? Lia asked, still astonished.

Paddy explained that he knew the owner of the company. The firm had six helicopters, several of which were always either in the air or standing by on the ground. They could get a bird in the air over London anytime. Usually they ferried corporate coshes from one meeting to another, but Paddy sometimes ordered last-minute jaunts. Helicopters were only supposed to fly specific routes in London airspace, and they weren't allowed to land just anywhere, but for a special premium the owner was willing to take the risk.

Elza listened to the conversation, looking pale and glancing at her watch. Lia checked the time. They had three minutes left of their original two hours.

The lift arrived at street level.

'Paddy and I shouldn't be seen with you any more,' Lia said to Elza. 'You should go back to the beauty parlour alone.'

Elza nodded without saying anything.

She's scared. She's scared to death.

'I'll see you tonight in the corner shop on Vassall Road,' Lia said. 'I'll be there around eight o'clock. We'll meet there, and I'll tell you what to do. All that's required of you now is to stay calm.'

'I'm not the one to worry about. The question is whether Henriete and Ausma can stay calm,' Elza said. 'Tonight, eight o'clock, at the shop.' Then she crossed the street.

Lia and Paddy waited a few minutes. They saw a large, black van pull in to a space at the bottom of the stairs leading to the shopping centre. Lia recognised the driver: the bald man, Olafs Jansons. Unintentionally she flinched, drawing back behind Paddy as she remembered her latest narrow escape from the thug. Elza and three other women came out of the shopping centre and climbed into the van, which turned into the flow of traffic and disappeared from sight.

'What happens now?' Paddy asked.
'I don't know,' Lia said. 'I don't have the faintest idea.'

36

Mari answered Lia's call immediately. She listened for a moment and then interrupted. 'How much time do we have? Until eight tonight? Good.'

Mari was at the Fitzroy Museum and asked Lia to meet her there. Paddy got a few hours off, which he was glad to take.

When she reached the museum, Lia purchased a ticket and walked up to the hall between the fourth and fifth galleries.

Mari was sitting in her usual place, on the bench in front of *Double O*. Her concentration was total as she watched the circles of film flitting in the air between the enormous fans.

Here she can be at peace no matter what happens.

Lia sat down beside Mari and told her about the events of the day so far.

Mari listened in silence, and Lia noticed that her expression didn't change at any point. She seemed indifferent to the price of the helicopter ride.

Lia handed her Daiga Vītola's picture. She did not need to say who it was. Mari looked at the picture for a long time and then lifted her eyes to the whirling piece of art.

Her face was serious, and when she finally looked at Lia, Lia could see the deep sorrow in her eyes. Mari still did not say a word.

What is she thinking? I can't make it through this by myself.

'All we have are hard choices,' Mari finally said. 'I've been trying to think whether we have any way to handle this so that Vanags will definitely end up in jail and the women will definitely go free. But we don't.'

It was possible that the police would find evidence against Vanags, but there was a serious chance that they would not be able to connect him to the murders. Having Vanags remain at large would be dangerous for them all.

Mari had also attempted to clarify what the Latvian women's status was in Britain. She had called a lawyer who specialised in immigration rights. The situation was difficult and ambiguous, the solicitor had said. Daiga Vītola's family and the Vassall Road prostitutes might not be allowed to stay in Britain and might be deported to Latvia.

If the women did not make their presence known to the authorities and attempted to stay on in the country on their own recognizance, their lives would remain difficult. They would have to stay in hiding, and they would not be able to keep in contact with relatives or friends. If information of their whereabouts got out, Vanags would be able to find them.

Lia understood. There was no expedient that would resolve the women's situation outright.

Is this what this is like? We research. We plan. We risk our own safety. But even with all that we can't do any good.

'Can't we help them get away to somewhere else?' Lia asked.

'Of course we can. But where do we draw the line? If we help them, why don't we help the women at the three other brothels as well?'

They could give the women money to get by for a while. They could help them engage lawyers, but none of them were going to be granted asylum. People in Latvia were not living in extremis.

'Latvia is a perfectly reasonable place to live. At some point our assistance has to stop,' Mari said.

She motioned to the installation in front of them.

'We have to remember that the Baltic is also like this. They have art, artists, normal life. Perfectly normal people. If Elza and the others return to Latvia, their life there might be just fine.'

These women had been injured in a way that had changed their lives. The prostitutes had all taken a risk coming to London, and that gamble had turned out badly. Lia and Mari could ameliorate the situation somewhat but not completely.

They could not ensure these women a good future. That they had to do for themselves.

'This is a question of fairness,' Mari continued. 'We dispense fairness, not justice.'

Lia realised that Mari was speaking from experience.

She has been in situations like this before.

But they had to get the women out of mortal danger, Lia insisted. The most important thing was to get the prostitutes and Daiga's family to safety. Everything else would happen if it happened. Perhaps Vanags would be convicted for his crimes.

'We'll help the women out of danger, and then they can decide what to do. At least they'll get to choose themselves,' Mari said.

She stood up.

'Have you also been thinking about Fried all this time?' Lia asked.

'I've been thinking about everything.'

On the way to the Studio, Mari sketched out the strategy.

They called Paddy in to talk it over. By six o'clock, the plan was ready.

Lia wondered whether she could go home for a bit to take a breather, but time was too short. She stayed at the Studio and found a place to rest in the Den. Lowering one of the hammocks from the ceiling of the dining area, she climbed in.

She could see a strip of dark sky and the industrial buildings across the way. A warm light shone on the walls, coming from the large windows of a warehouse that had been converted into a gallery.

She heard the sounds of work echoing through the Studio. Mari walked from room to room, talking to the others. She conversed quietly with Berg, giving him instructions for the following day.

Lia thought about what she would soon have to do. Just a little while before it would have frightened her, but now she was strangely relaxed.

Just after seven o'clock, Lia set off towards Oval. On the way she received a call from Paddy. According to the plan, he had followed Kazis Vanags and checked that he would no longer be on Vassall Road when Lia arrived in the area.

At a quarter to eight, Lia found herself a dark spot across the road from the corner shop.

Time passed slowly. Eight o'clock arrived with no sign of Elza.

At six minutes past the hour, Lia saw Elza walk down the street and enter the little shop. Lia quickly followed.

Between the shelves, Lia related her suggestion in hushed tones. The plan was simple. Elza listened carefully. When Lia was finished, Elza had only one question.

'And then what? Where do we go?'

'You'll have to decide that yourselves.'

Elza nodded. She took Lia gently by the shoulder.

'Thank you,' Elza said, embracing her.

She turned and began filling her shopping cart with cigarettes and fruit. In her hand she held a white piece of paper with a list.

Cigarettes. Tabloids. Bananas. And something for starting a new life, Lia thought.

37

The next morning at 9.40 they set the plan in motion.

Lia was sitting with Paddy in a car on Vassall Road. First thing that morning she had rung *Level*'s company doctor to report she had the flu. The female doctor had ordered three days' sick leave, which Lia accepted without guilt.

The signal came from the top floor of number twelve. A window opened and a hand appeared holding a small white towel. The hand waved the towel several times.

Lia watched in the rear-view mirror as two men climbed out of the vehicle behind them. Large, both in jeans and leather jackets, Alan Scott and Fergus Anderson were security professionals whom Paddy used regularly.

Paddy got out of the car and went with them into the stairwell. Lia stayed in the car and counted the seconds.

Up the stairs, twenty seconds. To the door. When Elza opens it, quietly inside.

Regroup outside the toilet, ten seconds. Charge in – five seconds, maybe ten.

They surprised the Vassall Road guard sitting on the toilet.

The signal at the window had come from Elza. They took down the guard in the unlocked bathroom, not giving him a chance to grab his weapon or call Vanags.

At 9.47 a.m. the window to the flat opened again. The same white towel was waved.

Lia exited the car, locking it. After climbing the stairs to the top floor, she waited outside the door. She didn't ring the doorbell, to prevent the neighbours from noticing that anyone had called.

Paddy let her in. On his right temple was the beginning of a bruise, apparently from a fist.

The mood in the flat was tense. Elza and the three other women were standing in the middle of the large front room staring at the guard, who was lashed to a chair. Elza looked relieved, the others startled and frightened. They hadn't known in advance what was going to happen.

The guard was a young man of compact build. His trousers hung open, and his face also bore the marks of a struggle. Fergus Anderson had covered his mouth with three layers of thick duct tape.

Getting that off is going to hurt.

The guard's eyes roamed nervously, moving from woman to woman and then focusing on Paddy and his broad-shouldered sidekicks. Lia he looked at most intently.

He's thinking that because I came last, I'm in charge of all of this.

Lia pulled out her mobile and rang Berg.

'Two minutes,' Berg said.

Elza spoke to the women in Latvian. Lia could not understand the words, but knew what Elza was explaining. The women had to decide now, quickly, what they wanted to take with them.

Where are we going? they asked.

Elza had ready the response Lia had given her. To a safe place for a few days. After that they would have to take care of themselves.

The women collected their belongings in a state of shock, but Lia could see that the sight of the guard, bound and cowed, had done them good. It was a signpost to freedom.

At the window, Paddy motioned for Lia to come and look. They watched as a large, white camper van rolled onto Vassall Road. Amidst the cars it looked like a ship gliding along. There was still space for it to park though, because at this time of day many residents had already departed for work.

The move from the flat took place in a tumult of tension and confusion. Originally they had planned that Paddy and his assistants would leave immediately. But now Paddy had changed his mind.

'That bloke is so slippery that he might get out of those ropes pretty quick.'

They decided that Scott and Anderson would stay to guard him for at least half an hour. No customers usually came to the flat that early.

Lia led the women down the stairs. Knowing the seriousness of the situation, they did not make a sound.

They carried their hastily packed bags to the camper van, where Berg was waiting. Paddy watched their progress and then went to his own car, ready to follow them.

Berg beamed at the women.

'Welcome aboard! We're going to have a lovely couple of days together,' he said loudly.

Despite her tension, Lia had to smile. Berg was the perfect contrast to what the women had just left behind.

Berg watched while they all found seats, and then he moved up front. Lia started to come up next to him, but Berg shook his head.

'You're needed back there.'

Of course. He's right.

Lia returned to sit with the women. As the vehicle started and glided slowly forwards, she introduced herself. 'I'm Lia. From Finland.'

It was a strange drive.

The women peered out the windows at London. They had all been in the city for years, but still they pointed at the famous sights as if they had never seen them before. Soon Lia understood what was new to them: they were driving through it all for the first time as free women.

Now they look like places they could actually visit some day.

They headed for Catford. On Sangley Road, Berg parked the camper van a little distance down from number 182 for safety's sake.

Lia and Berg asked Elza to accompany them, and Paddy joined them on the street.

'Mr Helicopter,' Elza said in greeting.

'Just call me Paddy.'

At this, Lia realised that they had never had time to be properly introduced.

Paddy said he had just called Rico, who was in Leyton keeping an eye on the Eastern Buffet. Everything was in good order. Kazis Vanags was in his shop.

They circled the building again to the back garden. With Paddy in the lead, they approached the rear door of the house cautiously.

Lia nodded to Elza, who knocked on the door. Elza only managed to say her name and a couple of sentences before a cry came from within.

They all jumped. Then they realised that it was a joyful noise. Daiga Vītola's daughter Ausma began speaking.

'They want out right now,' Elza said. 'They're just afraid because they were told that the doors and windows are primed with explosives.'

Lia glanced at Paddy and Berg. They had remembered the threat as well.

'I still don't believe it,' Paddy said.

They had described the place to Berg earlier, and it did not take him long to come up with a solution.

'Inside there has to be a fuse box with a mains breaker. Ask them to turn it off,' he told Elza.

While the women searched for the master switch, Berg fetched one of his tool boxes from the campervan. This one contained more gadgets than his basic tools.

From inside the house, the women announced they had switched the electricity off.

Berg pulled out the small device Lia had already seen him use at Gareth Nunn's flat. Berg pointed the gadget at the house, and lines appeared on the small display.

'Since the mains electricity is off, there shouldn't be any sources of current inside. Unless the bomb has its own battery or its power is connected somewhere else,' Berg explained.

Slowly he scanned the door and windows. No sign of an electrical field showed up on the device, just the same flat line.

'Clear,' Berg said.

Of course it was possible that a booby-trap that didn't require a power source had been attached to the door or window. But no one really used anything like that any more. They were bloody-minded systems that tended to decide on their own when to explode.

'I'm ready to bring them out.'

From his pocket, Paddy produced the set of lock picks he had used previously to open their route to the helicopter. After looking at the lock, he chose a tool.

The lock resisted. Paddy worked intently, and a minute later came a click as the bolt opened.

Paddy pushed the door wide open, and they looked at the two women standing together, wrapped in each other's arms in fear.

When no explosion came, the women's expressions relaxed. The younger of them let out a shriek and threw herself at Elza.

The older woman stared at them all. Then she burst into tears.

Getting the situation calmed down and Henriete and Ausma Vītola out of the house took about ten minutes.

At first they were talking so feverishly with Elza at the back door that Paddy led them all inside to avoid attracting additional attention. Then they had to collect their things. They did not have much, but they hadn't packed since they had not known when they would be getting out.

Before leaving, Henriete also wanted to thank Lia, who was embarrassed by the outpouring of gratitude. After shaking Lia's hand several times, Henriete took her in her arms and hugged her.

Lia stood in the unfamiliar house, which had been these women's prison for so many months, and embraced Daiga Vītola's mother. She had to wipe tears from her eyes.

Now I know why I had to do this. If only for this one moment.

When Henriete and Ausma were finally ready, Paddy carefully closed the back door of the house. They moved back to the campervan. Elza and Henriete were speaking together seriously.

They're talking about Daiga. And about what will happen now.

When the three women waiting in the vehicle saw Ausma and Henriete, a renewed wave of frenzied conversation and hugs ensued. Everyone was talking over everyone else.

Lia could see there was no point in attempting to convince the group to sit quietly in their seats. Elza noticed her concerned expression.

'You sit there in the front seat,' Elza said. 'We need a little time to work some things out, and no one will have time to translate for you.'

Lia abandoned the commotion in the back to sit with Berg up front.

Berg started the camper van, and this time Paddy drove ahead of them, as if to break a trail, leading them towards the main road that would take them out of London. When she glanced in the rear-view mirror, Lia saw the group of women sitting close together talking, holding each other by the hands, laughing and crying.

If only for this one moment.

38

When they had been on the road for approximately an hour, Paddy rang Lia.

Scott and Anderson had notified him that they had closed up the flat on Vassall Road behind them. They had bound the guard again, but he would probably get free during the course of the afternoon.

'That's enough,' Lia said.

She then rang the police exchange and asked them to connect her to Detective Chief Inspector Peter Gerrish.

'I have a tip about the Holborn Circus and Hyundai murders.'

'We have other officers collecting public tips. I can connect you to...'

Lia interrupted.

'You ask Gerrish whether he wants to accept a tip from Lia Pajala.'

Half a minute passed and then the call went through.

'Gerrish.'

'This is Lia Pajala. Do you remember me?'

'I do. What do you have?'

'A tip. The one I talked about before.'

She told him that in Leyton was a shop named the Eastern Buffet that sold precisely the same combs they had found with the remains of the woman in the white Volvo.

'Is that so? Interesting. Is that all?' Gerrish asked impatiently.

'No. The first victim's name was Daiga Vītola and the second's was Anita Klusa. They were Latvian prostitutes.'

The line fell silent.

'Where did you get this information?'

'That I can't say. But in about an hour I'll be able to tell you more. Then you need to be ready to make an arrest. It would be best to do it quickly, because he's most likely behind both murders.'

'Hold on. You know of someone who could be a suspect for both murders?'

'Yes. But I can only tell you more in about an hour. You just prepare to make the arrest.'

'Why do you think you can order the police around?'

'I don't think anything of the sort. I'm just offering you tips. In return for what you told me before.'

'If you have reason to suspect someone of these women's murders, it is a crime to delay providing that information to the police…'

'I'll ring you in an hour. Be ready.'

Lia rang off. Mari's plan required self-confidence, and, from somewhere, Lia found it.

She rang Mari's number and gave a report on events so far.

At 12.52 p.m. Paddy pulled into a campsite, followed by Berg with the camper van.

The Twineham Green Caravan Site was small, and it was so close to Christmas that no one else was there. It was a stark sight: a few bare trees, a concrete building for the showers and toilets, and the site attendant's hut. The camp host was astonished to have so many vehicles show up. Berg parked on a pitch near another, smaller camper van, which was waiting at the edge of the campsite area.

Lia and Berg told the women in the back that for the next few days they would have the use of the smaller motor caravan as well as the larger one they were in. All told the two vehicles held beds for ten.

'Berg and I will stay here with you,' Lia said. 'Berg does snore, so we may have to cast lots to see who sleeps with him.'

The women were excited to get out and stretch their legs, even if the place was just a bleak caravan park.

Lia and Berg learned Elza's companions' names: Alise, Kamilla and Rozalinde. The women also wanted to tell them the names they used as prostitutes. The name had to be simple so the client could remember it, and it had to sound Eastern European. Kamilla had chosen to be Anya. Alise was Elena. Elza was Olga, and Rozalinde used the name Katya.

Amidst all the buzz of conversation, it took Lia a moment to realise something was wrong.

She couldn't see Daiga Vītola's mother Henriete anywhere.

Attempting to contain her anxiety, she searched the area. Kamilla and Rozaline were smoking outside the large camper van. Elza and Daiga Vītola's daughter Ausma were sitting talking in the smaller vehicle. Berg was chatting with Alise about British television shows and adjusting the large camper van's TV aerial.

Lia checked both toilets. No one.

Paddy was sitting in his car making a call on his phone. Lia waited for him to finish and then went to tell him what was worrying her. Together they went through the entire campsite and both camper vans again. There was no sign of Henriete anywhere.

'I don't think she's disappeared here at the campsite,' Paddy said.

He had been in his car the whole time and could see the camper vans and the people moving about around them. If Henriete had gone off for a walk, Paddy would have noticed.

'Let's ask Elza,' Lia suggested.

They could see instantly that Elza knew what was up.

'No, Henriete isn't here. She decided not to come.'

'Where? When?' Lia demanded.

'When we left Sangley Road. She wanted it that way.'

'Why? What does she intend to do?'

'I'm not sure. I imagine she intends to have it out with Vanags over Daiga and Anita's deaths.'

Lia and Paddy stared at each other, speechless.

'Damn it. Does she have a weapon?' Paddy asked.

Elza nodded.

'What weapon? Where did she get it?'

'A pistol,' Elza said. 'I don't know what kind. It was the Vassall Road guard's gun. I took it when you tied him up.'

'Damn, damn, damn!' Paddy cursed, turning around on the spot.

'I looked for a gun, but when I didn't see one, I assumed that he didn't have one,' he said to Lia.

'Do you know that Henriete could end up dead because of this?' Paddy snapped at Elza.

Elza looked at him and then at Lia for a long time.

'I know, and so does she. She decided this herself.'

Lia felt as if the entire situation had turned upside down. She rang Mari and explained the new state of affairs.

'Do you have any specific idea what Henriete intends to do?' Mari asked.

Lia asked Elza, who shook her head.

'Good,' Mari said. 'She probably won't go out looking for the Eastern Buffet, since she doesn't know London. But she could be waiting on Sangley Road to see whether Vanags comes there after hearing the prostitutes escaped.'

'And I'm supposed to ring Gerrish and tell him about Vanags soon.'

'Ring him now. Ring right now. Maybe they'll have time to arrest him. And in the meantime, you can pick up Henriete and get her to safety.'

Lia's hand was shaking as she dialled the police exchange number again.

'Detective Chief Inspector Peter Gerrish. He's expecting my call. This is Lia Pajala.'

Reaching Gerrish took only a moment. Lia began telling him Vanags' name, but Gerrish interrupted.

'The owner of the Eastern Buffet shop you mentioned. We looked it up. Why do you suspect he killed these women?'

'That's what my source told me. That's all I can tell you. I don't have any evidence.'

She gave Gerrish the address to Vassall Road. The police were sure to find evidence linking at least one of the murdered women to that flat.

'Pick up Vanags from his shop for interrogation. And his companion from that flat.'

'Do you know whether he's armed?'

'No, but I would assume the worst. You have to hurry. I assume he'll try to destroy any evidence in the flat.'

Gerrish thought for only a few seconds.

'We're going to speak again,' he said and then rang off.

Lia rang Mari back.

'Go to Sangley Road. Henriete may not listen to you, but she's sure to listen to Elza,' Mari said.

Elza did not resist when Lia asked her to come along. Paddy, on the other hand, was reluctant.

'We aren't a strike force of some kind. We're talking about a woman who's been held prisoner for over six months and is out of her mind with grief. And Vanags might be there too. Not a good combination.'

But he didn't have any better suggestions.

'Let's go. And hope nothing has happened yet.'

Leaving the other women for Berg to keep track of, they set off in Paddy's car.

The mood in the car was tense. The journey still took more than an hour, even though Paddy sped most of the way. Mostly they were quiet, lost in their thoughts.

'I don't know whether Henriete knows how to use a gun,' Elza said. 'She asked me where she could get one. I had it in my purse just in case. I hadn't thought of giving it to her.'

Lia could see on Paddy's face that he felt like shouting at her. But Paddy controlled himself.

They were only five kilometres from Catford when Lia's mobile rang. It was DCI Gerrish.

'Kazimirs Vanags isn't at the Eastern Buffet,' he announced. Vanags had left the shop about an hour earlier, in a terrible rush, had said the young woman who stayed to watch the place.

'That's bad news,' Lia said.

'Where else can we find him? Will there be others at the Vassall Road flat, and are they armed?'

'I would imagine he would have gone there. And yes, there could be others. He seems to have several assistants who help him run the prostitution ring, all of whom you might call professional criminals.'

'Right. If you hear anything...'

'I'll ring you straight away,' Lia said.

Paddy swore again when he heard that Vanags had escaped the police.

'This could go badly wrong for a lot of people now.'

'But not for the women at the Twineham Green campsite,' Lia said. 'He won't find them there.'

Elza cast Lia a small, thankful smile.

Paddy parked the car on a side street near Sangley Road and turned to speak to Elza.

'I've already taught Ms Pajala here a little about operating in dangerous situations and how to take instructions. We're not just rushing in there. You both walk behind me and only talk if I say it's OK.'

Elza nodded.

From the outside, number 182 looked just as deserted as before in the pallid afternoon light.

Paddy walked slowly round to the back garden and approached the door cautiously. Lia and Elza followed behind him. At the door, Paddy motioned for them to crouch against the wall on either side of the doorway.

'Ask if anyone is there,' Paddy said to Elza.

'*Henriete, vai tu tur esi*?'

No answer.

Elza made to stand up, but Paddy stopped her with a wave of his hand.

'Again.'

Elza raised her voice. '*Henriete? Vai tu tur esi*?'

A reply came from somewhere inside the house. '*Elza, tu*?'

It was Henriete. Elza engaged in a short conversation with her and then translated.

'She says we should come inside. She says there are things we need to know.'

Paddy and Lia looked at each other hesitantly. Lia grabbed the door handle. The door opened, although Paddy had left it locked.

When they stepped into the living room, they heard Henriete moving around in the adjoining room.

'Come here,' Henriete yelled in English.

Paddy pushed the bedroom door open. They saw Henriete standing against the wall. From her left shoulder ran a trail of blood.

Henriete was holding a large handgun, aiming it across the room. She would not for a moment take her eyes from the point she was targeting.

'Come here,' she said again.

'Not as long as you have that gun,' Paddy said. 'If you put down the gun, we can come in.'

Henriete understood without an interpreter. She smiled and said something in Latvian.

'OK,' Elza translated. 'Stay there. I just want you to hear this.'

From the other side of the room came a cough. It was the man Henriete was covering with her gun.

'Is it Kazis?' Elza asked.

No answer.

'Kazis Vanags, are you in there, you son of a bitch?' Elza screamed.

From the bedroom came male laughter.

'I'm here,' Vanags said. 'You and the girls decided to run off.'

Lia recognised Vanags' voice from the time she had visited his shop. The sound made her heart pound even harder.

He sounded as if speaking was difficult. But still his tone carried a threat. He spoke to Elza as the owner of an animal might, intent on disciplining his pet for its foolishness.

'Elza, you know running away is one of the things you get punished for.'

'Ask her what she wants,' Paddy said to Elza.

Elza obeyed.

Henriete's reply was long, and as she listened, Lia's blood ran cold seeing Henriete's expression.

She means to kill this man.

Finally Elza interpreted the answer.

Henriete wanted Vanags to pay for Daiga's death. She had been waiting for him outside. She had known he would come here after hearing his whores had escaped. She knew that he would come here intending to kill her and her granddaughter.

When Vanags had come to the door, Henriete forced him to enter at gunpoint. Inside he attempted to overpower her. He turned and slashed at Henriete with a knife. She fired three shots. Two hit home. One shot to the arm, another to the chest.

Henriete added something.

'She says it isn't enough yet,' Elza interpreted.

Hoarse laughter came from the bedroom. Vanags said something to Henriete in Latvian.

'He called her a mother of a whore,' Elza said, her voice dark with anger. 'This is a very bad insult in Latvian.'

I'm not surprised.

Lia swallowed and tried to get Paddy's attention. They had to try to defuse the situation. Paddy shook his head: too dangerous.

Henriete spoke to Vanags in her halting English.

'I want you tell to them same thing as to me. Tell them how you kill Daiga and how you kill Anita.'

Vanags coughed. His breathing was laboured.

'Tell them,' Henriete ordered, shifting her grip on the pistol.

'Very well,' Vanags said. 'I killed Daiga, because Daiga was stupid. I told her many times how things work in our houses. But she was always arguing. I was ready to kill her before, but then she was still bringing in money. Then she smuggled you here, her old mother of a whore and daughter of a whore. Then I thought why should I look at this ageing whore who isn't making me much any more and thinks she's something. So I shot her.'

Lia, Paddy and Elza listened in silence. Tears were running down Henriete's cheeks. She stared at Kazis Vanags along the barrel of her gun.

Vanags described how he had been transporting Daiga's body in his car at night to dispose of it. Olafs Jansons was with him. Jansons had seen a building site at the side of the road. There was a steamroller.

'Jansons suggested that flattening her beyond recognition would be the perfect punishment for a mouthy whore. We put Daiga on the road and I drove over her with the steamroller. Back and forth. At least ten times. It was hard shovelling all that shit off the road.'

Once the men had collected the remains of the body, Vanags had decided that they could use it to teach a lesson to his other whores.

'To you, Elza, and the others. So we got the Volvo and put her in the back.'

Henriete used one hand to wipe her eyes and nose.

'And Anita?'

Vanags was quiet for a few seconds before answering.

'Doesn't everyone already know? Anita escaped from Creed Lane with Loreta. We caught Loreta and killed her. Anita managed to hide. Then she made a mistake. She got in touch with her brother in Latvia. The brother told everyone that Anita was having problems in London. We found her, and I shot her to smithereens. With a machine gun.'

Vanags went silent.

'How?' Henriete asked. 'Tell everything.'

They had a warehouse for storing imported goods, Vanags said. In the middle of the warehouse was a large concrete pit for getting underneath lorries in order to service them. They had taken Anita down there. They turned on all of the warehouse lights so she could see where she was and that she couldn't get out. She had seen that Vanags had a machine gun. In the warehouse they had dozens of Soviet PKMs stored for sale.

'I told Anita to try to escape. She just stood there. In the middle of the pit.'

Vanags had fired a burst in front of her. She jumped and started running. Vanags kept her moving by firing short bursts after her as she ran from wall to wall in the confined space.

'She fell. And then I shot her to pieces. First from a distance and then up close. The head came off and the legs almost did too, at the ankles. It made such a fucking mess. And we made an example out of her, same as Daiga. But not in a Volvo. We put her in a Hyundai. We aren't stupid like Anita. We don't leave stupid clues.'

Lia, Paddy and Elza could not see Vanags as he spoke, but they did not need to. They could hear the mockery in his tone.

'Why did you kill them?' Henriete asked in English.

'Why? What a stupid question,' he replied, laughing.

'Why did you kill them?' Henriete screamed.

His answer was brief.

'They didn't obey. My whores obey me.'

Henriete shifted her stance, standing straight instead of leaning against the wall. She drew herself up, keeping her eyes glued on Kazis Vanags. She began speaking again, this time in Latvian.

'*Bestija*!' she said. '*Bestija*!'

Henriete spoke quickly, spitting words out of her mouth. Elza didn't have time to interpret or say anything.

Henriete closed her eyes. When she opened them again, she fired three quick shots.

It happened so quickly that none of them could brace themselves for the sound. Lia, Paddy and Elza instinctively hit the floor.

The shots were like small explosions. They filled the house. The pressure reverberated through them all.

Complete silence fell. The force of the blasts had blocked their ears.

When they looked up, they saw Henriete still standing there, unmoved.

Paddy looked at Henriete until he could make eye contact. The rage of a moment before had disappeared without a trace.

'OK?' Paddy asked.

'OK.' Henriete said the word slowly and carefully.

Henriete tossed her pistol aside. Paddy stood up and entered the bedroom. Taking a handkerchief out of his pocket, he picked up the weapon and walked around the door.

He's making sure Vanags is dead. Can a person survive gunshots from that close range?

A moment later Paddy came back into view. Lia saw the answer in his expression.

'We have to leave now,' Paddy said. 'We can't do anything here.'

Lia and Elza stepped into the bedroom. Elza went to Henriete and took her gently in her arms.

Lia stared at Kazimirs Vanags' corpse on the other side of the room. Her first reaction was to look away, so much blood had spattered everywhere. But she ordered herself to see this thing.

Vanags was half sitting against the wall. Henriete had probably hit him with all three shots. The bullets had ripped holes through his chest. His head hung to one side, frozen against one shoulder.

'The neighbours may have heard,' Paddy said, and Lia understood. They had to leave.

She and Paddy quickly conferred. What should they do with Henriete?

'She's just murdered a man,' Paddy said. 'The first shots, when he attacked her with the knife, could be considered self-defence. But not those three. This is clearly murder.'

'But she killed the man who killed her daughter. And he kept her and her granddaughter prisoner for months. He was the man who intended to force her granddaughter into prostitution,' Lia said. 'Let's go back to Twineham Green to the others. We need time to consider what the right thing to do would be.'

'I don't know if extra time will help with that,' Paddy said.

They concealed Henriete's shoulder wound with a coat, and then Elza led her firmly but tenderly to the car. Paddy wavered over what to do with the weapon Henriete had used. Removing a murder weapon from a crime scene was a serious felony in itself. But the gun had Henriete's fingerprints on it.

In the end he decided to keep it.

No curious neighbours were visible outside the house – apparently the shots had not been loud enough outside for anyone to raise the alarm.

Elza and Henriete sat in the back seat of the car, Henriete leaning against Elza as though all her strength had abandoned her.

Lia sat in the front. Paddy leaned over from the driver's seat and placed something in the glove box. It was Henriete's gun.

'Do you know what she said?' Elza asked.

Lia and Paddy understood what Elza meant. Henriete's words to Vanags a moment before she shot him.

'She said, *bestija*, beast. She said, "Now you go to hell. And when I follow you there, I will kill you again. I will always kill you again. I will kill you a thousand times."'

Silence fell inside the car.

They were just about to leave when Paddy stopped.

'Who knows how long it could take the police to find Vanags' body. If no one heard the shots, the police have no reason to search that house.'

Lia understood the problem.

'The police will be wasting time and resources looking for a man they'll never find. And in the meantime, Vanags' comrades can escape or cover their tracks.'

'Vanags' car has to be here somewhere,' Paddy said. 'We should take a look at it. We may be able to use it to get the police interested in the house.'

Lia and Paddy found the car quickly. It was only parked fifty metres away. They tried the doors, but of course they were locked.

'Vanags must have the key,' Paddy said. 'We have to get it.'

Lia waited on the street while Paddy returned to the house. He did not linger at the unsavoury task any longer than necessary. Within a minute he was back, and Lia did not ask anything.

Paddy opened the car, glancing through the interior quickly and then inspecting a bag that had been left on the floor.

Lia kept an eye out for passers-by. A moment later, Paddy emerged from the car holding something which Lia recognised as a sat-nav.

They could not take it with them, since the police would need it in their investigation. But Paddy wanted to download the information in its memory so they would know where Vanags had driven to. Paddy had a program on his computer which could copy the data.

He headed back to his car, and Lia stayed to watch Vanags' car. The street was quiet, with no one in sight.

Lia saw Paddy turning on his laptop in the front seat of the car and explaining something to Elza.

A breeze picked up, and Lia started to feel cold. She opened the door of Vanags' car to get in. Then she saw a figure in dark clothing quickly approaching Paddy's car.

The bald man. Olafs Jansons.

A lot happened over the next twenty seconds. Lia tried to scream, but a paralyzing fear choked her voice.

Jansons was holding a pistol in his hand and pointing it straight at the windscreen of Paddy's car. He was about twenty metres away, ready to shoot.

He means to execute them right here on the street.

Lia threw herself into the car and slammed the horn on the steering wheel. The warning was high-pitched and loud.

The sound made Paddy lift his eyes from the computer screen. At the same time, Olafs Jansons turned for a fleeting second to look back towards the sound. Paddy's headlights flashed, and Lia understood that he had started the car. She saw that Paddy did not have time to turn around.

Jansons was approaching them on the pavement, but then suddenly changed course, loping into the middle of the road and continuing towards the car.

He's trying to stop them from driving away.

Paddy's car careered into motion. Jansons stopped reflexively, and then he shot. He fired two shots towards Paddy, who was driving directly at him.

Jansons dodged by spinning to the side. Lia saw the shots smash through the windscreen. She could not see Paddy, Elza or Henriete.

The car darted down the street, and when it corrected its direction, Lia understood that Paddy must still be in the driver's seat. He had crouched down out of sight. Jansons shot at the car again, but then lowered his gun. He turned around, still in the middle of the road, looking for eyewitnesses.

Only when he started walking quickly towards Lia did she realise that she was still blasting the horn. She raised her hands, and the deafening wail stopped.

She had barely had time to even think of fleeing. Olafs Jansons was already standing a few metres away and raising his weapon towards her.

Paddy sat up carefully in the driver's seat and slowed down. They had sped off down Sangley Road, leaving the bald gunman behind, but Paddy could not see the street properly. The gunshots had thoroughly shattered the windscreen.

He glanced into the back. Elza and Henriete were huddled out of sight on the floor.

'Are you alright?' he yelled.

Elza raised her head and looked at Henriete.

'Yes,' she said.

After rounding two corners, Paddy realised he could not go on.

He braked and then stopped the car completely at the kerb.

'What now?' Elza asked.

'Lia.'

There was no feeling in Jansons' eyes, Lia thought. The way he looked at her, she could have been inanimate.

Jansons pointed his weapon at her, but that was not what made Lia powerless. Instead, it was the tension in his bearing. He knew that something was going very wrong. Three people had just slipped out of his grasp, and he had no room to let Lia escape as well.

'Door open,' he said.

Lia pushed the front door, which had never clicked shut, the rest of the way open.

Jansons moved to the side of the car to get a better line of sight. Lia realised he was also holding his pistol behind the door so no one else could see it.

She considered whether she could kick or hit him in a way that would make him drop his gun. She abandoned the idea immediately.

They stared at each other for at least twenty seconds. Lia saw that Jansons was weighing his options. Then he nodded towards her feet.

'Open the boot. The lever is under the seat.'

Lia felt under the seat until she found the lever, which she pulled. When she heard the boot lid pop open, she realised what was about to occur. Her chest clenched as if someone had sucked the air out of her.

Jansons did not need to say anything. He motioned once with his gun. Lia slowly climbed out of the front seat.

She felt Jansons press the barrel of the pistol into her back and butt her into motion. Lia stepped behind the car, the barrel in her back the whole time. Jansons shoved the boot the rest of the way open. Again he pressed Lia with the barrel of the pistol, and Lia knew what he wanted.

She tried to focus on breathing. It was getting so hard.

I have to climb in the boot, just like Daiga and Anita.

This is where I'm going to die.

Jansons prodded her again, more forcefully this time. It hurt. Lia leaned against the edge of the car. Her back was aching. Her hands were shaking.

Suddenly a blow came from above and she did not think anything any more.

Paddy evaluated the situation.

The car was still fit to be driven, and he could steer despite the broken windscreen. Elza and especially Henriete were in a state of shock, but neither of them had been hit. And the cut on Henriete's shoulder was not bad. They were in no immediate danger.

But Lia was.

The bald gunman could already have killed her. But if he hadn't, what would he do?

'Do you know the man who shot at us?' he asked Elza.

'Yes. Very dangerous.'

Elza briefly described Jansons: the most hardened type of criminal.

Paddy had to make a decision.

'Stay here in the car and keep quiet,' he said, climbing out.

As he started walking back towards Sangley Road, he checked the pistol in his inner coat pocket. He took out his mobile and dialled Mari's number. He needed reinforcements.

Lia lay in the luggage compartment of Vanags' car trying to calm her breathing.

The pain in her head was so intense that it made her curl up in a ball.

She was not sure how much time had passed. She looked for her mobile in her coat pocket, but it had disappeared. Jansons must have taken it.

Carefully she tried the boot lid catch. It wouldn't open. She remembered hearing the car's automatic locks clicking shut. Of course he had locked the doors. There was no emergency release.

Where had Jansons gone? Did he not mean to kill her after all?

The automatic locks buzzed. Jansons had returned.

Lia did not have time to do anything before she felt the car rock. Jansons climbed in, locking the doors again immediately and starting the car.

He's taking me somewhere. I can't get out.

Paddy crouched low behind another car parked on Sangley Road and watched while Jansons started Vanags' car and drove off. There was no sign of Lia.

Jansons had just returned from the house. He had come out very quickly after finding his boss shot through the chest. But where was Lia?

Paddy watched as the car disappeared. He rounded the house again. He knew he had to act quickly, and ignored the need to take precautions. The back door was still unlocked, and Paddy held his weapon at the ready as he ran through the rooms.

His instincts told him Lia was not there even before he had checked the house. There was only Vanags' corpse in the downstairs bedroom.

Paddy exited through the back door and went to look at the place where Vanags' car had been. Still no sign of Lia. So she was in the car, with Jansons.

On the way to his own car, he rang Mari again and briefly related the situation. They had never had an emergency like this before, but Paddy heard Mari's reaction from her voice: she set her feelings aside, acting as a rescue worker would, concentrating on the facts.

Elza was waiting in the car, ashen-faced. She had sat up, as had Henriete, who was holding her eyes shut.

'Lia isn't there. Jansons probably took her with him. Do you know where he could be going?' Paddy asked.

Elza thought for a moment.

'Jansons is in charge of a place in the City where five women work. But I don't know where he lives.'

'It's unlikely he would take Lia anywhere with other people.'

'Yes. They must have some warehouses. Kazis talked about the one where he killed Anita. I don't know where it is.'

Paddy looked at the GPS he had taken from Vanags' car, which had been thrown on to the floor in the recent getaway.

'This knows,' he said and picked up the sat-nav.

The drive took at least fifty minutes, Lia thought.

In the dark and close atmosphere of the boot she tried to concentrate on the passage of time. That gave her something to think about. Something other than what was happening.

Lying in the boot was pure torture. Her head hurt, and she did not have space to stretch out her arms or legs. They had all gone numb.

The engine roared in a wall of metallic sound, filling the entire space.

One second. Two seconds. Three seconds.

Periodically she counted off the minutes. Absurd thoughts ran through her head.

How long does thinking the word 'second' take?

She felt every braking and acceleration. The motions of the car tossed her about. At times she felt nauseated and worried she would vomit.

When the sound of the tyres changed and the car began swaying even more, Lia realised they had turned off the road.

A sudden braking and a stop. Jansons switched off the engine. The automatic locks opened with a whine.

Lia tried the boot again. She couldn't prise the catch open from inside. And she wouldn't have had time to get anywhere anyway.

Footsteps in gravel moved around the car, and the boot opened. Jansons pointed his gun at her. The sudden light hurt Lia's eyes.

This was what it had felt like for Daiga, Elza and all the other women when they were smuggled into Britain, Lia realised. Only much, much worse.

Paddy searched the GPS for locations Vanags had stored in memory.

Twenty-one places in London. Paddy quickly recognised the addresses Vanags visited every night: Vassall Road, Sangley

Road, the Assets club. But Jansons would hardly take Lia anywhere so populated.

Paddy searched the locations on the outskirts of London stored in the GPS. There were four: in Chatham, Harlow, Rickmansworth and Sutton. Was one of those the place?

He called Mari, who was at the Studio and immediately took the phone to Rico.

Rico typed the addresses into his search programs.

A minute passed while Rico gathered information about the type of structure at each address and what occupied it, as well as aerial photos of each.

'I would rule Harlow out because there are so many companies housed around there,' Rico said.

'We're probably looking for a warehouse. The one where they killed Anita Klusa,' Paddy said.

Rico and Mari sifted through the information as quickly as they could.

'Sutton. 1392 Kimpton Park Way. That has to be it. The only business registered there is Vanags' Riga Trade. That's the only one that looks like a warehouse from the outside.'

Paddy immediately entered the address in his own sat-nav and started the car while he was still on the line with the Studio.

'We're ten to twelve minutes behind.'

Mari said she had reached Alan Scott and Fergus Anderson. They were on their way, but getting to Sutton would take time.

'And the police?' Mari asked.

'If the police come, we'll all end up being interrogated. That would make it more likely for Jansons to be arrested, but I don't know whether it would help Lia at all.'

This was a decision neither of them would have liked to make. But time was short.

'No police,' Paddy decided. 'Not yet. If there is anyone besides Jansons at the warehouse, then we'll call in the authorities.'

The warehouse contained big, dusty machinery, lots of boxes and a few chairs. Lia had to wind her way through it all as Jansons forced her inside.

Lia saw the concrete pit in the middle of the hall. Her knees sagged. The pit looked smaller than she had imagined and more frightening.

Jansons ordered her to walk down into it.

Slowly she descended the concrete ramp. She had only taken a few steps along the bottom of the pit when Jansons said, 'Stop,' in a clipped, commanding tone.

He talks that way to take power, to keep me in his grasp.

Jansons inspected his mobile phone for a moment. He kept one eye on Lia as he read his messages.

Lia saw on the edges of the concrete pit the steel grates that could be placed over it, allowing for cars to be serviced from below.

She realised what the dark marks on the floor and walls of the cement pit were.

The brightness of the fluorescent lamps lighting the warehouse made the dried bloodstains look blackish brown. There was blood everywhere. In the centre of the pit, along the rough concrete floor ran a wide, dark trail. Someone had sprayed water into the pit to wash the blood away. The dark stream had run down to a shallow drainage trench along the centre of the pit. Lia made the mistake of looking at the drain hole. The wire grille was full of bloody gunk and small bits of something unidentifiable.

This was where they had killed Anita Klusa. This was where they had shot her apart with a smuggled machine gun.

Lia closed her eyes, but that made her even more afraid. She opened her eyes and looked straight ahead, fixing her gaze on the wall above the pit. All that had on it was dirt and grease.

They forced Anita to run when they fired. I won't run. I won't run even if he tells me to. Or will I be able to stop myself running when he shoots towards me?

Jansons pointed his gun at her. 'Sit.'

Lia sat on the concrete floor. She tried not to look at the bloodstains.

She couldn't help thinking about Anita Klusa.

Less than a week had passed since her murder. In that time the bloodstains had already stopped stinking in the cold warehouse. It just smelled musty.

Jansons slipped his mobile phone into his pocket and looked at Lia. She couldn't tell much from his face. Lia understood that for both of them, their options were running out.

Paddy parked his car a few hundred metres from the warehouse. He identified it easily: several other industrial buildings were close, but only one had light shining from its windows so late at night.

Paddy had learned from Scott and Anderson that they were still half an hour away. Too long.

He rang Mari and reported the location of his car. She could guide the reinforcements in.

'If they can't contact me, their first task is getting Elza and Henriete to safety. Then they can come looking for Lia and me.'

After ringing off, Paddy turned to look at Elza. 'You stay here.'

'We will,' Elza said firmly.

Paddy set his mobile to silent and climbed out of the car. Switching the safety off on his gun, he started walking towards the warehouse.

Kazis Vanags' car was parked out front. Paddy approached the car, scanning the area.

No one was inside. The boot was open.

'Who do you work for?' Olafs Jansons asked.

Lia stared at the man standing before her on the edge of the pit and thought about what would be the right answer. Was there any answer that would help?

'You aren't with the police,' Jansons said.

'No, I'm not,' Lia said. 'I've been looking for a woman named Daiga Vītola.'

Jansons eyed her closely.

'Why?'

'I wanted to know why Daiga Vītola was killed.'

Jansons' expression did not change.

'Who killed Vanags?' he asked.

Lia kept her mouth shut.

'It wasn't you,' Jansons said.

'No. It wasn't me.'

'Who was it?'

'A woman Vanags had hurt.'

Was that a smile Lia saw flit across his lips?

'There are many women like that. Dozens. Who was it?'

Lia did not utter a word.

I don't want to say Henriete's name. If there is any justice in the world, I won't have to say Henriete's name.

Jansons' phone beeped, and he stopped to read the message that had arrived.

Another moment. I have another moment left.

Henriete Vītola opened her eyes.

She looked at Elza, who was sitting next to her, and Elza saw that Henriete was back in this world.

'How are you?' Elza asked.

'Not well. But that doesn't matter. What are we doing here?'

'We're waiting to see whether the Finnish woman is dead. Lia. Olafs Jansons took her into that building there. Paddy, the bodyguard, went to see what he could do.'

Henriete looked somewhere far away.

'Finnish Lia is there,' she said. 'Who is Olafs Jansons?'

Just like Kazis Vanags, Elza said. Just younger. A man who has killed many people, but has just not had time to kill as many as Vanags. The man who keeps women in slavery at a brothel in the City, and the man who came up with the idea to crush Daiga's body with a steamroller.

Henriete looked straight ahead for a long time.

Then she opened the rear door of the car and slowly got out. Elza saw that she was favouring her left arm, the one Vanags had cut.

Henriete opened the car's front door and leaned in. She opened the glove compartment and fished something out. Outside she straightened up, holding the pistol in her hand. The gun's magazine was empty.

'Do you have any bullets?' Henriete asked in Latvian.

Elza swallowed.

'Yes.'

'Where?'

'In my bag.'

'Give them to me.'

Elza stared at Henriete. She extended her handbag to her.

'This is not good,' Elza said. 'Everyone is going to die.'

Henriete took a small clip from the bag and slid it into place in the handle of the gun.

'I already died,' she said. 'I died when they took Daiga from me.'

The text message made Jansons impatient.

Lia could see it in his face. He started typing into his phone but then he stopped.

It's bad news. Maybe he's heard that the prostitutes from Vassall Road are gone. He's worried about his own girls.

'Who was that man? The one driving the car,' Jansons asked.

Lia remained silent. She could see this made him even more annoyed.

'You have ten seconds to start talking.'

Jansons raised his gun. Now it was pointing directly at Lia's face.

How many bullets does he have? Has he reloaded since he shot at Paddy's car?

'I'll talk,' Lia said. 'He's my friend. He wanted to help me.'

'Where did you take the whores?'

Shuffle the deck. Bluff.

'I don't know. I really don't.'

'I saw you at a nightclub and on Vassall Road. Where did you take the whores?'

'I wasn't in charge of that. I just wanted to get Daiga Vītola's mother and daughter free.'

Lia looked Jansons straight in the eyes. She looked at him so she would not have to look at the gun. She saw how his face went hard.

He's going to shoot me soon.

'For the last time,' Jansons said. His voice was cold and sharp. 'Where did you take the whores?'

A thundering noise split the air. Lia realised that the blast had not come from Jansons' gun. There was a puff of cement at his feet, and he collapsed with a yell.

A bullet had struck Jansons in the right leg.

Lia threw herself as flat as she could. She saw Jansons hesitate for a moment and then jump into the pit. As his right leg hit the floor, he snarled in pain.

Lia turned to look behind her. Who fired the shot?

She couldn't see anyone over the wall of the pit.

Then Jansons was next to her, grabbing her by the arm and dragging her up. Pressing his gun to her throat, he drew her close to him. He turned Lia between himself and the gunman as a shield.

Everything went quiet. All Lia could hear were the pounding of her heart and Jansons' panting.

At the back wall of the warehouse, behind some storage shelves, she saw movement. Jansons stared at the head that flashed between the shelves and then withdrew behind them. Lia recognised Paddy.

They heard Paddy's loud voice.

'Let her go. Let her go, and you can go yourself.'

Lia felt Jansons' grip on her tighten. He pressed the pistol even harder against her neck, into the spot where the back of her head met her spine.

Silence fell again.

Jansons took a step back, drawing Lia with him. He walked backwards, slowly, favouring his right leg. He forced Lia to follow pressed against him.

Lia tried to slow him down, but his grip on her was too strong.

He knows that Paddy won't shoot as long as I'm between them.

Slowly they retreated towards the end of the concrete pit and then up the ramp.

'Stop!' Paddy yelled.

Jansons only sped up his steps after making it up the slope to the main warehouse floor. He glanced at the route to the door.

Lia felt the hard barrel in the back of her neck, and infinite sorrow filled her suddenly.

He's going to get away. He'll take me to the car and lock me in the boot again.

'Stop!' Paddy yelled, but Jansons already knew that Paddy wouldn't shoot and continued moving towards the door.

At the door, Jansons paused.

Lia could feel his uncertainty. He shifted her position in front of him slightly. Lia guessed what he was thinking. Paddy was far away on the other side of the room, but were there reinforcements outside?

Jansons cracked the door with his elbow and then glanced out. Lia saw a glimpse outside as well and her heart fell in disappointment.

No cars. No police. No one.

Jansons waited for a second and then made his decision. Placing his good left leg in the opening, he levered the door with his back and dragged Lia outside with him, glancing nervously back in Paddy's direction as he did.

Then the door behind Jansons swung open suddenly and he faltered, trying to keep his balance. Instinctively he loosened his grip on Lia to prevent himself from falling, and Lia collapsed to the ground. Jansons was not able to stay on his feet. He spun, dropping awkwardly to his knees and trying to stop his fall with his hands, searching for the attacker he expected to lash out at him.

Outside the door stood Henriete Vītola, pointing a gun at him.

Lia saw Henriete's face as she looked at Jansons.

Jansons lifted his weapon, but Henriete was too fast.

She pulled the trigger so many times that the magazine emptied and the pistol began clicking ineffectually in her hand.

When Lia opened her eyes, she saw Jansons' bullet-riddled corpse lying across the threshold, half outside and half inside.

Henriete stared at the body and the forming pool of blood.

Henriete looked at Lia, and Lia knew what she was thinking.

Bestija. The beast had been felled.

39

They were led to the car.

Elza held Henriete under one arm. Paddy supported Lia on his shoulder.

Nothing hit me, Lia thought. *I'm fine.*

Henriete shot both of them. She is the strong one here.

A little later she thought that if anyone were to see them, they would seem a strange troupe.

In the car Lia and Henriete were placed in the back seat. This time Paddy put the weapon Henriete had used in a bag, which he took to the boot of the car.

Paddy also went to retrieve Lia's mobile phone. He found it in the warehouse, in the pocket of Jansons' jacket. He returned Vanags' sat-nav to his car after wiping his fingerprints from the device.

They set off towards the Twineham Green campsite in a silence broken only by Paddy's call to Mari.

They were safe, Paddy said. Lia, Henriete, Elza, all of them. Olafs Jansons was dead.

Mari announced she was setting off to meet them and would tell Scott and Anderson to stand down.

When Paddy pulled into the camping area, it was already late in the evening.

The camper vans waiting in the darkness were an unreal sight. The light from their windows shone far into the surrounding fields, and when Paddy stopped the car, they all sat there for a moment to take in the effect. It was as if the muddy, deserted caravan site had come to life, and the circle of light around the camper vans seemed to be protecting them.

The mood in the larger camper van was warm. The women had all called home to Latvia during the day. The vehicle had been filled with weeping and squeals of joy. Berg had made food – pasta and vegetable sauce. They had opened several bottles of wine.

When the women saw Henriete and her bloody shoulder, a concerned confusion broke out, but Elza informed them that no one was in any danger and all Henriete needed was a little patching up. As if by mutual agreement, none of them told what had happened.

Henriete smiled at everyone who spoke to her, but she did not reply, seeming to have slipped into a half sleeping state.

Paddy cleaned the wound on her shoulder using the first aid kit in one of the camper vans. The cut was not deep, and he was able to bind it relatively tightly. They gave Henriete painkillers and water. Within half an hour she had fallen asleep on the bed. Ausma sat next to her grandmother and held the hand of her unhurt arm.

Lia sampled the wine Berg poured for her, wondering why she felt so strange.

Berg boiled another batch of pasta so Lia, Elza and Paddy could eat. Soon they heard the sound of another car outside. It was Mari.

Lia realised she had never known that Mari owned a car. Or perhaps she had rented it. She was too numb to give the matter any more thought.

Mari and Paddy went to the other camper van to talk through everything that had happened. They considered whether to take Henriete or Lia to a doctor, but neither seemed to be in need of that level of help. The best thing for them now was sleep.

Elza came to tell them that the women were doing relatively well. After seeing Henriete and Lia's state, they had put off thinking what would happen to them later, accepting that first they simply had to get through the present moment.

When Elza left, Paddy asked, 'What will we do with Henriete?'

'Nothing,' Mari said.

None of them wanted to give her up to the police. They were sure to ask Lia about Vanags and would also find Jansons. But Henriete had suffered too much, and Mari could not see any reason she should have to go to jail.

They rejoined the group in the larger camper van.

Lia asked Mari to come to her. She was extremely tired, but wanted to talk.

'How are things with Arthur Fried?'

'Don't worry about that. I'll take care of Arthur Fried. There's nothing you need to worry about now.'

'Good. Now I'm going to empty my head of thoughts,' Lia said, showing her wine glass. 'It feels like I have a lot to get flushed out. Do we still have any wine left?'

Mari poured her a full glass.

'I've been thinking about you,' Lia said.

'Really?'

'Do you know what kind of person you are? You're a *työihminen*.' She needed the Finnish word to express how at one with her work Mari was.

Sometimes people would say that someone was a *hyvä työihminen*, a good work person, Lia continued. But the adjective was pointless. If someone was a *työihminen*, that word alone said how responsible and competent she was.

'And you are.'

Mari nodded and allowed Lia to express everything running around in her head. Lia's thoughts wandered here and there, but she did not speak at all of the day's events.

As Lia began to nod off, Mari moved on to chat with Elza and the other women. She made the acquaintance of everyone in the whole group, except Henriete who was fast asleep.

Then Mari left for home, and the others also began to move towards their beds. The small camper van became the men's quarters and the larger the women's. The women were a little crowded, but everyone preferred things this way.

Lia fell asleep quickly. Berg had given her a sleeping pill, because, despite her exhaustion, she didn't think she could quite fall completely asleep.

Berg was the last one awake and made the rounds of both vehicles before going to bed, checking that all the doors were locked. He did not really fear anyone coming to such an out-of-the-way campsite, but he was used to looking after important people.

40

On Wednesday morning, Lia woke up to Berg shaking her awake.

'You're going to want to see the news,' Berg said, pushing a coffee mug into her hands.

Lia sat up on her small bed in the camper van and squinted at the morning news broadcast. Two seconds later she was wide awake.

The lead story was that Fair Rule was suspected of supporting groups convicted of staging racist attacks using secret money transfers. The police had made a surprise raid on the party headquarters, seizing computers and files. The office would remain open, but party secretary Gallagher had already announced that their work would be slowed down until the issue had been resolved.

The reporters had interviewed Gallagher because Arthur Fried was incommunicado. The police had asked Fried and Gallagher to appear for questioning regarding the irregular support payments.

Lia looked in Berg's face for an explanation.

'Wasn't this supposed to come out a couple of days from now? What happened?'

Berg shrugged.

'I moved up the schedule,' Mari said when Lia reached her on the phone.

Mari had asked a favour of a private detective she knew a few days earlier and arranged for the information to be given to the police immediately.

'It felt right. The Latvians' case came up. You, Paddy and Berg are there now. And that's as it should be. You need to be there.'

Arthur Fried would be instituting counter-measures to survive the tax evasion revelation. Mari had wanted to give him something new to think about as soon as possible. If Fried was spending all his time responding to enquiries regarding racist groups, he wouldn't have time to plan a rescue operation for his reputation.

'That will give us at least a couple of days. Then I need you back here. And Paddy and Berg too of course. How are you doing?'

'I don't know. I feel sort of numb.'

'Take it easy. Call me whenever you want. Even if you just want to talk.'

The day was unique in every way.

Lia watched the news, which was filled with analysis of the latest Fair Rule scandal. Many of the commentaries suggested that the party had fallen into a tailspin from which it was unlikely to recover, at least not before the general election.

As she watched the news, images from the previous day also flashed through her mind. Being forced into the boot of a car. The bloodstains on the concrete pit in the warehouse. Henriete Vītola with a pistol in her hand. Kazis Vanags' and Olafs Jansons' limp bodies.

That the news was not full of those pictures felt strange to her. Suspicions of racism directed at a political party seemed insignificant compared to what had happened to them.

Over the course of the day, Lia, Berg, Paddy and the six Latvian women formed a strange family. They busied themselves preparing food and playing card games together. They talked a lot, but not a word was said about the previous day.

The father and mother of the family was Berg, who listened to and bolstered them all up. Elza and the other women from Vassall Road were the sisters, unfailingly loyal to each other.

Lia learned much about each woman as the day wore on. She soon found it difficult to connect them to prostitution and everything else in their past. She thought she could sense shadows of the past now and then in the melancholy with which they regarded certain things. The way they threw themselves headlong into games and jokes made it seem they wanted to forget all of that.

Paddy was the family's mischievous older brother, who turned out to be a master card player and dominated every game. Under his direction they played a long game of poker with Paddy circling the table doling out advice.

Lia was unsure what was going through Ausma Vītola's mind. She participated in everything they did together, but she was quiet.

Two days ago she heard about her mother dying a gruesome death. She's had to live for months in a locked house, not knowing what would happen to her. She's just a girl, and the world has already showed her cruelty in all its forms.

Henriete and Lia were objects of protection and nurturing, and they accepted it all with gratitude.

Lia surreptitiously watched Henriete's condition. She sat with the others, but did not participate in the games and only spoke when directly addressed.

In her eyes there was something very serious and resolute. Lia believed she knew what was in Henriete's mind: She had decided to survive.

In the afternoon, while most of them were napping, Elza approached Lia.

'How are you doing?' Elza asked.

'Pretty well.'

Lia said she was seeing nightmarish images even when she was awake but was starting to feel fine otherwise.

'How long do we have to stay here?' Elza asked.

'Not long. Until tomorrow. Tomorrow everyone has to decide where they are going.'

Lia and Mari had thought about housing the women at the campsite for longer if necessary. But there was no sense putting off decisions they would have to make eventually in any case. That wouldn't help anyone, and the possibility that one of Vanags' criminal associates would pick up their trail was always there. They had to move forward.

'Right. I'll talk to the others,' Elza said.

At around four o'clock, a woman in her forties pulled up to the caravan pitch. Fiona Gould was the lawyer specialising in immigrant rights with whom Mari had spoken before and whom she had hired to advise the Latvians.

Lia expected that the question about their future would dampen the mood, but the opposite was true.

Fiona Gould was quite something. She spoke in a loud voice and laughed even louder, and everyone found her both extremely professional and sharp-witted. She described the women's options precisely and realistically.

That they were Latvians, EU citizens, theoretically gave them certain rights in Britain. The problem was that most of them had entered the country secretly and none of them had passports – Vanags had taken them. Four of them had worked as prostitutes, which was legal in Britain in itself, but since they had worked under pimps it was not. Laws had been broken, but who was actually culpable was unclear.

They were exceptional cases. It was obvious that they had no right to asylum, because Latvia was a stable country. Even the fact that they had been held captive did not make any difference – it could matter in the cases against the men who had kept them prisoner, but it would not bring them a new life in London.

Fiona Gould did not sugar-coat their prospects.

'Of course I'm duty-bound to advise you to follow the law and present yourselves to the authorities. However, it is possible that you will be deported to Latvia. Latvia may be an EU country now, but that happened recently enough that you still needed a permit to live and work here for so long. Even if the authorities allow you to stay, you won't qualify for state benefits for twelve months, so living and looking for work will be very difficult. Should you stay illegally, your situation would be even worse.'

Hundreds of thousands of people came to Britain in search of work each year, many of them illegally, Gould said. Estimates suggested that within less than a year about half of newcomers returned to their homelands or went elsewhere because life in the country had proved too difficult.

A return to Latvia could be the better choice for most of them. Especially if they had friends or relatives there.

The women considered their options. None of the quartet from Vassall Road wanted to return to the brothels, which was a big relief for Lia. If one of them had wanted that, their escape from their pimps would have caused them serious difficulties.

They had a difficult decision to make. Originally they had come to London voluntarily as sex workers. But then to all intents and purposes they had been turned into prisoners and had had to make what they could of their lives, living in constant fear. Their previous lives they had mentally set aside.

For them London had been a jail, but it was a prison surrounded by potential wealth. The thought that the city could offer something else fascinated them. A return to Latvia meant returning to loved ones, but also to the difficult questions that had led them to London originally: how would they survive, how would they earn their living?

Lia asked them about their work on Vassall Road and how the customers had treated them. She wanted to understand what they had been through.

The women replied briefly and seriously. Yes, the work had been punishing, and in their free moments they hadn't had the energy for anything more than staring at the television. No, the customers had not been violent, but some were certainly clumsy, heavy-handed, a little vile, treating them with the contempt they thought a whore deserved. They were all thirty years old or more. That was old for a prostitute, since most men wanted women in their twenties. Often they had been sold at a discount: before 5 p.m. was happy hour and regulars received their own mark-downs.

Before long Elza pulled Lia aside and asked her to put an end to her questioning.

'You're asking this for yourself. It won't help us. You're a lovely person who has helped us in an unbelievable way. But now let us be. That's how you can help,' Elza said.

Lia understood. They had made difficult choices. They were ashamed of what had happened to them and that they had been prisoners. Talking about it only underscored the difference between them and everyone else. They had to break loose from their experience and cope with everything new that was ahead of them.

Fiona Gould overheard Lia and Elza's conversation.

'Don't think you've done anything wrong,' Gould said to Lia. 'This happens when you help people. You can't go any further into people's lives than they want. The person doing the helping often thinks that helping is also about becoming friends. It doesn't work like that. You have to be content to help and also stay a little bit removed. It's better for everyone.'

Like Mari said that time. This is about dispensing fairness.

By the evening the women's choices were becoming clear. Elza and Ausma wanted to stay in Britain, at least for now. Finding work would be a problem, but both were ready to do the basic manual labour that might be available: cleaning or routine task in hospitals and restaurants.

Henriete, Alise, Kamilla and Rozalinde wished to return to Latvia.

The problem was that all six women needed passports. Without those, seeking work in London or travelling to Latvia would be difficult. Even though Latvia and Britain both belonged to the EU, the UK was not part of the Schengen Area which meant you had to show your passport at border control.

Paddy knew how the issue could be resolved. Before he told them, he asked Fiona Gould to go out for a walk.

'This is one of the things you can't be involved with,' Paddy said.

Through her contacts, Mari could obtain fake passports, Paddy told the women assembled in the camper van. They had done it before, and now they just had to get them more quickly than usual.

The women received this information with great relief. Without delay Berg began taking passport photos of them with a tiny camera and recording their dates and places of birth, the exact spelling of their names and their physical descriptions.

'Where will the passports come from?' Lia asked. She remembered her and Mari's meeting with Big K, the snitch, who had connections to the criminal underground.

'It's better not to know,' Paddy said. 'It isn't important to know everything. Let Mari handle this.'

Berg emailed the women's pictures and particulars to the Studio.

Berg sighed. 'This will be expensive,' he said quietly to Lia so the others couldn't hear. 'Six Latvian passports, express delivery. Making them on this schedule will be a small miracle.'

But Mari did not bat an eyelash at the cost. She was only interested in getting the matter settled.

Once the question of the women's future had begun to resolve itself, the mood eased again. The day's discussions with Fiona Gould and the acquisition of passports had dispelled the women's uncertainty.

And, strangely enough, Lia also felt recharged by what Gould had said and the improvement in the women's situation.

There is the law – and society. Yesterday we went far outside both. Today we're crossing those lines again. But soon I'll be back inside.

In the evening they had a party in the large camper van. Fiona Gould stayed and sat with them, making herself at home.

Berg acted as bartender, mixing drinks from what they had to hand. Ausma was DJ, searching the radio waves for songs. The others played cards, smoked, drank and laughed. They talked loudly, English and Latvian mixing fluidly.

Lia was the only one who occasionally sought out the quiet of the smaller camper van in order to watch the TV news. The downward slide of Fair Rule and Arthur Fried dominated the entire night. On every channel, from one broadcast to the next, one question recurred: why was Fried staying out of the public eye?

Fried had not given a single interview since the allegations of his party's support for racists and his company's tax avoidance had come out.

'Fried has long been considered a skilful politician and media strategist, but now he looks more like a coward or lightweight,' observed the host of a Channel Four current affairs programme.

Lia believed Mari would be pleased but didn't ring her. She wanted to focus on her big new family at the Twineham Green Caravan Site.

41

The breakdown came during the night, a little after one o'clock.

Lia had not been able to sleep at all. She had decided to try to get through without sleeping pills. She had stayed quietly in her bed, listening to the sounds of the other women sleeping in the camper van. Light snoring, breathing, rolling over. The air was stuffy – the ventilation was not nearly sufficient for seven sleepers.

Lia's upper body clenched. It was as if an enormous steel beam had fallen on her. Eventually she couldn't stand the pressure in her chest and throat any more.

She had to get out, into the fresh air.

She climbed out of bed, feeling her way to the door and opening it. The night was black.

The campsite lights had been turned off. The moon was dark. Lia could only just see where she was stepping.

She took a few paces, but then realised she had left the door open. She turned to close it, but suddenly she could not move.

The weight had not disappeared. Now it was around her, pressing in on her from every side.

She felt faint. Her legs buckled. She found herself falling.

Lia collapsed to her knees. Her reactions were still functioning well enough that she managed to get her hands out in front of her as the ground rushed up.

She had fallen into darkness. Her head pounded, and the only thing she was able to think about were bloodstains.

Bloodstains on the concrete pit surrounding her. The remains of another human being.

The scream came from deep within her. Lia did not know she was screaming, but then next to her a bright light flashed and someone came running and grabbed her.

This only made Lia scream more. Her agony was naked and intense.

Paddy ran to Lia with a torch in his hand. When her scream turned to a howl of terror at his touch, he released his grip.

Lights went on in both camper vans, casting cones of light onto the black ground. Lia was on her knees, leaning on her hands, as if someone had struck her down. Paddy knew what had happened.

The trauma from two days before had broken through.

Elza and Berg came out but stopped when they saw Lia. Ausma hid behind Elza, staring on in terror behind.

They heard Lia gasping for breath. Suddenly she stopped screaming. She stayed on all fours on the ground, her body shaking, coughing and trying to get oxygen.

Cautiously Elza approached Lia and lowered herself to the ground in front of her.

Paddy illuminated Elza with his torch, so Lia could see who she was. Lia stared without recognition, but gradually her expression changed. In a torrent of tears, the fear began to escape from her.

Elza touched her carefully with her hand, and Lia moved towards her, looking for refuge.

Mari answered the phone immediately, as though she had already been awake.

Paddy briefly explained the situation. They had managed to get Lia laid down, with blankets under her on the ground, and her breathing had stabilised.

Elza was sitting next to her, holding her hand.

'I was afraid of this,' Mari said.

Frightening experiences had to come out, but Mari had hoped they would discharge more peacefully, over time.

'I'll call a psychiatrist. I know one who specialises in victims of violence.'

'How can you get a psychiatric specialist on the phone in the middle of the night?'

Mari said she had already called her twice about Lia and Henriete. The psychiatrist had encouraged her to wait, because people reacted to catastrophes and threats in such different ways. Sometimes thrashing them out with other people just made the problems worse. But the danger of a strong reaction had always been there, so Mari had arranged for her to be able to ring her acquaintance for aid at any time.

Mari rang Paddy back a few minutes later.

'Take her to hospital.'

The psychiatrist had decided that due to her respiratory distress, Lia had to be taken to hospital, but not by ambulance, which might intensify her fear. And not in Paddy's car, because that was the one they were using when it all happened.

'Take one of the camper vans to Princess Royal Hospital Haywards Heath. It's closest. I'll call them right now. We have to get Lia breathing properly first. Then we can think about other things.'

Paddy carried Lia to a bed in the smaller camper van. Lia did not react to Paddy's touch.

'Breathe,' Paddy said to her. 'Concentrate on breathing. We'll get you help soon.'

Elza also went. Berg stayed with the women in the other vehicle. No one could sleep after being awakened so upsettingly, so Berg began making tea.

The A&E department at Princess Royal Hospital was expecting them. They also knew they were accepting a traumatic shock victim – Mari had arranged everything over the phone.

The orderlies retrieved Lia from the camper van, and within a matter of seconds had her inside. They connected machines to monitor her vital signs, and the nurses also began checking her pulse, temperature and pupillary response.

Paddy hesitated to give the hospital Lia's real name and personal information, but secrecy would have been pointless.

The doctor made significant progress in only a few minutes. He seemed like a competent professional. Joe Alderite had clearly been working in A&E for a long time and was used to extraordinary situations.

'What sort of mental trauma?' Alderite asked.

'Kidnapping. She was in mortal danger for several hours. But she doesn't want to involve the police.'

Alderite's eyebrows went up and he wrote some notes.

'And who are you?'

'A colleague from work. One of the people who helped her out of the situation.'

Alderite moved into the examination room where Lia lay. Paddy left out that Lia had also recently been in close proximity when two people were shot to death.

A bad case of shock, Alderite announced when he returned. Lia's breathing was stable, but her EEG and pulse showed that all was not well by any stretch. She was in an overstimulated state that was too much for her body. She was unresponsive when spoken to. Alderite guessed that responding to speech was too great an effort for Lia right now.

Because Lia had no known illnesses and her general state of health was excellent, Dr Alderite believed that slow, carefully monitored care would be best for now. Lia had been put on an intravenous drip, but she was only being given mild sedatives. They wanted to leave room for more medication should the situation change.

Paddy and Elza stayed at hospital to wait, and half an hour later Mari arrived as well. After a short conference, they decided that Mari would stay on watch at the hospital while the others returned to the campsite.

When Mari announced at the hospital reception that she was Lia's next of kin and wanted to monitor her recovery, they asked for her personal data as well.

'What relation are you to the patient?'

'Her sister.'

42

Mari sits in a room at Princess Royal Hospital and looks at Lia lying on the bed.

Lia is sleeping, or resting in a state reminiscent of sleep. She does not seem to be aware of where she is or that Mari is by her side.

Lia's breathing is deep and unbroken. Mari watches her unceasingly.

Mari has seen traumatised people. Lia's condition isn't the worst, but it is serious.

The question Mari must resolve immediately in order to move forward is whether Lia is here because of her.

No. She is not.

Lia is lying in a bed in hospital, with a liquid solution of sedatives slowly dripping into her veins because in April in the City of London on her way to work she saw a white Volvo and was incapable of passing by that car and its monstrous contents without something changing within her.

Mari is partially to blame. She participated in making this possible. Lia met death, first last April at a distance and now face to face, and it was painful for her.

Mari looks at Lia and evaluates the situation. She thinks that Lia will pull through.

If the events of the previous days had happened to the Lia she was just a little while ago, she would surely be in a worse condition now. But Lia has changed, as she has seen herself. She is better prepared for bad things to happen now.

People handle problems according to the scale they are accustomed to.

For many people, seeing a murder or having someone point a weapon at them would be completely incomprehensible. And so it should be. But for Lia, overcoming that sort of fear is already within reach.

Mari's own scale for processing shock and fear is wide, exceptionally large. It grew in situations that caused her an almost paralysing amount of pain and anguish, but she passed through them.

The night slowly marches on. Mari sits next to Lia and watches her.

Early in the morning before dawn she leaves the room for a moment to visit the toilet and to ask the nurse whether she can use her mobile phone in the room. After receiving permission, she returns to the room. She sits down and takes Lia by the hand, the one without the IV tube. Lia does not wake up.

Mari begins scanning the news online with her phone.

Lia is next to her and Arthur Fried is out there somewhere far away – but Mari has a hold on him as well.

43

Lia awoke to a clinking sound. She opened her eyes ever so slightly and tried to focus her gaze.

A hospital room.

She realised she was drugged and lying in a hospital bed. Next to her sat Mari eating breakfast from an ugly yellow tray. Mari noticed her move.

'Sorry. They don't have plastic mugs. Just these porcelain cups that clatter,' Mari said.

Lia smiled, trying to get herself back up to speed. Then she remembered.

The bald man. The car boot. The gunshots. The bloodstains. The camper vans. The family of Latvian women. The lawyer, Fiona Gould. The feeling of safety. That feeling disappearing.

A quiver ran across her face.

'Everything is fine,' Mari said quickly. 'There's no problem. The doctor who examined you said that he wishes he were in as good a shape as you.'

Lia stared at her, and as she slowly gained control of her thoughts once again, she smiled.

'*You* should take care of your health,' she said. 'All that time indoors at the Studio. Not good.'

Lia was not hungry, but Mari helped her drink some juice.

Lia asked about the situation at the caravan site. Mari quickly gave her the bare facts so Lia would not fret too much: Paddy and Berg were still there. Most of the women would leave that day. Their passports were almost ready, and Maggie would arrange their travel.

Elza and Ausma would likely remain at the campsite for a few more days, and Lia could see them soon if she wanted and if she had the strength.

'Everything is fine. And you don't have to do anything.'

At the door a nurse appeared, saying that the doctor would be coming in five minutes to check Lia's status before he ended his shift. The nurse was happy to see Lia sitting up in bed and talking.

Mari said that she was leaving.

'Rico or someone else will come by. You won't have to be alone for long.'

'I don't want to stay here.'

'I imagine they intend to keep you for observation for a little while. If they try to move you to a room with other people, tell them you need your own room and that I'll foot the bill.'

Lia laughed.

'Maybe I want to stay after all.'

Mari said she would arrange a meeting for her with a crisis therapist.

'You're quite enough,' Lia said. 'You and your mentalist tricks.'

Mari was unwilling to make light of the situation.

'I'm a psychologist, not a psychiatrist. And besides, I'm part of the problem. I feel responsible for this, at least in a small way. Not completely, because you wanted to investigate Daiga Vītola's death yourself. But I had my part in it. And I'm sorry for that. I'm sorry that you're here in hospital.'

Lia waved her hand.

'I'm fine. I've got this far by myself. Get out of here.'

The doctor was prepared to release Lia from hospital almost immediately. Her vital signs had been stable all night, and she answered all of his questions with clarity and good humour, reflecting a return of mental equilibrium.

Lia pronounced the doctor's name from his badge and asked him where he was from.

Alderite said he came from the Philippines.

'How much do you know about it?' he asked.

Imelda Marcos' shoes, Lia said. The Philippines had had female presidents, like Tarja Halonen in Finland. And karaoke.

'You all love karaoke, like most Finns, unfortunately.'

'Don't you like music?' Alderite asked in amusement.

'Yes. But karaoke isn't music; it's just the noisy side of drunkenness.'

The doctor laughed.

'You're ready to leave.'

However, he would not let her go without a clear plan for ongoing treatment.

'You absolutely must talk to a therapist and probably keep going for a good while. The intensity of your stress reaction tells me that the situation you experienced was really bad. You don't just get over things like that. Your sister said that she already has a crisis therapist lined up.'

My sister?

Lia took a deep breath while she formulated her answer.

'Thank you, Doctor. I'll be sure to take your advice. My sister is actually one of those people I'll probably need a therapist to survive.'

'She seems like a very capable woman,' Alderite observed. In addition to her own contact information, Mari had left at reception the number of her solicitor, whom the hospital staff could contact if necessary. Mari had even given them the name of the taxi service they should use if Lia was discharged.

'Apparently she's already paid the fare,' Alderite said.

'Of course. That's the kind of sister she is.'

After Lia had had a chance to shower and eat, Rico appeared.

He was glad to see Lia on her feet. What did not delight him was that Lia wanted them to go to the Twineham Green Caravan Site.

'Mari told me to take you to see the therapist.'

'Mari probably has it all set up,' Lia said. 'But first we're going to the campsite.'

One of Rico's good qualities was the ability to play things by ear, so they set out for Twineham Green in the taxi Mari had booked.

The two camper vans at the campsite were in upheaval. Bags were being packed, contact information was being exchanged and goodbyes were being said. When Lia and Rico arrived, all of the women wanted to hug Lia and hear how she was.

Lia hugged everyone and said her goodbyes to the ones who were on their way home. Seeing this recently fledged family before they began scattering to the wind was important for her.

All six Latvian women cried, even Elza and Ausma who were staying in London.

The hardest thing for Lia was saying goodbye to Henriete, Daiga Vītola's mother. Her eyes were hard, and Lia knew the source of that hardness was her grief.

She's lost her daughter and been imprisoned with her granddaughter. And she's killed two men.

I'm having attacks that make it impossible to breathe. She isn't.

I'll probably recover from this. She won't.

They did not talk much. Henriete mostly just repeated one thing: thank you. Lia had no way to reply to that other than by embracing her long and hard.

Paddy offered the ones who were leaving a lift in his car, whose windscreen he had had repaired. He would take them to London, where they would begin their long three-day journey by bus. Fly-ing would have been faster, but passport control was stricter at airports.

Elza and Ausma would stay at the caravan site alone in the meantime, since Berg wanted to go home for a bit.

Lia and Rico took the taxi to the address Mari had given them. Rico accompanied Lia to the waiting room and said he would wait until the session was over. Lia did not resist.

The psychiatrist, Elizabeth Brooke, had been expecting them, so Lia only had to wait fifteen minutes to get in.

Brooke was a small, slender woman, who looked at Lia kindly through large glasses.

'I'm fine,' Lia said. 'I'm sure I'll need help, but I think I could start off more slowly.'

'I heard a little from your friend about how dangerous the situation was you were in. Can you tell me more?' Brooke asked.

She reminded Lia that she was bound by doctor–patient confidentiality regarding everything Lia might tell her unless an extremely serious crime was involved.

How do you define extremely serious crime? Lia thought.

She said that her life had been in danger and that she had seen other people die. She did not say how she had ended up in these situations or exactly what had happened.

'You seem quite brave talking about such shocking things. You're speaking quite calmly,' Brooke said.

Lia nodded.

'I imagine that probably has something to do with feeling like… like I was doing something that was worth it. That it was worth what I went through.'

'Why?'

Lia thought of the four Latvian women who were on their way back to Riga, and of Elza and Ausma at the small campsite in Twineham Green contemplating their new life.

'I can't talk about it. But it was worth it.'

They talked for an hour, and it was easier than Lia had expected. Brooke respected Lia's decision to keep most of the details to herself.

Mostly the psychiatrist asked about everything else in Lia's life. At the end of the hour, Lia realised why.

She's figuring out what my life is like and giving it back to me. Sending me back to the safe version of myself.

Talking to Brooke, Lia found that the great anxiety she had been carrying was gone. The previous night's outburst had drained her dry. Now it felt so far away.

They arranged to meet next one week later. As she was preparing to leave, one question remained in Lia's mind.

'Can what happened last night happen again? Do you think it will keep coming back?'

'That's impossible to say. People react to these situations in such different ways. Usually getting past them takes time. But I think you're doing remarkably well given the circumstances.'

Rico escorted Lia to the taxi and home to Kidderpore Avenue. Sensing that she did not want to be walked all the way to the door, Rico said goodbye and asked the cabbie to drive on.

Lia walked into her basement flat. She was home. She showered again and changed her clothes.

It was three o'clock in the afternoon.

She called *Level* and said she was getting over her flu and was well enough to come to work the following day.

She intended to turn on her computer and read the news, but then she changed her mind. Instead she lay down on the bed and tried to work out how she was coping.

She thought about the bald man, Olafs Jansons, and the weapon in his hand. She thought about falling the previous night at the caravan site.

No tears came. No panic came.

After waiting a few minutes, Lia found herself wanting to get out and move about. She got up, dressed and put some money in her pocket. Along her North End route was an award-winning falafel shop.

44

Arthur Fried made his move on Friday morning at 7.20 during the live broadcast of the ITV breakfast show.

This was the first interview request he had accepted since knowledge of his businesses' tax evasion and Fair Rule's support for racist organisations had come out.

The female host tried to ask Fried several pointed questions, but the five minutes he spent on screen still ended up as a monologue. He had two messages.

The first was that he was innocent and had been unfairly stigmatised. If he was guilty of any mistakes in his business activities, they were unfortunate accidents for which he offered his deepest apologies. Other people handled the party's support payments, but as party leader he took full personal responsibility for rectifying the situation if any illegalities came to light.

Fried's second message was that two days earlier he had been ordained a minister.

'This is why I have kept silent,' he said, looking directly into the camera. 'After these allegations emerged, I had to prove to myself what kind of person I really am. Am I the man I believed I was? Honest, upright, keenly aware of his duties? Or am I two-faced and hard-hearted as some have accused?'

This contemplation had lasted several days. He had spoken with his wife and his family, as well as the pastor of his church.

'I also cried. I cried alone and with my wife,' Fried said.

A glint appeared in the reporter's eye. This was brilliant TV. News reports would be replaying Fried's words all day.

'I cried because I realised that I had failed,' Fried said. 'The success of my party has made me rush forward, overlooking things that I should have handled myself.'

After these meditations, Fried had felt the need to cleanse himself.

'When you correct your path, I feel it's always best to do it in a way that really changes something.'

As a prominent member of the community in good standing, the pastor of his non-denominational congregation had welcomed his desire to enter the lay ministry with open arms and he had given his first sermon the previous day to a small audience in the group's chapel.

'I've never felt so relieved. I know that I'm on the right path now. And I intend to continue as party leader, holding firm to the sense of justice I have now reaffirmed in myself.'

Mari rang Lia immediately once the interview had ended.

'Masterful.'

Fried had not admitted to a single crime, instead shifting all the blame to others, whom he also did not name. He had repeated words such as deep, right, duty – putting across the feeling that he had really reflected on his life.

'And taking orders was a brilliant con. It's complete rubbish but looks important on the surface,' Mari said.

Anyone could become a minister in some churches. There were dozens of loosely affiliated evangelical Christian congregations in Britain, and ordination often required little more than a desire to serve in the church. Some organisations even allowed you to order your priesthood online.

'Isn't that too transparent?' Lia asked.

Mari guessed it wouldn't go down very well with the media or anyone who already thought Fried was suspicious. But it might fool the people Fried needed now: Fair Rule supporters.

Not announcing the interview in advance had also been an expert feint. If anyone had known about it, speculation about Fried's intentions would have been rife. Now it came as a surprise and the first reports of his return from seclusion would just repeat what he had said. The interpretation would come later.

Mari's evaluation was spot on, Lia discovered when she reached *Level*. Everyone was talking about Fried.

'A minister!' Sam laughed. 'That was the best bit of theatre I've seen in ages.'

But in their editorial meeting, Fried was placed at the head of their topics for the next week. The political reporter, Timothy Phelps, was assigned to find an incisive angle to approach it from.

Too bad I can't give Tim what I have. Sarah Hawkins' video isn't going out until next week.

After her long absence, the office felt like a boisterous place. The approaching holidays were keeping everyone busy, especially since they were all also making preparations for Christmas.

Lia hadn't had time to give the holiday a second thought.

As she slogged away at her layout work, she felt better than she had in ages. She had slept well. If she had returned to those recent moments of danger in her dreams, she didn't remember it.

During the day, Sam and Timothy came to say that they had missed her.

'And you aren't Miss Finland any more. We have a new name for you,' Sam said.

'Is that so? Well, what is it?'

'You're our Lia Detector.'

'And that means… what?'

'You're a lie detector. A bullshit alarm.'

Sam said that a lot of people in the office had been waiting for her to get back so they could have her do their layouts. They wanted her to comment on their writing because she never let anything slide.

'Hmmm. A BS alarm. I suppose that's a compliment,' Lia said.

'It's a huge compliment, Miss Detector.'

In the afternoon, Mari rang again. Elza and Ausma would be leaving the Twineham Green Caravan Site that day. Elza had rented them a small flat. It was rather expensive, but they would only be there to begin with and Maggie would help them find a cheaper place. They especially wanted to thank Lia again.

Mari gave Lia Elza's number: she had bought a mobile phone and a prepaid SIM so as to keep the name of the owner confidential. Elza and Ausma had to be careful that their continued presence in London did not come to the notice of Vanags' and Jansons' accomplices.

Lia rang Elza during her lunch break and talked with her and Ausma for some time. They sounded calm but expectant. Fiona Gould had prepared them for what their job search would be like.

'Little problems aren't going to scare us away.'

Lia asked Elza to ring her anytime.

'Thanks. Maybe one day we can go for coffee at some really smart place. I'll buy,' Elza said.

At half past three, Lia's phone trilled again. Unlisted number. Lia answered with trepidation.

'Detective Chief Inspector Peter Gerrish here.'

Oh bollocks.

'Good afternoon, Chief Inspector.'

'Likewise. We would like to question you about any information you have concerning Kazimirs Vanags. We'll send a car round to pick you up.'

Such a quick departure in the middle of a working day would be difficult, Lia objected.

'You'll want to come down here right now,' Gerrish said. 'I don't want to arrest you, but we can do that too if necessary.'

Lia rang Mari immediately.

'Do you think you can handle it?' Mari asked. 'We can always have our solicitor delay the interview.'

'I think I can do it. But it would feel better if someone else were there with me. In case they ask something surprising.'

'Would Paddy work?'

Lia thought for a moment.

'Actually, I'd like Fiona Gould.'

Fiona didn't know everything that had happened, but she would know when Lia had the right not to answer a question.

'I'll handle it. Wait a few minutes,' Mari said.

Soon Mari rang back and announced that Fiona would come by cab to the Wood Street police station.

Lia begged the AD's forgiveness for having to leave so early even though she had just returned from sick leave. Taylor did not seem to take it amiss.

'Christmas errands?' he asked.

'Something like that,' Lia said.

Gerrish had sent an unmarked car, Lia noticed with relief, and no one in the office was there to see her getting into the car waiting on the street.

The driver was young, a plain-clothes cop, who introduced himself briefly and said he would drive Lia to the City of London Special Constabulary. He didn't try to strike up a conversation along the way, and silence suited Lia too.

Fiona Gould was waiting outside the police station, and seeing her made Lia feel more confident. The young driver called DCI Gerrish down.

Gerrish then led them to his office, which was still dominated by the same familiar chaos of paper and files.

DCI Gerrish quickly made it clear that Lia was not suspected of any crime. On the contrary, they believed she had information needed to solve four homicides.

'Four?' Lia asked.

'Come now. That can hardly come as a surprise to you,' Gerrish said.

Of course he was referring to the killings of the two Latvian women, Daiga Vītola and Anita Klusa, he clarified. And the deaths of two career criminals, Kazimirs Vanags and Olafs Jansons, also of Latvian extraction. The police had found the men based on Lia's tip that Vanags was involved in the women's deaths. They had investigated the places where their databases claimed Vanags had businesses or other interests, and Jansons' body had turned up as a result.

Lia stated that she was unable to answer any questions regarding the men's deaths.

'But the two women. Them, I might know something about.'

'Where did you get your information about them?' Gerrish enquired.

'From a Latvian prostitute. She knew them both.'

A rigorous interrogation ensued. Who was this prostitute? Where had they met? How had Lia found the pearled comb at the Eastern Buffet? Why had she gone to the shop?

Lia's answers were succinct. She had thought through beforehand what she would say. She did not tell him Elza's name or describe her in detail. She said she had run into some Latvian prostitutes at the Flash Forward club and met with one of them in a café at the Westfield London shopping centre.

She did not mention visiting Vassall and Sangley Roads, and claimed she had only heard about Vanags from this prostitute. Olafs Jansons was a mystery to her. She remembered that a young woman had served her at the Eastern Buffet. Only through the prostitute's story had Lia learned that the shop's owner was a hardened criminal.

Whenever Gerrish attempted to ask about Vanags and Jansons, Fiona Gould intervened.

'Ms Pajala said at the outset that she is unable to answer any questions regarding these men.'

The questioning lasted well over an hour. Gerrish took one break and fetched them coffee and tea.

He kept the pace of the conversation brisk, and Lia sometimes had a hard time arranging her words. But Gerrish did not accuse her of anything. His approach was exacting but not bullying.

He knows I know much more than this. But he believes I'm more on his side than against him.

Gerrish taped the conversation on a digital recorder and made notes on his computer. At the end he leaned back in his chair, clicked the file closed and stretched his arms. Making himself more comfortable, he slurped down his cold tea.

'Thank you, Ms Pajala,' Gerrish said.

Lia relaxed instinctively.

But the recorder is still on. He wants me to think the interview is over, so I won't think as carefully about my words.

Because Lia had answered his questions so willingly, Gerrish wanted to describe how he believed the murders had occurred.

The police did not have any evidence about who had killed the Latvian women. The cars they had been found in did not contain any evidence linking them to Vanags or Jansons or any fingerprints extant in the police records. But in the warehouse where they had found Jansons' body, they had also found the machine gun used to kill Anita Klusa, as well as indications that she was killed in a concrete pit in the same warehouse.

Lia shivered.

The flat on Vassall Road had contained ample evidence that someone had been running a brothel there, and interviews with the clients had confirmed as much. Finding them in order to question them had been easy: the police simply waited inside and opened the door when they arrived. Daiga Vītola had apparently worked there. Strands of her hair had showed up in two rooms, and the tiny key found with the remains of her body fitted an empty suitcase they had found at the flat.

They had not made contact with the women or pimps who had worked out of the flat. They were interviewing neighbours, and that might still yield new leads.

'We also found three other brothels Vanags was involved with.'

Lia raised an eyebrow.

The police had located the brothels using a sat-nav they had found in Vanags' car. The addresses stored in it had led to all sorts of interesting finds, including dozens of illegal guns. In the brothels they had found fourteen women in all, twelve Latvians and two Russians. The list of crimes of the men guarding them seemed long.

'What will happen to the women?' Lia asked.

'They'll probably be returned to their home countries. We've brought them in to take their statements. But once that's done, I think most or all of them will be deported. They've been working here illegally without the proper paperwork or paying tax.'

They had also been able to link Olafs Jansons to the place Anita Klusa's body had been found. CCTV on Ludgate Hill had recorded the moment when the blue Hyundai had driven into the area. The pictures did not show the car's driver, but Jansons' bald head was clearly visible a little later walking in a crowd of pedestrians along the street.

The same gun had been used to shoot Jansons and Vanags. The police hadn't found it though.

'They were shot at close range. Almost execution style. That could indicate an internal power struggle or an attack by a rival gang.'

There was also another theory about the gunman, Gerrish said, inspecting Lia closely.

In addition to that of the victims, the police had found blood from another person at the house on Sangley Road.

The cut on Henriete's shoulder. Will they catch her because of that?

'Upon DNA analysis, we discovered that the person the blood came from is a near relative of the Holborn Circus victim. Daiga Vītola.'

Gerrish waited to see what kind of impression this revelation would make on Lia.

'Do you know anything that could explain that?'

Lia shook her head and remained silent.

'I have a theory about what happened,' Gerrish said. 'I'd like to hear your views on it.'

The Chief Inspector believed that the men had not died at the hands of their partners in crime or their competitors. He believed that Daiga Vītola's sister had killed them. She probably had a sister who worked as a prostitute with her, and this sister had shot the men out of revenge.

Lia considered Gerrish's theory.

'Interesting idea,' she said. 'But I don't know whether Daiga had a sister. The prostitute I met didn't say anything like that.'

Gerrish met Lia's gaze. He did not give voice to the thought she could see in his eyes: right then. So be it.

Gerrish announced that he considered the course of events mainly settled.

'These two men may have killed the two prostitutes and some person or persons took revenge by killing them. We still have additional evidence we need to sift through.'

Gerrish ended the meeting by turning off the recorder and standing up from his desk.

'Thank you. We'll be in contact if our investigation reveals anything else.'

'Is that necessary?' asked Fiona Gould. 'Ms Pajala has been more than forthcoming. Repeating things of this nature doesn't improve anyone's peace of mind.'

'I'm sure it doesn't,' Gerrish said calmly. 'But Ms Pajala had voluntary dealings with people connected to the case. We found two dead bodies based on her tip off. We're going to have more questions.'

Let them come. I can handle it.

Lia thanked Fiona outside the police station and stored her mobile number in her own phone.

She was home on Kidderpore Avenue by seven o'clock, feeling dog tired. She had survived threats to her life and she had survived a police interrogation, but now she was just an exhausted hound following the hunt. *Piski.*

She felt a strong need to be close to someone. To Mari she could have said it, said the word *piski*, and Mari would have understood.

But she did not have the energy to talk to anyone now. She did not want to talk about the police interview, the Latvian women, Arthur Fried or anything else.

She drank a cup of tea and went outside. Every now and then, St Luke's held evening masses or other events, and Lia had half expected that so close to Christmas something would be on. But the lights in the church were off, and it was closed.

She stepped into the park. In the winter the trees were bare and dreary, but the statues shone dimly in the white haze created by the streetlights.

There was nowhere to sit by Poundy the Dog, but she leaned on him and laid her hand on his neck.

Us piskit, *mongrels, you and I.*

She thought of Daiga Vītola, the woman whose picture she carried in her wallet. She thought of Detective Chief Inspector Peter Gerrish, who had interrogated her.

Lia sat at the feet of the Elgars, the artist couple. She tried to see herself from outside, a small blonde woman sitting in a cold winter park. Sitting there she realised what she had accomplished. She had caught Daiga Vītola's murderer.

Before now that idea had never solidified. All the death and fear – with all that she had been unable to think clearly about what had happened. But undeniably, irrevocably, she had been involved in the work that solved the murders of Daiga Vītola and Anita Klusa.

Finding their killers had not atoned for the women's deaths, only perhaps offered some comfort to their loved ones, and even that comfort was cold and cruel.

But something of what had begun the previous spring when Lia saw the white Volvo on Holborn Circus was ending.

She sat there for a long time, looking at her home. Lights shone from almost every window in the building, including her own. That sight had always made her feel more at ease, as it did now as well.

45

The weekend was a relief.

As she wandered the city on Saturday morning, Lia found herself glancing around.

She did not know who or what she expected to see in the throngs of people. She did not feel in danger, but at the edges of her consciousness something nasty flickered from time to time. Memories Lia did not want to contemplate but which stayed with her. She knew she needed something else to think about. As she walked in the Christmas crush on Tottenham Court Road, she remembered that the Fitzroy Art Museum was only a few streets away.

The friendly woman at the museum desk recognised Lia, who purchased a ticket and then climbed the stairs to the second floor. She half expected to see Mari sitting on the bench in front of *Double O*. But the bench was empty. Only a few people meandered through the galleries.

She sat down on the bench and looked at the installation. As the black tape circles floated in the current of air, the quiet sounds made by their fluttering and the blowing of fans reminded Lia of something.

She closed her eyes, listening. Sitting here before with Mari, she had never concentrated on the sounds the artwork made. She had just looked at its unreal beauty.

The soft rustling of the ribbons felt strangely familiar. She knew she had heard the same sound – but where? It had happened long ago, when she was a child. At summer camp, with the fans humming on a hot day? At that big lake in Kajaani. What was its name? Lake Oulujärvi? Oulujärvi, she was sure of that, but her memory did not return anything else. It was too far back.

Is this how Mari experiences this too? The piece doesn't just include the new thoughts it evokes but also all the memories it calls to mind.

Lia sat on the bench for a long time. When someone walked up, she snapped out of her reverie. It was a gallery guard, a man of about fifty, who had a name tag on his coat: John Norman.

The guard smiled and cast a glance to make sure he was not disturbing her. Lia smiled back.

'This piece always makes people stop and think,' Norman said.

'Indeed it does. I must have been sitting here for half an hour.'

'More like a full hour,' Norman said and smiled again.

'A friend showed it to me. She spends a lot of time sitting here.'

'I know her well,' the guard said. 'Once she asked me to tell her how it works. Whether we have to throw the ribbons in the air in the morning or do something else to start them moving, and how they stay between the fans.'

'Well, how does it work?'

'I asked her whether she really wanted to know. Whether it wasn't more beautiful when you didn't know how it worked. She said I was right. Sometimes you don't have to know how something works, just that it does.'

'That's a beautiful thought.'

Norman smiled again and then glanced back towards the galleries, intending to continue his rounds.

'How many times have you seen her here?' Lia asked.

'Many. Ms Rautee visits quite frequently.'

The guard said Mari's family name with considerable familiarity. Almost as a Finn might do. Perhaps Mari had told him how to pronounce it properly.

At the museum they almost considered Ms Rautee part of the staff, Norman said buoyantly.

'Last year when this piece was set to go to the warehouse, she was here day after day watching it. For hours. And then she joined the museum foundation and made a donation to make it a permanent exhibit.'

Lia tried not to show her astonishment.

'Yes, she is a friend of the arts,' Lia said.

'It's people like Ms Rautee who make it possible for museums to stay afloat. I asked her why she didn't just buy a copy of the piece for herself. There are a few in different places around the world. The artist certainly would have sold her one, and it would have been less expensive for her. She said she wanted it to be here. That she wanted to share it with everyone. But she didn't want her name on a plaque next to it or anything. Most donors do.'

'That sounds like Mari,' Lia said.

'I was surprised,' the guard said. 'She likes it so much. You don't often see a person crying when she looks at a piece of art.'

Lia looked at Norman, lost for words. Crying?

'Sometimes she cries when she sits here. You know… quietly, to herself. I don't know – maybe it isn't appropriate to talk about it. But you are her friend.'

'Yes, yes I am.'

Norman nodded and set out on his rounds. Lia sat for another moment.

When she left the museum, it was already past noon. It was Saturday, with six days until Christmas. She had not done any shopping. She hadn't bought anything for anyone. Not even for her family at home in Finland. She had been putting it off, thinking that if she couldn't manage anything else, she could just make a charitable contribution in their names online. A goat for a family in Africa or something.

She rang Mari.

'What are you doing tonight?'

'Hmmm. Nothing in particular. Paddy and Rico are here at the Studio, and we were thinking…'

'Not tonight. You can work during the day. Come to my place tonight. In Hampstead.'

'To your flat?'

'Yeah. We'll have a Christmas party. I want to buy a present for someone. Even if it's just something small.'

A few seconds of silence followed on the phone.

'That's the best idea I've heard in months,' Mari said.

Sometime after seven, Lia suggested. She would get something to eat, and Mari could bring the wine.

'I have stronger stuff at home already if we need it,' Lia said.

'You bet we will. Kidderpore Avenue?'

'Yes. Near the corner of Kidderpore and Platt's Lane. The door to the stairs is locked, but just ring when you get here.'

As she opened the outer door, Lia could see that Mari had understood the intended nature of the night's event perfectly. She was dressed in one of her best frocks, a dark brown silk. Lia knew that Mari had purchased it years before on a trip to Vietnam and liked it very much. Lia was wearing her best skirt and expensive tights. She had put on her party make-up.

Mari's arms were full, including two wine carriers that weighed so much Lia had to laugh.

'These are going to be proper office Christmas party *kännit*. We'll drink expensive wine but save on renting the party space,' she said.

Mari giggled.

She stood at the door of Lia's flat looking in.

Lia had decorated as best she could. She had wrapped strands of white cotton string here and there to represent snow. She had placed Christmas baubles in selected spots. The room's main illumination, a boring square ceiling lamp, had been covered with transparent paper with star-shaped holes. It gave off a soft light, which pardoned the room's many other faults.

Lia looked at her flat and knew how it appeared. A little box of a student flat, with Christmas thrown together on a shoestring.

But Mari made herself at home with an enthusiasm that filled the space.

'Lovely,' she said. 'Is there space in the fridge for the whites?'

There wasn't room in the refrigerator, so they took the white wines outside to the building's bicycle shelter. Mari had the champagne already chilled.

That night strengthened many things.

It was a return to the previous summer, to the evenings and nights they had spent out on the town.

They ate the food Lia had purchased. She had wanted to offer better in honour of the day than what she could rustle up in her own mini kitchenette: pesto salad, bouillabaisse and lime sorbet.

From the champagne they moved on to other wines. The selection Mari had brought included a companion for each and every dish. After dinner they gave each other their Christmas presents.

'Can we open them right now?' Mari asked.

'We have to,' Lia said. 'Otherwise Christmas won't come.'

From Lia, Mari received two DVD sets: the collected works of the Aardman animation studios and a selection of Lars von Trier films.

'Marvellous. Thank you.'

Lia knew the films fitted Mari perfectly. Warmth and hardness, both taken to extremes.

From Mari she also received two gifts. One was a set of novelty plastic cubes with flashing lights inside for putting in drinks. Of course they had to mix drinks to use them immediately.

The second gift was a £600 airline gift card.

'That's enough to get you to Provence. Or wherever else you want to go,' Mari said.

Lia was at once moved and taken aback at the expense of the gift.

'That includes your bonus for your work at the Studio,' Mari said.

That was a passable excuse. Unanimously they declared that the gifts were exceptional and that Christmas had indeed come.

Lia wanted to show Mari her view of the park. Turning off the lights, they gazed at the church and sculpture garden standing in the dark.

'Do you want to go out?' Lia asked.

Mari nodded. Getting dressed for the outside, they went out to the park. Lia amused Mari by telling her the stories about the statues she had read over the years.

The story of the Elgars was full of romantic sacrifice. Caroline Alice had set aside her own literary career to marry Edward, a composer prone to violent mood swings. Her family and friends considered her husband too lower class, but Caroline Alice endured both her relations' muttering and her husband's outbursts.

'She was sometimes heard agonising over how caring for a genius was a full-time job. But to counterbalance it, he dedicated his compositions to her.'

Mari sighed.

They looked at St Luke and Florence Nightingale. Lia felt a pure, peaceful joy: Mari was enamoured in just the right way by everything.

As they walked back to the flat, Lia was also relieved. Mari was the first visitor she had hosted in her small home. Mr Vong didn't count, and he had mostly only visited to help mend things.

They settled down on Lia's bed in amongst the pillows, drinking and talking. About work, about people, about everything.

Had Mari done anything regarding Paddy, in a dating sense? Lia asked.

'No. Who knows if we're cut out for it?'

Lia understood without asking any more. Mari and Paddy had a sort of battle or playing field between them, in which they made little moves and approaches now and then, and which everyone who knew them, including themselves, could see.

Mari changed the subject: how did Lia feel after all that had happened that week? Lia said she liked the idea that she could turn to the psychiatrist at any time, but she felt as though she would manage without the help.

'My head says I should be more distressed than I am. But I'm not afraid. Or worried. I'm just... relieved.'

'Good,' Mari said.

She said she had been watching the effect of Arthur Fried's ordination in the media. At first the news had been received with suspicion. The lead editorials in the papers had declared Fried's new religious fervour a publicity stunt they could not see stopping the party's downward spiral.

And the new minister would be seen in an entirely new light the following week when Sarah Hawkins' video came out, Mari added.

They toasted this with French wine labelled with a picture of a pious monk.

'I've never told you that I first met Fried more than ten years ago,' Mari suddenly said.

They had met in the United States, in Texas in fact. Mari had been touring the country and seeing the world, while Fried was on business.

'We met in a bar. Everything happened fast. I almost went to bed with him.'

Lia's wine nearly went down the wrong pipe.

'I know,' Mari said. 'It's totally unfathomable.'

Arthur Fried hadn't been the kind of man then that he was now.

'It was purely sexual. He came to chat me up. For a moment he was very attractive.'

Lia listened silently while Mari told the whole story.

There had been none of the reek of religious hypocrisy around Fried then. None of the cruelty they both sensed in him now. Mari had just seen him as a businessman, an entrepreneurial, quick-witted chap.

'I was attracted by his ability to get straight to the point. His energy. He said straight away that he was looking for a one-night stand. He seemed genuine – now it feels stupid, but for a moment I believed him.'

Mari had also recognised something disturbing in the man. As she chatted with him at the bar, she had tried to sense what kind of person he was.

'He was evasive. He wouldn't talk about himself, just America and everything he had seen. That was smart. He probably didn't want to talk about himself because he was still married to Sarah Hawkins at the time. Although their marriage must have already been on the rocks.'

After seeing Mari's interest, Fried had asked whether she was into any kinky stuff.

'I realised what was bothering me. There was a desire in him to subjugate, but it had nothing to do with pleasure.'

Mari had made it clear that she wasn't interested. Fried had become indignant and called her a little whore, who didn't know what was good for her.

'He moved on to softening up another woman at the bar, and I left.'

Mari had looked into who Arthur Fried was. She did not like what she found. She had begun tracking Fried's political activities and gradually become convinced he was dangerous.

'He is a rare person.'

Fried was both extremely gifted and evil to the core. Mari believed that he had no ability to feel sorrow or empathy, or any deeper interest in other people at all. The place where those things should have been in his personality was simply blank, creating a hole he filled with experiences of wielding power.

They did not return to Fried again that night.

It was a good night. They drank a lot, but their time together was about more than drinking and laughing. It was more about all they had shared in recent months.

Lia showed off her travel guide, *London, Good For You!* Mari's reaction to it was the same as Lia's had been: first confusion and then enchantment. They read the best parts out loud. The chapter 'You Don't Say, London' related surprising items of cultural and historical interest: Mozart had composed his first symphony at the age of eight in London, on Ebury Street in Belgravia. Until 1916, Harrods sold cocaine, which was considered medicinal. The 'Rock bands favoured by the youth', The Beatles and The Rolling Stones, had played at the same show in 1963 in the Royal Albert Hall, at a charity fundraiser for the Printers' Pension Corporation.

As she laughed with Mari, out of the corner of her eye Lia saw both of their reflections in the darkened window. Next to them floated tiny lights, the flames of the candles Lia had lit. She imagined Elza there with them.

A moment later another form appeared alongside them in the reflected scene. A dark-haired woman Lia had never met. She had only seen her photograph, which she carried with her always now. Daiga Vītola. Brave, reckless Daiga sat with them, drinking and having fun.

The fear was also there, hovering next to them, the spectre of everything that had happened. But the fear was manageable now. By living through all that had happened since the spring, Lia had begun to develop the strength to cope with her fears. Even what had happened in Finland all those years ago, the memories of a relationship turned dangerously sour, felt different now. One phase of life among all the others.

Lia heard their laughter ringing from the small room's walls. It was a sound she had never heard in her flat.

At ten o'clock she noticed another sound. She waved to Mari to tell her to be quiet.

'Mr Vong!' she whispered, and Mari fell silent, an expectant smile on her lips.

They heard a steady murmur. Water running into the bath. The sound echoed hollowly off the porcelain surface, amplifying it into a muffled roar that filled Lia's room like small rapids in a stream.

The rushing stopped. Mr Vong had turned off the tap. A couple of tiny splashing sounds came as the last drops fell into the water. Complete silence fell. They heard Mr Vong lowering himself into the water. Mr Vong and his nightly bath.

Mari began to say something, but Lia hissed, 'Quiet.' A moment passed.

A rumble. Another.

Lia covered her face with her hands to stifle a laugh, and when she peered through her fingers, she saw Mari gasping for breath in pent-up delight.

Mr Vong was passing his evening gas, which echoed under the water clear, tight and dull like the skilful playing of a brass instrument. They shook with joy.

A sensuous intoxication had settled over them. The wine blunted their senses like a blanket enfolding them.

Mari wanted to get home while she still had the strength. Lia offered a share of her bed.

They repeated the Finnish word, admiring its beauty: *Siskonpeti*. Sister bed. It brought to mind quilts dug out of the back of the cupboards, the tiny flats of bygone days and the ties of friendship – both those just created and those strengthened over years.

But Mari declined. She needed her own, familiar surroundings.

They ordered a taxi and collected Mari's presents and other things. They looked at the clutter that filled Lia's small home. Food and plates, bottles and glasses, wrapping paper and candle stubs.

'Best Christmas party ever,' Mari said, hugging Lia.

Lia escorted Mari to the outer door and watched until she climbed into the cab. Then she walked back to her flat as steadily as she could, checked that the candles were all out and collapsed into bed.

Her mobile rang on Sunday morning before eight o'clock.

When Lia saw the name *Sarah* on the display, in an instant her head cleared significantly.

'Hello?'

'Lia?'

Sarah Hawkins apologised for calling so early, but she had business that could not wait.

'Lia, you can't publish that video. I'm so sorry. But that's my decision.'

'What? Why?'

'Some things have happened. I don't believe that releasing it is right any more. You can't publish it. And I want all the copies back for myself.'

Lia was trying to catch up. They couldn't stop the release any more, she objected.

'Yes, you can. It's my story, and if you release it, I'll tell the papers that it isn't true.'

'Why have you changed your mind?'

'I've been talking with people. My sister. And Arthur.'

Sarah said she had met with Fried, but did not want to talk about it in any more detail.

'I'm truly sorry for all the bother you've been through. I'll pay for the hotel myself.'

'Are you still at the hotel? This isn't about money…'

'Yes, I'm here. But I'm planning to go back home today.'

'Did he threaten you?'

The line went quiet.

'Let's not go there,' Sarah said. 'This is just my decision. It's best for me and lots of other people as well.'

'Sarah, I'm going to ring you back in five minutes. We have to figure out what we can still do now.'

'Fine. Just so long as that video does not come out.'

'Ugh. You can't call so early.'

'Mari, we have a problem.'

They decided that Lia had to talk to Sarah immediately.

'If Fried has threatened her, tell her that we have to put a stop to him now,' Mari said.

Lia had to make Sarah feel safe again so she would dare to oppose Fried. They had to take Sarah to a different hotel. If Fried had offered Sarah money, Lia could offer her more.

'I have enough,' Mari said.

'Yes... Yes... Yes,' Lia answered as she searched for clothing in the chaos of her room.

'Tell Sarah about the other women Fried has hit and all the ones that are being hit in other families.'

It would help if Sarah didn't feel alone and believed she was acting in others' best interests as well. Lia, Mari and everyone else at the Studio would be there to support her the whole way through.

'Can we publish the video if she denies it herself?' Lia asked.

'No. Of course not.'

Doing that to Sarah would be wrong. And if she claimed the video was manipulated, in the worst case scenario the scandal could play to Fried's benefit.

Snatching up her keys and phone, Lia said she had to order a taxi now.

'OK. I just don't understand how Fried found her. We were so careful,' Mari said.

Sarah Hawkins opened the hotel room door looking serious.

'I think it would have been best to handle this over the phone,' she said.

Lia stepped in and tried to catch her breath.

'How did Arthur get in touch with you?'

Sarah gestured at her new mobile phone. She had given the number to only one person, her sister.

'I had to give it to her in case something happened.'

When Fried had been unable to find Sarah, he had gone to her sister and made her believe that Sarah had left home because she was in some sort of trouble. The sister had given Sarah's number to Fried.

'Arthur called and said that someone was running a malicious smear campaign against him. I didn't believe him at first. But it was strange that so many things were happening at once. First there was the story about his tax irregularities. And then there was the thing about Fair Rule supporting illegal groups. When Arthur heard that I had made a video, he said that it was part of the same campaign. I don't know everything he's done, but this does look an awful lot like someone is intentionally digging around in Arthur's past,' Sarah said, watching Lia's expressions carefully.

'Unfortunate things like this come out all the time. Someone finds them and publishes them,' Lia said.

'I know. And I still believe everything I said on that video. But I've decided not to let it out. You haven't given it to The Wall yet, have you?'

'No,' Lia said. The video was supposed to go to the group two days later. They had only told the head of the organisation that they would be sending a report of domestic abuse involving an important public figure and that it was likely to cause a stir.

Why had Sarah changed her mind, Lia asked.

Sarah closed her mouth and looked away.

'I don't want to talk about it.'

'Why not? Did he threaten you?'

Silence.

'Did he hit you?'

'No. No, not that.'

Silence.

'This is an ugly, difficult business. I chose the lesser evil of the options I had.'

Arthur Fried had promised Sarah money. And threatened her.

'He threatened to hunt me down if that video came out. He would hunt me as long as it took to find me and then beat me so that I would never walk again. And my sister. And my sister's son.'

Dear God.

'I know what you're thinking, Lia. That a man that violent can't be allowed to go doing it any more. But I believe Arthur. If he says he'll take revenge on me and my sister and my nephew, he'll do it. He said that if the video came out, he wouldn't have anything to lose. His career would be over, and he would make sure that we would pay.'

The alternative was £100,000. Fried had promised it in cash, delivered immediately, in addition to an increase in the sum he had been paying her every month.

'I didn't know that I had a price,' Sarah said. 'I didn't know that I would be able to make a choice like that. That I would deny the truth for money.'

'It isn't that simple. I know that,' Lia said. 'I know a little about what it means to be afraid. It isn't about being rational. Anyone can make decisions out of fear that they would never make otherwise.'

Sarah nodded. Lia thought about what she could offer Sarah and what sorts of arrangements would be required in order for her and her sister's family to live in safety.

Sarah glanced at her watch. Lia realised that she was waiting for something.

'Sarah, when did you have this conversation with Arthur? Was he here?'

'Last night. He called me around eight and then came here. We talked for a long time, and he left around midnight. He said that he would come back this morning and that he wanted me to collect all of the copies of the video so I could give them to him. And that's what I've decided to do.'

She keeps repeating that she's made her decision. She's trying to convince herself.

'Sarah, would you mind if I made one call?'

'Not at all. But Arthur could be here any minute.'

Lia wanted privacy, so she left the room. She walked to the end of the corridor where an alcove window looked out across the city. She rang Mari and told her the situation in hushed tones.

'One hundred thousand is a lot,' Mari said. 'And we have to offer more, or something other than money. But I can handle it either way. Not right this second, but within a few days.'

'Are you sure you want to pay that much? And what about the security arrangements?'

'If we don't have the video, Fried could recover from this. Paddy can help make the security arrangements. He's done the same sort of thing before.'

It might also be possible to publicise Fried's threats, Mari suggested. If they had any evidence, they could release that with the video, and then the police would have to come to Sarah's aid. Mari did not know offhand what they would need for Sarah to qualify for state witness protection, but the protection would work out either way, whether through official channels or through the Studio.

Lia saw movement at the other end of the corridor. It was Arthur Fried with a large briefcase in his hand. Fried went to Sarah's hotel room door and swiped a keycard in the lock. The door opened, and Fried disappeared into the room.

'He's here,' Lia whispered into the phone.

'Oh shit,' Mari said.

‘I have to go back to Sarah’s room.’

‘Anything could happen in there. Wait. I’ll ring Paddy to come to you now.’

‘Ring away, but I’m going in now. I’ll keep the line open so you can hear what happens.’

Lia strode back to the door and knocked loudly. A few seconds passed before Sarah answered.

Arthur Fried was standing in the room behind her. Fried’s briefcase was on the bed where he had been in the process of opening it. Lia pushed her way into the room without waiting for Sarah’s permission.

Sarah and Fried had clearly been engaged in a heated discussion, which Lia’s arrival had interrupted.

‘I don’t know how he got a key,’ Sarah said. ‘I don’t understand how the reception desk could have given someone else a card to my room.’

‘Easily,’ Fried said. ‘I told the tart at the desk that I was your boyfriend and that I had a gift for you. She would have given me a key to her own room if I had asked.’

Lia saw how upset Sarah was.

‘Is the money in the briefcase?’ Lia asked, stretching her neck to see through the crack.

She saw thick stacks of notes. Maybe there really was £100,000 in there.

‘Who are you?’ Fried asked quickly.

Lia glanced at Sarah: apparently she hadn’t had time to tell him that she was there.

‘My name is Lia Pajala. And this is my mobile phone,’ Lia said, raising the phone. ‘On the other end is a person listening to every word we say and recording it all.’

Fried didn’t miss a beat.

‘You seem familiar. Have we met?’ he asked.

Of course he wouldn’t remember me from his campaign office. I’m far too ordinary a person to bother remembering.

Lia had to give an explanation so Fried would not realise how organised the effort against him was.

'Yes, we've met before. I work for *Level* magazine.'

Arthur Fried's eyes narrowed.

'I thought Sarah was being press-ganged by some trashy rag. I didn't know *Level* was wallowing in the gutter now.'

Lia thought for a couple of seconds about how to proceed. Raising her mobile and holding it about a foot from her mouth, she began dictating loudly.

'It's Sunday morning at 10.35 a.m. We're currently in the Ibis Hotel in Earl's Court. In the room with me are party leader Arthur Fried and his former wife Sarah Hawkins. Arthur Fried has just arrived with a large amount of currency, presumably one hundred thousand pounds...'

'Bitch,' said Fried, stepping towards Lia and slapping from her hand the mobile phone, which flew across the room.

Lia had only just thought of darting after it when the blow came. Fried slammed her to the floor in one quick, savage stroke. More out of surprise than pain, Lia curled up in a ball. Instinctively she raised her arms to shield her head.

She heard Sarah's cry.

'No!'

This shout made Fried stop short. He stared at Lia, poised to attack.

'No,' Sarah said, giving Fried a look that left no room for interpretation. If he hit her again, their agreement would be over. Fried stepped to the bed and closed his briefcase. 'Gather your things,' he said to Sarah.

Sarah hesitated. Then she walked into the bathroom to collect her personal items.

Arthur Fried and Lia looked at each other. When the shock of the assault had passed, all Lia could feel was the speed of her pulse. She was not afraid, which astonished her.

'You won't succeed,' she said to Fried.

He looked back silently.

'There are too many people involved. Sarah, and her sister knows too. And me. And the person listening on the other end of the line,' Lia said.

Fried glanced at the mobile lying on the floor. He walked over to it and switched it off. Then he looked at Lia again.

'Whore.'

'Bribing and hitting people aren't going to get you out of this,' Lia said. 'You're going to get caught.'

Fried did not say anything. Lia saw him weighing up whether striking her again would be worth it or not.

Just then Sarah returned from the bathroom with a hastily assembled make-up bag. She rushed to pack her clothes. Only a few items remained in the drawers, since her suitcase had already been almost ready.

A sharp rapping came at the door.

'Hotel security! Open up!'

Lia realised that Mari must have rung the hotel. That was a faster way to get her help. For a moment none of them moved or said anything. The knocking turned to pounding on the door.

'Open up immediately!'

'Why? What seems to be the problem?' Sarah replied to the guard.

'We've received a report of an assault. Open the door immediately or we will enter with our own key.'

Sarah looked at Arthur Fried.

'Everything is fine,' she said to the guard.

'Open the door immediately. You do not have a choice. We have a protocol to follow. We must inspect the room.'

Lia raised herself from the floor, first sitting and then slowly climbing to her feet. The whole time she kept her eyes on Fried on the other side of the room. He was standing stock-still.

'You won't succeed,' she said to Fried.

Sarah opened the door, and a young, stern-looking guard barged in. In his hand was a radio transmitting something made unintelligible by static.

'I'm in,' the guard said into his radio.

He stared at the three people standing in the room and looked around.

'Is everyone all right?' he asked.

Sarah nodded. The guard turned his eyes to Lia, who gave him a quick smile.

'Everything is fine,' Lia said.

'Sir, are you all right?' the guard asked Arthur Fried.

'I'm perfectly fine,' Fried replied.

The guard apologised for his intrusion but still checked the bathroom. As he returned he eyed the bag Sarah had just packed.

'Are you leaving?'

'Yes.'

'We received an alert that someone's life was being threatened in this room. Do you know what that could have been about?'

'No. I don't know.'

Fried stepped in.

'This may have something to do with me being a public figure.'

With this, he walked up to the guard and shook his hand.

'Arthur Fried, Fair Rule party leader. I've been in the press lately due to some unfortunate allegations. It may be that this is more of the same. You know what sorts of psychopaths follow celebrities around.'

Recognising Fried, the guard nodded.

'My apologies for the disturbance. When we receive a report of danger to anyone's life we are obliged to act as we did.'

'I understand completely,' Fried said, smiling at the guard. 'It's good you have these protocols. And an effective staff. But truly, nothing has happened here. And if any representatives of the media ask about this incident, I depend upon your discretion.'

The guard quickly withdrew from the room.

'You haven't changed,' Sarah said to Fried. 'I thought it last night when we talked, but now I know. You're never going to change.'

Without answering, Fried fetched his briefcase. He threw Lia's phone on the bed and picked up Sarah's suitcase.

'Let's go.'

'Sarah, do you understand what you're doing?' Lia asked.

Sarah did not say anything. She simply turned to follow Fried out the door.

'Bring the video to Sarah's flat by three o'clock. Every copy. If anyone keeps a copy or it comes out in the press, you know what I'll do,' Fried said.

Lia stared at the door as it closed after them.

When Lia arrived back at the Studio, she found that Mari had called Paddy and Rico in for an emergency meeting.

'That was a bold move,' Mari said.

If Arthur Fried had said anything within earshot of her mobile phone that could prove his bribery or intimidation, perhaps they could still have published the video. Now they couldn't.

They all agreed that the biggest problem was not security for Sarah Hawkins and her family. They could arrange that easily enough. The problem was that the video would end up helping Fried if Sarah refuted its contents publicly.

'Fried and Sarah would say that the video was doctored, that we spliced it together. As we did. But they would make it seem like the video wasn't the truth,' Rico said.

All the work they had done to produce it would turn against them. For example, removing the background noise could be used as evidence that the speech had been manipulated as well.

'We can't use it,' Mari said. 'That's done now. Fried's won this round.'

They agreed that Lia would take Fried three DVDs with copies of the video.

'It doesn't matter how many copies you take,' Rico said. 'We could make thousands of them if we wanted. But it'll be easier for Fried to think he's got all of them if you only take a few.'

Of course the Studio would keep a copy, Mari said. Rico would have to make sure it was kept under lock and key so no one on the outside could break in and download it.

Rico looked shocked at the very suggestion that Mari thought someone could break into the Studio's data systems.

'That won't happen,' he said.

'Still,' Mari said. 'We can't take the risk no matter how unlikely it is.'

Sarah Hawkins had suffered so much already. They had to respect her by doing as she asked. But they would keep a copy in case she ever changed her mind.

Paddy volunteered to drive Lia to Sarah's flat and monitor the meeting from a distance.

'What now?' Lia asked Mari.

'Now we think,' Mari said.

On Ferndale Road, Paddy stayed in the front garden while Lia rang the bell. Sarah opened quickly, as if she had been waiting by the door. She glanced at Paddy, but did not ask about him.

Lia walked inside. Arthur Fried was waiting in the kitchen at the table. He and Sarah had been drinking tea. It all looked so oddly cosy.

Lia set on the table a binder containing three plastic sleeves, each holding a DVD.

'Is this all the copies?' Fried asked.

'It's a digital recording. These are all of the copies we've made of it.'

Did they still have a master? Fried wanted to know.

'No,' Lia lied. 'We deleted it.'

Fried nodded.

'You can go. I hope *Level* can again someday rise above the crude cesspool of vituperation the red tops churn out.'

Lia smiled.

How long did thinking that one up take you, Arthur?

Lia did not say anything to Fried as she left, but she did shake Sarah's hand. Sarah was unable to speak, and Lia could feel the trembling in her hand.

Paddy drove Lia home.

At Kidderpore Avenue, he asked, 'How are you doing?'

'What do you mean?'

Her encounter with Fried had not exactly been easy, Paddy said. Less than a week had elapsed since the events in the Sutton warehouse. Lia had been interviewed by the police. She had been through things that would shake anyone up.

'I'm fine. Really. I'm surprised by it too. But I wasn't even afraid today. I mostly just felt like laying into him, but I'm not quite that stupid.'

'You're a tough girl.'

Lia snorted.

'Yeah, I'm a regular badass.'

'I know how it feels,' Paddy said seriously. He had been shot at and beaten several times.

'The first couple of times I was wetting myself. But then hitting just turned into hitting. It lost its mystery.'

That happened in this line of work, Paddy said. But everyday life went on, if you didn't get hurt too badly. Over the years Paddy had feared less and less, but he had become extremely careful all the same.

'I decided that at least my life wasn't going to end accidentally, because of some bumbling small-time crook.'

‘Maybe I’ll get used to it too. Although I don’t think I’ll ever get used to gunshots.’

‘You can practise that. We’ll go to a range sometime and you can learn to shoot.’

That made Lia smile.

‘Thanks. Just a little while ago I would never have believed it, but that sounds like a great idea.’

46

Mari sits in her office at the Studio and stares at her computer monitor.

Onscreen updates from the news wires scroll by, relating events in Britain and around the world. But Mari is not looking at them.

She is thinking.

Arthur Fried sneaked ahead of her and frightened Sarah Hawkins into keeping mum. Fried now has space to breathe. But Fried knows that he has to do something to save his career.

Losing Sarah's video was a big setback for Mari. She can't replace it just like that. It was Plan A, and usually Mari has other backup plans, a B and usually a C as well. That is how her head works. A backup for the backup for the backup plan.

That is how she ensures success. Her mind develops a plan, considering the target from every possible angle, and that is why she achieves her goals.

But this plan will be hard to replace. Perhaps impossible.

Time could simply run out. Only a few months remain until the election, leaving Fried free to do any number of things to restore his reputation and squeak into Parliament.

Mari's thoughts run in circles, repeatedly landing on the same themes: the politician, his ex-wife, the video.

It isn't good, and Mari knows it. She has to get free of what she had before. In order to solve the problem, she has to think of something else, she has to find something new.

Mari knows that Rico is hunched over a keyboard in his office. Berg is tidying up the Den. Paddy is doing his own work. Maggie is free, waiting to be ordered what to do. Lia is dropping in at *Level*, jogging and generally recovering. They all have their place.

Mari's place is here and her task is resolving this. Her mind has always produced a solution. Always, before long, some thought has started to take shape.

Mari continues to think.

47

Monday was full. Lia had a big pile of stories to lay out, and immediately after work a meeting with her psychiatrist.

On her way to Brooke's office on the Tube, she found that despite it all, the day seemed to be missing something. This was supposed to have been the day when Sarah Hawkins' video went to The Wall, shocking the women who worked there and leading to immediate publication.

This week Fried was supposed to fall.

Her conversation with Elizabeth Brooke expunged all such thoughts from her mind. Brooke carefully walked Lia through her state of health, how she had been sleeping, had she been using any medications and other items that would reveal possible symptoms of stress.

I should have them, I suppose. But I haven't noticed any myself.

Lia talked with the psychiatrist about a question that had been bothering her: when you saw a death, was it OK to be satisfied sometimes? If they were evil people, was it wrong to mostly feel relief at their deaths?

'I doubt there's any one answer to that,' Dr Brooke said. 'That takes us to the outer limits of morality and the law. But I should think it was strange if relief was not one of the acceptable reactions to that.'

At the end of their meeting, Brooke said she was happy for Lia.

'Your attack last week was so severe that I would have expected you to be doing significantly worse. But it is possible it was a unique episode. If you continue doing this well, perhaps you won't need any more extensive treatment. And in that case we wouldn't need to continue meeting long.'

Lia did not tell her about Fried punching her the previous day. Mentioning the incident did not feel necessary.

I didn't burst into tears at Arthur Fried's feet. I didn't have a panic attack. I didn't have any nightmares.

Frightening me isn't so easy any more.

At home she considered the week ahead. A few days until Christmas. One more day at work before her short holiday. No plans.

She rang Mari. 'What's up?'

She heard Mari laugh.

'Same old, same old. Thinking. Weighing options.'

'Do you have any Christmas plans?'

'No. I haven't had any all autumn and I still don't. I doubt I'll go to Finland. I don't think I could stand a family Christmas. I'll probably be boring and just continue doing this.'

'Thinking?'

'Yeah.'

'Couldn't I interest you in anything else?' Lia asked.

'Like what?'

'Well. Running. Films. And there are still clubs with bands. Or we could go to some charity's soup kitchen to hand out Christmas meals. To the poor. Anything other than just being.'

'Thanks. Some other time, definitely. But not right now. Not this Christmas.'

'Well, let's stay in touch. Maybe we'll come up with something.'

Lia guessed that would not be the case.

Tuesday was busy at the *Level* offices, especially since amidst all the rush everyone took a break to drink the wine and eat the food the magazine had bought and wish each other a happy Christmas.

Lia also wished editor-in-chief Matt Thomas well, not feeling the slightest bit false in doing so. Months had passed since Mari had revealed Thomas to be an utter idiot, but Lia had had barely a moment's time to dwell on it. She had begun to give in to the idea that at some point she would have to change jobs.

At home on Kidderpore Avenue nothing awaited her.

Two days until Christmas Eve.

Lia pulled out the airline voucher Mari had given her. Six hundred pounds. She looked up the airline's website and searched the last-minute deals. All that appeared to remain was expensive departures and destinations in which she had no interest.

Then she noticed a flight to Helsinki. A Christmas Eve morning departure to Helsinki with a return on Boxing Day, price a cool £589 including tax. How was it just that price? But Lia did not want to go to Helsinki to celebrate Christmas with her parents.

Now that she thought of it, she realised what a long time had elapsed since she had last rung them.

Her father answered in Espoo after only two rings.

'Hi. It's me,' Lia said.

'Lia? It's nice to hear from you.'

Her mother was out just then, gone to the shop, her father said. To get potatoes. Apparently they were having beef and mash the following day.

Lia could hear the sound of Finnish television in the background and knew that her dad was sitting in his favourite chair where he could see both the telly and out towards the sea, where a strip of the Baltic was clearly visible.

Lia asked after their health. Her mother had been in for a check-up due to some back pain, but the results of the tests had not yet arrived. At long last, her father had been able to get out and run, since his legs were cooperating again.

'You ran the shoreline trail, where the geese are during the summer?' Lia asked.

'Yes, that's the one.'

'I've been busy. I've met some new friends, and work is a lot... well, it's just a lot,' Lia said.

She briefly informed him that she would not be able to come to Helsinki that year.

'I'm only taking a couple of days off.'

This explanation suited her father well enough. Work. Work could earn you forgiveness for nearly anything.

'How are things at work?'

'Fine, fine. Something did happen a little while ago that showed me what a ghastly beast my boss is though. The editor-in-chief. It isn't a problem otherwise, but I have started thinking that I might not be at this magazine for ever.'

Lia regretted this slip immediately. A note of concern came into her father's voice.

'But you have such a good position there. It wouldn't do to switch just like that. It's always a good idea to try to keep a good relationship with your boss, no matter what he might be like.'

'Oh, our relationship is fine. But I'm not willing to take whatever he dishes out.'

'There aren't many good bosses out there anywhere. You just have to stick it out.'

'Thanks, Dad, but I'll handle it myself. I'll decide whether I'm staying there or not.'

The phone went silent.

'Where is this coming from?' her father finally asked. 'That you're talking this way?'

'I don't know.'

'Does it have something to do with these new friends? Who are they?'

Lia sighed.

'Perfectly respectable people. Normal people. One of them is a Finn. A Finnish woman.'

'Well, that's good. With Finns you always know what you're dealing with.'

As the call was ending, as she was sending her love to her mother, Lia knew positively that she did not want to visit her parents for Christmas. She did not want to feel weak. But she also knew she would seriously regret not sending them anything.

Online she found some appropriate CDs and a DVD box set of a BBC nature series, paying nearly £100 to have them delivered wrapped via courier the following day, Christmas Eve.

That was a trifling sum for peace of mind.

Lia spent Christmas at home on Kidderpore Avenue. She bought good food and listened to her favourite albums.

She thought about the Baltic Sea and her parents' view of it. She thought about that same sea extending to Latvia.

Four women had returned there from London. They were home for Christmas, and although Lia did not know whether their return had been joyful or miserable, that thought alone brought tears to her eyes.

She sent Mari a text message: had she heard anything from Latvia?

Everything there was well, Mari replied presently. She had heard from Ausma, who had called her grandmother Henriete in Riga from London. All four women had arrived home safely and were with relatives. Henriete was well. She had told her family that Daiga had died in London. Upon hearing, her ex-husband had come demanding Daiga's things for himself. Henriete had thrown him out.

Lia laughed with tears in her eyes at the thought of Henriete Vītola tossing her no-good son-in-law out on his ear.

Lia went out for long runs on Christmas Eve and the day itself. It was perfect. Sixteen kilometres on Hampstead Heath, which was full of happy sights: families playing with their children, the elderly sitting on benches for the few moments the chilly weather would allow, dogs dragging their owners along.

After her run on Christmas Day, she rang Mr Vong's doorbell.

They played cards for seven hours. Mr Vong asked whether Lia would mind if he played Christmas songs on the radio in the background, since he had this lovely little world radio in the shape of a duck. Lia had no objections. She enjoyed every moment. Thankfully Mr Vong was not one of those people who would have had to bustle about offering Christmas delicacies or things to eat in general. They simply sat in peace playing and drinking tea.

On Boxing Day evening, Lia went out into the city, to a sports bar named Goals, and in half an hour found herself a man. Ollie was fun, intelligent and just as disconnected from Christmas tradition as herself. He also turned out to be good in bed. As they lay on the broad mattress of their chain-hotel room, Ollie suggested that they stay the night.

She ate breakfast in the hotel with him. Staying till the morning deviated from her habits but felt good just then.

I could get used to something like this. I could bend my routine sometimes for this. Sometimes.

She popped home to change her clothes, and when she arrived at *Level* she immediately saw that something had happened. People were standing in small clumps around their desks talking about something, and it wasn't updating each other on their holidays.

'What's going on?' Lia asked Sam.

'Matt Thomas is leaving.'

He had been named deputy editor at the *Daily Express*. Thomas' resignation from his current post had been effective immediately he announced it, because he was off to another media company. The board of *Level*'s controlling company had called an emergency conference in the middle of a holiday morning to decide on a replacement.

'Oh. Wow,' Lia said.

'No kidding. Thomas is still in his office. We're trying to

work out whether we should throw some sort of improvised send-off. And how to handle all the work.'

Lia sat down and allowed the significance of this news to sink in.

Almost instantly she was ready to help organise Thomas' farewell party. Assigned to get the cake, she went to a nearby supermarket and purchased the largest one she could find.

Matt Thomas emerged from his office at eleven o'clock. He had made several calls over the course of the morning and hastily collected his things.

He was delighted to see the cake, coffee and sparkling wine the staff had thrown together.

The mood during the party was sociable, but Lia thought she could see that she was not alone in being relieved at Thomas' departure. In the middle of the celebration, news came down that the board had decided to name Timothy Phelps *Level*'s interim editor-in-chief, until the position could be filled permanently. The bubbly went around again.

Timothy was congratulated on every hand, and Matt Thomas gave a brief speech in which he mostly complained about *Level*'s circulation prospects.

'Matt, out with it. Did they lure you there, or did you apply for the position yourself?' Timothy Phelps asked.

'They rang me,' Thomas said. 'I didn't even know the *Daily Express* was looking for another editor. But they made me an extremely convincing offer. And I've always thought at some point I would end up at a big paper like that.'

Self-conceited cretin.

Lia watched Thomas grinning and considered Tim's question. It felt important. What was so special about Matt Thomas that the *Daily Express* would be interested in him? It was a big tabloid that banged out sensationalist headlines that competed for a different readership from *Level*'s. It was a completely different game. A dirty game, some said. And newspapers usually promoted from within.

This started to bother her.

She rang Mari. They had not talked at all over Christmas or afterwards other than exchanging texts.

'How's it going?' Lia asked.

'Work,' Mari said. 'I took some time off on Christmas Day though.'

Lia reported what had just happened at her work, that the editor-in-chief was changing.

'Is that so? That's interesting,' Mari said.

Lia paused for a second.

'Did you know about this?'

Mari's reply was slow in coming.

'Yes.'

'Did you arrange this new position for Thomas?'

'I played a role in it. But Thomas really did want to move to a larger paper. All I had to do was help a little.'

'How did you do it?'

Mari said she had put out feelers earlier in the autumn to see which papers were seeking people for management. Some positions were listed publicly, while others were doing their searches quietly. The *Daily Express* position was in the latter category. One of Mari's acquaintances had dropped a hint to the publisher that Matt Thomas might be interested in a new challenge. Thomas was thrilled to be invited for an interview.

'He probably thought the background interview we did with Elevate had something to do with the choice. And in a way it did.'

I should have guessed. It was too good to be coincidence.

'Do you feel bad somehow that I helped Thomas leave?' Mari asked.

'No. But it doesn't feel like it should. And I have the feeling that I owe you a debt of gratitude. Even though I didn't ask for this.'

'No, you don't owe me anything.'

Matt Thomas was happy because he was getting to move forward in his career, Mari said. Thomas' ideas and attitude would fit in better at a member of the tabloid press whose main goal was sales and circulation than *Level* did. And Lia would have the opportunity to consider whether to continue in a job she liked. All of her options remained open.

'You could still leave, if you want.'

'That's all true,' Lia said, trying to control herself. 'But can you understand how this makes me feel? That you're playing around with my life. Opening up new opportunities for me. Not letting me do it myself.'

'I guess you could see it that way,' Mari said. 'But that's how I am. I organise things the way I want them to be. In a way, everyone does it, but I take it further than most.'

'And of course I appreciate what you did. But if you'd asked me whether I wanted you to...'

'You probably would have said that you didn't,' Mari said. 'You wouldn't have wanted it because you think that life isn't supposed to work that way. Thomas should have found a new job just by chance, with no one else having a hand in it. It's a question of free will. Did Thomas change jobs out of his own free will and choice? Yes, he did. Only the circumstances were changed; I changed them. Lia, you and I probably have different views on how life works. I think that hardly anything in the world ever really happens out of free will. Someone or something is always guiding everyone's choices. There are times when I want to be the one doing the choosing.'

'But when it's a question of my life, I want to be that person, not you.'

Mari admitted that it was a perfectly justifiable hope.

'But I have to say that there are always going to be things that I don't ask your opinion about. And nowadays I already ask you about an awful lot. And that's important to me. But I don't always intend to ask.'

They ended the call. The discussion was going nowhere. They each had their work to do, and arguing depressed them both.

An uncomfortable feeling hung over Lia for the next few days. Matt Thomas' departure was a good thing, but Mari's part in it was troubling.

As interim editor-in-chief, Timothy Phelps immediately moved to make changes, surprising and inspiring the staff. He delegated some editor-in-chief responsibilities to other members of the team, but no one's load grew too much. For example, he encouraged them to work in pairs on developing content for their regular columns. Lia enjoyed sitting with Sam for half the day bouncing around ideas for subjects and visual themes for the magazine's small feature stories.

Tim's natural transition into the routine of being editor-in-chief was a joy to see. Lia did find it a little embarrassing that she had once gone to bed with the man who was now her boss. But Tim had always treated her well, and he did so now as well. He also did more work than anyone else in the office. His face burned with the intensity of someone whose career had just taken off, but instead of trying to get ahead by trampling on other people, as Thomas had, Phelps valued others' contributions.

At times Lia felt thankful to Mari for what she had done. At times she was infuriated that Mari could arrange things the way she wanted them to be.

She did not ring Mari, on principle, in order to protest. And not a text or email came from Mari. Sad to say, Lia knew the silence was not the result of Mari feeling she had done something wrong.

She's just concentrating on something else.

48

The news broke on the 2nd January. The first versions were already spreading through the media by 6 a.m.

It was a conundrum for all of them. The subject matter was so unbelievable that they each had to publish their own piece as soon as possible, but the accuracy of the report was difficult to evaluate. One after another the online media, TV news and printed papers moved it to the top of their stacks.

The most arresting headline came from the *Daily Mirror*. They had just barely squeaked through a reprinting of their front page. Filling it were the words: 'Fried beat the Woman Without a Face.' Above was a clarification: 'Prostitute says.' Beside this stood a picture of a smiling Arthur Fried.

Millions of people saw the front page of the *Daily Mirror* that day because many of the TV broadcasts also used it to illustrate the story. However, the *Mirror*'s piece was the bluntest version of the same information everyone had received.

It dawned on Lia quickly that the stories were all based on a bulletin she had also received from a very familiar source: the battered women's advocacy and domestic abuse prevention organisation The Wall. The bulletin had been sent overnight to hundreds of news outlets, including *Level*.

In the communiqué, the chairperson of the organisation, Karen Llewes, reported that she had in her possession a video that had shocked her and the other staff deeply. They had decided to hand over the video to the police immediately.

'But in order to prevent this serious matter from getting lost in the bureaucratic shuffle of police investigations, as so many incidents of violence against women do, our organisation also decided to release the video to the press,' Llewes wrote.

The video was available for viewing on their website. Because public interest in the story would be so large, The Wall had moved their site to a new server that could better handle the load.

By mid-morning, no one needed to go online to watch it though, since it was running in a near continuous loop on every TV channel that covered the news.

However, some people wanted to see the original as well. In the afternoon, The Wall issued a new statement that the video had received over 900,000 views so far. Financial donations were flooding in. In order to prevent publication of the video seeming like a fundraising operation, The Wall had also posted links to six other anti-domestic violence organisations on its site with an admonition to support them as well.

Lia watched the video again and again.

The hardest thing to get used to was seeing Elza speaking in it. The press release gave her first name, and she introduced herself at the beginning of the video.

Lia stared at the familiar face, which filled almost the entire screen. The video was short and simply produced. Elza sat before a white background and talked.

Her words left the viewer stupefied.

'My name is Elza. I'm from Latvia. I'm a prostitute and I've been working in London for many years. When I came here it was my own choice. I wanted to work as a prostitute. But from the beginning the conditions I was forced into were very difficult, and I want to stop working like this now.

'Before I finish, I want to talk publicly about a man who was my client, Arthur Fried. Arthur Fried is a very bad man. He's well-known in Britain and portrays himself as a good, religious man, but I know that he is evil.

'He beats women. He's done it to a lot of girls, and I know two prostitutes he left black and blue.

'One of them was my best friend, Daiga Vītola. Daiga was the woman who was killed and left in the boot of a white car in the middle of the City last year. In the newspapers they called her the Woman Without a Face.

'Once when Arthur Fried hired Daiga, he hit her several times. Daiga asked him to stop, but he said he would pay extra and kept on doing it. He said he liked Daiga's cries. They helped him hit her harder. He only stopped torturing her when other people came into the room because of her screams.

'We didn't know that Arthur Fried was a famous politician then. After that I heard from a lot of prostitutes that he had hit them. I've heard that he's hit other women in his life as well.

'I wanted to say this publicly because men like Arthur Fried don't deserve to walk free. When this video comes out, I'll already be out of the country.

'How do you know what I say is true?

'Ask Arthur Fried. And look at this picture.'

The video switched from Elza's face to a photograph showing a side view of a naked male figure on his knees straddling a naked woman. Looking closely at the picture, one could easily recognise both Arthur Fried and Elza. Fried's penis had been removed from the image with a blur. The photograph stayed up for twenty seconds, after which the video cut back to Elza again.

'I don't want to blackmail Arthur Fried. I'm not asking for money. I'm giving this picture to him completely free of charge, through the media.

'My friend Daiga Vītola died in a horrible way. Before that her life was horrible too. She was a wonderful person and she deserved to have a decent life.

'I'm going to go looking for a life like that somewhere else now too. My first step is this video.'

At the end of the video, the telephone numbers and URLs of three victim support groups appeared on the screen.

It was amazing work. But watching it was troubling. It troubled Lia that the story was so appalling and visceral. And it troubled her that she knew it was not true.

Most people did not doubt the veracity of the video for a moment. Elza's narration was so stark and felt so sincere that disputing it felt impossible. The photograph increased the feeling of reality.

Even the experienced staff at *Level* believed it instantly.

'Good God Almighty,' said Timothy Phelps. 'Fried is finished now. The good minister is going to a special circle of Hell now from which no one in politics ever returns. All the angels in Heaven couldn't redeem him now.'

Cries of protest over publication of the video also arose quickly. Online comments and phone calls came in to The Wall criticising the organisation as ethically irresponsible.

According to the news, the police were considering whether to ban The Wall from keeping the video on their site. It might be a case of gross criminal defamation, and simply displaying the video could be construed as a crime. But the threshold for such censorship was high, and the ban had to be handed down by a court.

And besides, stopping the video would have been impossible. Within a matter of hours it had been copied to countless other sites. Declarations of opposition to Fried and his class of criminal attracted hundreds of thousands of sympathisers. Television crews interviewed men and women on the street about how their attitudes towards Arthur Fried, domestic violence and prostitution had changed. The entire country was talking about it.

The comic John Blatt tried to use it in a joke.

'Is hitting a prostitute domestic abuse? Don't ask me. I just wish my domestic circle was as wide and sexy as Arthur Fried's,' Blatt joked on a live broadcast on Channel Four.

Blatt became the day's second, lesser bête noire. Most of the live audience sitting in the studio exited in the middle of the broadcast in protest over the joke, and dismayed feedback flooded in.

Arthur Fried did not appear in public. Dozens of reporters and cameramen camped outside his house, but no one had any solid information about whether he was even home. He had visited five cities over the previous week in an attempt to shore up voter support for Fair Rule. Now no one could get in touch with him.

That evening at six o'clock, a press release left the party office. It contained just two sentences: 'Party Leader Arthur Fried is deeply shocked by the slanderous attack recently made on his character. He condemns all violence of any sort and believes that the truth will emerge in the police investigation.'

Everywhere these statements were interpreted as containing no direct denial from Fried that he had hit women and the prostitutes mentioned in the video.

During the 9 p.m. BBC News broadcast, the political correspondent observed that unless some miracle occurred, Fair Rule's election hopes and Arthur Fried's career were finished.

'We call memoirs containing revelations of this sort kiss-and-tell books. Now we've entered a new era. This was a kiss-and-kill video. I can't see any way Fried could return to politics after this,' the reporter said.

Lia watched the evening news at home. The case had also made the international channels. CNN seemed to relish showing clips of it with accompanying expert commentary.

Although no one anywhere suggested that Fried had anything to do with the death of Daiga Vītola, many people found the abuse alone incomprehensibly cruel.

This has to be Mari's best work ever. She's got Fried after all.

Lia did not ring Mari. She did not ring anyone at the Studio. She guessed that at least Rico, Berg and Maggie had been involved in making the video. But she was not sure whether she wanted to know.

Lia did not know how to regard the video. It was both beautiful and grotesque.

Truth and lie perfectly entwined. So tangled together they become indistinguishable.

After watching her face tell this shocking story all day, Lia wanted to talk to Elza herself. Taking out her phone, she looked up Elza's brand new number.

To her surprise, Elza answered immediately.

'Lia? Is that you?'

'Yes, it's me. Where are you?'

'In London. I haven't left yet. How are you? How do you feel?'

'I don't know. I don't know what to think of this video.'

'It's great, isn't it? It's everywhere. I just saw it on al-Jazeera and a Polish news show. I have cable TV here with at least two hundred channels.'

'Elza, why did you do it?'

Lia heard her laugh.

'Why? Come on, you should know. Because of your friend, Mari. She showed me Arthur Fried's ex-wife's video. The one you couldn't publish.'

Of course.

'But Arthur Fried never hit Daiga. He probably never even met her.'

'No. But he hit so many other women that it doesn't matter. Daiga won't mind. Daiga would want us to make him suffer as he should.'

Elza was clearly thrilled. She explained about the filming: they had done it in the same place as Sarah Hawkins' video, and Elza had collaborated with Mari on the script.

'I would have wanted more make-up for the shooting, but everyone else didn't think it was a good idea. They wanted me to look normal.'

How had they made the image of Arthur Fried with Elza? Lia asked. Was it genuine?

'Of course it is!'

Elza sounded almost insulted.

'Mari found out where Fried was. He was on a speaking tour in Yorkshire, and we found him in Leeds.'

Everything had happened in a matter of days. Elza flew to Leeds with Rico and Berg in tow. Once in the city, they took a room in the same hotel where Fried was staying the night.

In the evening Fried was sitting in the hotel bar, keeping his distance from the other customers. He was drinking a lot. Elza approached him.

'At first he was surprised and then his guard went up. He guessed I was a reporter. I said I was just a lonely girl. He asked whether I was in the business, and I said I was. He asked my price and whether I knew who he was. I said I didn't know and I didn't care. I was damn good, Lia. He really thought I didn't know who he was.'

Fried gradually forgot his suspicions and his interest in Elza's offer grew.

'The best was when I gave him the key to my room. He stared at it and said that usually the deal was to go the man's room. I said that if he thought I was too forward, maybe what I needed was the right man to teach me my place.'

A fleeting flash had lit up Fried's eyes. Elza had dangled just the right piece of bait: a woman who needed a tough, hard man.

They went to Elza's room. Elza made sure that Fried was drinking the whole time. By the time they had their clothing off, Fried was so drunk he was staggering.

'He came and sat on me. What a big oaf. We were taking pictures the whole time.'

The room had been so full of hidden cameras they could have captured Fried from any angle they wanted. Rico and Berg had spent the whole day installing and testing them.

'It wasn't even actual sex. He couldn't do anything,' Elza said.

Fried had groped and slobbered on her, and she had let him long enough to get the shots they needed. When Elza said she had had enough, Fried tried to hit her, but he was no danger by that point. Fried collapsed on the floor, and Elza called Berg and Rico to drag him to his own room.

'Fried thought they were hotel staff. He pushed money at them to try to shut them up.'

Elza had an abnormal amount of experience of what men were capable of – and what to expect of them. But Arthur Fried was in a different class.

'He's just like Kazis and Olafs. Not the same kind of criminal, but still empty inside the same way. He's not human and he never will be. Something important is missing inside. He's like an animal. *Bestija*.'

And Elza herself? Lia asked.

'You can't stay in Britain any more, since the whole country's just spent the day staring at that video. The media and police will be hunting you down to get more information.'

Elza said she had no intention of staying. She was moving to Canada. Mari had procured her a new counterfeit passport in another name.

'I'll get to make a new start in Canada. Ausma is coming with me, and she already has a new passport too. She's just coming for a trip, to think about what she wants to do. We have the means for that now.'

Where had Elza received her money from? Lia asked.

'Your friend doesn't mess about. I would have done it for free, but Mari wanted to pay. I need the money, and she needed the video. Everybody wins.'

My friend. Everybody wins.

Elza said she would not be reachable on that number after that day.

'It isn't a good idea for me to keep this one, and I'll be getting another number in Canada anyway. Actually, your friend has already arranged it all.'

My friend has already arranged it all.

49

The next morning, the Fair Rule party secretary, Tom Gallagher, called a press conference in London. The agenda contained only one item: Gallagher announced that the party office staff had decided unanimously that they could not continue working under Arthur Fried's leadership.

'The work of the party has experienced such significant setbacks over recent months that simply surviving has been an enormous task. The news we all heard yesterday made continuing impossible,' Gallagher observed.

Fried was still party leader, because only an official party conference could make a change in leadership. However, the message was clear: the party's other officers no longer stood behind Fried.

One hour after the press briefing, Gallagher announced that he had received a communication via telephone that Fried intended to resign his position in the party effective immediately.

'In our conversation we did not discuss yesterday's news or the video that has received so much attention,' Gallagher wrote in his release.

Most people interpreted this to mean that their conversation had dealt with precisely that, but that whatever they said they did not want made public.

The video was still gathering views on The Wall's website. Based on the newspaper reports, no one believed any more that Arthur Fried had a political career ahead of him. His chances of receiving any sort of public position whatsoever were considered nonexistent.

The police had announced that because they could not locate the woman in the video, they would investigate the matter by calling Fried in for questioning. However, they had not been able to reach him yet.

Lia went to the Studio around midday.

She first glanced into the Den and a few other rooms, but could not find anyone. She did know that Mari would be at work.

'Hi,' Lia said as she entered the room.

'Well hello,' Mari said in delight.

Lia headed directly for the couch. It felt as though an awfully long time had elapsed since they last met. The Christmas party in Lia's flat and then a quick meeting at the Studio after Arthur Fried had succeeded in cowing Sarah Hawkins.

'Tell me why Fried won't come out in public,' Lia said.

The answer came with lightning speed.

'Fried doesn't know what to say. He doesn't dare deny that he hit a prostitute named Daiga Vītola, because he's hit so many prostitutes in his life. He doesn't remember them all, and never knew their names. He's afraid that if he starts issuing denials and evidence crops up somewhere, he'll end up in court for the abuse. And he can't tell the truth. Nothing could sound worse right now than for him to say: *I don't believe I hit that woman*.'

Lia nodded.

'So you gave everyone else the day off. Since the Fried job was basically in the bag,' she said.

Mari's gaze was very sharp.

'No one needs me to give them days off. Maggie, Rico and the others can decide perfectly well for themselves when to take rest days and when to come to work.'

Lia thought for a moment.

'Are you satisfied?' she asked.

'With what?'

'You know with what.'

'Yes, I'm satisfied. Very satisfied. We won.'

'I'm not satisfied,' Lia said.

'I can tell.'

'Doesn't that matter to you?'

'Yes, of course,' Mari said. 'But I have no intention of allowing it to ruin my own satisfaction.'

'There's a cold side to you too. You separate everything into such nice, tidy boxes. And then you go on acting as if those things aren't connected, even though they are.'

Mari considered this for some time.

'True,' she said. 'Sometimes that's necessary. But luckily that isn't the only side to me.'

'The video was marvellous,' Lia said.

'Thank you.'

The mood, the rhythm of the speech and some of the words had been taken directly from Sarah Hawkins' exposé. That was why it felt like a real victim's story. It did a wonderful job of combining Daiga Vītola's story with references to the sad experiences of other real people. Feeling anything but strong emotion towards the woman talking on the video was almost impossible. Pity, admiration, empathy. It was a masterpiece of planning.

'Arthur Fried will never talk his way out of this,' Lia said.

'Indeed.'

'That video is a lie.'

'Indeed.'

They were both silent for a second. The conversation was starting to feel dangerous. As though they might say something irreversible.

'I wanted to be part of this when it was true,' Lia said. 'I can stand bending the rules. And altering circumstances. I can survive being afraid. I don't know if I can survive lies.'

'We only lied about one thing,' Mari answered immediately.

Their lie was that Arthur Fried had never hit Daiga Vītola or Elza. Mari had used Daiga Vītola's name because Arthur Fried was so close to escaping. Her plan had been in danger of collapse. They had needed something sufficiently big.

'You exploited the shock value of Daiga's fate.'

'Yes, I did.'

'It's insulting.'

In what possible way? Mari objected. According to her friends, Daiga Vītola had been a woman of exceptional courage and strength of will. She had been held in sexual slavery for years. She had endured the abuse of her customers. Then she had been shot and driven over with a steamroller. How could a person like that ever be insulted by her name being used to expose a violent misogynist?

'Elza absolutely wanted to do the video, and Daiga probably would have too,' Mari said. 'And you should have heard what they said about it at The Wall.'

'Don't think you know what everyone else wants. You don't. You don't know what I want.'

Mari looked at her long and hard.

'Actually, I do know what you want,' she said. 'You want to be a part of this, and you also want out. And right now what you want most is out. And that's... sad.'

Something was moving in Lia's throat.

'It was a big lie,' she said.

'Yes, it was,' Mari said. 'And it was worth it.'

Lia left Mari's office. She went along the Studio corridor to her own office, but stopped at the door.

On the desk were her papers and files. Daiga Vītola and Arthur Fried. She wanted to stack them and put them away somewhere, but she could not help staring at the large, orange circle on the floor.

She knew that when she stepped on it, news of her movements would travel to the Studio's computers. And to Mari.

Lia switched off the lights and walked out of the Studio.

50

Lia goes to work. The mood at *Level* is good: on 7th January, Timothy Phelps is chosen as permanent editor-in-chief, and at long last everyone has the feeling that the magazine is doing well. Lia's work is more relaxed. She knows that she is in no rush and that her most important work, thinking, will sort itself out if she just gives it time.

Lia visits the psychiatrist. She has not had any more panic attacks, and after four meetings they decide that the need for treatment has passed.

Lia is still waiting to receive a summons for more police interviews. It doesn't come. One morning she receives a telephone call from Detective Chief Inspector Peter Gerrish. He asks whether the Latvian prostitute speaking in the sensational video published by The Wall, Elza, is the same woman from whom Lia received her information. Lia thinks for a moment and then replies. 'Yes.' Gerrish asks whether she knows where Elza is. Lia thinks for a moment and then replies. 'No.'

Sometimes she thinks of the women's life in Latvia. At other times she thinks about Fair Rule, the party that has fallen off the British political map.

Lia runs almost every evening. She knows which streets will be slick in Hampstead at any given time, and she likes her winter running shoes' grip on the road. It is different from other times of the year. She feels like a cat. A feline whose footfalls never fail.

She travels London by bus, train and Tube. Almost she feels as if she has moved to a new city. She has come to know a new side of Londoners: even amidst the throngs, they are calm and usually polite. She lives in a metropolis where people can still be at peace.

She does not go to bars at night for men. It's no time for that. Perhaps the time when she went looking for one-night stands has passed entirely.

She does not go to the Studio. She misses Rico, Maggie, Berg and Paddy.

She misses Mari unimaginably, but that feeling mingles with a gnawing indignation, and that is why she does not go to the Studio.

She misses what she was at the Studio.

Her weekends are empty, and that emptiness is difficult to fill. She decides that it is not particularly worth trying to fill it anyway. Often at these times she goes to sit in the sculpture garden.

Lia talks to her favourite sculptures. She reminisces about the past with St Luke and talks about the future with Florence Nightingale. She does not imagine them answering. She answers for herself.

Lia adjusts to life without the Studio.

An evening comes when she realises that she has to decide. She has been living without being able to make any decision, she cannot continue evading the issue eternally.

That night she stands next to Poundy the Dog, the most faithful listener of the lot. The sculpture shines in the winter night. During the day it rained, and now the crystallising moisture is creating a thin, resplendent coat of fur on the dog.

Lia has become accustomed to this life, but it lacks something. She has to choose.

She looks at Poundy the Dog expectantly. She has probably talked to him dozens of times. High time for him to say something. Poundy doesn't say anything.

Lia stands in the park staring at the silent dog. In that moment, she knows at least one thing she wants: a pint. Perhaps two or three.

Removing her mobile phone from her coat pocket, she sends a message containing a single word. '*Janottaa*.' I'm thirsty.

Only thirty-eight seconds elapse before Mari's reply arrives, and during those thirty-eight seconds Lia thinks about how she is not sure what she is choosing but knows that she could not choose otherwise.

Biographical note

Pekka Hiltunen is a Finnish author, whose debut novel in 2011 immediately became one of the most acclaimed first novels in Finnish literature. The psychological thriller *Cold Courage* was nominated for the *Helsingin Sanomat* Prize for Best Debut of the Year, a rare feat for a thriller. It won three literary prizes in Finland, including the Clue Award for Best Detective Novel of the Year, and it has been nominated for the Scandinavian Glass Key Award 2013.

Critics have pointed out that Hiltunen's thrillers, called the Studio-series, started a whole new phase in Finnish crime lit. They combine global political topics with a smart urban setting and a nod to classical trickster novels.

Hiltunen also writes in other genres, and his books have been translated into six languages, including French and German. His forthcoming work *BIG* deals with the tricky problem of the worldwide obesity epidemic. Following a twenty-year career as a journalist in 2010 he received the Best Writing Editor Prize for his magazine articles. He specialises in extensive articles tackling social and political topics

Hiltunen is a keen traveller, and most of *Cold Courage* was written on a year-long trip around the world. He loves the monthly supplements of quality British newspapers and devotes any free time to his two hobbies: holidaying away with his partner at a summer cottage by a small Finnish lake and inventing themes for imaginary surprise parties he wishes he could throw.

Coming Soon

Black Noise

by

Pekka Hiltunen

The Second in the Studio Series

Read on here for an exclusive extract
to find out what happens next...

I.

Personal messages from the Devil.

Those words rang in Lia's head all day. When the blank videos started appearing online, they were like personal messages from the Devil.

Lia had spotted the little news story about the videos in her newsfeed in the morning when she arrived at *Level.* Apparently someone had hacked the YouTube accounts of two English teenagers to upload the videos. The teens didn't know each other, they lived in different parts of the country and they didn't have the slightest idea why they were targeted or who had done it.

The strangest thing about the clips was that they were essentially blank – no video, no audio. Just a black screen.

A reporter had interviewed one of the teens. He said the videos scared him. Staring at the silent darkness had felt strange at first, but when the nothingness just went on and on, it turned frightening. It was like getting coded messages or personal threats from the Devil, the boy had said. That was why he contacted not only the YouTube admins but also the police and a newspaper. In the picture, the boy looked more pleased with the attention he was getting than racked with terror.

As a joke, the stunt was dismal; as vandalism, ineffective, but it was still assumed some significance must lurk behind it.

The hacker had uploaded ten blank videos under each teenager's name, their lengths varying from a couple of minutes to nearly six. The videos had been taken down, and YouTube representatives were currently investigating how the hack had occurred.

A marketing stunt? Lia thought.

But what company would want that sort of publicity? And YouTube would be sure to take anyone to court who hacked accounts for advertising purposes.

By the end of the day, Lia still couldn't work out what the videos were about. She left the office early because she had another, less orthodox job, to do before the evening.

After leaving her magazine's building on Fetter Lane, she pulled on her gloves. They felt soft and protective, signalling that something new was happening.

Lia wore gloves when she ran only on the chilliest winter days. She had a runner's circulation and a Finn's tolerance for cold. It was March, and London was already past the worst of its bleak spring, but now she had to have gloves. With them on, she wouldn't leave any fingerprints.

She looked at the thin, white fabric. The touch of cotton on her skin made the change concrete. She had entered into a new phase of an undertaking which had required long, painstaking planning. Now it was really happening, and there was no turning back.

Lia had chosen her gloves with care. She had looked at the range of a few department stores and chosen a brand sold at several. Even if they left fibres behind, tracing them would be impossible.

She checked the envelopes one more time. There were five small ones, their addresses printed on labels, their stamps affixed with glue. Three were larger, thicker envelopes, prepared in similar fashion. Each envelope, label and stamp was different.

Reclosing the plastic bags she was using to protect them, she placed the envelopes in her rucksack.

Lia had decided to run her errand. She had checked the locations of the postboxes and post offices online and carefully planned her route so the envelopes would be processed by different sorting facilities and arrive on three different days. If someone ever investigated the letters, connecting them to each other would be difficult.

Starting in the City, running the route would take her a good three hours, but this felt like a good use of her time. Every last detail had to be perfect. A person's entire life was at stake, and the Studio and its people would also be affected.

My dear, strange band. My dear, peculiar second home.

The Studio had given her day-to-day life a new dimension, caring for other people. You could commit to that more than other things. Lia wanted to do her day job at *Level* magazine well too, but for more selfish reasons, to be a strong professional. At the Studio she was doing things for other people, and they became important emotionally. Doing them she became stronger as a person.

Running through Clerkenwell and Finsbury, she headed towards Islington. Her favourite street happened to fall along her route. On Essex Road her eyes took in every little launderette, shoe shop and funeral home, everything she had time to see as she ran seeming to touch her lightly and spur her on as she passed.

The rucksack on her back grew lighter as she dropped each envelope in its appointed postbox. An almost melancholy feeling came over her. There went everything they had collected and composed so meticulously.

Whenever she stopped at a traffic light, she continued jogging slowly on the spot. People smiled, and Lia knew how she looked: a young, blonde woman out for an evening run. Energy in motion, silent determination.

She thought of the envelopes she had posted and the routes they would travel. Each of them had a different destination but the same purpose.

In her mind she saw the letters' journey. Postal workers fetching them, piling them on to moving conveyor belts, machines sorting them and sending them off in different directions. Then they would be delivered around London and the surrounding area. The envelopes would travel in post trolleys in buildings, making their way to secretaries' desks and then to their intended recipients.

How long would they wait to be opened? And when they were opened, would they serve their purpose?

She dropped the last envelope near Primrose Hill. The round, red postbox swallowed it without a sound.

Home was a few kilometres away. Accelerating, she felt her breathing speed up. Her step was light, so light she was almost floating in the air. As if she were breathing herself forward in the darkening evening.

When Lia arrived in Hampstead, she could recognise every hedgerow and garden gate. She knew exactly where and how to run so she wouldn't need to slow down and could keep her heart rate steady at just the right level. On her street, Kidderpore Avenue, she finally slowed to a walk.

Right now she was powerful. An unusually long and winding run, just the right amount of exertion and the euphoria that accompanied it. The knowledge that the envelopes were on their way and that important things had been set in motion.

Her warm body. The chill evening. The contrast produced a physical pleasure that tickled a special place somewhere in the depths of her brain.

Stopping at the small park next to her building, Lia started moving through her familiar post-run stretching routine. Next to the large, dignified statues in the park, her slender body was like a fragile blade of grass. But Lia felt vigorous, confident and utterly alive.

That evening she didn't notice the news that someone else had discovered their YouTube account had been hacked. The devil had sent more of his messages. Another ten videos had been uploaded to a Scottish woman's account, again showing nothing but black silence.

2.

As soon as Lia opened the door to the Studio, she heard quick, alert steps start towards her.

Tap, tap, tap. Well-groomed claws barely touched the floor. Kneeling, Lia accepted all the warmth a dog's greeting could give.

Gro always knew when she had arrived before all the others did, perhaps even a split second before the Studio's surveillance systems. And Lia always wanted to greet Gro as thoroughly as he wanted to greet her.

'You're going to spoil him rotten,' Mari used to say. 'What kind of a guard dog is he going to be now?' But Lia defended herself saying that she was only petting and wrestling with him, not feeding him too much or teaching him bad habits. In reality Mari was almost as taken with Gro as the rest of them.

Gro was Berg's dog. Berg was the Studio's carpenter and set designer, who could create almost anything for their operations: documents, identity cards, tools, objects. If necessary Berg could create a whole flat that looked like it really belonged to someone.

Sixty years old, Berg was half Swedish and had named his dog after the former Prime Minister of Norway, Gro Harlem Brundtland. Berg wanted a woman's name for his girl dog that exemplified Scandinavian values.

'Gro doesn't sound very dignified,' Lia had said, teasing him. 'It sounds more like a dog's growl.'

'But I know where the name comes from,' Berg had said. 'Since she has a name I respect, I never say it without that respect.'

Why not some Swedish woman? Lia had asked. Greta Garbo? Ingrid Bergman?

'No,' Berg had said. 'She looks like a Gro.'

In addition to serving as prime minister, Gro Harlem Brundtland had been a doctor, a party leader, director-general of the World Health Organisation and much more. Her black and white namesake had a more diverse background: the breed she most closely resembled was a pointer. She was a stray Berg had picked up at an RSPCA shelter. After teaching her basic obedience and building her trust at home, he had gradually introduced her to the Studio's team.

At the Studio Gro lived in the Den, which, despite its name, was an enormous space. That was where Berg worked, and it took time for Gro to learn not to chew on things she found on the shelves and desks and not to sniff at the cupboards in the kitchen in the corner of the room.

But the dog worshipped Berg, and before long she learned her boundaries in the Den and the Studio at large. Eventually Berg even trained her to stay out of the kitchen.

Following a brief discussion, Mari had agreed to let Berg replace some of the Studio's interior doors with lightweight swinging ones so Gro could move from one room to another by pushing doors open with her muzzle.

'It'll be easier for her to guard the place this way,' Berg argued, although they all knew the Studio didn't actually need any more guarding. The CCTV cameras, motion sensors in the floors and computer surveillance were quite sufficient.

Two areas were off limits to Gro. One was Rico's large office, dominated by dozens of computer racks and other delicate devices.

'Gro Harlem is welcome in my home any time but not near these cables and instruments,' the Brazilian IT genius had said. Calling the dog by her full name amused him, what with its entirely non-Scandinavian reference.

Gro was also never allowed in Mari's office. Lia wasn't entirely sure why, whether it was meant as a sign of deference to Mari's position at the head of the Studio's little team or whether she just wanted to be left in peace, but Gro accepted this rule quickly too. Even though Mari's door was often open, Gro never tried to go in.

'She recognises natural leadership, who the pack leader is,' Mari once observed to Lia, who was slightly irked to have to admit to herself that Mari was right.

Even though Gro had been a stray with some trust issues, she settled into life at the Studio significantly faster than Lia had herself. For the dog it took a couple of months, for Lia it had taken most of a year.

The Studio was a place the likes of which Lia had never imagined existed, and yet she couldn't talk about it to anyone. It was a large, eight-room space occupying nearly an entire floor of an office building in London's Bankside, and the jobs its occupants did were always interesting and unusual. Mari always chose projects that would move the world in the direction she wanted. Sometimes it was behind-the-scenes charity work, but sometimes the jobs were stranger and more frightening.

For Lia the Studio was like a second home or office where the lines between friendship and work overlapped and intertwined. By day she worked at *Level*; in the evenings and on the weekends, she spent most of her time on Studio business.

Mari was her best friend, an exceptional woman who had suddenly appeared in her life after nearly six years living in London. Their shared Finnish background united them, along with an ability to drink with abandon when the opportunity presented itself and a feeling that although they made their way through life on their own they had to be thankful for true allies. Berg and Rico worked for Mari, but like Lia and everyone else at the Studio they were also Mari's confidants. The team's two other members were Brits: Maggie Thornton, an actor in her fifties, who did background research and played characters in their operations as necessary, and Paddy Moore, a security specialist and private investigator.

Lia did not know how many of the Studio's jobs required specific detective skills or led to illegal acts. Although she and Mari had become quite close, Mari remained tight-lipped about much of what her group had done over the years.

Lia stepped into Mari's office and Gro returned to the Den, back to her master.

'How did it go?' Mari asked.

'Well,' Lia said, taking her usual place on one of the large sofas in Mari's office.

She knew such a brief report wouldn't be sufficient for Mari, who always wanted to know everything down to the tiniest detail. Lia had learned that it usually paid to tell Mari everything, because even the smallest-seeming bits of information could turn out to be worth their weight in gold once they had percolated for a while in Mari's brain.

So Lia recounted the letters' progress over the previous day, which she had tracked using the Royal Mail's online system. Of the five thin envelopes, three had been delivered today to the editorial offices of large newspapers. The rest would arrive tomorrow. The three larger, thicker envelopes were still en route, one of them on its way to the editor-in-chief of a magazine and two to the offices of TV channels.

They had considered the number and manner of delivery of the letters for a long time, weighing the likelihood that each editor would make the contents public and which media outlets it was most important to reach. They debated whether to approach the newspapers by email or using more old-fashioned means. They decided on letters because these days those always made more of an impression on their recipients than electronic communication, and concealing the true identity of the person sending a letter was easier.

Each of the five thin envelopes contained a letter to the editor. They all dealt with the same topic, although they were each written differently and sent under a different name.

Mari had written them with Lia's help. From her day job at *Level*, Lia knew a little about what kinds of opinion pieces newspapers and magazines wanted to publish, but Mari had only needed a little help polishing them. Making sure each had a unique authorial voice was critical so the letters could never be connected to each other.

Together with the Studio's other employees, they had also created contact information and an online history for the writers. If the newspapers checked up on them before the letters were published, the enquiries would come to the Studio. There Maggie and Rico were prepared to play the appropriate parts on the phone or via email.

Newspapers rarely checked opinion-letter writers' information, Lia knew. Mostly only when politically significant issues were in play. The editorial offices of the larger, more prestigious papers did look online and in the telephone directories to verify whether the senders existed. But seldom did that lead to even a phone call.

In the thicker envelopes were larger packets of information, and creating them had required more of the Studio. They had needed to set up an entire foundation. It was very small, built so one person could operate it, but on top of needing a website it also required press releases with a range of dates and references to it elsewhere online. Berg and Rico had handled that.

All of the preparations had taken a little more than a week, in which time quite a bit of other planning also went on. That still amazed Lia. She had been working with the Studio for more than a year but still struggled to keep up with the rest of the group.

'What now?' she asked Mari. 'Just wait for a couple of days?'

Mari nodded. Now they waited until the letters served their purpose. Then the next stage would begin.

Lia had learned at the Studio that Mari's plans worked. And although waiting felt hard, she knew it was easy for Mari. She would use this time to plan too, always something new. For her, the world was a place that could be changed – you just had to choose what you wanted to change.

Fortunately Lia knew what to do while they waited.

'I'm going for a jog,' she announced and then left to make two creatures happy for the next two hours: a dog and herself.

3.

They waited for Craig Cole a few blocks from his flat so he wouldn't think they were pushy.

Cole walked briskly. He had hidden his red, puffy face behind dark glasses. The swelling of his face was not a result of drink, Lia and Mari knew. This was a man who now cried every day. Sometimes several times a day, without the dignity or self-control that had been central to his life up to this point. Until the catastrophe struck.

Craig Cole had become a man who cried every day when a fourteen-year-old girl named Bryony Wade had called in to a live broadcast of his radio show and announced before an audience of millions that Cole had made advances on her.

Of course BBC staff had screened that call just like all the other calls to the show three weeks before. An assistant producer talked with Bryony Wade before connecting her to the broadcast. She was supposed to request a song by Justin Bieber and chat with Cole about her friends' favourite websites. Instead she dropped a bombshell. She said that her parents had encouraged her to call and say that the family intended to go to the police.

'You dirty old man,' Bryony Wade said live on the air. 'You should be in prison.'

Cole's twenty-six years in radio did not save him. He lost the critical moment by thinking that the call had to be some sort of sick joke. This sort of thing simply didn't happen.

'Come on, Bryony,' he said. 'We've never even met. I think it's best we end the joke right here.'

'Last night you shoved your hand under my sweater and touched my tits,' Bryony said. 'You promised me money if you could grope me. You dirty old man. I'm only fourteen.'

Under our three imprints, Hesperus Press publishes over 300 books by many of the greatest figures in worldwide literary history, as well as contemporary and debut authors well worth discovering.

Hesperus Classics handpicks the best of worldwide and translated literature, introducing forgotten and neglected books to new generations.

Hesperus Nova showcases quality contemporary fiction and non-fiction designed to entertain and inspire.

Hesperus Minor rediscovers well-loved children's books from the past – these are books which will bring back fond memories for adults, which they will want to share with their children and loved ones.

To find out more visit www.hesperuspress.com
@HesperusPress